THE TRUTH ABOUT NIGHT

THE TRUTH ABOUT NIGHT

THE MERCI LANARD FILES

Amanda Arista

THE TRUTH ABOUT NIGHT
Editor: Aimee Ashcraft, Brower Literary & Management

TABLE OF CONTENTS

CHAPTER ONE

Ethan stood over me and shook the remaining ice in his coffee mug nearly drained of its whiskey. "There is a party going on here, Merci. In our honor."

I couldn't stop reading the mayor's deposition the DA's assistant had faxed me—totally off the record. My anger churned, another storm brewing on my horizon, or perhaps it was only the echoes of this last tempest. "He's denying Cartwright Construction offered him bribes. I mean, we found proof and he's still lying."

Ethan sighed and sat on the corner of my desk, stretching his long legs out before him. "We got Cartwright. The Mayor is three seconds from going down himself. Let the police handle it."

He snatched the faxed pages from my hand and replaced them with my untouched mug of celebratory whiskey, which had been sitting forgotten on the desk. I studied the navy blue cup that read "World's Best Partners" and chuckled. The matching set had been a congratulatory gift from Emily, his wife, after we landed our first eight inches above the fold. The Cartwright bribes were just the latest in our long history together.

Which is why I knew that he would understand.

"There are some things learned best in the calm, but most are learned in the storm."

Ethan rolled his eyes at my Willa Cather. "It's a party, Merci. Take three seconds to appreciate what you've done."

"Correction: what *we've* done," I said as I leaned back in my chair. "Without your picture of the mayor's tan line from his watch,

I wouldn't have thought to even raise a question about his family vacation to Hawaii."

"But you were the one who cracked the travel agent, got her to admit that Cartwright was the one who booked and paid for it all."

"And the rest is front page."

"Above the fold."

I grinned at that accomplishment and took a whiff of the cheap whiskey our boss had bought for the celebration. "Hayne's got the good stuff in his office. You know that, right?"

"Yeah, but it's an office party. Isn't the liquor supposed to be cheap as long as the company is good?" He lifted his mug toward me for a toast. "To staying out of trouble?"

I clinked mine against his. "To staying out of trouble."

I took a sip of the whiskey and winced. It burned all the way down to my empty stomach. It made the store-bought chips and salsa at the party almost appetizing.

Ethan laughed. "Come on, Merci. Let's go be social. I think Hayne wanted you to give a speech or something to fire up the newbs."

It was my turn to roll my eyes at the suggestion. "There is not enough alcohol in the world. Have we forgotten the Founder's Roast when I was asked to speak?"

Ethan's brown eyes widened and his mouth opened. "Oh, God. That's right. When you joked about the Board Director's new boat costing as much as his second wife's boob job and it turned out to be true? I'm not sure he ever fully recovered." He laughed, taking a childlike glee in remembering one of my less-than-stellar moments. "Why don't we have video of her chasing him around with a purse?"

"Nondisclosure?" I shook my head and spun the coffee mug in my hands as I surveyed the newsroom.

Ethan liked these kinds of things, the family of the newsroom, the camaraderie, the celebration of a job well done. It just wasn't my kind of scene. I was more of a one-on-one person. Big crowds made me nervous.

"Go. Have a good time. You know I don't play nice with others."

"Yes, you do, Merci Lanard. Underneath all those layers and sarcasm, you want to help people."

"Correction: I just want to get paid."

He scoffed. "Correction: You want to make the world a better, more honest place."

I couldn't correct him there. "I do want to make *Philly* a more honest place but rehashing the investigation for the newbs isn't going find out why the mayor is denying proof about accepting bribes for city bids. We still have work to do."

Ethan groaned in frustration, but I saw the playful glint in his eyes the moment his thoughts and tactics changed. "But what if rehashing this story inspires one of the newbs to dig deeper, work longer, go harder. What if telling this story makes them make the world a better, more honest place?"

I just looked up at him, eyebrow raised. "Is that seriously the story you're trying to sell?"

"Yes, and I'm sticking to it."

I snorted. "Did the cheap whiskey kill that many brain cells?"

"Nope." His smile beamed down at me. "Well, maybe."

"No wonder you didn't last two days on Metro and Hayne punted you behind a camera."

Ethan set his cup down on the desk. "Please, Merci. I just want one drink with my best friend before everything hits the fan again. Can't you just put it on pause for one night?"

Truth was, I didn't know if I could. Not without whiskey to drown out the building storm of questions I was already preparing for the mayor. I just didn't work like that. But for Ethan, I could try to drown them out, but this cheap shit was not going to cut it.

"One drink. And only if we can convince Hayne to toss this crap and get the good stuff."

"Done," he said quickly and he sprang off the corner of my desk.

Ethan's infectious smile pulled me from my chair but only halfway across the newsroom floor where the rest of the staffers were busy congratulating themselves on the paper's part in getting another corrupt institution exposed and completely scooping the competition.

The phone in my back pocket buzzed and I pulled it out. I didn't recognize the number that flashed across the screen, but I rarely did. When a person needed to spill secrets, they never did it with caller ID. "Lanard here."

"It's Benny."

I stopped my trek across the newsroom and turned away from the party. It wasn't just that my favorite informant was calling, it was that he sounded stressed and shaky over the static of the payphone line. "What is it, Benny?"

"You up for another hit?" he asked.

My skin tightened and tingled in anticipation. "What you got?"

"You know those new players in town?"

"Yeah." I tried to play it cool, but my skin sizzled like butter on a hot skillet. Ethan and I had heard whispers and pulled together half-strewn stories of those who had survived a new menace on the streets and were willing to talk for a few bucks. We matched that to an uptick in missing persons around the time that these guys started really pulling their weight. It's why I'd asked Benny to look into them. Ask a few questions in the darkness where even I couldn't go. See if there was a connection between the two. "You find them?"

"Better. Got Names."

Lightning crackled through me. Names meant addresses, paper trails. It meant the hunt was on and Ethan and I could sniff it out.

"Can we meet?" he asked.

I found myself back at my desk, grabbing my messenger bag from my bottom drawer. I didn't have a choice in the matter. The storm within me would never settle. No matter how many mayors we exposed or how many drug rings we took out, it would never be calm skies. "Where and when?"

"Tonight. Cambria and Rosehill. There's an empty corner store."

I jotted down the location in my notebook already out on my desk and waiting for the next story. "You and your abandoned stores, Benny."

"Can you make it?"

I scanned the room. The party was in full swing now with Hayne booming out a story—probably something about his heyday before he was editor-in-chief—and Ethan was laughing along with the rest of them. No one would miss me in this celebration.

I glanced down at my watch and calculated my exit strategy and the traffic. "Hour?"

"Sure." Benny slammed the receiver down and I jumped at the sound.

Something had him wound tight, but then again, who knew what he was high on this week.

I double-checked my bag for my usual tools: audio recorder, roll of cash, and a Taser, because you never knew what you might be walking into.

Ethan strode quickly across the floor when he saw me sling on my coat. "You are not seriously going to get in the Mayor's face about his deposition tonight. What happened to the one drink?"

That is what you get with two years of side-by-side work in a handful of perilous situations, a person who could call you on your shit because he knew you better than you knew yourself.

He loomed over me, his hands on his slim hips. "I thought we were going to stay here, drink bad liquor, and take one night off."

I defiantly dropped my notebook into my bag. "Benny said he has a lead on those new guys we keep hearing about and wants to meet." I was playing dirty. I knew that Ethan was as interested in the story as I was. "Names, Ethan. New doors to knock on, trails to follow."

He wasn't buying it. "The names will still be there tomorrow, Merci. And doors don't go anywhere."

I closed my messenger bag and rested my hand on the top. "You don't need to come. I got this. It's just Benny."

"Everyone's better with a partner, Merci." He recited Hayne's cardinal rule as he ran his fingers through his hair and it flopped back across his forehead. "I was supposed to help Emily set up her classroom for the open house tomorrow."

"And you can. It's a simple face-to-face, Ethan. I just need to know he's not lying."

"Right. No one can resist that Lanard Charm." Ethan snorted. "The girl who always gets the truth."

He wasn't wrong. The Charm, as Ethan had jokingly named it, wasn't just the sweet smile I developed while people yelled at me, though sometimes that was enough to get under their skin. It was the years of watching people lie their tails off, studying lips and eyes and arms, and being the one to catch them in their deceit with hard-fought proof. It was the sizzle of looking someone in the eye and knowing they wanted to lie and not letting them, not giving them room to breathe to even get the lie out. It was knowing the truths I needed and never stopping until I knew the whole story.

And he was right, I always got the truth.

I watched as Ethan weighed the party and his obligations at home against another night fighting the good fight. The argument raced across his brown eyes.

I tried to soothe them. "I can get the names by myself and we can run them in the morning. You can go home and have a spontaneously romantic night with Emily."

"Should I call your lawyer before or after that romantic night?" Ethan's gaze landed on me, that friendly, wide face usually so welcoming etched in concern. His voice was low, pained. "You really can't stop, can you? Not even for one night."

The silence after that statement echoed between us. I licked my lips of the cheap whiskey and confessed, because I couldn't lie to him. "You know I can't, Ethan."

The obsession for the truth wouldn't let me sleep if I didn't go, chase, hunt. Moving toward a story, seeking out the truth, was the only thing that eased the electric-like anxiety in my brain when the compulsion of a story hit, quieted the millions of questions milling around in my brain. Where others only saw the tenacity of a journalist, Ethan had seen what really happened when it wasn't sated. The obsession. The compulsion. The sleepless nights. The empty bottles. Another less glamourous bonus of being partners.

"We can still have that drink." I held up my mug and gulped down the rest of the whiskey and took a moment to recover from the burn.

"What kind of partner would I be if I let you go alone." Ethan exhaled and examined his mug. "So much for staying out of trouble."

He finished off his whiskey and coughed out the sting of the liquor, before setting his mug down to mirror mine. "I'll call Emily on the way."

I slung my bag over my shoulder, ready for the night, and crossed my heart. "Tell her I promise to have you home at a fairly decent hour."

Ethan laughed as he grabbed his coat and camera bag from his desk across from mine. I heard the clink of his filter cases as he made sure he had everything he needed. "Right, you mean like for her birthday when we were supposed to meet her for dinner and we ended up bringing breakfast tacos?"

"But we brought enough for her whole class with a dozen roses. And cake. I think we've made it up to her by now."

He smiled, giving into the thrill of the chase. "Ladies first."

As the two of us walked out of the newsroom, I vaguely heard Hayne yelling across the newsroom as the elevator doors shut, but my boss yelled so often it was ambient noise.

It didn't matter. That sizzle hummed along my skin now I knew I wasn't going to have to go this one alone. He was right. I was better with my partner. And Ethan and I would solve this like we had solved everything else.

...

"Where the hell is he?" I checked my watch for the twentieth time in the past thirty minutes, then rubbed my hands up and down my biceps. I could see the fog of my breath in the darkness of the abandoned corner store. "We promised to get you home before bedtime."

"It's Benny. He's always late." Ethan adjusted the woven strap of his camera over his shoulder, seemingly impervious to the cold. "Have a little patience."

I huffed. "You know I don't do patience. Especially when I'm freezing."

Ethan chuckled. "It's Philly in November. What did you expect?"

He untied his scarf and pulled it from the collar of his coat. He looped it over my head and threw one end over my shoulder. "Two years of stakeouts and you never remember a scarf."

"Why would I need to when I've got you?"

For a moment, I was enveloped in the body heat still lingering on his scarf. I snuggled in, letting the itch of the wool scratch at my neck before I wrapped it around tighter. It smelled better than the mix of dust and decay that filled the disintegrating store.

Ethan shook his head with a chuckle and started walking around the small convenience store. He lifted his camera and snapped a few shots of the worn counter and the bulletproof glass still in place. He checked the pictures on the view screen and then clicked away some more.

I wrapped my arms around my chest tighter and sank deeper into his scarf as I watched him walk across the striations of golden light on the white tile. He did this a lot, taking random pictures, switching out lens. I never saw the pictures he took, but he had to have enough images of light and darkness to fill a gallery.

Ethan dropped the camera from his face, head cocked as if listening to the night.

"Something is coming."

"What?" I scanned the place. In the dim streetlight, I didn't see anything, but Ethan standing there listening, his camera still cradled in his hands.

I never got my answer. The light vanished. Not like streetlamps going out, but more like something had stolen the light and pitched us into a swimming pool of black. I couldn't see my hand as I reached out into the sudden cool of darkness. "Ethan?"

"Merci," he called back.

"We need to get out—" Ethan's voice was cut off by a hard grunt.

Hands out before me, I shuffled toward the sound of Ethan's voice when a hulk caught me in the midsection and slammed me down on the floor between the empty shelves. My head cracked against the linoleum and bright starbursts flashed in my vision.

Rough hands rolled me to my stomach and a knee rammed into my back, grinding my ribs into the ground.

"Run, Merci!" Ethan screamed.

I fought with everything I had against the thing on my back, kicking my legs and screaming, trying to get a foothold on something to turn or spin, but I was pinned to the floor like a bug on a collector's mat.

Another figure knelt by my head and wrenched my left hand up between my shoulders. I cried out as the pain tore through my side and left me momentarily unable to wriggle away. I could still scream, though.

"Ethan!"

Fingers grabbed my hair and slammed my face against the hard floor once again. Bright spots swam through my vision, taking a longer respite than before. My head began to spin like I'd downed an entire bottle of whiskey, bile rising in my throat. For a moment, I couldn't feel the rest of my body, but I could hear the distinct rip of clothing. I knew the truth of what happened to a woman surrounded by a gang of men.

A burning sensation flew up my arm and the pain reached across my blind eyes in claws of red lightning. I couldn't tell if I was kicking, but I willed everything in me to fight once more.

"Hurry," the one on my left said.

A scream filled the night and I could feel my attackers freeze, my arm still pinned behind my back.

"Get him," the one on the right barked.

My arm was released as the second man left. I seized in a breath and choked on blood running down my throat. I blinked a few times, trying to see anything. What was happening to Ethan. What this thing was doing to me. I tried to pull away from the fingers wrapped like tourniquets around my arm.

The man on my back dug his knee into my shoulder as he continued furiously shoving the arm of my coat up as far as the wool would allow, then ripping my sleeve. His breathing quick and labored, he grabbed my forearm and fire sliced into my flesh,

I cried out and the attacker delivered a sharp punch to my kidneys and I knew I was out. A gasp leapt from me as paralyzing pain seized my body again.

I heard the staccato sounds of fists meeting flesh, echoed by grunts of pain and exertion. Ethan was fighting, taking out all the others. He would save us.

Then it all went silent.

The men, the shadows, the thing holding me down, vanished as quickly as they had appeared and I was left, sputtering for air on the cold tile.

As soon as I could manage a lungful of air, I called out Ethan's name.

A groan was my only response.

My left arm gained feeling first, and I pushed myself up from the ground.

Light slowly returned to the abandoned space. I had to blink a few times as the world came into focus. The first thing to take shape was a puddle of my blood on the white tile where my face had been. I curled my legs to me. They worked, but my side was tender. My head still spinning, I frantically searched to find Ethan.

He was sprawled on the ground not ten feet away at the front of the store. It felt like ten miles as I dragged myself across the floor.

Blood was everywhere, on the floor, on him, like thick crude oil in the low light, the scent of pennies replacing dust.

"Ethan?"

He hissed out something. I leaned over him to find a stream of blood flowing from his throat. Or where his throat should have been. A long gash ran from his ear down to his chest, and blood flowed out in waves.

As quickly as I could, I wrapped his wool scarf around his throat and put his head on my leg. My right hand seemed to be the better working one as I called 9-1-1. I gave the dispatcher my location and didn't bother with her instructions to stay calm. I threw the damn thing across the floor and began a chant I'd heard before.

"Just hold on, Ethan. Hold on."

I kept my hand pressed against the wound, but nothing in triage class could have prepared me for this. Bullet wounds I could handle. But this? No amount of gauze was going to fix this trench of gore down his neck. I wasn't even sure there was enough neck to fix.

The truth of the situation seeped into me as I held him, brushed a curl from his forehead, matched his short, panted breaths with my own. Ethan was going to die. I knew it from the odd angle of his head as he looked up at me, the way his eyes couldn't seem to focus on mine.

I bit back the sob forming deep within my chest.

Ethan smiled up at me, his teeth bloody. "You're not going . . . to cry on me, are you . . . Lanard?" His deep voice was no more than a whisper between us.

"Contrary to what they say, I do have a heart." I didn't know if the cool streak on my cheek was a tear or blood.

"Tell Piper … I'm sorry," he bubbled.

There were a million things that I needed to say, needed to tell him, but my brain stalled at the unknown name on his lips.

"Take this."

His bloody, shaking hand grasped at his shirt and I had to help him find the silver medallion around his neck. He didn't have the strength to break the chain, but he pressed the pendant into my palm and curled my fingers around it.

"Let Emily know … I loved her."

His last breath caught half-formed in his throat, and I felt him die. His body went limp in my arms, and the warmth of him slipped away until he was nothing.

…

Ethan's funeral was that Saturday. I must have stood in front of my closet for an hour. Just standing there in my towel. My entire wardrobe was comprised of jeans and boots and comfort. It was the wardrobe of someone who jumped fences and skulked around at night. Nothing was right for where I was going in full daylight.

Finally, in the back, I found a short black satin dress my mother had bought me for a cousin's wedding. I didn't think it would fit anymore and was surprised at how roomy it was after I zipped it up. I found a pair of black tights, no idea where those came from, and tried to fasten my only pair of black heels.

My hand shook as I worked at the buckle. It could have been the three cups of coffee I'd had that day to keep me warm, but I knew the truth was simpler than that. That's the nice thing about the truth: it's mostly simple and straightforward. And when you happen to be a girl almost entirely composed of the stuff, when truth drives every fiber of your being, it's easy to know exactly what is really going on in your head. I was lost. My right leg was gone and I'd been limping around in circles.

I'd burned out. I'd been chasing leads for three days straight. Talking to people I knew, paying off people I didn't. Trying to dig as hard as I could as fast as I could to find Benny before the trail ran cold. He'd disappeared; it was like he hadn't even existed. But he wasn't dead yet—the assistant at the ME's office confirmed that.

Three days and I had nothing, except a wicked hangover and sore knuckles from knocking on doors. The life seemed to have drained out of me, and I was hollow as I stared at my reflection in the mirror. I wasn't able to cover my black eye or the busted lip with makeup. I wore my hair down to cover the gash on my forehead and the finger-shaped bruises around my throat. My black cardigan worked fine to cover the bandage still on my right arm.

I held on to Ethan's medallion dangling from my neck, and must have stared into the mirror for another twenty minutes before Hayne rang the buzzer. I dropped the silver chain down the front of my dress and left.

He didn't say anything as we drove. I think he was in the same headspace as me. My brain remained eerily quiet, and there was a ringing in my ears, like I'd been to a rock concert. Maybe it was always there, and I'd never stopped long enough to notice it. I noticed it now. Maybe this is what failure sounded like.

I'd been too far too many funerals. But this one was more like the first, my father's. I'd ridden in the town car provided for my family that rainy morning and the distance between my mother and me on that leather seat had felt like miles. It hadn't gotten any shorter in the years since.

At the cemetery, we made our way slowly from the graveled parking area, up the hill to where two sections of rowed white chairs stood against the almost too green turf laid out.

Hayne guided me down the middle aisle of the seats, passed the rest of the staff from the newspaper, his hands hovering at my shoulder and elbow. The ringing in my head muffled the kind words of other reporters as I walked through their ranks.

It was my father's funeral all over again. Near strangers giving me condolences that I wasn't sure I'd earned.

Dot had saved us a few seats in the front section, a strange understood place of honor for the editor-in-chief. The white folding chair wobbled under the weight of my still packed and ready-to-go messenger bag.

"I'm sorry," Dot said as she sat in the wooden chair beside me. Hayne's daughter was eight years younger than me, and looked up to me like a big sister, though today of all days, I wasn't sure I deserved that.

Ethan deserved that, I didn't. I'd lied to him. I'd promised he'd get home at a normal time, and now he was never going home.

"I couldn't believe it when Dad told me you were actually upholding the HR violence moratorium and hadn't been at work."

I took a moment to appreciate that Hayne was covering for me. Telling lies in my stead. "Yeah, well, even ace reporters have to let broken ribs heal."

"Geez, Merci," she said. "Dad said the cops stopped by but they didn't have any leads?"

Hayne cleared his throat and put his hand on his daughter's shoulder. "Leave her be, honey."

Dot pressed her lips together quickly, stopping the barrage of curiosity I knew came naturally to her.

Before I could say anything further, a figure blocked out the sun. At least it was sunny today, and on the warm side. I hadn't brought a scarf with me.

"Merci Lanard?" he asked.

I had to shield my eyes from the bright light behind him. The man was tall, as tall as Ethan had been. His dark curls did nothing to soften his angular features, and the casual hair stood out in sharp contrast to the black suit. My gaze fell to the white rose in his long fingers.

"I'm Emily's brother, Levi. She was wondering if you'd like to dedicate a flower during the service."

I swallowed as I searched for Emily. Her tall frame was standing in the front row surrounded by sorrowful faces and wrapped in comforting arms. God, Emily. What was I going to say to her? Hallmark hadn't made an *I'm sorry I got your husband killed* card. I had been unconscious in the ER when she had come to identify the body. So today was the first time I'd seen her since she, Ethan, and I had birthday tacos a few weeks ago. Had it only been a few weeks? That seemed like another life. One where Ethan was alive and we were laughing. Not this new sudden existence where he was dead and she was so far away.

Levi offered me the white rose. I stood and my hand shook as I took the long stem.

"You can stand in the front. He always did think of you as family."

As if this entire day wasn't going to be painful enough, the truth sliced into me like a razor. I was now alone. The one person I had to rely upon, to trust, was now gone, and I was alone. My constant who I'd talked to every day for two years, had holiday meals with, bought birthday presents for was gone, and I was alone.

Today of all days, I had been wishing that one fact might stay away, might remain in the numbness, in that hum in the back of my brain.

Levi escorted me to the end of a row of black-clad people also holding white roses. Just as I found my footing next to him, the pallbearers brought out the casket from the back of the hearse. I had seen the car sitting there, its sleek black finish gleaming in the unusually warm November morning. But it wasn't until six men pulled the mahogany casket from the back of the car that the thought occurred to me: his body had been there the whole time. Like he'd been listening to us, still with me as I stood there in uncomfortable heels. Like he was still there mocking me.

Whatcha all dressed up for, Lanard?

The thought hit me like a punch to the stomach, and I flinched.

A hand landed on my shoulder. My heart leapt. For an instant, the world went black again, and I was seized by a million hands on that cold, hard floor. I gasped and flung my arm at the assailant.

My forearm connected with something real, and with the connection, the spell was broken.

My vision returned to the present, and I found Levi putting his hands up between us. "You okay?" he asked.

I took in a few deep breaths to keep my heart from lodging in my throat. "No." I didn't lie. Couldn't lie. Not here. Not in front of Ethan.

My heart was still racing when the men carried him past me. As much as I wanted to, I resisted reaching out to touch it. I knew the truth. Ethan wasn't there. What made Ethan special was not trapped in the box. What made Ethan *Ethan* had slipped out of him that night.

A white handkerchief appeared to my right. It took me a moment to reorient myself to the present, rather than the past and pain.

"You've hurt yourself." I heard the concern in Levi's voice.

A rose thorn had pierced my palm.

I took the bit of white and pressed it against my hand. What was I going to do without Ethan? Even now I needed the Band-Aids he always carried around, the first aid kit he always had stocked with alcohol wipes, latex gloves, and more supplies than an entire Boy Scout troop put together. How many times had he patched me up? How many times had I patched him up?

I wondered if that was a family thing. Was everyone in his family so prepared, or was it specific to Ethan? I inspected the line of people with white roses, and none of their faces were familiar. Why were they not familiar? Why hadn't I asked more about him? His family? Why was our relationship primarily based around our work?

Ethan's loved ones were called forward to put the roses on the casket. I barely heard the minister. I was taking in everything about the people standing with me, and fresh questions began filling my brain. How did Ethan manage to keep these six people holding white roses a secret? Two years working together. Why didn't he speak more about them? How had he managed to keep it all in? Especially with a person like me sitting next to him for two years. A person whose job it was to pull out the darkest sins from people.

Correction: Had I ever even asked?

I followed the line of people to the side of his casket, my movements more automatic than intentional. Tension rolled across my shoulders. As my turn came at the side of the casket, I squeezed the rose too tightly, and again, the thorns pierced the soft mound of my palm.

I made another promise to him, one that I would never break.

I will find them, Ethan. I will find your killers, and they will not hurt anyone ever again.

I placed my rose on the top of all the others, and I walked back to my spot in front. I paused before Emily and ready to say something, anything. Her brown eyes were red, the tip of her nose shiny where she had already wiped off her makeup. I searched for the right words, but all I had in the moment were the cadre of limping apologizes and trite condolences. Nothing truly conveyed exactly how I felt for what had happened to her husband. The apologies I needed to make for the late nights and the missed dinners. That, of all the people here, we might be sharing the same severed leg feeling.

I just sighed and kept walking back to my chair at the end of the row.

The service concluded, and I watched, still as a headstone, as they lowered his casket into the ground, my blood-covered rose on the top.

It wasn't until Emily walked away, her arm wrapped around a tall blonde woman, and the crowd began to disperse that I realized I'd stopped breathing, as if seeing if I could survive under the ground, if we could switch places.

I sat back down on one of the chairs, my energy draining into the earth, the questions settling for a moment, the muffled silence returning, as I felt him leave me again.

This was it. Ethan was gone. He wasn't coming back. Just like Dad never came back. It was just me. Abandoned again.

I heard the sounds of a scuffle, and I looked up from the hole in the ground to see Emily's brother glaring down at a man half a head shorter than him. The strange man's eyes were fierce and his face flushed. Their voices were nothing more than growls and gravel on the wind.

Where there is family, there is drama. Or at least, that is what I'd been told. This wasn't my fight. Let these strangers handle it themselves.

I pushed myself up from the wooden chair and walked to the parking lot. Hayne, Dot, and the rest of the staff were waiting for me when I finally made it to his car.

Dot fussed over my hand, taking the white handkerchief and inspecting my palm. She held it tightly until she was sure that it wasn't going to bleed anymore, prattling on about a new literature professor she had who was completely dreamy, as if thoughts of a cute boy could help distract me from today. She was too good for this world.

Hayne's brow had been furrowed when he'd picked me up that morning, and the furrow hadn't smoothed out yet. "We're going over to McTaggert's."

"I thought Irish wakes were the night before the funeral."

"Shut up and get in the car, Lanard."

As I read the others, I knew the truth. Just like they had rallied in the newsroom, they were rallying at our favorite bar because they didn't want to be alone any more than I did.

Hayne walked me to the passenger side and opened my door.

"She's lying!"

The words echoed across the parking lot, and everyone turned. They turned because it was a show; it was a spectacle at a funeral. It distracted people from their loss and own sense of mortality.

I turned around because this voice felt like someone sliding a blanket across my skin. The static in my brain rose to greet this new sensation, as did the hairs on the back of my neck.

The man I'd seen fighting with Levi stormed across the parking lot straight toward me. Hayne tried to step between us, but I restrained him with an outstretched hand. I'd never hidden behind Hayne before, I wasn't about to start now. I would face him as I faced all threats, head on.

When he stopped before me, my skin singed under his teal-blue eyes and the anger that poured off of him. He glared at me, the arch of his eyebrow giving a wicked articulation to a presence that felt bigger than his body. Who was he? What were he and Levi fighting about? Why had he called me a liar? The questions started circling around in my brain and the sizzle to answer them was like Frankenstein's monster being brought back to life.

"You're lying about what happened that night."

My body reanimated with the new electricity running through it. I took my time with my answer as I collected details. The who's and what's of the situation. Accent was Scottish. Couldn't be family. He was smaller than Ethan. The suit was new from the smell of it. And, seriously, those eyes were as deep as an ocean trench.

"I never lie about anything," I answered, keeping my voice steady and my nerves calm.

He thrust his finger at me. "You got him killed."

Oh, the game was on now. A smile played across my lips as the current danced around my head, tingling and tightening the hairs at the nape of my neck, "You really want to do this here?"

"Yes. Here." His glare deepened. "I need to know."

It was comforting to feel the familiar chill down my spine as I slipped into interrogation mode.

"Did you see the initial police report?" I asked.

"It was a load of shite."

The police report didn't have much in it because I didn't have much to tell. Even now, after three days of reliving it in my head, there was very little I could articulate about what had happened. And I'd never give up Benny as my informant—his ass was mine. "What do you think happened?"

"Ethan was targeted. Either by your stupidity or—" He snapped his mouth shut as the words nearly spilled out of him.

"Or what?" My voice somehow remained calm though I was vibrating on the inside with anticipation, like a high schooler with their first cup of coffee.

Tension filled his jaw and his entire body as he restrained himself from speaking.

I bit my lip to keep the questions inside. Who was this man? Why did he think that Ethan's death was on me? What did he think happened that night? They were all right there, the questions, beating against the inside of my skull like a swarm of angry bees against a window.

He took another step toward me. I watched his lips, the flush of his cheek as he spoke. "I will find out what happened."

I didn't back down. Never backed down. "No, I will. He was my partner."

His nostrils flared, and his knuckles went white at his sides. "Aye, but he was my brother."

It was like steel bat to my midsection, and all the air left me in one quick assault.

Ethan never mentioned a brother.

In two years, I'd only known Emily. And as I spied the sea of unfamiliar faces that watched us, I didn't know any of them. Not any of the other family members who had dropped a rose on his casket, not half of the attendees who hovered around, watching horrified as our argument escalated.

I took a step back and into Hayne, and his soft hands held my shoulders.

Ethan lied to me?

How could he? I'd told him everything. Everything about my father, my mother, the hunt of a story. Embarrassing high school stories and first loves. Everything.

And he had lied about having a brother.

There was one question in the swarm that had not been silenced by the man's confession and the barrage of betrayal that threatened to pick me up and sweep me away. One that seemed to persist its way to my lips. "Who's Piper?"

And like that, the other people in the parking lot stepped in. It was no longer me and this wrecking ball, but Levi and the blonde and then a bear-like man hauling my accuser across the parking lot.

Hayne stepped in front of me, blocking my view, preventing me from chasing after him. "We need to go."

"Ethan lied to me."

Hayne shook his head. "Come on, Lanard. It's been a rough day. Let's get a drink."

I let him maneuver me back into the car, one question repeating over and over in my head: How had Ethan lied to the girl who always found out the truth?

CHAPTER TWO

"Lanard, I got it." Steven the IT guy brought me Ethan's laptop. He set it on my desk. "It had a 128-bit encryption, pretty good stuff, but I'm better."

"So not the usual stuff you guys pre-load on the machines?"

Steven shook his head as the screen booted up between us.

I shoved my keyboard aside and pulled the laptop in front of me. Ethan's desktop picture was of him and Emily on one of their monthly hikes.

I shot Steven a small smile. "Thanks. I owe you."

"Owe me? I thought Hayne approved this to get his pictures?"

"Right. Totally legit. Now don't you have something else to hack?"

Steven disappeared into the background clattering of the newsroom as I started digging through the files. Technically, it was a company computer. Technically, it was part of an active investigation. And technically, the newspaper had paid Ethan for the images, so they were company property. But probably not meant for my eyes.

Ethan would forgive me for investigating his family. After the funeral, I couldn't shake that Ethan had lied. Emily and Ethan had omitted a huge part of their lives from me, a brother. It trumped any story about the Mayor denying some meaningless construction bribes.

Ethan would understand that I needed answers if I was ever going to sleep without alcohol persuasion again, even if Hayne might not. Ethan would understand that I would stop at nothing to find the truth. And right now, the questions of why Ethan was hiding a brother drove my search toward his family.

I scanned through the files and was able to crack his email archive without IT help. He'd always been so romantically faithful, so of course the password was his wife's name and their anniversary. I scanned through his emails, searching for new names.

Unfortunately, it seemed that they weren't into email. Ethan's messages were mostly newspaper HR spam and links to hiking websites from Emily. Nothing had a suspicious vibe. Nothing pointed to a secret life that would get him killed.

I opened his picture files and found one called "ML." I double-clicked it, and my stomach dropped. It was full of pictures of me. Weird side shots when he was testing the lighting of places, odd shots of me laughing, and a few of me thinking. I opened one where he'd done some camera trick that made me look like I had a red halo or maybe the sun was setting behind me. I checked the time stamp. Two weeks before his death. In fact, there were quite a few from that time period and all of them featured me, surrounded by that same strange red aura.

"Lanard."

I jumped at Hayne's voice and slammed the laptop shut. I spun around in my chair to see him walking toward me, his arm around Emily's shoulder. I rose as they stopped at my desk. I needed to be on my feet for this encounter.

My stomach immediately twisted into knots along with my tongue. I didn't know what to say. I'd comforted a million victims' families before, but those crime victims had never been my friend. The last time it was just Emily and I, we'd had a "girls' lunch," and over sandwiches, brainstormed ways to keep Ethan from growing a beard. Now we only had two feet of tile and a bag of her dead husband's things.

"Mrs. Rhoades came in for Ethan's possessions and Steven told me you had his laptop."

I grabbed it from my desk and clutched it to my chest. "It's company property and part of an active story."

Emily's doe eyes brimmed with tears. There was no denying that Emily was gorgeous. Tall with golden skin. And she was somehow more beautiful now as the grieving widow. It made me feel like Orphan Annie as I stood before her.

"It's his laptop. I mean, it's his work. Our work. Why do you need it?" I asked.

Emily tried to answer, but nothing really came out.

Hayne interrupted her silence. "Merci, just give her the laptop."

Knowing there was no way I was going to win this, I handed it over. Emily took it and put it in a black canvas tote, where I saw the contents of Ethan's desk: his extra shirt, his stress ball, and his "World's Best Partners" coffee mug probably still smelling of whiskey. It took everything I had not to ask for that back and I'd fill it with regret for not having that last drink with him.

"Did you happen to see a silver medallion?" Emily voice wasn't shaky, but wasn't as strong as I remembered it. Definitely wasn't strong enough to keep a classroom of thirty third-graders in check.

I gulped. The medallion bounced against my stomach in response to Emily's answer. I shook my head. I wasn't ready to give that part of him away yet.

Her shoulder's slumped. "It must have gotten lost at the hospital."

She turned to go, but I wasn't done yet. There was something still unfinished as I stood there feeling like the kid with her hand in a cookie jar, a very bloody cookie jar.

"Emily, I... Ethan told me to tell you that he loved you." I couldn't say why that truth came out just then, but something inside me pushed me to share this bit of Ethan. It was as if talking about him might keep him alive for a little while longer, and keep *her* with me a little longer so I didn't lose her too. And those are the words that came out, the truth taking the place of the lie I'd omitted about the medallion.

"Why would you say that?" Emily asked, staring at me as if I'd asked about the proper way to eat a cockroach.

I flinched at her reaction. "It's the last thing he said. 'Tell Emily I loved her,' and 'Tell Piper I'm sorry.'"

Emily pressed her lips together and shook her head. Her eyes sparkled with tears as they locked with mine.

"Who's Piper?" The last time I'd asked, a group of people had pulled me away. But it was just Emily and me now, the two people who had to want to know what happened to Ethan.

Emily bit down hard on her lip and her chin quivered. She was keeping something from me. Was it about his family? Was it about his death?

The electricity started to brew again in my head and sizzle down through our connection, pressing her for the answer, pushing the question at her. "Do you know who killed Ethan?"

Emily turned and ran. She didn't just look away, she ran away from me and across the newsroom floor, clutching the black canvass tote to her chest. Her feet saved her from the truth.

"Please, Emily. Talk to me!" I yelled after her.

Hayne's hand clamped down on my shoulder. White-hot pain from my still-healing ribs ran across my vision and I froze. Hayne pulled me back and grabbed my arm. It didn't budge as he dragged me into his office like a petulant child being hauled to the principal's office.

I didn't stop fighting until my ass hit the familiar leather cushion of the hot seat. My heart pounded against my ribs, and I put my head in my hands, running my fingers through the curly mess that had become my mourning hair.

"I know you're grieving, but for Christ's sake, Merci. That was his wife."

As soon as I heard him shut the door behind me, I retorted. "She knows something, Hayne."

"She wasn't the one who killed him."

"Then why not just answer the question?"

"She doesn't have to!" Hayne pointed a knobby finger at me as he leaned against the desk in front of me. "Yes, he's dead. Yes, you're grieving. But you need to consume something other than Jack Daniels and get your head on straight."

I took in a deep breath, until the electricity that danced between my shoulder blades settled and my heart reached a fairly normal pace. "I just don't understand. Emily should want me to find out who did this. Why run?"

Hayne knelt down before me and I stared into his concerned gray eyes. "Grief manifests in different ways. You of all people should know that, Merci."

And I did. Perhaps a little too well. Greif over my father had manifested into a mad dash to college to take over the family business without a second thought. To work for this city just like my father had all those year ago. This grief, well, I wasn't sure what it looked like yet.

"I've been meaning to say thank you for writing up the article."

"I can still sling words around when I need to." Hayne shook his head. "Maybe you need some time. Go see those cousins in California. Go visit your mother."

I frowned and sat up. Hayne knew how I felt about my mother. How her country club couture could stay on her side of the state line and my chaos could stay on mine – and neither the twain shall meet. Why would he mention her now?

"Don't take me off this, Hayne. We were on to something. Our informant was going to give us names that connected City Hall to a new gang and the missing girls in the Trade Streets. We were so close."

That was a lie. And the lie's flavor filled my mouth—a rotten sort of lemon flavor that made me wince. It was times like these I hated being a journalist's daughter who had the truth preached to her for her whole life, to the point that she couldn't lie without repercussion.

A compulsion that had manifested in a psychosomatic reaction to self-deception. Or at least that's what one of my old shrinks said.

"Why shouldn't I take you off this? We don't want you going all Teddy on us."

I set my jaw, pain flaring up the side of my face as I glared at my boss. This was not going to be the event that sent me off the deep end and into Sunnybrook for a mental health vacation. We both knew that.

A tingle ran down my spine as Hayne shifted under my gaze. "You can't let him die for nothing."

Hayne sighed as he crossed his arms over his chest and looked away. They always looked away. I hadn't met a person yet who could withstand the Lanard stare.

Hayne held his hands up in surrender. "I'm not putting you on leave. But I need you to take care of yourself. I've already lost one staffer. I can't lose you, too."

I leaned back in the hot seat, the old metal squeaking out a protest. He wasn't going to lose me too, but from the outside, I'm sure that wasn't as evident. "I can promise you one hot meal in the next twenty-four hours."

"Thank you." He studied me with those tired gray eyes. "I know there was a lot you two didn't tell me about your process, things you researched that never made copy, and I respect that. If you think that one of those stories pissed off someone enough to go after you, then you need to get after them first."

My mind went blank for a moment, as I tried to comprehend what he'd just said. "What?"

He rose, pulling himself away from me and sat in the other chair, where Ethan usually sat while I was being read the riot act. "I have never seen anyone in my life face down danger like you do, and then do it again and again. One win on the heels of another. Its uncanny."

For some reason, this was hard to hear. Partly, because it made me sound reckless, but mostly because I didn't do that alone. But I was going to have to now. I didn't have my wingman, and the loss was wincingly fresh again. I rubbed my arm keep the ghost chill of my severed limb at bay.

Hayne gave me a reassuring face. He didn't give actual smiles, but this face was as close as he got. "If anyone can find his killer, your instincts will get you there. But you need to sleep and eat actual food, drink something that isn't whiskey."

But with sleep came dreams, and the dreams reminded me how badly I was failing at the only thing I was good at. I'd exhausted all possible avenues that weren't putting an APB out on Benny, and Emily wasn't exactly forthcoming with any information.

I took in a deep breath. Hayne was right. I needed to trust my instincts. They had gotten me this far. And if I could trust anything else in this world, I could trust my instinct to get into trouble and find the truth.

I stood up from the hot seat. "Okay, Chief."

Hayne was slightly confused at my answer, but gestured for the door.

"Oh, and, Lanard?" Hayne called after me as he went back to his side of the desk.

"Yeah, Chief?"

"One more outburst like that, I'm putting you on the Lifestyles pages."

...

I lifted the whiskey to the second man to buy me a drink that afternoon and threw the two fingers back. The first drink came with a thank you from a regular who I'd helped out with some unfair rezoning legislation, but this mysterious Romeo at the dark end of the bar was just a nice man who wanted to cut down on my tab. Poor sap. I set the empty tumbler down, still staring at the police reports.

"Whatcha working on this time, Lanard?" Bill asked as he took my tumbler and put it in the washer under the bar.

I glanced up. "I'll know it when I see it."

The bartender nodded and popped open a few more beers for the other patrons. He came back to lean against the bar before me. "I don't know if I told you personally the other night, but I'm sorry about Ethan. He was a good guy. You two were a good team. He'll be missed."

I looked away from the work before me and kept my eyes open, drying the water gathered there. Where my gut reaction was to say "Get bent with your bar towel," my inner voice, Ethan's voice, was like a warm hand on my shoulder.

He was trying to be nice. And this is one of the few bars you haven't been thrown out of.

I cleared my throat. "Thanks, Bill."

He poured me another drink and set it on the bar before me. "Let me order you up a cheesesteak for dinner."

"I'm good. But thanks."

He nodded and moved over to another sorry soul on a stool down the way. I went back to work too.

I'd called in a few favors with the police, the tax assessor's office, and the elementary school where Emily worked to get employment records, police reports, and anything I could to ease this nagging suspicion. Not even my obsessive truth-seeking could quiet the ache of going behind her back. I didn't want to investigate Emily and her family like this. I'd much rather just ask her to her face, get the honest answers, feel the communication flowing between us, as easily as it did before, but the other day had shown me that neither of us was ready for the questions I needed to ask.

What was Ethan really hiding from me? Why didn't he tell me about his brother?

Hayne had said to listen to my instincts. My instincts were telling me that if Ethan was keeping secrets, there had to be a reason. And that reason might be as dangerous as drugs or missing people. Could even be something on par with shadowy killers who appear out of nowhere.

And this brother? The one who spoke with such sound and fury? Nothing. Without a name, he didn't exist on paper. There was no record of Ethan having a brother, and yet his voice in my head kept me awake at night, with the shattering of Ethan's friendship.

There was definitely something strange about the Howard family, Emily's family. Longevity for one. The establishment papers on her brother's construction company were filed in Pennsylvania in 1970, making Levi Howard at least fifty, and he hadn't appeared a day over thirty-five. The Howard Construction Company had been at the same location for nearly thirty years until Levi filed for a rezoning of an old warehouse to be the new front for his business ten months ago. I matched a police report to his old office location for a B&E.

What could have scared Levi into moving? Surely it was something more than a little B&E. But what? Corruption, drugs, bribes, human trafficking?

It's not drugs until you find a crack pipe.

I smiled. Ethan said that to me on more than one occasion. I had this habit of writing the endings to the articles, of knowing the truth of the stories before we had evidence on everything. It infuriated Ethan that I assumed the worst every time, though nearly every time I was right.

I sighed and took a sip of the whiskey. If Emily Howard Rhoades was involved in something nefarious, it didn't show in her work; her school employment had been exemplary. When I'd called, her principal said that because Emily always took long weekends for their monthly hiking trips and was still out on bereavement leave, she was running low on her vacation time and was in jeopardy of losing her job. But I knew from the tone of the man's voice that he would never fire Emily.

On a general search of the police database cross-referenced with her name, I'd stumbled upon a report detailing vandalism to the school where she worked. Only her classroom was ransacked. Desks overturned, windows broken from the inside, spray paint on the walls, yet nothing taken. It was definitely a surprising find. Could this be the evidence I needed that the Howard family *wasn't* on the up-and-up? Two break-ins in less than two months?

"Hey."

What I couldn't figure out was why there wasn't a bigger inquiry? Practically nothing had been reported. Of course, my dad would have said that two break-ins made a coincidence, only three made a pattern.

And more importantly, Ethan hadn't mentioned a word of it to me. That stung, and damned the family further. You'd think it would merit a mention during a seven-hour stakeout when we were talking about our college heydays or my little psychosomatic thing that happened when I told a lie. God, he had loved that. Especially the descriptions of some of the flavors.

Bill rapped his knuckles on the bar in front of me. I jerked my head up. He hitched his thumb over to my right.

My mysterious Romeo was standing beside me the bar. His eyes were trained on me, and there was a quirk to his lips, but all I could do was stare at his greasy, slicked-back hair and his terrible plaid blazer.

"Can I help you?"

"I wanted to know how that drink is."

I inspected the drink still in my hand. "Pretty good."

"What about the one before that? The one I sent over."

I snorted. This guy was seriously trying to hit on me? In the middle of the day? In that get-up? "Pretty good."

He moved to take the stool next to me, but I put a hand on his chest and pushed him back. "Listen. I am absolutely positive you are a spectacular guy, but I'm really not interested right now. So if you'd like the six bucks back for your conversation starter, I'm sure Bill could put it on my tab."

He smiled down at me. "You really are a ballbuster."

"Excuse me?"

"Everyone knows Merci Lanard always gets her man. I mean, look at how easily you took down Cartwright. Seems pretty little lonely at the top now, though."

I instinctively balled my fist and flexed my forearm, making the wound flare to life. The pain spread up my shoulder and heated my cheeks.

Last bar you haven't been kicked out of, Ethan repeated in my head.

I forced a smile. I needed to keep my head. Truth was, this wasn't the first jerk who hadn't gotten the hint, and it probably wouldn't be the last.

"Listen," he continued smoothly. "How about you come with me, we have a few drinks, and I'll let you see if I'm the man you're looking for."

"Unless you're responsible for the death of my partner, you're not the guy."

"How do you know?" he said with a smile whiter than it should have been, wider than it should have been.

It was the ugly smile that jogged my memory, the notion that there were too many teeth. He'd been snooping around the Mayor's office a day late and a dollar short on the Cartwright construction bribe story. "I know you. You're from *The Teller*. Mitchell, right?"

There was a moment of panic in his eyes as his ruse crumbled. "I want to know what happened that night."

I laughed in his face. This sad excuse for a reporter was trying to scoop Ethan's attack? "You couldn't find a headline at high noon."

Bill stepped in and probably prevented lawsuit number five. "Why don't you leave the lady alone?"

"Why should I? She's got her own editor publishing lies. Someone has to tell the truth to the people of this city."

I dropped my chin and looked up at him, the thunder rolling through my temples. "Are you seriously going to question my story?"

The electric sizzle started between my shoulders and seemed to travel to where my hand still curled around the whiskey tumbler.

"Someone has to."

"Merci, I think you should go," Bill said.

"Why? I'm not insulting the integrity of your clientele."

Bill had to pry the tumbler from my left hand. I turned to my neighborhood bartender and my anger dissipated a fraction as he held me within his calm blue eyes. "Ease up, Lanard," he said softly.

But what I heard was Ethan's voice telling me to stay out of trouble. I didn't have back up like I used to.

Mitchell stepped forward quickly. He reached for the inside of my sleeve and caught the edge of the white bandage that peeked out of my shirt.

"What's this?" he demanded as he tore the medical tape and gauze from my arm.

Fire flew up my forearm, and I clutched the wound to my chest.

"Article didn't mention you getting cut. You're hiding things, Lanard," Mitchell waved the bloody gauze between us.

I looked down at the still red and raw wound on my arm. There was a faint memory of a surgery resident making the small, clear sutures on my deadened skin. I ignored it mostly for the past week.

White tape dangled, half torn off and exposing the strange mark. Blood started to ooze out of the straight, deeper middle portion of it. The hook at the end seemed still tightly sown back together. The gore, the fresh blood froze my thoughts for a moment as I looked at wound like it was on someone else's arm.

Bill came to my rescue with a white towel and more expletives flung at the reporter than I had ever heard strung together in one breath.

The man clenched his jaw and left the door barely on its hinges as he stormed out.

I held the towel to my arm and my arm to my chest and exhaled through the fresh pain.

"I'm sorry about that, Merci," Bill said as he returned to his proper side of the bar. He pulled out two clean glasses and poured whiskey into each.

"Great. Am I driving you to drinking too?" I asked him as I sat back down on my stool, surveying the scattered papers.

"I hate guys like that."

I laughed. "You run a bar frequented by guys like that."

"You're different from those ambulance chasers, though. You fight hard. You drink like a fish, but you care. Guys like that are only in it for the acclaim."

I snorted. "Yeah, some acclaim. Look where it got me, got Ethan."

Bill shook his head and sipped his whiskey. "You will never convince me otherwise, Merci."

I made a wish that Mitchell wasn't the last man to buy me a drink in a bar, and threw back the amber liquid. I'd made a promise to Hayne and at least I could keep one promise this month. "Cheesesteak, extra whiz?"

"Coming right up."

CHAPTER THREE

I'd gotten myself into some interesting spots before. In the closet during a sexscapade starring the former governor. Hiding out in an air duct for a day to catch corporate espionage. Kidnapped by a serial rapist. But never had I ever found myself climbing a tree during a full moon to watch a bunch of people go camping.

Ethan and Emily had gone camping every month. He'd even pack up in the middle of a story and leave for three days. Middle of the week. National holidays. Ethan hadn't lied to me about that. I knew they went hiking and camping often.

I'd been rethinking what I knew about Ethan, what I could prove, what I had seen with my own eyes. He went camping with his wife; I'd seen the pictures. He loved puns; I'd been the victim of his jokes for two years. He held more than a few cheesesteak eating records at local restaurants; I'd been there for most of them. He listened to hours of me talking through my frustrations with my mother. He planned something silly to do on my birthdays and always made sure to call me on major family holidays.

That was all I had so far. I couldn't prove the rest of who he really was. So I did what all good reporters do—searched for more proof. I'd looked through my notebook to find Ethan had taken his last foray into the forest just over three weeks ago. They were due for another visit on Friday. So since Emily wasn't going to talk to me, I had to get the information with an old-fashioned stakeout. So in no time, I was waiting outside Emily's place, and, sure enough, she took off that night with a large pack tossed in the back of her Jeep, and I followed her straight here.

I had assumed they were camping at the plethora of local national parks around Philly. But that's not where we were now. I'd followed her car out to the large property I'd found while digging through the Howard Family holdings. Just an hour outside of the city, the property was just land. No buildings and no real roads or electricity or plumbing running to it.

So why did a city family of construction workers, who built for a living, need a significant chunk of undeveloped land? The storm started brewing and I wanted to know—no, needed to know—what they did every month.

So here I was, up a tree. Following where my instincts led me.

I found a steady branch and sat on it, leaning against the broad trunk. The night was bitter cold, and I was aware of my cloudy breath as I perched. My position in the tree was high enough that I could see a group of people mulling about on the crest of a hill. Not a lick of camping equipment in sight.

Why camping? There was certainly nothing appealing about sitting around, freezing in the woods on a November night and certainly nothing that needed to be done every twenty-eight days out here.

I pulled my coat collar up around my ears against the frozen night. I'd forgotten a scarf again.

For a moment, I hurt. My entire body ached with grief again as I sat alone in the tree. As desperate for answers as some of the mothers I've talked to, the ones who were trying to figure out how their sons got involved in crime in the first place.

As if it was carried on the breeze, I heard Ethan's voice.

Lanard, pity party of one.

I chuckled despite myself. That's right. I didn't have the right to feel self-pity. I was alive and there was a story to chase. I could be on the verge of witnessing something that would open the door to why Ethan was killed. Drugs. Human trafficking?

Through my binoculars, I saw Levi, Emily's brother, standing at the center of the clearing at the top of a wooded hill, bathed in full moonlight. It was easy to make out other figures through my binoculars. So the "camping" was a family thing. It wasn't just Ethan and Emily, but the entire crew? But where were the tents? Was this one of those survivalist cults?

Levi took off his shirt and any estimation of his age was thrown out the window. He was ripped, totally buff, the moonlight defining every abdominal. In fact, as most of the others followed suit and shed their clothing down to the bare essentials, I could make out lots of very in-shape people. The group, maybe forty now in total, peeled off layers of clothing. What was happening? Correction: Was this a nudist survivalist cult?

Levi seemed to be addressing the group, but I was too far away to make out his words. He extended his arms out and leaned his head back. The scent of puppies filled the air, and a hot brush of fur swept against my cheek and my cold hand pressed against my face as if to catch the softness. My whole body was immediately relaxed, like something hit a button inside of me that made me as limp as a rag doll.

Nearly losing my braced perch, I barely caught myself before I fell off the branch. The limb shook violently, sending dead leaves and twigs falling the twenty feet to the ground. My heart jumped in my throat at the vision of being splayed out at the bottom of the tree like a suicidal squirrel.

Frustrated, I positioned myself better on the limb and cursed my sensitive nerves. What the hell was that? I moved to note it to my audio recorder, only to find that it must have taken the dive to the forest floor without me.

I sighed. At least I had my binoculars.

The air was suddenly charged, like I'd run my socks over a mile of carpet, like when I knew that a story was going to break. I could still smell puppies around me as the hair on my arms stood on end and the nape of my neck prickled.

Levi was still standing at the apex of the hill, a clear shot for me to see. I watched patiently through the binoculars. Though for a moment I thought they'd fogged; one second, Levi was clear, in the next, he was blurry, and in the third, a huge wolf with black fur and a sharp, angular snout stood proudly.

He looked straight at me, his gaze piercing through the branches.

I gulped.

Levi had turned into a wolf.

The others began to shimmer, and animals began to fill the clearing, pacing and running and chasing each other. People faded into wolves, dogs, a mountain lion. A few hawks began to circle overhead. It was hard to miss the huge black bear that lumbered over the top of the hill then disappeared into the tree line.

The wind wrapped a howl around me. My skin goose bumped, and I shivered in my coat on my little branch in the middle of the woods surrounded by animals, most of them carnivores.

I knew that sound. The memory of that scream had jolted me awake for the past two weeks. The primal scream that Ethan had emitted, the scream that had drawn the men off my back.

The truth left me white knuckled and gasping.

It hadn't been a scream that night. It had been a howl.

Ethan was a werewolf.

Magic was real, and I'd just seen it with my own two eyes.

Ethan's family were werewolves, and I had followed them out in to the woods. Alone. With nothing more than an audio recorder, binoculars, and a stun gun, my usual arsenal. Nothing with silver or anything smart like a gun or knife.

How do people protect themselves against bears? Was it to make a loud noise or just stay up the tree? But I'd seen large cats, too, and mountain lions were very adept at climbing trees. In fact, that's where they preferred their prey. I was going to die. I was going to be eaten by my deceased partner's family for following my insanely dangerous instincts again.

I listened to the night. The scent of puppies had dissipated a long time ago, and I couldn't hear anything padding around in the forest over the sound of the whirling blood in my ears.

A twig snapped, and the wind carried a rustle that seemed to dance around me and disorient the direction it might have come from. Perhaps staying in the tree was better.

I looked down at my feet to secure my bearings on the branch and saw a man at the bottom staring up. Still and pale, his large eyes shone in the moonlight, like a predator on a night vision camera.

Exposed and drowning in a fear, I froze. I could feel my heart lodge in my throat as I contemplated a defensive move. Drop something? My binoculars? God, how could I have been so stupid to climb a tree in the middle of the night with nothing but an audio recorder and a Taser?

"Lanard?"

I would have known that voice anywhere. The man from the funeral. I readied for battle and kept looking for a weapon.

"What?" I called down.

"What the hell are you doing here?" he called up.

"Are you one of them?" I looked to the crest of the hill, remembering what I had just seen. Humans that turned into animals, and I already knew how vicious he could be in human form.

He shuffled around the base of the tree. "You've got to come down."

"Answer me."

"Yes, and so was Ethan."

And I knew it. I couldn't refute it now after what I had witnessed. He was telling the truth.

Werewolves were real, and Ethan had been one of them.

And I was stuck up a tree in the middle of the woods. But somehow, climbing down seemed the most sensible option. It wasn't like I'd ever gotten into anything I couldn't charm my way out of. Except the IRS investigation. I was going to be audited for the rest of my life after that one. And the whole nearly getting beaten to death by people whose faces I couldn't see while my partner's throat was slit. There was that.

But up until this moment, this particular adversary had only berated me with words, and words I could fight with. Teeth not so much.

The climb down was not as graceful as the climb up had been. My foot slipped on last knob before the ground, and I stumbled out of the tree and straight into him. He caught me and righted me quickly.

I didn't have to look up at him; he was my height. But what struck me was how warm my face was before his, like standing in front of a space heater. I would have stayed there in that warmth for the rest of the night. Ethan has been just as warm.

Jarred by the painful comparison, I pushed myself away and brushed the dirt from my hands and jeans. "What are you doing here?"

He scoffed at the question. He took a step closer, and I wanted to take a step back, like part of me knew that close was not a safe place to be with him. "We need to go," he whispered as he surveyed the woods.

I didn't budge, except to reach for the recorder in my pocket, before remembering it was somewhere beneath the tree. "You called me a liar."

He glared at me.

"You said I got Ethan killed," I pressed further as I searched for my recorder.

"From where I'm standing, your instincts get you into dangerous situations."

"From where I'm standing, you and your family look a lot like monsters."

It was the word, like I'd plucked the one word from all of creation that stung him like a bee, and he flinched.

"It's not safe out here for you."

"I was fine up in my tree."

His gaze shimmied up the tree and down with it came a confession that I was not expecting. "There is a lot about our family Ethan never told you," he finally said.

"Like that he had a brother or that he was a werewolf?"

"Both."

I wanted him to be lying, but he wasn't. He didn't turn his head away or cover his mouth with his hands; his eyes moved naturally around the situation. He was telling the truth. Or his version of it.

Play nice, Lanard. You're out of your league here.

Dammit. I hated when Ethan was right. What did I know about people who changed into animals? I had no clue where to start with this piece of information, let alone with how to trust this man in front of me.

He nodded and extended his hand. "Rafe MacCallan."

"Merci . . ." and I trailed off because as I touched his hand, I was met with another wave of warmth, and a soft, intimate brush of silky fur against my neck. It left me breathless and my knees went weak for another moment.

Like lightning, MacCallan held on to my hand and scooped his other arm around my waist, bringing me close to him again.

"Are you all right, Miss Lanard?" he asked as I gained my footing.

I blushed only for a second before embarrassment turned into anger. I never faint and now I'd come close twice in one night. I took a step away from him and shook it off, regaining my solid footing, physically and mentally. It was probably hunger. I was trying to get food on a regular interval. Yet another thing that Ethan did, regulate my food cycles. He was always hungry.

With the pale of his skin and the bright of the moon, MacCallan managed one of the most pronounced furrows in the history of eyebrow furrows. He gestured back in the direction of the road. "Better be getting you back to your car."

"Not without my . . ." I scanned the forest floor for my device and found it just on the other side of MacCallan. Still recording. So if I was eaten tonight, at least it would be well documented.

I followed the broad sway of his shoulders as he moved easily through the tangled underbrush, and noticed he was only wearing a long-sleeve black cotton shirt. No jacket or anything else to keep him warm.

During our silent hike, he paused a few times, and I watched as he listened, turned his head and cocked it at a funny angle. Just like Ethan had done that night.

Ethan was a werewolf.

If I just kept repeating it to myself, maybe it would sink in.

We broke the line of the trees to a small parking lot. I recognized Emily's Jeep that I had followed. I pointed down the road to where I'd hidden my little four door on a small side drive parallel to the gravel road I'd crept down hours before my entire world view had shifted.

MacCallan kept peering into the tree line and perhaps he could see into the dark.

Maybe now we were out of the woods, I could get a little more out of him. Just a few simple, general questions. Something to orient me with this new information. Something simple that might help him open up to me, answer the gathering questions pressing down on me.

"Are you naturally hot blooded? I mean, it must be thirty degrees out here and none of you were wearing . . ." My brain flashed to the sheer amount of nudity I'd just witnessed. "Um, coats," I covered quickly.

"It's cyclical. Our body temperatures rise under a full moon," he said smoothly.

"Like a fever?"

"Almost, but nothing is communicable unless in animal form."

I stopped, startled at his meaning. "Communicable?" I asked. "Like a disease?"

"We talk of it as a disease because there is no real vernacular to describe it. In this language, at least."

There were too many questions. Even if I rapid fired this interrogation, there was too much to know, too much that I had to know to move forward to even ask the next question. I wasn't going to sleep. I had a two-year friendship to rethink, a magical community to explore, and a new gang to start hunting. My instincts told me Ethan's death was somewhere in the crosshairs of that mess.

I went back to the basic of journalism, BUILD RAPPORT 101. "Can I buy you a burger?"

...

Sam's was this great little place off the highway back toward town. From the private property, it was only a short fifteen minutes to get there. I ended up at Sam's more often than I wanted to, but people felt cozy in the little, twenty-four-hour mom-and-pop diner. It was easier to spill secrets in this remote locale. The vinyl seats had become a confessional booth to many as I sat and listened, rarely even having to ply my charm at all.

I scooted into my usual booth in the corner of the long restaurant and watched as MacCallan sat across from me in the hot seat. He had the same grace as Ethan, that effortless smoothness I'd never been able to explain. Until tonight. It was the animal in him. The wolf coming through.

Under the fluorescent lights, I got a better look at him. He was closer to my height than Ethan's, his shoulders broader than mine. His hair was dark brown, like Ethan's, with faint red highlights I knew shimmered red in the sun. As he scanned the menu I had memorized, I watched him turn over the laminated list and noticed he had good, solid hands. Ethan's has been long and spindly, like him. My Grand-Mere had told me that was the measure of a good man, that he had to have good, strong hands.

I slid off my coat, warm for the first time in hours. I glanced down and spotted blood on my sleeve, and my heart raced at the sight. It was all I could see, all over my hands, all over my shirt and jeans, the table. Like a scene from a horror movie, splashed up on to the window and across the table.

"Excuse me," I managed out before I ran for the bathroom.

I leaned over the porcelain sink, my head against the mirror, and took in three deep breaths, trying to get my heart to stop pounding. I had to force my gaze up to my reflection. No bruises, no gashes along my neck. I was fine. No wounds. I was fine.

Well, I wasn't really fine. The bandage on my arm had leaked through to my shirt. The damn thing wasn't healing. But then, I hadn't really given it a chance, definitely hadn't followed the aftercare recommendations.

I dropped my bag on the sink and opened it, digging through for the small first aid kit I'd nicked from Ethan's desk. One of the few things Emily didn't take home, probably because she knew that I needed it more, having witnessed some of the scrapes that we had been in.

I carefully covered the old bandage with a new one and taped down the edges. Once patched up, I washed my hands.

"I'm fine," I told my reflection, but the sour taste in my mouth told me the truth.

I took out my ponytail and raked my fingers through my hair to find some semblance of order in the curls. I put it back into a bun and then dug out some lip balm from my back pocket. I patted my face with a damp paper towel. I couldn't do anything about the dark circles under my eyes. I was presentable enough for this conversation. I might feel like shit, but there was work to do, there were stories to write, promises to keep. And I now at least one of Ethan's family members seemed willing to talk to me.

MacCallan shifted in the booth as I slid in across from him.

His gaze stayed with me as I settled. "I ordered some coffee."

"Perfect."

The waitress came back with two mugs and a hot carafe. She poured the steaming brew and slid them over to us.

"Thank you, Vicki."

"You're welcome, Merci," the woman nodded before she went to attend to a few other customers.

"Come here often?" he asked with a raised eyebrow.

"People like their privacy when discussing personal matters." I lined up two creamers and three packets of sugar—visual reminders of the big questions I needed to ask him—I was pretty sure he wasn't the type of informant who wouldn't take kindly to me jotting down notes about werewolves.

He took in short breaths and kept licking his lips. He rubbed the knuckles on his left hand and spun a signet ring on his left hand. He must have turned the coffee cup around a million times. If I didn't know better, I would have pegged him as a guilty informant. He'd done something, or was just about to do something.

Only one way to find out. Start asking questions. "So how did a Scottish boy end up with a brother from the Midwest?" I asked as I dumped in one sugar packet and stirred.

The familiar sizzle cascaded up my back, and pressure swirled behind my eyes. I settled into interrogation mode and relaxed.

He finally turned toward me, and I caught his gaze. I knew I was being analyzed, assessed, sorted. My skin hummed under his heavy scrutiny, and the weight of it pushed at me from all sides. But this, in the hum of the hunt is where I lived. I couldn't be certain about him.

But he still wasn't talking. I tried another question to ease us into the conversation where I could tease more information from him and calm the static forming in my brain from a lack of answers. "Why didn't Ethan tell me he had a brother?"

"You'll have to ask him."

"Why do you think he never told me he had a brother?"

He finally picked up the coffee cup. "Perhaps his literature professor brother wasn't anything to tell his work friend about."

I winced. Work friends. We were so much more than just work friends. Or were we? I was sitting across from his brother I hadn't even known existed. Trying to get answers to questions that I could have never imagined.

"The police have been around to talk to all of us," he finally said.

"Yeah, I got my social call, too."

He took a small sip of the still steaming cup and put it back on the saucer. "Emily showed me the initial police report from that night. It was brilliant work of fiction."

I nodded and it jostled the hornets' nest in my brain, sending a few questions out to buzz around as I dumped in a creamer reserved for the next question. "What do you think happened that night?"

"I think Ethan was targeted."

"Why?" was all this award-winning reporter could come up. "Because he was a werewolf?"

I wasn't sure if my confession techniques were that strong, or if the literature professor just needed to weave a story. The narrative came flowing out of him easily, without the need for my normal interrogation tactics, the incessant questions, the direct eye contact. "Technically, the term is Shifter. Ethan was the Riko of the pack, the protector. Emily is the Shala, the teacher. Recently, the pack had some dangerous run-ins with Warlocks and—"

Finally, a word I understood. "Like the motorcycle gang?"

MacCallan shook his head, but his eyes never left mine. "Actual Warlocks with magic. About five years ago, there was a major turf war, and we ran the Warlocks out of town. I need to know if he was targeted by a regular gang because of the story you were working on or if these Warlocks are back in town."

There wasn't a shade of doubt in his eyes. He'd stopped fidgeting and actually grown more confident in the way he looked at me. But Werewolves and Warlocks? Was he serious?

I sat back in the booth. "If there are werewolves and warlocks in Philly, I think I would have run into one by now."

"We've had thousands of years to learn how to disappear within society. You'd be amazed at what we can get away with."

"What else is out there? Are there other magical beings?"

"Oh yeah. Outside of shifters and warlocks, there are Elementals – they have influence over the elements. Fey can glamour, warp your senses, play with time. Guardians are like Superman with special powers. And those are just a few of what I know to be in Philadelphia."

I closed my eyes. Why wasn't I sick to my stomach? Why wasn't I afraid? This was insane, right? There is no such thing as werewolves or warlocks or guardians, oh my.

And yet, I'd seen it tonight. I'd seen Levi standing as a man and then a moment later standing as a black wolf. I'd felt it in the air, and it had nearly knocked me out of a tree. Magic was real, and I was just going to have to wrap my brain around it to get to the bottom of the story, because this was the only reason that I could think of as to why Ethan would lie to me.

I opened my eyes and blinked away desert-like dryness. I focused on MacCallan, and the familiar tingle trickled down my back as my gaze locked with his. "Why are you telling me all of this?"

MacCallan maintained our steady connection, something not too many people could do, withstand the Lanard stare. "The pack doesn't want to believe this was a premeditated attack. But something dark is happening here."

"What sort of dark?" Was it the same sort of dark that made informants disappear from the streets and hunted down journalists?

"I don't know. Levi's got them thinking they are safe and secure and won't let us investigate."

"Wait. So, Emily's older brother is your pack's leader?"

MacCallan nodded. "Ethan was feeding Levi and the pack information from the police and the stories you guys worked on. We all knew you were trying to sniff out a new gang in town."

The betrayal of it all temporarily distracted me from his impossible story. Ethan, my best friend, my family, had died in my arms, and yet, he'd been going behind my back, feeding my stories to someone else? Just the idea of it made my gut wrench.

Why would he do something like that? After everything that we had done together, everything I told him about me, didn't he trust me enough to tell me his secret? I forgot the line of questions queued up to the right of my coffee mug. "Why didn't Ethan ever breathe a word of this to me?"

"Pack law has it that humans can't know of our existence, so both of us could be executed if the pack finds out that you know."

The idea of execution actually made me feel a lot better about the situation. I was back in familiar territory.

I studied him. His youthful face betrayed by the small lines around his eyes, the sparse gray at his temple. Nothing about him told me he was lying. In fact, I only saw a mirror of my own grief in the dark circles under his eyes.

He seemed to scrutinized his hands, running his finger along the deep lines in his broad strong palms, over the callous on the right middle finger. A writer and not a typer. When he finally spoke, his voice was low, his tone a mixture of defeat and determination. "Even Piper told me to leave it alone."

There was that name again. It even distracted me from the note of betrayal still humming around me. Piper. The name that echoed on Ethan's lips night after night as I watched him die again and again in my arms.

"Who is Piper?" I asked and I let myself dump in the packet of sugar that would make my coffee palatable.

"She is the Den Mother," he said simply, like I was supposed to know what all that meant. Like I was supposed to know what *any* of this really.

But before I could issue a second question, one that would pry out exactly what a Den Mother was, his face grew hard and the furrow between his brow deepened to oceanic trench depths. It paused my usual compulsion.

"Even she told me to drop it, to take some time to run it off, get some sleep, but I need to know the truth. I need to know if it was your investigation or the Warlocks, if his death was magical or not."

Well that was familiar, wasn't it? When there were that many people saying look the other way, there really was something to look at. My father had taught me that.

"I know this sounds insane," he continued, "but magic is real and werewolves are not just on the telly. I know that it is hard for a person like yourself to accept this."

"A person like what?" I asked.

"A journalist."

I counted the remaining packets of sugar, the questions all lined up and ready to be asked. I was a journalist, one of the best, and MacCallan was offering information. Information about Ethan. But at what cost? What was I going to have to pay to get the answers I needed to sleep peacefully again? What would he have to pay for disobeying pack law and coming to me?

"I won't be able to print a story about people who think they're animals, and I'm not thinking the police force is up to it, so how would I bring his killers to justice?"

"You'll leave the justice to me." His truth rambled down my spine like a stick along a picket fence. "If the cause is magical, I will take care of it. If it was your story, it's your responsibility. But we need to find out who is responsible."

"Are you giving me an ultimatum?"

"Think of it as a trial partnership."

I scoffed at the idea. "I'll investigate the new gang, but I can do it on my own."

He shook his head. "You're one human. And they nearly killed you along with Ethan. You don't know what you're saying."

"And you don't know who you're dealing with, Professor." I grabbed my mug and finally took a sip of the hot, sweet coffee. "Maybe I should investigate how a big piece of a national park reserve was quietly sold to a private family?"

MacCallan ran his tongue along his lower lip and I had finally nailed down his tell.

"Maybe I should investigate the B&E that caused Levi to move his business?"

He leaned back in his seat and dropped his hands to his lap. "You don't need to prove to me that you are a good investigator, Miss Lanard."

"But you do need to prove that you are a trustworthy informant."

"Informant?" He looked like he'd tasted a lemon.

"You have information I need about Ethan's life that could have led to his death. That makes you an informant."

"No, Miss Lanard. We are in this together. Partners."

I laughed. "Never, Professor."

There was a shift in the air, a subtle heat that passed across the table like someone had lit a gas burner on the stove. I didn't need to see his hands to know his knuckles had gone white; the clench in his jaw was familiar enough. I was telling him to sit. I was made of *do*, of *fight*, of *chase*, and perhaps the man across from me was made of the same thing. Maybe he couldn't work through it without getting his hands dirty as well.

My resolve melted, for both our sakes. "We work together on this, but on my terms, following my instincts on this one. You might know about full moons, but I know this city, how it ticks, and I won't have you getting under my feet."

MacCallan looked at me long and hard, and I matched his stare without breaking his gaze. Even as a body-wracking chill ran clattered through me, I didn't turn away.

"You know, if you stare an animal in the eyes like that, it's considered a test for dominance," he said in a low voice.

"I am not testing your dominance."

"Are you sure, Miss Lanard?" he voice was low, gravely. It tickled the spot just behind my ear.

"I am sure, Professor MacCallan."

Vicki the waitress came back and snapped us out of our staring contest. I was momentarily lost in his accent as he ordered the biggest burger they made, cooked the rarest that it could be cooked and still stay together as a patty. Thinking about eating it made me sick, reminded me of the animal hidden beneath his unassuming exterior. I pulled my bag, hiding the stun gun, a little closer.

"And the usual for you?" Vicki asked.

"Hold the onions." I handed her the unused menu.

After Vicki walked away, we stared at each other for a few more moments before I needed to get the conversation started again. "Feel free to ask me questions too. I need to know everything about Ethan's world, but that doesn't mean the information only needs to flow one way."

This was a game I'd played with a few other informants. Let them loosen up, made them feel like they had an even hand in all this. But perhaps with MacCallan, it would provide that needed disclosure, maybe build some trust if we were really going to solve Ethan's murder together. Ethan and I had taken six months to find our stride. MacCallan and I didn't have that kind of time.

"You've made the front page enough for me to get the general gist."

I snorted. "Of what? Ace Reporter?"

"Danger addict and chaos magnet more like."

"*Chaos is the law of nature- order is the dream of man*," I quipped.

There was a glint of approval in the literature professor's eyes.

"If you didn't have questions, you wouldn't have agreed to burgers."

I cleared my mind and focused on MacCallan. There was a familiar banter here that reminded me this was a walking, talking part of Ethan right in front of me. He knew the side of Ethan that I didn't, but considering the amount of time Ethan had spent on the job, there was likely a good part of Ethan that maybe MacCallan had never gotten to see.

"Why aren't you scared? I just told you monsters were real."

So he wasn't going to start with the basics: what's your favorite color, where did you grow up, what was your first pet. Maybe he sensed the urgency in assessing our potential to work together as well. This was his test and he was just about to find out how good a student I really was.

"I am scared, but it won't stop me. I'll do anything to figure out who killed Ethan."

"Including climbing a tree in the middle of the night."

"I was fairly convinced the Howard family was just growing pot or trafficking drugs, but I needed proof. Werewolves were the farthest thing from my mind."

MacCallan laughed. "Levi could use some, but he's too uptight to try it."

Vicki delivered our food and he devoured half the burger before I could even realize what was happening or that I was staring at the way he devoured the burger and the dainty flick of his tongue to get a bit of ketchup from his lips.

I managed a few bites of the salad. It was my turn now.

"How exactly are you and Ethan related?"

He finished chewing. "Mum and Da were high school sweethearts. Had me in the seventies when marriage was passé. Da came to America, fell in love, and had Ethan. Ethan kept his mother's name."

At least now I had an explanation as to why my searches for him hadn't panned out.

He put down his burger and took a sip of water. "I'd imagine you spent a lot of time together, investigating crimes, etcetera."

I nodded. "We saw each other nearly every day for two years, and when we didn't see each other, he called me to make sure I wasn't in trouble."

"Even on full moons?

"Even on full moons."

His insecurity floated on the surface of those ocean-blue eyes. "And he never said a word about any of us, of this?"

"I only knew Emily. Knew some stories about Daisy, his mother."

"Doesn't that make you a bad reporter?"

"No," I scoffed. "It makes me a self-centered ass hat." I shook my head. "How does a person miss all that? Never ask?"

MacCallan sighed. "From personal experience, you'd be amazed at what you can hide if you have to, make two completely different sides of yourself."

"*Nature gives you one face and you make yourselves another?*"

MacCallan's dark brow arched beautifully over his teal eyes. "Tenacious and a Shakespeare fan?"

"Which side am I seeing now? The rakish professor or the dutiful brother?"

MacCallan shook his head. "Neither, actually. I follow the Polonius way of thinking. *To thine own self be true.*"

I studied him carefully. "So you're telling me what I see is what I get?"

"Something I'm sure you don't encounter on a regular basis, Miss Lanard." A wide smile spread across his face.

He was attempting to disarm me with it, and with his next question revealed why.

"What really happened the night Ethan died?"

I pressed my lips together as if that could hold in the truth. I didn't want to tell him. Every time I thought about it, it took longer and longer for the nightmare to fade from my mind's eye. But I couldn't lie to him. It was more than my complete aversion to lying. This was his brother, and as much as I told myself that Ethan and I were close, we were not blood.

"Girls started going missing on the Trade Streets. Whispers started floating around about a new gang in town. We were waiting for a regular snitch of ours who said he had information when we were attacked. I didn't see anything. Guys came at both of us. And they vanished as fast as they came."

Even as I told him the story, I saw everything in a new light. The darkness that had come over us—could that have been a spell that stole my vision? And the unnatural strength—could it have been some sort of preternatural being? Ethan was strong and in really great shape, yet those guys took him down. Could Ethan really have been killed by something paranormal? By Warlocks?

"What's wrong?" Rafe asked.

Nothing could get out of my mouth. The questions about that night raced, the truth and the trauma were coalescing, scattering my thoughts in a million directions at once. If a mild-mannered photographer could be a werewolf, how many others were hidden in plain sight? How was I supposed to catch a bunch of Warlocks? Even if I did get the information MacCallan needed bring them to justice, could I stop them before they tore through more people in my city?

MacCallan slid out of his booth and into mine with a movement so smooth that I didn't see him, only felt his warmth when he asked, "What's wrong?"

I turned toward him, his heat pressing against me, ridding the entire booth of oxygen. He was there, around me, suffocating me with that warmth and that concern in his blue eyes. I pushed at his chest, trying to get him away, but he didn't budge.

"Calm down. Take a deep breath."

But I couldn't, not with the questions pushing against my brain and the press of his heat against me. I was trapped in a shrinking room, paralyzed. I couldn't think about anything but the memory of Ethan's blood on my hands and the possibility that I might never have the chance to make them clean again.

Warm fur slid against my skin, even against the unexposed soft centers of my side and neck. My entire body relaxed as MacCallan reached out to gently turn my face toward his. I fell into his ocean-blue eyes, exhausted.

"Deep breath." His voice was nothing more than a whisper between us.

I did as I was told, expanded my lungs, took in the air, then slowly let it out.

"Again," he prompted.

I was lost somewhere in the left quadrant of his right eye, picturing the clear bay outside the resort hotel where I'd spent a week eons ago on my last vacation. I took in another breath and let it out. "What is that? Why do I feel fur?"

"It's my power, my energy. I can expand it outside of myself. We call it brushing, and it's how Shifters greet one another, get a sense for another's feelings."

I wasn't sure I understood everything that he was saying, but the longer he talked, the calmer I became and the less I thought I was going to puke.

"Good."

It was only then that I grew aware of his soft hand on my face. I pulled away and turned to look at his empty booth.

He slid back a few inches but didn't return to his side of the table. "What happened? Your heart was racing a mile a minute."

"I'm fine." I wasn't. This lie tasted like extra-soured sauerkraut.

"No. You're not. I could hear it across the table."

I took a sip of water, trying to convince myself that my hand wasn't shaking before I looked back at him. At his pale skin, his dark hair, and those amazing blue eyes. Of course, he could hear my heart beating. He was a werewolf. It was probably one of those perks. They did stuff like that. Big ears. Big eyes. Big teeth. My heart speed up in my chest again, and again, his warmth spread over me.

A deep furrow sank between his brows. "Were you having a panic attack?"

I shook my head, but there was a very real possibility it wasn't only a panic attack, but some strange cross-section of panic and obsessive seeking. It had happened before, this suffocating barrage of questions bottlenecking and strangling me.

God, I needed a drink. Too bad the hardest stuff in Sam's Diner was the black coffee.

Since I couldn't sate the need in my head, I could feed it with the story. I needed to focus. Like a figure skater focuses on one spot to keep from getting dizzy. And I really didn't want that one spot to be why being next to MacCallan made everything go still. Why I could still feel his hot hand on my cold cheek?

"If we are going to work together, we need a plan of attack," I said to the wall.

"Aye."

I took a sip of my coffee. It was still warm and sweet. "I need to find Benny. He's the one that called us out that night."

"Who is this guy?"

"One of the best informants I've ever cultivated. I haven't been able to get in touch with him since."

"Why wasn't that your first step?"

I scoffed. "Because someone confronted me at my partner's funeral and my instinct told me to go investigate why his family had their tails up their asses."

I thought he might snap at me, but he chuckled instead, then sighed. "Wolf puns were a running joke between E and me. Who could pull off the cheesiest before the other cracked?"

I smiled knowing that part of my Ethan was true. "He was like a non-stop Dad joke factory."

I looked at my watch. It was nearly three a.m. "Do you need to go get your shift on? Why aren't you all furry under a full moon? I'm mean, if that's a real thing and not just in the movies?"

MacCallan's gaze dropped to the table. He slid out of the booth to stand at the end of the table.

I kept pushing. It's what I did. What I could never not do. "Why didn't you shift with the pack? Why were you watching like I was?"

He struggled. I saw it in his jaw and the lines of muscles down his neck as they disappeared into his tense shoulders. "I've been assigned as the pack's official watcher. Someone has to be available during the full moon in case something happens."

"So, you don't get to shift with everyone else?"

"No."

"When do you get your monthly shift?"

"When the pack leader says I can," he finally got out between clenched teeth.

My brain jumped to a sour conclusion, but I finally had some validation of what I'd suspected: something was going on with this family. They were actively separating MacCallan from the rest of the pack. It explained the fight at funeral and why I was the only person he could confide in.

"Do they blame you for Ethan somehow?"

MacCallan sighed and looked out the windows into the dark of the night. "Blame isn't the right word for it."

I understood the tremor in his voice, and it made me want to reach out to him. I wasn't the only one who had lost a person that night. He had his own bag of grief to carry around, and I could not deny him the opportunity to do something with it, even if that was something stupid and not particularly well-thought-out.

I slid out of the booth. "Care to join me?"

"Where?" MacCallan asked.

"Ethan always said that a good story really only starts in one of two places: The City Morgue or Rome. And at this hour, the city morgue is closed, even to people like me."

"What's Rome?" he asked.

I smiled. "My naïve little professor. You have to experience Rome to understand it."

He paused, studying the wall for a moment. "As much as I want to, I need to get back, watch over the pack, but I'll be free at dawn."

Four hours until sunrise. I couldn't get into too much trouble. I grabbed my mug and gulped down the rest of the coffee. It seemed to fortify me for the night ahead, for chasing this renewed purpose—find Benny. And with that renewed purpose the world felt right again. I was doing what I needed to do: chase.

"If I run into something that looks like it bumps in the night, I'll call."

He grabbed a napkin and pulled a gold pen out of his pocket. He wrote his name and two phone numbers on the white paper. See, old school with the pen and paper.

I pulled out my cell phone and programmed the numbers in it before he even finished writing.

He simply nodded. "Good night, Miss Lanard."

I watched him walk away. It wasn't until he disappeared across the highway and into the dark of the woods that it occurred to me that I had just been sitting across from a werewolf.

CHAPTER FOUR

Just after 4 a.m., I parked under a streetlight and double-checked that my rolls of twenties were securely on my person and that my stun gun was equally accessible. All trade leads to Rome. If you wanted drugs, you went to Rome. If you wanted sex, you went to Rome. If you wanted information and were willing to pay the right price, you went to Rome.

The smell of the bar brought back memories of Ethan and me. Our first story was a dead sex worker found in the trade streets. In the beginning, it was rough. I was stubborn and Ethan was a pushover. I thought I had been saddled with the biggest Jimmy Olsen wannabe. He'd had quite a learning curve when I'd taken him down to the red-light district to interview a working girl for leads the police didn't want to pursue. It had taken us a long time to find a good stride, for him to finally get over his incessant need to question every step of my process and learn to trust my instinct for trouble. Once that happened, we were golden. Partners who thought just alike enough to get along and just different enough to keep the angles fresh.

And I was back here two years later talking to my regulars about another dead body. Alone this time.

I ordered a whiskey, kept my eyes down, and bided my time. Atlanta had to wait until her pimp came around for his cut, but she eventually said goodbye to the girls and joined me at the end of the bar.

She adjusted her bra as she sat down. "Almost didn't recognize you without that hot photographer following you."

I tried not to wince, instead I threw back the two fingers of the cheap whiskey. It didn't make the sentence any easier to say. "Ethan was killed."

"Damn. That's a loss. I would have climbed that boy like a tree."

I chuckled. Ethan would have turned bright red with that comment, which was probably why the girls around here loved to say stuff like that to him. The wholesome All-American from the Midwest.

"What do you need, honey? Name it. Drugs? Boys? Girls?"

"Information."

Atlanta rolled her eyes. "Always the hard stuff with you."

I pulled out the roll of twenties. "Same deal as always?"

Atlanta flicked her gaze down at the cash then back up at me. "Last time I talked to you, some cop came sniffing around. Nero was not happy."

I sighed. Officer Rutherford. He was always trying to find my sources. That beat cop was always at the right crime . . . but the wrong time and a roll of twenties short for my stories. I always punted him any information I got that could take down the real bad guys though—as long as I got the byline. "We got the guy that beat up Georgia. Beat up all those girls."

She only raised an eyebrow. "And some of those girls went downtown for a stretch."

I pulled out another roll of twenties. "I'll double your fee."

Atlanta waved her fuchsia nails in my direction, a magician's flourish, before she took the rolls off the bar and made them disappear into a secret pocket in her bra. "What can I do you for?"

I focused on the questions I needed, the truth that I needed—where was Benny and what happened that night. The static filled my brain, that itch to chase, and I brought my gaze up Atlanta's glittering top to look into her eyes. There was still an innocence to her, and a fierce loyalty, right there in her golden-rimmed eyes.

"Have you seen Benny around anywhere?"

Though willing to talk, she was hesitant. I could feel it between us, see it in the nervous twitch at the corner of her lips still stained red at the end of her shift. Of course, she would still be hesitant. Despite the cash, there had been a cop sniffing around, and that was never a good thing in her line of work.

"I know you are hesitant, but Ethan died while we were trying to find out more about those missing girls you told us about. The new gang in town."

Her pupils dilated as she relaxed into the truth. "Heard Benny's running with a new crowd."

I knew the bait of my own truth would hook her, now I just needed to keep her on the line. "Really? I thought he was Dawgs 'til he died." Could this be why his loyalty to me had faltered? Benny had been with the Dawgs since his first arrest. What could make him change colors like that?

"'Bout two months ago, he's stats flashing around some new income. Got himself a girlfriend. Pretty steady girl actual. They had an all-out about his business a few weeks back."

"Benny had a girlfriend?" I asked.

She licked her lips. They always did. There must have been something about telling the truth that made people thirsty. "Yeah, works the mini-mart on 22nd. She stays over on Cumberland. He might be there."

"Got a name?"

"Tiara, friends called her Tay-Tay."

I recorded the name and address she gave me.

The bartender came to pour us another round and announced last call, though we were all here past legal last call. I looked down at the second drink of the night and sighed.

"What happened to picture boy?" Atlanta asked. Her tone was maternal, the same she'd used to convince the girls to talk the last time Ethan and I had stopped by.

"We got attacked two Wednesdays ago by a group of men. He didn't make it."

Atlanta slid her hand slowly over the black lacquered bar and patted my arm with her long nails. "He was one of the good guys. As much as we razzed him, we knew you two had our backs."

I nodded. "Thank you, girl."

"You know," she started as she pulled her hand away. "There were some strange lights off Chavez. We thought it was just another rave in those abandoned warehouses. Couldn't hear anything though."

Despite my brain being a little fuzzy because of the insomnia and whiskey, I sharpened and listened to her. "Besides the strange lights, did you see anything out of the ordinary? Something that the trade streets don't usually get? Like a gang of men dressed all in black?"

"That's not strange for the trade streets."

She was right.

"Anything else?"

"No, it was a slow night."

"On the first of a month?"

"Yeah. Like too quiet. Back home, we used to get tornados and everything would get real quiet right before one hit, it was sorta like that." Atlanta sipped her brandy. "New blood's got a lot of people trippin'."

I raised an eyebrow. Ethan was always right. The good stories always started at Rome. Atlanta was one of those who had tipped us off about a new presence shaking up the usual trifecta of gangs. I'd scratched her information down in my notebook as I gathered the whispers together, trying to see the bigger story. "Really? What else have you heard?"

"Savannah met this catch. Couldn't stop talking about all the things he promised her, and then she vanished."

"Savannah with the blond hair? I saw her last month."

Atlanta nodded. "One night she was here, and then she was gone."

That was fast. These girls were family. He must have promised her the moon to get her to leave them. "Anything you can remember about this guy?"

Atlanta thought, chewing on her bottom lip. "Nothing special. Benny brought him around."

Benny. Maybe all roads were leading back to Benny. "Did you file a missing persons?"

Atlanta laughed. "Some weeks, you and picture boy were the only people who cared about us, Merci."

My anger threatened to snap the plastic Bic pen into pieces. I had to put it down on my notebook and stretch out my fingers to calm down. "I have to, Atlanta. You are part of my city, born and bred here just like me. Granted its morally-questionable underbelly, but a living soul."

She clinked my glass with hers and tossed back the remainder of her drink in one gulp. She rose, adjusted her bra again, settling her two new rolls of twenties, and looked down at me. "This new blood is another fad. The new ones get hot and then fade out. The old vices will always stay in business."

I smiled. "Here's to job security."

...

The numbers on my watch blurred in the slowly rising sunlight. Was that a five or a six? I rubbed my eyes. My entire worldview had changed in a matter of hours and I was running on fumes. I need to go home, I needed sleep.

I wished I could write off everything MacCallan had said as one huge lie, but he'd been telling the truth. It clung to me like the warm smell of sandalwood and sage that had surrounded me in that booth. Werewolves were real. Ethan had lied to me about what he did once a month for the past twenty-four months because he'd have to kill me if he told me.

Right now, Benny seemed like the most solid thing in my life.

I took a sip of the to-go coffee and scouted the apartment building across the street. Benny could be in there. Benny—who was either scared or dead or, worse, a traitor—could be in there with a myriad of answers for me. About Ethan. About this new gang. About the missing people.

Or this could be my fourth B&E charge. Though in this neighborhood, I'm not sure anyone would notice.

The real question was, should I call MacCallan? He wasn't a cop. He wasn't a reporter, but he was Ethan's brother. He had every right, possibly more than me, to stick his nose into everything that might have gotten his brother killed. And if it was something strange, something like what I saw last night, then I would need his help.

Everyone's better with a partner. Ethan's words echoed in my small car.

I looked at the time. It was past dawn now. MacCallan was technically free unless there had been some sort of pack emergency. Someone had gotten treed and couldn't get down.

I smiled to myself, but it faded fast. Ethan and I would have made so many jokes about it if he'd only told me. The puns could have lasted for days, but the pack had rules.

My thumb scrolled back to the newest number on my phone. With a deep breath and a shake of my head, I dialed it.

"MacCallan," he answered.

"Lanard. Up for sniffing around for an informant?"

I heard a car door shut and his car turn on. He must just be leaving the little shindig in the woods.

"You've already got a lead on your guy?"

I scoffed. "I am a professional, MacCallan."

"Where are you?"

I gave him the address, and he said it would be nearly forty minutes before he got there.

I could barely wait twenty. He'd just have to catch up.

Here's to staying out of trouble.

The buzzer on the door was broken, but the label next to 3C clearly read 'Tay-Tay." The glass door that should have needed to be buzzed had shattered so long ago that there wasn't even any glass littering the ground. So it wasn't technically breaking and entering if the entry was already broken.

I slipped under the metal handle, the only barrier in my way, and into the foyer. No need to give Benny any sort of heads-up that his favorite journalist was trying to pin him down. The other denizens were also silent on this particular crack of dawn, save for someone in 2A watching old cartoons.

The building was old and smelled of years of cigarette smoke. It only got worse the higher I climbed along the central stairwell, hot air rising on this cold fall morning and making the cigarette smell new again. I crept along the third floor hallway, paused outside apartment 3C and listened.

I couldn't hear anyone inside, but Benny kept the same schedule as I did, so he shouldn't be awake at this hour. But Tay-Tay might. And Tay-Tay might not know exactly what to do if she found herself eye-to-eye with Merci Lanard.

I took a deep breath and knocked softly on the door. The slight pressure pushed the door open a few inches, and my heart jumped in surprise. In a neighborhood like this, I would have had seven chains on the door, yet this one was ajar.

I calmed the swarm of questions in my head, trying to bat them away with explanations. Maybe Tay-Tay had run out to her car to get something or had come back in after leaving for work and that's why the door was unlocked. But the apartment stayed silent.

And then I got a whiff of something, like dust and garlic and rotten ground beef.

Unless Tay-Tay was a particularly bad cook, there was only one thing that smelled as rank as that.

I turned my head to suck in one last breath of the suddenly refreshing smoke smell of the hallway and toed Tay-Tay's front door open.

The light from the hallway illuminated the layout of a normal apartment. Small and old and messy, but normal. Foyer table full of bills, coats hanging from a rack. I recognized the black one that Benny had worn the last time I saw him, that large Eagles emblem that hung off him like a trash bag. Atlanta hadn't steered me wrong. This was the place.

I readied my phone in one hand and my Taser in the other.

I stepped in and called out, "Benny? Tay-Tay?"

Silence echoed back to me, and I took another step into the apartment. My eyes adjusted to the dim dawn light filtering in through the door to my back and what looked like a patio door further into the apartment. My nose was not going to adjust. The putrid garlic smell was only getting stronger.

A bistro table held to-go boxes piled high with lo mien, but even the worst place in town couldn't create this smell.

I scanned the apartment. Couch, TV, stereo system. All still here, despite the open door.

"Benny?"

There was a grunt in the shadows behind me. My instincts flared and my trigger finger flinched as I spun around.

MacCallan caught my wrist, and the crack of the Taser's prods sent a white glow across his freckled cheek and electrified his blue eyes.

"Calm down there," he said.

I released my trigger finger and the lightning stopped. I could taste my racing heart in the back of my throat. "When I called, you said you'd be forty minutes."

"Traffic was light." He slowly let go of my wrist. "Do you know what that smell is?"

I resisted taking a deep breath—despite needing to calm my nerves. "Of course I know what that smell is."

"Shouldn't we call the cops?"

"In a minute. Don't touch anything, walk in straight lines behind me."

I turned around and surveyed the apartment again. There was a purse on the chair by the couch. Women's shoes underneath the table, same place I put mine. But no men's shoes. Benny's coat might have been by the door, but his shoes were not.

From the layout, there was only one more room to explore, the bedroom. I knew the truth about what I was going to find in the bedroom.

One foot in front of the other, I made my way toward the back of the apartment. Rafe's heat pressed against me as he followed closely.

It was on the bed, tangled up in sheets like a rowdy night gone wrong. From the doorway, I could make out a foot and maybe an elbow sticking out from under the white sheet with yellow flowers. Someone had covered up the body.

"Stay here," I whispered to Rafe.

I took another step into the bedroom. Morning light slipped through the windows, and I was glad that no shadows hid in the corners. With one more step, I stood at the end of the bed. I reached toward sheet, but Rafe came to stop my hand.

"I've seen dead bodies before," I assured him.

"What about evidence? What about—"

"I need to know if it's Benny."

He pressed his lips together and released my arm, standing next to me, shoulder to shoulder, a united front against the dead, against what might be under that sheet.

I rummaged around in my bag for a glove and pulled out the familiar blue latex.

An arch formed in Rafe's brow.

"I've seen dead bodies before," I repeated as I snapped the gloves on.

I slowly reached to pull the sheet from the bed. It wasn't what I expected.

I'd seen dead bodies before. I've seen them freshly bloodied. I'd seen them bloated and floating and spread out across the highway like jam. But I'd never seen anything like this.

It was an experiment human beef jerky. The skin was tanned and dried—all of the moisture completely drained from it. The dress seemed starched, then freeze dried to the figure. The arms jutted out to form sharp angles and her legs were splayed wide, but feet touching. The lips peeled back from white teeth. But the hair was perfect. Long, dark hair splayed out against the pillow made her look like she was peacefully floating in water, like driftwood.

I could feel Rafe flinch, and I didn't need my eyes to tell me that he had not seen as many dead bodies as I had.

"What's wrong here?" he asked.

"Everything."

"Walk me through it."

"Why?"

"Because I might have a few preternatural skills that will help," he snarled.

I deserved that. Slowly, I walked him through everything that I saw. "There are no fluids. The bed is clean except for that dark spot there." I pointed out a place on the sheets that could have easily been spilled cocoa instead of blood.

Rafe slunk around the corner of the bed, light and smooth, like he didn't want to disturb a single thread of carpet.

"How long could it have been here?" he asked.

"No more than seven days?" Atlanta said they'd had a big enough fight last week to echo through the chain of gossip.

Rafe leaned over the dark stains on the bed and sniffed, and for the first time in a long time I was actually disgusted. I turned away and noted the trinkets on the dresser. Jewelry, big earrings, and a picture of Benny and his girl.

I snatched it from the mirror.

Carefully, I looked back to Rafe, where he stood by the bed.

"Blood," he said.

"That is a relief," I answered. "But from where?"

He reached toward the body with an open hand.

"Don't touch it," I snapped.

"Magic lesson number one, Miss Lanard," he said smoothly. "*Wanderers*, people with natural abilities, have heightened physical senses. And some can tell if something magical happened here, like me."

I waited and I watched. Ethan hadn't done any of this with me, but it didn't mean he hadn't used some of his senses before. He'd hidden other things from me, so why not this? The night of our attack flashed back. Ethan had heard something coming before I noticed anything. Before the Shadow Men came. Maybe he had used his super-skills and I'd just never noticed.

I really was a self-centered ass-hat.

MacCallan's voice quietly soothed away a few of my rougher questions as he narrated exactly what he was doing. "My magical abilities allow me to expand outside of myself, increase my own senses, to feel the energy in others, in places. And sometimes that is residual energy from spellcraft."

He focused on her body and, though it was slight, I felt a shift in the air; the room's stifling stench lessened and I got a whiff of sandalwood with the garlic.

And as I watched him, he paled and pointed toward her upper torso. "There's something on her arm. Some magic on her."

I tiptoed around the room and stood close to him.

"Where?"

He pointed and I leaned in as far as I dared. I could see a mark, a shadow of something that at some point had maybe been a brand or a tattoo. But I couldn't make out an actual shape. The skin was too dry and wrinkled.

"Well, you got magic, I've got tech."

I pulled out my cell phone and its camera had enough pixels to get details. I took a few shots of the arm. There was something there, and I was comfortable zooming in on the picture. I really couldn't make out exactly what it was. Something with a line and a cross maybe?

I went back to the picture of her and Benny in my hand. She didn't have a tattoo there when this picture was taken. I went back to the foot of the bed and took a few shots of that as well, stretching as far as I could to get as aerial a shot as I could muster.

I heard a door shut somewhere in the complex and a mother yelling for her daughter.

I shoved my phone in my back pocket and pulled off the blue glove. "We need to scoot."

Rafe looked back at the body. "Who is she?"

I licked my lips. And I shouldn't have. I could taste the oily decay from the air. "Her name was Tay-Tay, and it's time to lay her to rest."

Rafe and I left the apartment and he followed me down to my car, but I didn't get in—not yet. I was going to smell like dead body for the rest of the day. The stench had worked its way into my coat, into my pores, like rotten French fries. My face I could wash, my car upholstery I could not. I needed a moment to air out my coat and my thoughts.

This was a second dead body associated with Benny. Benny whom I had worked with a hundred times, whom Ethan had worked with. And now another person was dead and he was still on the wind.

I took another lungful of air and let out a cloudy breath into the cool morning.

"I'm going to call this in to a police friend of mine. He's going to rake me over the coals, so you need to not be here when he shows up."

"What am I supposed to do? There's a dead body with something magical on it." He started to pace in front of me.

I felt the truth in his words, and my own wound started to itch. There was something rasping underneath what he said, like a puppy needing to get outside. He needed to do things and there were still too many questions spinning around to get a direction to act in. He was just as compelled as I was to keep doing until it was done. It was all so familiar, so I used familiar words to calm him down.

"Walk me through it," I suggested.

His entire being changed. They were the right words. He stopped before me and stood up a little straighter. He really was a professor to his core and this was something he could teach me, because heavens know, I don't speak magic.

MacCallan put his hands on his hips and studied the neighborhood. "Everything has energy, a spirit, a chi, whatever. Places, people, even things—they all hum with that energy."

He pointed toward the apartment. "That place, didn't have an ounce of energy left in it, except the essence of something on her arm."

I furrowed my brow, doing my best to follow. "So you're saying that whatever sucked that body dry of water might have sucked the energy out of the place as well?"

"Either way, magic was used and a woman is dead."

The deal between us ran across my brain. "And if it's magical, it's yours. If it's not, it's mine. Are you going to go to the pack?"

"No," he said quickly. "It's not enough. They would crucify us and we'd never be able to find the truth of what happened to Ethan."

Part of me was relieved that he wasn't going to fight me on staying with this story. Not that he could have really done anything to keep me from investigating. Not that anyone or anything could keep me from chasing this story.

"Since you can't go to the pack, do Wanderers have books? Those dusty grimoires in all those movies?"

He sighed. "It's not all like the movies, but yes, we have our own references."

"Great. Then research what would do that to a body. I'll stay here, call Rutherford."

He leaned against the car. "You need sleep. You're frayed around the edges."

I scoffed. "How the hell would you know?

"Call it a perk." He looked one last time at the apartment. "No matter how hard you think you are, Miss Lanard. Even you need to rest. Any maybe something to eat that isn't rabbit food."

What was it with the men in my life making sure that I ate? "After the cops, I'll go home, get some sleep, and then I'll follow up with the M.E. and see what she can get from the body."

He grumbled, but eventually stood, luckily upwind of me. He still smelled like the woods, the pines that he had probably brushed up against. "Call me when you have something."

...

Natasha was the prettiest M.E. technician I had ever worked with. She was blonde and tall and thin and wore shades of pink that left streaks across my retinas. It was late enough in the morning that people were actually beginning their work for the day and short staffed enough that no one notices a civvie sneaking into the building.

"Hello, Merci," Natasha chirped as she slid a body into a locker and shut the door.

"How do you shove around these bodies in those heels?"

Natasha smiled and regarded her pink shoes lovingly. "You get used to it. Even have special soles so I don't slip."

I plodded after her in my boots as she bounded across the lab to her walled-off office. Even her office had way too much pink for my taste. But despite all the blush tones, Natasha loved to tell the stories of the dead. It was why she was down here instead of on a pediatric ward cheering up the entire floor. It was why she was a kindred spirit.

We sat down across from each other, like we had a hundred times before.

"How are you doing, Merci?" Natasha asked. "I made sure they handled Ethan with care. I wish I could have done more."

Everything within me tensed at seeing his body again in my mind's eye. Imagining him wrapped up in that cold bag, under a sheet like the one yesterday. Each time it happened a little faster, the fresh sting got a little duller, being slowly replaced by the cool sadness of loss.

"It's okay, Natasha. I appreciate all you do."

"So what brings you to my level of the underworld today?" She smiled.

"Rutherford sent over a dead body yesterday."

"Tiara Henderson?" Natasha cocked her head. "You usually don't want to hear about the weird stuff, Merci. You're more of a *just-the-facts-ma'am*."

The skin between my shoulders tingled, and it wasn't just as her very bad impersonation. "Life has been strange enough lately for me to want to make the leap, but you've seen everything under the sun. What makes her death weird to you?"

Whatever I said turned on a light behind Natasha's already bright blue eyes. "To get the full weirdness, we don't start with Tiara Henderson. We need to go back a week."

Natasha fluttered her hot pink nails over her computer keyboard, bringing up her database of the dead. "Last week, John Elroy Mitchell was found on a doorstep in a residential neighborhood."

"Wait. I know that name." Why did I know that name? I flipped through the mental Rolodex in my head of informants, but came back blank.

"He had a picture of a family in his breast pocket. No names on the picture but a family. A wife and two kids. Wouldn't know it by the gross examination. He was emaciated, to the point his teeth were falling out and they couldn't even match a dental. His skin was leathered like he'd been in the sun for years. He was marked as a drug overdose, but his clothes were fairly intact and this picture was in perfect condition."

I frowned. "His family never reached out to find him?"

"You're not getting it. The picture was perfect, like brand-new. Not even old enough to be considered a missing person."

Natasha turned the computer screen to me and I stared at the man from the other night at the bar. The one who had attacked me and ripped off my bandage.

"He's a reporter for *The Teller*. I had a fight with him last week."

Natasha nodded. "I know. Before and after," she said as she clicked the arrow key on her keyboard and I was face-to-face with something from National Geographic's Ancient Egypt explorations. It was Tay-Tay all over again. The weathered skin, the strangely perfect hair and the sunken eyes not even juicy enough to wink.

"The same thing happened to him?"

Natasha nodded. "Now do you understand the weird?"

I was beginning to understand it with every passing minute of this week.

"Why didn't you call me about Mitchell when you found out he was a journalist?"

Natasha pressed her lips together, and her eyes went soft and doey. "I thought you might need your space after Ethan, and I couldn't bear to call you with another dead reporter."

Poor thing did have a point. The normal human reaction to a loved one's death would be to grieve, not hunt down dead bodies in the middle of the night. But I've never been a normal human.

"Do you have pictures from the Mitchell scene?"

"I do." She searched around more in the file and found the wide shot of Mitchell's body.

I leaned in to study it, still remembering the horrifying stench that had emanated from Tay-Tay's. Same strange position, same strange freeze-dried clothes.

Same ugly plaid sports jacket that he'd been wearing the night that we had fought. I leaned back in my seat with a thud.

"I saw him last Wednesday night. I had a fight with him at McTaggert's. He accused me of lying about Ethan's death."

Natasha's eyes went Betty Boop wide. "You might have been the last person to see him alive, Merci. They found his body Thursday morning."

"Seems to be a running trend with me." I rubbed my suddenly very cold arms. "Tiara Henderson had a mark on her arm. Got anything on Mitchell's?"

Natasha turned the screen back to her and clicked through a few things. "There was something. Couldn't really make it out during the examination."

Two bodies with two potential magical marks. This did not sound good at all. "Anything else about Tay-Tay?"

"The general state of the body was closer to something you'd see in a hot, dry climate. Dehydration beat out decomposition. But she had only been dead for a day or two max."

"How do you know?" I asked.

"I found a cell phone in her bra, still had a charge."

A cell phone with a charge would have a potential phone number to Benny. Electricity ran up my spine, through my already tingling shoulder blades and settled in the crown of my head.

I needed the numbers off that cell phone. Natasha had helped me tell the story of the dead a hundred times. Printing extra pictures was one thing. But a cell phone? This was a chain of custody thing that could get Natasha fired, and I didn't want that. So I gave her a bit of my truth to make my case as delicately as possible.

"Tiara Henderson's boyfriend is a suspect in Ethan's death."

Her eyes went wide again. "Oh my, Merci."

"Is there any chance her phone is still here? That you could help me solve Ethan's murder by seeing if there is a contact for this guy?"

I waited for her answer, waited as I watched her eyes search mine.

"Cops haven't picked up the evidence bag yet. Let me get you some gloves."

Pulling the phone numbers out of Tay-Tay's phone was surgery, a precise execution of gloves and sterile environments. I'd hovered over Natasha's shoulder as she opened up the phone and found a few potential numbers that I snapped pictures of with my own camera phone.

She didn't breathe again until she put the phone back in the plastic bag clearly sealed with ME tape.

I flipped through my notebook to see if there was any loose ends. There was nothing pertaining to these dead bodies, but my pages were still filled with the lost and missing. "What kinds of records are kept on those without autopsies?"

"Officially, not much. Time location, COD, and that's about it. But I remember all of them. Someone has to remember the unnamed."

"All of them?" I almost didn't believe her, but I saw the truth in Natasha's eyes.

She nodded as she reached into her desk drawer and pulled out a pink water bottle. Her fuchsia lips pinched around the straw and she took a long sip.

"So then our John Does that come through here, you remember those?"

Natasha nodded and her blond ponytail bobbed.

She didn't go to the computer this time. She rolled over to a tall filing cabinet and opened the second to last shelf. She pulled out a folder, which struck me as odd; everything officially on record was in the database. This wasn't official. This was an unofficial Natasha file, and by the size of the cabinet, there were a lot of unofficial things in there.

She handed the original file over to me without needing to look into it. "For example, John Doe, August Fifteenth. Official report chalked it up to exposure."

I flipped through the pictures. Stained clothing. Worn shoes. The body didn't have the same dehydrated look to the resent ones. It wasn't freeze dried or in a strange position. He was just dead, face down on a checkered tiled floor. "And the unofficial report?"

Natasha pieced her words together and her eyes darted through the files I knew she had stored in her mind. "Exposure seemed likely at the time, but it was August and the conditions of the body were not exactly conducive for that particular determination."

"How not conducive?" I asked as I flipped through the photos to find one of the face, to gain the identity of this lost soul.

"You know how you wear a pair of pants a few times and the knees stretch out?"

I nodded.

"The body was like that. Loose. Like it had been a man suit."

I shivered at the mental pictures. But I could see it in the eyes of the autopsy photos, like there was an extra gap between his gums and his lips, between his eye and his eyelids that looked stretched. "If you were a gambler, would you this John Doe is connected to my two?" I asked.

"No. Definitely not. I just wanted to let you know there has been a noticeable uptick in weird over the last six months."

"When you say uptick? What do you mean?" I asked.

Natasha looked over her shoulder. "I'm going to have to get a new filing cabinet."

I eyed the thousands of stories in those filing cabinets like a hive of questions waiting to be answered. "Have you mentioned this to the police?"

"Of course. It's my duty to get these people's stories told."

"Did they do anything about it?"

"Not exactly," she said simply.

"Then why didn't you tell me about some of these?"

Natasha sighed. "Don't get me wrong, Merci. You fight for this city, but even you can't solve every mystery in the world."

She wasn't lying. I couldn't do everything about all the dead, but I could do things about some. Specifically those who were connected to Ethan's death. I had two dead bodies to work with. This new lost soul was just going to have to wait until another day. I closed the file and put it back on her desk.

"I'm going to keep digging, keep figuring out what is going on. See that Tay-Tay gets a proper burial. Let me know if the family doesn't cover it and I will."

I walked out of the M.E.'s with two very strange cases, complete with pictures. I headed straight to the newspaper office. I'd missed evening pitch by about an hour, but at least I had one story that I could get words on. I needed a reason for Hayne to stop tiptoeing around me like I was a glass vase teetering on the edge of a shelf. I needed to show him I was back in the game.

After completely freaking out some poor newbie in the copy room as I printed out the pictures from my phone, I did every special trick in the book to try to figure out what was on Tay-Tay's and Mitchell's arms. The deterioration just made it too hard to see what had been there. My two tricks with photos and computers were nothing compared to what Ethan could have done with them. He could have re-pixelated and contrasted and brightened the pictures within three seconds and gotten me the image in three second.

I closed my eyes and just let the sadness watch over me, float around for three seconds in the abyss of loss. Yes, he had kept huge things from me. But he was still a part of me, a part of this team, and this half of the team needed help.

I tossed the photos of the bodies on Hayne's desk.

He jerked back like I'd thrown a rattlesnake before him. "Jesus Christ, Lanard. I was about to eat." Hayne tossed the Reuben he'd apparently been halfway through eating back into its paper tray and wiped his fingers on a napkin. "What is this?"

"Two dead bodies that the police are shoving under the rug."

"And you want to investigate?"

"I want to find out why every strange death in this city gets labeled as homeless and forgotten about."

He lifted and eyebrow. "You're going with a corruption story?"

I shrugged. Difficult to say at this point, but at least I had a lead. "Maybe. Can I run with it?"

Hayne frowned. "I thought you were digging into Ethan's death?"

"One of the bodies is the girlfriend of the informant we were meeting."

Hayne paled as he inspected the pictures for a moment then up at me. "Did you eat today?"

I pointed at the pictures. "I'm thinking it might be connected to the gang story that we were working on. Natasha said there's been an increase in unexplained deaths and we still have the missing sex workers."

"You're avoiding the question. Did you eat today?"

I shook my head.

Hayne pushed the sandwich toward me.

I sighed and sat in the chair across from him. If I was going to eat his sandwich, I might as well take a lecture from him as well. The minute I had the warm sandwich in my hands, my mouth began to water.

"So two bodies?" Hayne slid the photos around on his desk.

"The other was a journalist. John Mitchell from *The Teller*."

Hayne looked up at me with an arched eyebrow. I loved that arched eyebrow. It meant that I was going to get approval to work on the story. It meant that Hayne saw something worth investigating as well. It wasn't just my compulsions

"With Ethan, that makes two people related to newspapers have been killed in two weeks?"

I nodded, then took a bite of the warm sandwich and my eyes closed, as the one bite filled every inch of my suddenly starving frame.

Hayne frowned at the pictures. "Did you see these two were found in the same position?"

Honestly, no. I was too busy focusing on the alleged magical marks on their arms.

"It's an odd angle at best, not one that would have naturally occurred through a fall or a collapse and definitely not one that the person would have laid down in to die."

I stood up and looked over at the photos spread across his desk.

He lined up the pictures up to highlight their similarity.

I went to set down the sandwich, but Hayne blocked my hand and pushed it back at me. Then he grabbed a pen and a page from his printer. The stick figure wasn't exactly Picasso, but it matched the odd position of all the bodies. A strange T-shape with a diamond for the bottom.

I took another bite as I stared at the symbol. Why did that look so familiar? What was it about the shape that resonated in the back of my head? What did it remind me of?

"I'll call *The Teller*, see if I can convince that son of a bitch Rex to tell me what Mitchell was working on."

I licked my lips of the thousand island dressing. I knew exactly what he'd been working on: a story about me. "No need."

I snatched the drawing from Hayne and gathered the photos, the sandwich still clutched in my other hand.

"Thanks, Hayne!" I yelled as I went back to my desk in the open newsroom.

My instinct was to reach for the phone and call the only person who I knew spoke this sort of crazy. When you needed information, you went to an informant.

My hand hovered over the phone. I was being ridiculous. This was work. I needed him for work. But it would mean I would need to see him again, see the eyes that had invaded the five hours of sleep I'd gotten today and threw my entire reality askew.

I pulled my hand away. There was one more place that I could look before I resorted to that. No one had ever accused me of not being thorough and double-checking my facts.

...

Officer Julian Rutherford rolled his eyes when he saw me coming toward him. He'd been watching a pick-up game across the park, nimbly flipping a silver coin through his fingers. He quickly slipped it back into his pocket as I joined him.

I offered him the coffee and he looked down at it for a long moment before he took it. "You were the last person I saw on the last shift. Why are you the first person I see on this one?"

I loved the pinched rumble of Rutherford's voice when he was annoyed, which was pretty much all the time with me. "Why do I have to want something? Why can't I just enjoy a nice chat and cup of coffee with my neighborhood cop?"

I feigned innocence as I took a sip of my own coffee.

He surveyed the parking lot where I'd asked him to meet me. "Because you live over in Queens and this is Spring Garden. So what do you want, Lanard?"

Fine. Small talk wasn't exactly my strong point and neither was subtlety. "Do you happen to know a Detective Noakes?"

Rutherford shrugged. It was effective. The man was the size of a telephone booth and about as friendly. His shrug was a mile high and spoke volumes.

"He wrote up a crap report on a dead journalist. I wanted to get your take on him."

He snorted. "Are you serious?"

"As a heart attack." I took a sip of my coffee and set it down on the newspaper stand between us. "Isn't it protocol to at least do a basic Google search before you blame something on drugs and move onto the next crime?"

Rutherford looked down and I caught his glance. I locked eyes with him and wanted to yank the answers out of him. "What is the policy protocol on dead bodies?"

"Call in the M.E. Get the body picked up, and get back to the living criminals."

I stealthily slipped my notebook out to capture his answer. "So what would indicate a drug overdose?"

"Anything. Paraphernalia, bad teeth, rotten smell."

I scratched down the notes in my pad, breaking my gaze with Rutherford. So a body in a funky position wouldn't be enough to make it into a report, but the severe weathered conditions of the body would. Made me wonder what other suspicious things omitted from the reports.

He scoffed. "Scribbling away. You know all this stuff is always off the record. You got to go through the PR officer to get the real information."

"The real information is here, on the street corners. It's not behind some podium."

Rutherford nodded. "So you're back on the job?"

"Yep."

"Good. I heard the meter maids could you use again. Why don't you bother them?"

I knew what he wasn't asking me about, and I knew I wasn't ready to answer it yet. He of all people knew what being partners with someone meant; he knew the loss. I'd written the article about it. Almost made me appreciate him for about three seconds before I got back to work. "I really should get a badge with all the crimes I've solved."

"And all the crimes you've pulled? Is it three or four B&Es now?"

"Only three, thank you. The other one was a criminal mischief."

Rutherford shook his head. "Why are you chasing a dead body case?"

"Because there are ties to Ethan."

He choked on his hot coffee. "What? How do you know? What did you see?"

I waited for him to recover. "You know this town as well as I do. It's all connected. Every single pill and player in this city has got to be connected, and I'll hunt down every lead to get me closer to his killers."

Rutherford wiped his mouth with a handkerchief from his pocket and set his coffee on the newspaper bin. "I don't know, Lanard. You're pretty good with a headline, but there are things in this city that would eat you alive."

He surveyed the park across the street again, growing quiet for a moment, and so still he could have been made of stone, if it wasn't for the wild processing happening behind his dark eyes. "Noakes didn't do anything wrong. We've been told to wrap up cases faster. There are too many to get ahead of."

"So two dead bodies and—"

"Two?" Rutherford asked.

I nodded. "John Mitchell, a reporter for *The Teller*, was found in the same condition as Tiara Henderson from Saturday."

"And how do you know what the Henderson body looked like? You said you could smell it from outside."

I pressed my lips together. I didn't want the foul taste of a lie to get in the way of the sweetness of the coffee that I really needed to get into my system to keep going for the rest of the night.

"Damn it, Lanard."

I distracted him with the rest of my story. "Natasha over at the ME said she mentioned it the detective who brushed her off. So, I'm wondering why two bodies under similar strange circumstances would get stuffed?"

Rutherford bit down hard on his lower lip. It was his nervous tick. I had seen it only a few times in the two years I'd known him. Had it only been two years? It felt like Ethan and I had been working crimes for ages and Rutherford was always our first contact, the unfriendly face we could count on to do the right thing.

"When was the first time we met?" I asked.

Rutherford frowned and picked his coffee back up. "Some gang shooting, I think. Couldn't keep you on the right side of the police tape."

"Right. I think you called me a hair ball?"

"Angerball," he corrected. "Why'd you ask?"

I shook my head and finished my coffee. It was growing chilly and I shivered, even the coffee not enough to keep me warm. I needed a scarf. "You know how it goes. I'm reevaluating my life, things, moments to make sure I know the truth about what went on."

I stared down at my empty coffee cup. Where did that confession come from?

"I got you. If it makes you feel any better, half the force still thinks your kind are the scum of the earth, so not everything has changed."

"And you, Julie? You on the side of the guys who would rather look away than take a stand and really try to help this city?"

"I don't think you're scum, just more like an annoying little dog with a bone." Rutherford took a long swig of his coffee before tossing it in the trash. "I know firsthand you've saved some people with your stories, but your methods are going to get people killed."

I gulped.

"Maybe they already have," he continued. "You are not the only person who is trying to protect this city from itself. Saving it is not a one-man job. Think on that the next time you decide to accuse a police officer of not doing his job or hell, help him out. Give someone else a chance to do some good."

Rutherford turned and walked toward the group of boys loitering in the park.

"One-woman job," I yelled out after him. Or I had wanted to yell out after him.

The truth of it stuck in my throat like a vitamin too big to swallow. He was right. He didn't have to be such a bastard about it, but I had dragged Ethan out that night. Mystical war or not, werewolves or not, I was responsible for him being there.

And now the entire world was turned on its head; my brain hurt when I thought about it sober. I had put Ethan in danger with my focus, my obsessive need. I needed to be the person to solve this, to fulfill my blood-soaked promise.

I was going to have to call MacCallan.

CHAPTER FIVE

I ran my fingers through my curly hair and pulled it back into a messy bun. I second-guessed my jeans and changed into nicer boots. I made sure my eye makeup wasn't completely smeared and my breath didn't smell like Jack.

Just an hour earlier, when I'd finally sucked it up and called, MacCallan told me he was about to leave for the theater downtown. We arranged to meet at the coffee shop that doubled as the theater's concessions. Theaters were a little nicer than the usual dark corners and crack houses I was used to, so I wanted to dress nice. I didn't want to feel as exposed as I had at the funeral.

The lobby was full of people milling about during the intermission, but his wide blue eyes caught mine the moment I walked through the door. MacCallan stood and gave me a half wave from his booth in the corner.

I pressed through the crowd to find that he had already ordered a coffee for me.

His dress slacks and button down with the quintessential tweed blazer fit the part of the professor, a little different from what he'd worn during our last meeting. And he smelled nicer. He was here as part of an extra credit assignment for one of his classes, a theatrical reading of Chaucer. He blended in seamlessly with the crowd, whereas my attire was still a bit more leather and grass stains than was probably appropriate.

He extended his hand, as if we had never met before. "Miss Lanard."

"Professor. . . ." and I trailed off as I touched his hand and was met with warmth, a soft intimate brush of silky fur against my neck. I inhaled and braced myself against the table.

"Are you all right?" he asked.

I could still feel the heat of him down the entire length of my body. With a deep breath, I slid down into the chair and regained my wits.

"Fine," I finally managed.

This particular lie tasted like mealy worms in a dirt pie. Why was he reaching out with his animal to greet me? To remind me who I was dealing with?

I had a bag full of pictures to remind me there were darker things at work in this city than I could have imagined. But I was once again struck with the realization that I was sitting across the table from a werewolf. Neither of us was to be trifled with.

I tried to keep my eyes on the coffee, on the table, on the cute playbills framed on the walls, to keep my mind focused on work and not the fact that my body still hummed with something other than my need for the truth. I cleared my throat. "How did you manage a seat?"

He sat gracefully in the seat across from me. "Threatened to fail a few students if they didn't give me their table."

I couldn't help but chuckle. "Right."

He folded his hands on the table between us.

"Are you sure you want to do this in public?" I asked as I pulled out the folder of pictures and the sketch of what could possibly be the magical something that MacCallan felt on Tay-Tay's body.

"Thousands of years of hiding, Miss Lanard. In public is the best place to do it. No one will think twice at two people on a date."

My hand paused at the mention of the d-word. This wasn't a date; this was work. All work and no play is how you get inches on the front page.

I reached into the folder and only pulled out the rough sketch of the emblem. "I went to the M.E.'s office. There was another body.

Another journalist. When I compared the two bodies, they were both in this position."

I put it on the table between us and waited, leg bouncing. The truth was, I wanted this to be weird or just coincidental, though in my line of work there was always a cause and effect. But I didn't want this to get darker, get weirder, and I wanted the angles of the bodies to just be the angles that dead bodies fall into.

MacCallan frowned as he studied at the figure. He spun it around on the table between us, and his face became a scene out of a gothic novel. His eyes went from the teal blue of the Aegean to the dark gray sky over an English moor.

My stomach sank. This was magical and it wasn't good.

"The symbol is magical, isn't it? Is it related to Warlocks?" I leaned forward and lowered my voice. More than he knew balanced on the edge of my next question. "Does this mean there are Warlocks in Philly again?"

MacCallan looked up at me from the pictures. A shiver skittered down my spine as if I'd jumped into the icy blue ocean of his eyes.

"I can't believe I didn't see this when we were with the body."

I fought a gasp. "What does it mean?"

"Sacrifice."

My skin goose bumped. I didn't know if it was his meaning or his brogue, but I curled my hands around the warm coffee to chase it away. "Sacrifice to what? For what? By what?"

MacCallan shook his head. "I don't know."

I hated that answer so I pressed on. "Is it a spell? What else could mummify a person in under four days?"

He only shook his head again. "With the pattern, I'd say each body was part of a spell, but I'm not sure to what end."

I looked into those blue eyes, watched his calm hands hold the picture that would have rattled anyone without complete conviction. The realization washed over me again. Magic was real and there were Warlocks in my city, hurting my people. But that was going to stop now.

"What do we do next?" I asked.

MacCallan leaned back in his chair. "I take these to the pack to prove that we are not as safe as Levi thinks we are."

The questions started to stockpile in my brain, like traffic on a rush hour highway. The itch, the anxiety crept up my shoulders and seemed to squeeze my lungs. "And then what?"

"You move on to another story and leave this one to me. That was the agreement."

A laugh boiled up from the tension in my chest. "My ass. The agreement was about Ethan. We can't be sure that his death and these are even related. This is still my story."

"You don't know what you're dealing with here."

"You don't know *who* you are dealing with, Professor."

I snatched the photos and headed for the exit. How dare he think that I couldn't handle this, that I couldn't protect anyone? I stormed through the door and into the cold night air.

I nearly made it to the nearest crosswalk when a strong hand gripped my upper arm. Adrenaline flowed through me so fast that my vision went dark and couldn't catch up with my actions. I swung my fist at whatever was attacking me. It smacked hard against a face. The hand dropped from my arm and the shadow stumbled back.

When the adrenaline finally stopped, the tunnel vision opened, and I saw MacCallan holding his chin as he leaned against the theater's gaudy facade.

"I think I know who I'm dealing with now." He tested his jaw. "You've got a hell of an arm."

I looked down at my hand. No blood. There was no blood this time. Everything was okay. People had stopped and were watching, talking about the couple fighting in the street. The last thing I needed was someone calling the cops, especially with this folder of photos on my person.

I had to take a few deep breaths before my heart stopped racing, before the adrenaline subsided and let me think in a straight line.

"Are you all right?" I asked.

"Fine," he said as he pushed off the brick of the building. "Would you like to continue our conversation or just punch me again?"

"I'm sorry." The words fell out of my mouth. I never apologized for anything, so why was I now? It was strange, but this had been a strange evening—finding out there was a string of deaths and magic was the culprit.

He tested his jaw one last time. "It's my fault. I didn't think. You were attacked, and here I am grabbing you in the darkness. Of course you were going to react."

When he spoke again, his tone had changed. It was softer, like he was charming a jumpy horse and not a jumpy journalist.

"We agreed." He started. "If it was magical, I would handle it. If it wasn't, you would."

"That was about Ethan's death. This is bigger."

"Exactly. This is bigger. This city still needs you to investigate injustice, missing girls, new drugs, but you're out of your depth with this one. Hell, I might even be out of my depth on this one."

The cool air pressed against my fevered cheeks. "I have to know what is responsible for Ethan's death."

"You know I understand that."

He stepped closer, and his warmth, the same warmth Ethan used to have, seeped into me – a reminder that I was not the only person grieving here. We really were in this together, the pain of loss and the answer that would ease that pain. Neither of us was going to solve this alone. He just needed to be reminded.

"In the few days since you've told me about magic, I've already uncovered more than anyone in the pack has. More than you did by yourself."

I watched the press of his lips. He wanted to tell me something. I didn't need a special magical power to tell me that.

I continued. "I need more to see the big picture, see all the cogs in action. See what lives in the gaps between the stories."

There was a flash of recognition in his eyes at the words. "Appealing to my literary sensibility isn't going to get you anywhere."

But it would. The fight within him was lessening.

"You need me to help investigate. It's what I do. Ask questions. It's all I can bring to a magical fight, if that is what this is. You know one side of the city, I know the other. You're the one who said we have to work together on this to see the whole picture."

He let out a deep breath. The fight was over. "You make a very convincing argument, Miss Lanard."

Relief washed through me. We might actually be able to find out who killed Ethan. I might be able to sleep again. Plus, I was playing nice with others. Ethan would be so proud.

Rafe looked down at this watch. 'The reading is starting again in two minutes. Let's go back inside. We can finish those coffees with less people listening. Take a better look at the photos. Plan our next steps."

"Thank you, Professor."

We settled into the coffee shop again and he got us two new coffees. To the outside world, it probably looked mundane enough—but I was preparing to have my world shaken up like a snow globe. Again.

Rafe sipped his black coffee. "What do you need to know?"

I had a million questions that were all swirling around. Magic, Shifters. Warlocks. Spells. One, though, an older one, a stronger one, beat the rest to the front of the glass and got my attention. "Why was Piper so important to Ethan? What is a Den Mother?"

He adjusted in his chair. "She is a fount of Shifter energy and links us all together, keeps us safe."

"Who is 'all of us'?"

"Every Shifter across the world."

Whoa. "So what kind of shapeshifter is she?"

"She's technically human. She doesn't shift. But she can control the magical energy within any Wanderer—not just shifters."

"So she keeps you safe like she's a super, kick-ass Warlock fighter?"

Rafe chuckled. "Nothing of the sort. She's more like a spiritual Mother to us. Supports us, nurtures us." His smile faded. "Saves us from ourselves when we need it."

My mouth formed into an O, surprised. "But Levi is the pack leader, the Primo right? So if you took this information to Piper, it's like going above him."

"Levi won't listen. But Piper will listen to me, especially about this."

"Why?" The question jumped out before I would find a proper place for it in the list currently a line of sugar packets on the table to my right.

"Piper and I have known each other for a long time."

I suspected he could tell by the look on my face that I was going to need more than that.

He licked only his bottom lip and his thumbs tapped out a beat on the edge of his coffee. "About twenty years ago, there was a war, the Great Shifter War."

"I know my history, Professor. That isn't one of them."

"We've had over a thousand years of hiding in plain sight, remember? Humans don't see what they don't want to see, and frankly, it looked more like an impromptu Woodstock than a war."

I leaned back in my chair and trusted that my sensibilities, my instinct honed over the years, would tell me if he was lying. Though part of me knew that he wouldn't. Not about this.

"Every culture has its own version of the apocalypse, Ragnarok, if you're up on your Norse Mythology."

I smiled. "I am."

"Wanderers are no different. Ours is called The Last War, sounds better in Old Speak. A Demon, Jovan, wanted to jump-start The Last

War by starting the Great Shifter War, which according to prophesy would determine the side the Shifters would fight on when The Last War happens. He created a spell that called every Shifter from across the world. I was in university, working on my thesis when I felt the pull."

"Pull? Like how?" I asked.

He licked his lips. "Like a fish hook in my soul, dragging me across the world."

That was serious stuff. But I got it, in a way. How many times had I been caught in a story's net, and followed it to the ends of the Earth, like Captain Ahab?

MacCallan adjusted in his chair. "But the real prize was Piper. Jovan was using us to draw out her, to consume her power, and create an army of Shifters he could control."

I gulped. "But Piper won?"

"Depends on your definition of *won*." He looked down at the coffee. "If it had been an actual war, the two sides would have torn each other part. So she sacrificed herself before that could happen and he tore her apart instead. So entire Shifter nation put her back together, each giving her a piece of our power until she was whole again, and then some. Since then, she has connected us back together as one nation, through her, which makes her our Den Mother."

"So she's the only one of her breed?"

Rafe released a small smile. "Yeah. The only one of her kind."

"So you fought in the war with her?"

He bit down on his lower lip. Etched between his brows, the story had resurrected a crack in the glib, bookish façade. "I was there that day."

Though the story was over, his pain was not. For the first time, I didn't want to bombard him with questions, I wanted to alleviate that look in his eye. Get my rakish professor back to the banter we were so very good at.

"And this all happened twenty years ago? I already have a hard time believing you're old enough to be a professor. You don't look a day over twenty-five."

"Thirty-nine, actually. There are many perks to the shift," he said leaning back, a coy smirk forming on his face slowly as he returned to the here and now.

I would have never believed that he was thirty-nine. There was too much youth in his movements, in the gleam in his eye to be older than me. "Can I see your driver's license?"

He laughed but pulled his wallet from his back pocket and flipped it open for me to see. Sure enough, he had eleven years on me and nine on Ethan. And he didn't live in Philly. He lived in Aston. That was nearly an hour drive from here. Tucked in the slots of the leather wallet were also a Neumann university ID and a library card.

"If you drive so far, does that mean that there isn't a pack closer to where you live? Or did you just want to stay with Ethan?"

"I stayed in Piper's pack. Ethan found me here years later and stayed too."

"Because of Emily?" I asked.

"Mostly because of Emily, but having Piper this close has its advantages."

I fiddled with the next sugar packet by my coffee.

"Next question?" he asked, looking down at the line of accouterments.

Damn, he was fast. He'd already spotted my record-keeping system.

"How did you become a Shifter?"

He looked content and nodded. "I'm a Legacy. My father was a wolf, so I am, and so was Ethan. He passed it on to us."

He took a sip of coffee. "Are you single?" he finally asked.

I glared at him.

"What? Am I not allowed to ask questions this time?"

I pressed my lips together. I didn't particularly appreciate it when my interrogation techniques backfired like this, but I would play, as I had played before.

"Yes," I said quickly, and then moved on. "So it's spread to others like a disease? You used the word *communicable* before."

He smiled. "It takes a special sort of person to take to the shift after bitten. Not all victims who are bitten become Shifters. We don't even really know what it takes to complete the transformation." He didn't give me a minute to squirrel away the information before he jumped into his question. "Are you so dedicated to you work that you don't have time for a relationship, or is it deeper than that?"

A twinkle in his eye told me he was trying to press my buttons. Still testing my limits.

"My last relationship ended almost two years ago because I was quote too *morbidly obsessed with the truth* end quote."

"What does that mean?"

"He cheated on me when I was on assignment and I caught him in a lie." I took a sip of my coffee. "That was two questions. Staying warm on a cold night is a pro of being a Shifter. What are the cons?"

MacCallan took another sip of his coffee. "The high metabolism does get annoying. I could eat three rare steaks during the full moon and still be hungry. The whole hidden life thing, though…" He shook his head. "It really is against our law to tell anyone about this, but hiding who you really are all the time? It's brutal."

The ache of Ethan sat heavy in my stomach. I knew that this conversation should be about werewolves—Correction: *Shifters*—the string of dead bodies, and possibly what killed my best friend. Ethan's hiding his true nature from me was feeling less like a betrayal by the minute. Instead, I felt pity. After all, he carried this with him and couldn't share it. Couldn't share with his partner in crime.

He must have had an iron will, to have been able to keep it a secret from me. I was the women who got spontaneous confessions from near strangers. Or it was something more than just an iron will?

Did he use some sort of magic to keep it from me? There were too many questions, too many things I didn't yet understand.

I turned back to my sugar packets for my next question, needing to guide the conversation back toward solving a crime. "What are the cravings?"

"I don't think you want to know."

"I don't scare easily, professor."

He took in a deep breath and leaned across the table. "My animal is a wolf, a carnivore, and he craves what every animal craves, and when he's strong, I'll get cravings for raw meat, like fresh-from-the-rabbit raw meat."

He leaned in further and dropped his voice lower. I leaned in to join him.

"And sometimes, I have to run and hunt, and be free. I don't do caged well."

"No man does," I said with a raised eyebrow.

A smile played on his lips for a moment, then finally cracked through as he sat back in the booth. "You are a unique woman, Merci Lanard."

I really liked the way he said my name, the soft way it tickled between my shoulders blades. "Thank you. Your question."

He spun his coffee between his fingers. "What do you crave?"

I finished pouring in two packets of sugar. "Truth, justice, and a lover who doesn't leave the seat up."

MacCallan laughed, and as he did, that warm roll of fur brushed around me, through me. At least I was sitting down this time. There was a distinct drop in my stomach, but I recovered more quickly than before.

He had brought up relationships first, but now it was my turn. "How do relationships work for Shifters? How does it work with regular humans?"

"Only one way. You don't date people who aren't Wanderers." He shrugged and took another sip of his coffee.

I could see the moment that his question came into mind. He really was too readable. Just like Ethan. "What scars do you have?"

He was finally catching on to the game. Getting to the real gritty questions, which meant that I could go in for the harder questions as well.

Never one to back down, I unbuttoned the top of my Henley and pulled the material aside to expose my throat. Down at the base of my neck, just above the collarbone was a scar from a ring of teeth.

"Serial rapist took a bite out of me."

MacCallan's widened as he stared at the shiny ring on my neck.

"About a year and a half ago, I was investigating girls who were being taken and attacked, but not killed. I turned myself into bait and ended up finding the bastard," I said, putting my shirt back and buttoning those two buttons.

He just sat there, stunned. His blue gaze flicked from my neck to my eyes and back.

"And you still investigate? You still look into all the dark corners?" he asked softly, when his words came back to him.

"Evil is still evil, whether it's supernatural or not. If I can shed a little light in the darkness, then I've done my job."

MacCallan studied me like I was a textbook. "I've asked a few contacts to send me those dusty grimoires. See if I can find a spell that matches the pattern."

As tempting as it was to think about him flipping through large books in a tweed jacket, I knew that we didn't have the time for dusty books and discovery. "We can't wait. You have to take what we've got to Piper."

He sat up straight in his chair. "You're not even supposed to know about this. About us. If I take this to Piper now, the pack could find out you're involved now; you could be in real jeopardy."

"I'm used to being in jeopardy. Hell, I put myself in jeopardy most of the time. This is bigger than me. This isn't just Ethan anymore, it's the whole city."

He shook his head. "What is it with you and this city?"

I shrugged. "It's home. I feel connected to it somehow. I'm a Legacy," I smiled at MacCallan's term. "My father worked the news floor and now I work the news floor."

He gave me a half smile and nodded. "Okay then. I'll take it to Piper. See if I can figure out a way to not mention you."

"I am totally okay giving up the byline on this one if it keeps me from being executed."

I reached down into my messenger bag and gave MacCallan a folder with the pictures of the bodies in them. "Let me know what your Den Mother says?"

"Of course."

It was strange, handing over information. Usually I was taking it, stealing it, but I was willingly trusting him with part of a story. Not that I was trusting him with the originals, but still trusting him to help. For the first time, I was the informant and I really wasn't sure if I liked being on this side of the table.

MacCallan finished his coffee and looked down at this watch. "I need to go be a professor. What are your plans for the evening?"

"I nabbed a few numbers off Tay-Tay's cell phone. One might be Benny's new contact info. I'll check them out tonight."

"Do you ever sleep, Merci?"

I shook my head. "Not often and not very well."

...

I'd spent my night and part of my morning running headlong into a dead end on the numbers in Tay-Tay's phone. No one was picking up from my cell, my desk phone, Hayne's desk phone. Those numbers were going to be burned into my brain. I needed to step away from my desk before I broke something, so picking out expensive camera equipment sounded like a good idea. I fiddled with the camera that I'd signed out from the paper, looking through the view-finder and trying to focus on stuff close up and far away. The other staffers in the newsroom probably thought I'd officially gone off the deep end, but I'd discovered that with a decent zoom, I could read the lips of the people standing at the water cooler.

My cell phone rang. I jumped on it like a cat on a felt mouse. "Lanard here."

"Merci, It's Levi Howard."

Why was one of them calling me? After all, my knowledge they even existed was a huge violation of pack rules. Or perhaps this was just a social call on Emily's behalf. My mind replayed the scene of him changing into a large wolf, and I fought a shiver as I played it casual. "What can I do for you, Mr. Howard?"

"Piper wants to meet you."

My skin prickled at hearing the name. This was it. Maybe if I met her, it would fix the broken record in my brain that kept repeating Ethan's dying words. I needed to file at least that part of his death. But Rafe had warned of execution for those who trespassed into this world. Did she want to meet me so she could eat me herself? Surely not the Mother Theresa of Shifters.

"Why?"

"MacCallan told her that you'd found proof of Warlock activity in the city."

Well that was the understatement of the year.

"The Den Mother is violating pack law, but MacCallan's somehow convinced her you need to know everything to help us figure out if the Warlocks are back and if they are responsible for Ethan."

"Oh?"

"She can meet with you tomorrow."

My schedule was technically free, but I wanted to run this past Rafe first. Make sure this was a friendly call and not some firing squad. "Can you send me the address?"

"Actually, I'll drive you. We don't allow record of her location."

Now that was a level of security that I had not encountered before. But if these guys were really in a renewed turf war with a group that sacrificed people with magic, then maybe they needed to be that careful.

"I will pick you up from your office at two thirty."

He disconnected the line without a farewell. Seriously, what was going on in this pack? That was a story I was going to have to get to the bottom of. I dialed Rafe's phone number and waited. It rolled to voicemail. "Hey, it's me. Levi just called and said Piper wants to meet me. Call me back."

I hung up and tossed the phone on my desk. What else did I need for this meeting? I flipped Ethan's medallion around in my fingers, thinking. I had fresh batteries, providing I was going to get to even use the recorder. If they wouldn't let her address be written down, then they probably wouldn't let me record her. I had all the files I'd collected on the cases and the police record of the latest DB file that Rutherford had absolutely not dropped on the seat across from me as I drank coffee this morning at a predetermined location. I had everything I thought I would need to meet with the mystical mother of werewolves.

The game was afoot. Or would it be "a paw." I chuckled at my cleverness. Ethan would have loved that one.

My cell phone vibrated on my desk. Rafe.

My hand paused over the phone. Not MacCallan, but Rafe. The mental familiarity wasn't a good sign.

"Professor."

"I'm giving a test right now, so I've got to be quick. Levi called you? You're meeting her?"

"Tomorrow afternoon. Am I walking into a trap? What did you say to her?"

"Piper mentioned you first. Was relieved when I talked to her about it."

"Did you talk to her over the phone or face-to-face?"

"Face-to-face. She knows you're the one responsible for putting all of this together."

I sat down in my chair and lowered my voice. "He's picking me up at work at two thirty. Can you come? I want a familiar face there."

There was a slight pause. Only slight and I only noticed because I'd stopped breathing to hear his answer.

"I will see you there, Miss Lanard."

"Professor MacCallan."

I ended the call and back in my chair. Suddenly, I was surrounded by his scent as it wafted from my coat. The space behind my ears tingled and I sat up and away from the familiar smell. I didn't have time for that. I didn't have time to think about the fact that I had dreamt about that smell instead of blood last night.

...

Armed to the teeth with everything I would need for an evening of interviewing, I sat with my messenger bag on my lap and waited on a bench in front of my office building. I wasn't nervous. I didn't get nervous. I was only concerned that if I didn't make a good impression on Piper, I wouldn't be able to see this through. That I wouldn't get all the answers I needed, and the list of questions was getting longer by the day.

I did another double-check of my armory: audio recorder, lock-picking kit, file folder of dead bodies, and a Taser tucked away as well, in case anyone got frisky.

I was so deep into preparing my questions, into making sure that I had my bag all packed and ready to go, that I didn't hear Rafe walk up beside me. But I suddenly felt him, that same warm brush of furry energy preceded him. I found him standing at the end of the metal bench, hands tucked in his pockets, tie-less, and with a huge leather book bag hanging off one of his shoulders.

"Professor MacCallan."

"Miss Lanard." He sat on the far side of the bench and faced the street.

"So what am I really walking into here?"

Rafe leaned forward, resting his elbows on his knees and rubbed his hands together. "There will probably be about twenty people at her house. Emily has been staying there pretty much every night. Piper is amazing, warm, kind. I trust her when she says she wanted to bring you in on this."

I swallowed. That was a lot of people to consider, and it changed how I saw this going down in my head. I wasn't used to a crowd; they made me nervous. I worked better one-on-one. "Anything else?"

Levi pulled up in a huge black SUV before he could answer. I stood and straightened my jacket and slung my bag over my shoulder. Rafe rose beside me as did his energy; I could smell his scent on the wind.

"Could he have been any more conspicuous?" I whispered.

"Have you ever tried to fit a full-sized wolf in a two door?" he responded smoothly under his breath as Levi came walking up to us.

"Merci," Levi greeted me with a firm handshake.

"Levi." I thought it terribly formal considering we had met before. Maybe he had been put on his best behavior since Piper wanted to meet me? I returned the handshake and braced myself for his brushing, but it never came.

He turned to his pack mate. "Rafe," he said in a voice neither pleasant nor threatening, but he didn't extend a handshake and he didn't smile.

"Primo Howard," Rafe said lowering his eyes.

I was caught in the whirl of Rafe's warm fur and a puppy smell I recognized from the night I witnessed the shift. But at least I knew to brace myself on the armrest of the bench; I knew what it was going to do to the pit of my stomach.

Levi quickly swung his eyes back to me. I couldn't help but picture him in his wolf form, standing proudly in the center of the circle. I doubted that I would ever be able to see him as all man again.

"Are you ready?"

"Always." I forced a grin. Might as well be on my best behavior too.

Levi walked to his car and opened the front passenger door for me. I climbed in as gracefully as I could and he closed the door quickly on my heels.

I watched the side-view mirror as the men walked around the back of the car. Levi, the passion evident in his body language, was saying something to Rafe, and Rafe dropped his eyes once more. I glanced in the rearview mirror and wished I couldn't read lips.

From inside the car, I couldn't hear much, but I could make out that they were talking about me, something about pack and power. Rafe insisted that he had every right to be there. I lost the words as I watched Rafe shrink down when Levi snapped something in response. I looked away quickly when the men broke and went to their own sides of the car.

Both were quiet as Levi pulled away from the curb. We were heading back to the highway that would take us north of the city. I could see Rafe in the side mirror, and whatever Levi had said clearly upset him. He now sat silently in the back seat, his blue eyes focused on the distance out the window. Perhaps he really was in trouble for bringing a me into this.

My heart sank a little. What else could have instantly turned this loquacious man into a sullen child? Why was Rafe such an outsider to his own pack that he even had to involve me? It just added to the questions about a pack that didn't want to investigate the death of one of their members.

I had to get them talking about something. The dull roar of questions in my head was gathering strength, turning into a full-tilt thunderstorm as we got farther from the city. I needed to take the edge off if I was going to get through the next couple of hours, and I really didn't think stopping for a drink on the way there was an option.

"So what exactly does a Primo do?"

"Save your questions for Piper," Levi said abruptly. "Here, Put this on."

He picked up a black sleeping mask from the center console of the cab.

"Seriously?"

"Do you want to meet Piper or not?"

Clearly, there would be no questioning the blindfold. I was beginning to wonder how powerful this Piper could be if she could call the shots and Levi would obey.

With one last looks at Rafe in the back seat, I pulled the satin cover over my eyes and counted, measuring the miles of distance between me and my city.

CHAPTER SIX

Levi had already turned down three roads and crossed two bridges and we were still in a on roads off the highway. I was just about to ask if he even really knew where he was going, because I swore we had taken four rights, but I didn't discount that he was trying to confuse me to obfuscate her location. Just as I was losing faith in his internal GPS, he made a sharp left and we hit a gravel road.

"We are here."

I tore off the mask just as the tree line broke and we pulled up to a huge house. The driveway was long and manicured and we drove past several more SUVs as we pulled around to park in front of the house.

The three of us got out of the car, and I paused, gaping at the complete pastoral scene. The two-story, white farmhouse was surrounded by a clearing, which abutted a dense wood. A porch wrapped around the entire front half so a person could both watch the sunrise and the sunset from the rockers scattered around it. The place was so picture perfect it even had a rooster weather vane with a compass.

And yet here I was, about to walk into a literal den.

The more wolves to eat you with, my dear. Even in death, Ethan loved his puns.

Levi asked me to wait for a moment, then strode into the house, leaving me outside with Rafe.

I immediately turned toward him. "Is everything okay?"

"Fine," he snapped.

"I already know that you were fighting about me, so you need to tell me. Will you be punished for telling an outsider? There is a pretty big spectrum between forgiveness and execution."

Rafe watched me with those huge eyes, and something tugged just under my right rib. I was going to chalk it up to weather changes and recent injuries, and not a growing affinity. I focused on his answer.

"It's what Piper wants," was all he answered.

"But what Piper wants and what Levi wants are very obviously two drastically different things. Are you in trouble because of me?"

"No."

He was lying. His upper right cheek tensed up, he crossed his arms, his answer was short, and he avoided looking at me, instead finding the corner of the porch particularly interesting. The confident professor was gone, and I wasn't sure exactly who stood before me right now, but I didn't like him. So I told him. "You're lying."

"How do you know?"

"Because I do. Why do you drop your eyes when you speak to him? Does it go back to the pack dominance thing? Because you went above his head?"

"I can't talk to you about this." He walked off toward the tree line.

I would have followed him; when people lie to me, I usually beat them over the head with so many questions that truth becomes their only way out.

Levi called out from the porch of the house. I watched Rafe's retreating form for another moment, then turned to the country home. I took in a deep breath and put on my game face, squared my shoulders, and walked toward the porch. If Rafe wasn't going to help me out with this, then I would have to rely on the old Lanard Charm.

Levi held the door open for me, and when I walked in, I was met with the coziest house I'd ever been in. It wasn't so much the decor, which could be called clean, yet shabby chic; it was a feeling that hung in the air like the islet curtains across the windows. And it smelled like my grandmother's house, like something cinnamon was baking in the oven. As we walked through the sitting room, I fought the urge to curl up in the corner of the couch and read books as I had at Grand-Mere's house when I was little.

Now that was magic.

Levi led me into the bright kitchen where two people were brewing hot tea at a white granite island. An older woman looked up, and a warm smile spread across her face. Immediately, I knew this was Piper, the Den Mother. It was all in the sparkle of her wise, green eyes. The man with her was tall and dark, with yellow-green eyes that betrayed no emotion. He just looked at me and then back at the other woman.

"Piper, this is Merci Lanard. Merci, this is Piper Fantaye, our Den Mother," Levi introduced.

I extended my hand and Piper took it graciously. "It's an honor to meet you, Ms. Fantaye."

"Please, here it's first names only," she said, then gestured to the man, "This is my husband, Kye."

Kye nodded, not extending his hand. I mirrored his greeting.

"Can I get you some tea?" Piper offered.

"I would love some. Thank you," I said, adjusting the bag on my shoulder.

"Kye, why don't you and Levi let Merci and me chat for a while?" Piper asked sweetly.

When Kye didn't move, Piper gave him a stern eyebrow.

"If you need anything," he grumbled and he followed Levi into the sitting room I had just passed through. They were both unsure about this, keeping a close watch on their matriarch and the outsider who knew too much.

Piper shook her head and sighed. "Boys." She shrugged as she took the glass pot of tea and gestured for me to have a seat at the little bistro table by a gorgeous bay window, framed by frilly white curtains overlooking acres of property. "You save the world and they still think they have to protect you," Piper set up the two mugs with tea, milk, and sugar.

I thanked her and she took the seat across from me. My leg bounced and as soon as she looked over at me, my skin started to burn, like a sunburn all over my skin, crackling and dry. There were so many questions swirling through in my head like a dryer with shoes tumbling around.

"Now, Merci. Rafe told me you have discovered possible magical activity." Piper sipped her tea.

The story. The sizzle of it singed my neck, and I was ready to get to work, stronger than I had been in weeks. Focused with proof in hand.

"Yes, ma'am. I have the photos right here if you would like to go through them," I said reaching down into my bag.

She put her hand out and shook her head, her brows knotted together. "Rafe showed me enough."

I put the folder back into my bag and just sat there, feeling exposed under her wise gaze. If we weren't going to talk about the story, then why was I here?

"Ethan spoke of you often."

The mention of Ethan sucked the air out of my lungs and I couldn't speak. I don't know why it came as such a surprise. These were his people, whom he called family, of course his name might come up in conversation, but it still shocked me.

"The pack has not been the same without him, without knowing what really happened to him." She gazed out the window and cocked her head for a moment as if she was listening to something. She sighed, took another sip of her tea, and turned back to me. "Is there anything that I can answer for you? About us? About this world that will help you with his passing?"

I nearly laughed before my chest caved in with sadness, ached with this woman's consideration for my feelings, ached with loneliness at seeing all the people Ethan had to lean on. And I ached, knowing that the sense of home beneath this roof was something that would not come back with me in my cold townhome.

Even though I had written a hundred questions for her in my notebook, there was one question I'd rehearsed a thousand times today. Saying it now was more like muscle memory as I breathed it to life. "Why did Ethan keep this from me for so long, and yet with a few dead bodies, you jump at the chance to meet me?"

Piper stared at me as if I had zapped her with the Taser. She shook her head and forced a smile. "I'm sorry. Brain freeze."

The woman was lying. My interrogation mode hummed with it. The way she leaned away from me and cupped the mug squarely between us. The way her eyes crinkled and her lips thinned when she smiled. She was lying.

That wasn't a good sign.

"Kye, could you come here for a moment?" Piper called out pleasantly, but there was a new tension in her shoulder.

The man was through the doorway before I could blink. I sat very still, not quite knowing what was going on. I kept my hands as still as I could and forced my leg to stop bouncing through red flag number two.

"Put down your shield," Piper said to her husband.

Kye shot her a quizzical look.

"Oh just do it," she said in that exasperated wife tone.

I knew the moment he let his "shield" down. I felt it, as I'd felt Rafe and smelled Levi. But this was fur like silk against my cheek and it smelled tangier, more exotic. My hands clenched against the table, and I refused to faint, though the swirling in my stomach was greater than I had experienced before. He had to be twice as powerful as Rafe.

"Merci, ask Kye a question," Piper said softly, her eyes on me.

My mind raced. All these questions and I couldn't form my mouth around a normal one as I stared into his eyes. I finally managed, "What is your favorite cereal?"

Kye inhaled sharply. "Chex," he finally said.

I tore my eyes away from his and was left slightly spinning at the sudden disconnection.

"What is that?" Kye asked.

"I didn't believe it when Ethan told me, but he was right."

My skin went cold, and the previous sizzle was dampened like a wet blanket with her words. "Right about what?"

Piper relaxed, pulled her hand back to her tea, and put on that calming smile again. It didn't work for me nearly as well as it had a minute earlier. She inhaled slowly before speaking. "When you ask questions, I can feel magic."

The world stopped. Everything. Sounds faded. The lights from the kitchen ballast became too bright and everything else dulled into a blanket of white nothing.

The sweet scent of cinnamon brought me back the kitchen, back to the table, brought the world back into focus.

"Do you wander?" Piper asked, her hand on mine.

"No." The bitter taste of rotten lo-mien filled my mouth, and I suddenly was not sure about anything.

Magic? Me?

My brain twisted into a hurricane of questions, while my stomach became a stone. I sat heavily in the chair while my mind flew with the velocity of the truths I suddenly needed to know. What kind of magic? How strong? When?

"Why did he think that?"

Piper spoke softly, paced her words out slowly as if speaking to a scared cat under a chair. "He came to me about six months ago. After the IRS story. He told me about your process, your drive."

Oh, the IRS investigation. It was hours of going through public records and late nights and conversations that ebbed from silly to intimate. It was the first time that I told him about the storm in my head that happened when I got into a story, the sizzle of interrogation mode, how it was better than a hit of Ritalin to keep me focused on one headline at a time.

Piper continued. "I thought he was just proud of you, but then he told me about the actual interview with the IRS agent. I think that's when he really knew. He said you were able to get him to confess to what he did."

I flashed back that interview. The lightning in my brain had been full tilt for that story because it had affected the lowest income family in this agent's district, and I had been pissed. I didn't sleep for days while chasing that one, and the agent in question did give us everything we needed to publish the story. It seemed to fall out of his mouth, and my audio recorder gobbled it up and spit it out into headline news.

But it couldn't be magic. "We had proof. The guy couldn't deny it."

"Ethan called it *The Lanard Charm*, but I think it might be a type of ability."

Hearing our inside joke come out of her mouth, another wave of betrayal washed over me and brought the sizzle back to my skin. I had told Ethan everything about myself and he had turned around and told her. Even though I wasn't a big person on keeping secrets, this was my secret and he blabbed it to her.

Piper started to speak, and with it an ebb and flow of cookies and cinnamon wafted around me. "The Mother created us and gave us gifts. Each of us takes our energy and our magic to help the world. Please stop me if I am wrong here, but it probably starts with a buzz, a hum, a tingling of some sort?"

I nodded slowly, thoughts racing. Every shrink I'd ever gone to said my compulsion stemmed from the anxiety and guilt I felt after losing my father. I'd just chalked it up to journalistic instinct, that excitement while chasing a story. But it was magic?

"And then you have to do something, trigger the ability, and then you ask them a question, and they are compelled to tell you the truth?"

My ego shattered around me. The entire world grew silent as my entire world shifted axis again, the third time in a week. The words shuffled together like a new deck of cards, sticky and strangely out of alignment as they awkwardly fell into a sentence. "My dad said you always have to look an informant in the eye. Let them know you are serious."

Piper leaned forward over her tea. "So that's your trigger, looking someone in the eye?"

"How else are you going to know if they are lying?"

But that wasn't it anymore? I thought seven years in the field had taught me to spot a liar from across a football field, but it was really just a magic ability? Ethan and I tripled the numbers of spotlight articles together. His ability to sniff out a story and my ability to get the truth was nearly unbeatable. But it wasn't because I was good, it was because I was gifted?

The Charm, the magic, the whatever, began to rise along my skin, the familiar and yet now foreign sizzle making the hairs on my arms stand on end. Everything about me, my life, my career, every single interview I'd ever done glowed with a new light, an entire lifetime of magic in my brain.

Piper sat there quietly, patiently.

I bit my bottom lip to keep the questions from all jumping out at once. Finally, one question slowed down long enough to make it to my lips. "So it is a kind of magic, not some obsession?"

She nodded slowly. "Yes, but what is strange is how faint it is. The others might not be able to detect it."

Another question slapped against my tongue like a newspaper in the storm.

"So what am I? "

"I can't tell," Piper said, shaking her head, obviously puzzled. "Of course the obvious guess would be witch or guardian maybe, but I can't be sure."

My knuckles had gone white, my fingers pressing against the lace tablecloth. But I was still here. And they weren't tying me to a stake or anything. If she really was as genuine as she seemed, Piper might be the only person who could have some insight, who could actually help me control it, because the whiskey wasn't working as well as it used to.

"You're taking this quite well. Usually, when I break the news that people are Wanderers, they panic, freak out."

"I've known I was different my whole life," I said, my voice surprisingly calm. "I'm mean, not this kind of different, but you will find that I rarely panic and I have never freaked out."

"Then what do you do if you don't freak out?"

"Drink," I said frankly.

"I think I can handle that," Piper said standing. She took my teacup. "Will whiskey work?"

"No, I didn't mean..." I protested, but the woman continued across the kitchen.

"Nonsense, you deserve a drink. You've been through a lot, and it might help calm that storm you've got brewing in your brain."

I watched, stupefied, as she grabbed a bottle of Jack Daniels from the pantry and added a generous portion to my cup. She walked back across the kitchen, set the cup in front of me, and sat back down.

"My mother always said hot toddies were good for what ailed you," Piper said.

"My mother just said '*Shut up, you'll get yourself into trouble*'." I took a gulp of the tea and let it burn down my throat. The heat helped. It gave me something to focus on through the questions spiraling through my brain. "How did you know about the storm?"

Piper wrapped her hands around her warm mug and leaned forward. "Because of my resurrection, I'm pretty much made up of Wanderer energy, which means I can sense it more acutely than others." She searched for the word somewhere in the air above my head. "Like a lightning storm."

I took another large gulp of the cooling tea. Apparently hearing the truth about yourself made you thirsty as well. "So if I'm magic, it means one of my parents was magical, right? Rafe said something about being a Legacy because his father was a Shifter."

Piper smiled widely at the mention of him. "You are a quick study, but then again, Rafe is our resident scholar. Even though it was against the rules, I am glad you two found each other."

I studied my drink and swirled a few leaves that had gone astray of their bag. Rafe and I did work well together. And I had a million questions about him.

Piper continued with her story. "He was the Primo of a pretty large pack of wolves in Scotland before the ..." Piper trailed off, again searching for something through the window.

I wanted to ask a question so badly I had to wrap my ankles around the legs of the chairs to keep myself restrained.

Piper turned back toward me. "Go ahead, ask away."

My eyes locked on hers and I felt the connection, the sizzle between us, like I had million times before. "Before the Great Shifter War?"

Piper shivered for a moment, and I knew it was the magic taking hold. I'd just used a magical power on another person so powerful that everyone bowed to her. A magical power I'd been using on people my entire life. I wasn't exactly sure how I felt about that right now.

"Yes, before the War."

So Rafe was really powerful, too. He'd been able to feel my distress at the diner, like Piper was able to feel my lightning storm, but why didn't Rafe pick up on my magic? Because I'd never forced him to answer anything. We shared information. That wasn't like informants; that was more like partners.

I mentally replayed every interaction with Rafe. He had never even alluded to being a Primo, or of being anywhere but at the bottom of the pack totem pole. Squarely where Levi seemed to want him to be.

"I would have never guessed. I mean your husband, his power practically bowled me over. But Rafe's is so ..." I was actually at a loss of words.

"Gentle? Yes, I noticed that too. He's very restrained when it comes to his wolf."

"Maybe it's a British thing." I shrugged.

Piper laughed and laughed. The comforting sound soothed me. It wasn't until she stopped that I realized it was probably part of her power washing over me, making me feel safer.

"So you can feel our power?" she asked tentatively.

I nodded. "I can feel fur when Rafe is around, especially when he laughs, and you smell like my Grand-Mere's baking. But Ethan never let his slip."

Piper scrunched her nose. "So you can feel our power, use magic on us, and yet, I can't feel yours. You are a unique specimen, Miss Lanard."

"I have heard that more than once in my life."

She watched me, like Hayne used to watch me, to see what direction I was going to run, to see if I was able to run it. "Would you consider working with someone to hone your power, once we figure out what it is, of course."

"What do you mean *hone*?"

"Magic is like someone handing you Louis Armstrong's trumpet. The will and the power to play it comes from you, so you can't get good unless you practice, and as the pack's Shala, Emily, might be able to—"

"I'm good," I said quickly.

Piper stopped talking and just waited. Seemed like she also knew a few tricks about getting people to talk, because it worked.

"I know I need to deal with maybe being magical, but," I searched for the right words, the true words. "I'm not ready yet, and frankly, we don't have time. A day will let the trail go cold on these bodies."

Piper nodded and looked down at her mug of tea. "I understand."

"So maybe we can compare notes, and you can give me something more to run with. You guys know magic, but I know how to crack a story. We need to get on this now."

Piper picked up our teacups and placed them in the sink. "Ethan told me that you were special, something he'd never seen before." Piper leaned back against the counter. "It's why we need you. Rafe was just the only one with enough guts to do something about it. We need you to help us figure out what happened to Ethan, what's really going on in our city."

"And once we figure out who is behind the deaths, you'll swoop in and take them out?"

"I wish I could. Be on the front lines." Piper smiled, but there was a wink of sadness in the corner of her eye. "I've got too many depending on me to keep the Shifters together as one nation. If I put myself at risk, I put the rest of the Shifters in the world at risk too. It's why I need you. Need Rafe and the rest of the pack."

So that led to the next question. The one that I was actually hesitant to ask, because I knew what I wanted the answer to be.

"Can I still work with Rafe?"

Small crinkles at her mouth gave away her mirth.

I stood up and rested my bag on the table. "Please tell me if my instincts are wrong or if I am out of line, but Levi isn't exactly happy about bringing an outsider to this even if I'm a . . ." I struggled to get my mouth around the word. "Wanderer. I need someone who can answer questions without growling every time I need to know something. And Rafe's never lied to me."

"I want you two to keep up the good fight. For Ethan."

In that one instant, I knew I had to make good on my promise. I could trust her. More than that, I wanted to trust her. I wanted a place to come back to get the answers about me, but they had to take a second fiddle to the answers about Ethan's death.

I took a deep breath and went back to that night, the convenience store. I met Piper's gaze.

"That night. Ethan told me to tell you he was sorry."

Piper paled and tears sprang quickly to her eyes. "Sorry about what?"

"I don't know. I've been going over it in my head for weeks."

Piper put her hand to her heart. Perhaps the piece of Ethan had resided there. "Ethan was good. Wanted to protect his family, you included. There is nothing to forgive him for."

She moved away from me, toward a back door. "I need to get the grill fired up for dinner. I'm waiting for a few others to get here. Give me forty minutes and everyone can convene downstairs for you to present the case."

"To everyone? The whole pack? It's pretty gruesome."

"Everyone needs to know, Merci."

She slipped out the back.

I had to find out what was going on, not just for Ethan anymore, but for his family too. For this completely wonderful Wanderer in front of me. For the first person in a long while who seemed to accept me as I was. Well, second person.

I wandered outside and ducked into my coat. Piper and Kye were whispering about something on the back patio and an enthusiastic game of flag football was happening across the open backyard with some of the younger people here, not that everyone here didn't appear particularly young.

Rafe broke through the line of the trees on the back of the property. His hair was wild and his cheeks a little pink. He spotted me, and before I knew it, we'd gravitated toward each other, ending up on the edge of the backyard.

"Have a good chat with Piper?" he asked.

I wasn't quite sure what to say. "It was interesting."

"Are you okay?"

I was lost for a moment in his blue eyes. The words pooled in my throat with the urge to tell him everything, but I had to figure it all out for myself first, get my facts squared away. "I need to understand this more." I turned to watch the group of people at play.

He surveyed the scene with me. "Well, I'm not from these parts, but I think it's called football."

I chuckled. "A joke? Nice."

I watched his pack mates on the field, their lithe bodies running and tackling and bouncing around like they were all Cirque du Soleil performers. I recognized a few of the older ones from the funeral, but everyone looked different in sportswear. "They are all so athletic."

"They are, we are, at our core, animals," he said. "What else would you like to understand?"

After that little talk in the kitchen, wrapping my head about the fact that this instinct I'd honed was potentially a magical power was going to need more than a game of twenty questions. "I need a total magic primer, like an *Idiot's Guide* to being a wanderer."

Though I doubted he could produce one of those form a magical pocket, I went back to what I usually did, asking questions, piece everything together in small digestible bites.

"How does it work? The magic that shifters have?" I shivered and jammed my hands in my pockets. One of these days I would remember a scarf, maybe even manage gloves.

Rafe stepped around and stood upwind from me, blocking the breeze, but surrounding me in his woodsy smell, like he'd rolled around in pine needles. And perhaps he had. Maybe that's what he'd been doing in the woods.

"Each Wanderer has a specific magical ability given to us by the Mother. Shifters are able to use their magic to turn into an animal that fits their spirit."

I nodded; it was always nice when sources collaborated a story, when the gothic tales from my youth matched up with my current reality. "Piper said it was like a trumpet."

He smiled. "Piper's father was a Jazz musician, so of course she looks at it like an instrument. We all have our own way of figuring it out in our heads."

Mine was a storm. I knew that. Piper had already figured that one out for me. A lightning storm and I knew what it felt like to be electrocuted if the storm didn't get its way.

"I know it sounds strange, but mine is a book. It's how I visualize my power, open, then shut."

"Figures, Professor."

We watched the game for a few moments longer, and in the middle of a particularly long pass, one of the young men shifted into a wolf, twisting in the air to catch the ball in his mouth.

I gasped. It was within a blink, and at such close range. From there, it seemed to be a chain reaction, and the field was covered in a furry mass of wolves and dogs and a mountain lion all clambering around in play, ignoring the football now tumbling toward me.

Rafe stepped forward and stopped the ball with his foot. He popped it up with his toe and caught it. With a whistle, the pack stopped and turned their heads toward us in unison.

An ice cube of fear slid slowly down my spine as I stood in the predatory gaze of all those animals.

Rafe launched the ball back at them, and one of the wolves shifted back into his human form to catch it and run across the field for a touchdown.

I stared at the field as they all shifted back into their human forms, clothes and all. Playing like it was nothing.

"It is really always that easy?" I asked.

"No, it takes practice. But most of us retain our conscious mind, or at least most of it, unless something goes wrong."

I pressed further. "But what happens when someone doesn't learn? What happens if the magic takes over?"

Rafe frowned as he worked through how to explain it. "Someone new to the shift might be lost to the shift, temporarily losing their conscious minds to their animal instincts until their power is burnt out, like a battery-powered toy. We call it Moon Crazed."

And what happens when a person can't control the storm in their head? I already knew that answer. They get nosebleeds and black out. They lash out at themselves and others and do crazy things until the storm burns out and they are left lifeless on their couch for three days. It was the same magic, same consequences, same story I'd been living my whole life.

"Things don't go wrong very often. The pack structure sees to that."

I didn't have a pack to save me, but Piper had offered theirs. "Piper mentioned something about Emily being the Shala? And you said Ethan was a Riko?"

He shoved his hands into his jean pockets. "You don't forget anything, do you?"

"Mind like a steel trap this one."

He only half-smiled. "The leader, the Primo. The Rikos are the protectors. The Shalas are the teachers, to help younger wanderers find and control their animals." He turned to me. "Why were you and Piper talking about the Shala?"

My heart raced. I wasn't going to tell him here why I needed a Shala, not yet. I turned away from him toward the field. Who knew that watching shifter flag football could be so distracting?

"Piper just mentioned Emily could help me out with the investigation as well." This lie tasted like burnt hair and wood chips.

Wait. Could that be part of it too? I'd gotten the psychosomatic flavors of my lies for years, could it be my magic backhanding me for lying? God, there was so much I needed to know about this, about Ethan, and there just wasn't enough time.

I needed to switch topics. "You said that you watched over the pack when they shifted, so no one strays."

He nodded. "Especially the younger ones." He pointed to a set of tall, lanky twins. "The Sleators are fairly new to the shift, the two black wolf hounds, one got bitten and then bit the other one and the Shift took in both of them; they're up at the university with me. The wolves are all one family, the Thompsons, from eleven to eighteen, been shifting since their first full moon. Their mum runs this amazing sandwich shop in town."

"And the mountain lion?" I asked.

He paused for the name on that one. "She's new. I'm not sure I caught her name."

I watched them for a little longer, their exuberant play. "They are all so young?"

"Aye."

"I never thought of werewolves as kids."

"*Shifters*, Merci. And where did you think we came from? Under a cabbage leaf?"

I shook my head. I had never fully appreciated the width and breadth of what Ethan had been keeping from me, what he had been protecting. It wasn't just him and Emily, it was an entire generation of innocents he was protecting when he was passing along our information to the pack.

The anger at him passed through me and into the ground as the storm calmed. I was going to have be to that now, their information, their barrier against the darkness.

After a hearty burger and handful of salty potatoes chips that I wolfed down like a teenager, the call went out for the adults to gather in the entertainment room.

It was hard seeing Emily again, like a favorite toy that had been taken away but I wasn't sure that I'd earned back yet. I just didn't feel like I had the right to talk to her, and could imagine the many reasons she wouldn't want to talk to me. But I was acutely aware of her presence. I still mustered up my courage and walked toward the group of people gathered in the basement around a table. Correction: a Ping-Pong table. Someone had taken down the net to make for a better conference table.

"I thought things would be more formal," I muttered to Piper as she led me into the room.

"Why?" She shrugged. "We're people. People like Ping-Pong."

I clutched the folder full of pictures. This Ping-Pong table was never going to be the same again.

Others lined up around the edge of the green table. All shapes and sizes. Some of the faces were familiar from the funeral and some weren't. The tall blonde was there, the one who had led Emily away from the gravesite. And Levi, of course, scowling. Others didn't look thrilled to be there and their eyes darted from me to Piper to Levi. A man the size of a doorway took up nearly the entire end of the table, his arms folded over his chest, his face blank. Piper and Kye stood together at the other end, as a united pair.

I focused across the net line to Rafe standing there. He gave me a little nod.

With the Shifters surrounding me, I was the odd man out. Would they be able to smell a whatever-I-was in their mix? Rafe hadn't been able to, but I didn't want to risk it. These people weren't suspects or informants; they were here to help. I just would make sure I didn't look anyone in the eye or ask questions.

Right, like that was going to happen. I was so screwed.

"I'm sure you all have heard about Merci from Ethan," Piper started.

There was a general grumble of assent around the table.

"And, Merci, you know Levi, Emily, and Rafe, but you might not know our Prima, Cleo."

The tall blonde woman bobbed her curls at me.

"And our other Riko, Xenom."

The huge man at the end of the table grunted like a grizzly bear, his face not moving a single muscle.

"If you would," Piper said.

With a deep breath, I began. This was just like pitching a story to Hayne. The facts that I had already collected and then what we still needed to know. "While trying to investigate Ethan's death, I found two more equally disturbing murders. Both have been ruled as exposure, and you'll see why."

When I put the first photo down, Emily flinched. The second one made her turn away.

"Mitchell, another journalist, was found on the doorstep of the home he grew up in. Hadn't lived there in years. Cops assumed he was homeless due to the state of the body and moved on."

Levi interrupted. "Could it have been dried out and then moved there?"

I spread the rest of the photos out on the table. "Mitchell was gone for less than a week." I pointed at Tay-Tay. "Tiara Henderson, less than three days. She was the girlfriend of the informant that Ethan and I met with." I put the last picture on the table. "My contact at the M.E. says this type of weathering would have taken months to get that level of decay without any help."

The group stared at the two bodies before them.

"So what is the story that we aren't seeing?" Piper asked. She'd curled her arm through Kye's. It struck me that these were everyday images for me. Hell, I saw more pictures of dead people than live ones. But, even for the most powerful person in this room, gore was still gore and a corpse was an innocent lost.

"Notice the position of each body, arms out, neck stiff, legs bent in this sort of diamond shape? Same in both cases. Rafe's recognized the symbolic meaning behind it."

His blue eyes flicked up to me, slightly startled at being called on. I raised an eyebrow and nodded that he needed to take over.

"The shape their bodies are making is the Old Speak symbol for sacrifice."

One of young wolves gasped. Cleo hid behind Levi's shoulder. The bear at the end of the table flexed his muscles so hard that I thought he would rip his shirt. I watched as the others looked at Piper, who nodded for Rafe to continue.

"Now if we observe the state of the bodies, they appeared dry, completely desiccated. As if the life had been sucked out of them," Rafe finally said.

I listened to him carefully as he explained. "Two isn't enough to determine a pattern. But with the magical significance of the body, it could be a very intricate spell or an ancient ritual. One had a piece of magic still lingering on the body, and I've been reading the grimoires and, in theory, it could have been put on her arm while alive to be the catalyst for a spell that did this."

"What kind of spell?" I asked.

Rafe could only shake his head. "I don't know, but more than likely, we are looking at another one, and probably soon, within a week? My biggest concern is that they're being patient, which is something we haven't seen before."

Apparently, I was the only one able to articulate any questions, so I kept my eyes on the table, on the pictures, careful there was no chance my questions could expose me. "What was it like before, the last time you dealt with Warlocks?"

Levi actually answered the question. "Impulsive. Warlocks attacked a few of us. Got their asses handed back to them."

"Was this before or after your office was broken into?" The question slipped out completely under my radar. Against all the mental barricades I'd put up.

I could hear the familiar sound of teeth grinding. "I only ask so I can get a timeline of their activity."

"Before. We had no proof the break-in was them," he continued, "We thought they'd left town."

Rafe shook his head. "The magic on the Henderson body. It was fresh."

The others around the table started to shift uncomfortably. I wasn't sure if it was the magic or the dead bodies that were making them squirm, but neither one seemed to be setting right with this crowd. I felt bad about showing them this violence, especially Emily.

"Mitchell was found at his childhood home and Tay-Tay was found in in her apartment." I gestured toward the pictures for the rest of the group. "Could that be important to a spell? Something about home turf?"

Rafe shook his head. "Maybe. I'm not an expert in spells."

"I thought you were the resident scholar," I said.

A small smile crept across Rafe's mouth.

Levi didn't find it as funny and a small growl echoed across the space.

Piper rapped her knuckles against the table and pointed at Levi like a true Mother with the universal "No." She took control of the conversation by simply clearing her throat. "I'll see if I can get more books sent out here, but I don't want too many red flags raised. Last thing we need is the Cause coming in here and trying to get their claws in. Those do-gooders always seem to mess everything up."

There was a general consensus around the room. I was feeling like the new kid in class and almost raised my hand. "Who—or what—is the Cause?"

Piper flashed me a sweet smile. "They are a fraternity of a sorts, of different breeds of Wanderers who have pledged to protect the balance between humans and magic."

It sort of made sense, but Levi cut off my next question about them.

"I want us out in greater numbers," the Primo said as a hot wave of his puppy-scented power spread throughout the room, making my stomach flip-flop. "Keep in groups, but make your presence known."

"Are you trying to draw them out?" Emily's voice was high and tight as she spoke for the first time. Her dark eyes were wide and tear-filled. "Get another one of us killed?"

"No. I want these Warlocks to know this is our city."

Piper made a tsking noise. "I'm not entirely sure this is Warlocks, Levi. Something new might be trying to get into the cracks of the city. Just because it quacks doesn't make it a duck."

Emily shook her head and crossed her arms over her chest. It wasn't two seconds later that she left the table entirely, her footsteps echoing up the stairs.

Piper sighed as her eyes followed Emily out of the room. But she recovered and smiled warmly to the group. "Stay together. Try not to go anywhere alone until we know for sure what's going on. Thank you, all, for coming."

Piper and Kye left. A few others drifted away, muttering under their breath as they glanced at me or Rafe. Only Levi and Xenom remained.

I craned my neck to look up at the massive man and remembered the black bear that lumbered over the hill the night of the full moon. The spirit animal hadn't really been super creative with its form for this guy.

"So I guess you're running with the research?" Levi asked Rafe.

Rafe's eyes twinkled with a moment of amusement. These puns were getting out of hand. "I guess I am."

"I want to know everything you find."

"Yes, sir."

"You report to me and I report it to Piper. Got it?"

"Yes, sir."

Levi glared at me, then at Rafe, before nodding to Xenom. The two men walked upstairs.

As their footsteps sounded above us, I let out a deep breath. "That wasn't fun."

"Welcome to pack politics." Rafe leaned forward on the table, his hands braced wide and his head lowered.

I slowly moved to his side of the table to survey the pictures from his vantage point, trying not to enjoy the warmth that ebbed from him. I didn't want to admit that it calmed me, made it seem like not all hope was lost.

"Whatever happened upstairs, it sounds like she trusts you, believes in you."

"She does," was all I could say. The question was, could I trust myself, my instincts, anymore without knowing where the magic came from and where it would mostly likely end up?

"Then what's wrong?"

"I'll be fine," I assured. "I just need some quiet time." It wasn't technically a lie. I knew that in about five years and gallons of whiskey later, I would eventually be fine with all this.

"And you quiet time is working a murder story?"

"If you are going through hell, keep going."

"Really? Churchill."

I just shrugged.

He started to stack the photos into a neat pile before him, using a reverence that surprised me.

"Looks like we'll keep on working together," I ventured, "sanctioned by the Den Mother herself. Execution is officially off the table."

"Seems to be getting the job done." Rafe slid the photos back in their folder. "Well, it's coming up on Thanksgiving break, and then I've got three more weeks of school, but, frankly, it's all autopilot until their final presentations."

I chuckled as I took the file folder from him.

"What?"

"I didn't even realize it was Thanksgiving."

"So that's a 'no' to you having family?"

I turned to face the living room again. "Oh, I've got family, but they really don't like me all that much. Mom is still around, but would rather I keep my big city lifestyle to the big city."

"Last Wolf standing. It's only me for this holiday too."

"I'd imagine that the pack would put together a spread. This seems like a potluck friendly place."

He sighed. "Oh, they do."

I wanted to ask what had happened to warrant this shunning, but the words weighed heavy on my tongue. Something deep down almost didn't want to know and certainly didn't want to pull it out of him. It was the first time in my life I was okay with not knowing everything about everything.

My skin prickled with the realization, and I shivered.

But I pushed it aside. I had murders to solve and a sidekick to help. Like old times.

My cell phone rang and I had to dig through my bag to find it. "Lanard."

"It's Rutherford."

"Hey, Julie. What you got?"

"You know how you were hounding me the other day about weird dead bodies. Well, we got another one."

It was like he'd struck a tuning fork against my head; everything hummed with a gathering storm. "Please tell me I'm the first one you called."

"Haven't even called it in to dispatch. Wanted to give you a heads-up, because I *heard* you the other day, Lanard. I really heard you."

Shocked wasn't the right word to explain what I felt. It wasn't often that my rants changed people's minds.

"I wanted to let you know."

"Where are you?" I turned back around and started collected everything from the table. I needed to go. I needed to get there now.

When he gave me the address, my body froze with my arm stuck in my bag. "Repeat that?"

"I know. Where you and Rhoades were attacked. Reason number two I'm calling you in. Might lose my head for it, but I don't want this one to go unsolved."

My skin tightened and crackled as I tried to put together a plan. "I'm an hour out, Julie."

"I got you."

Tears nearly formed in my eyes at that. I hung up and gulped as I turned to Rafe. Even in the sizzle, his blue eyes seem to calm me, focus me. "There is another body."

Rafe paled and his lips parted.

"We might have a pattern."

I heard footsteps on the stairs and saw Emily hovering between this floor and the next.

I didn't know what to say. I was just about to go back to the place where her husband had died and it might be the proof we needed of a pattern. It was one of the few times in my life where I could actually believe the more the merrier. If everyone was looking, something would be found, right? Especially with their preternatural senses?

"There's another body," Rafe said

She hurried down the stairs. "What?" she whispered, when she reached us.

"Merci's just been called about another body. It makes a pattern," Rafe repeated.

"Just like you said."

I still had a million things to tell her. A million stories I wanted to share with her, to help her know that Ethan loved her with every breath he took. That I missed her secretly checking in with me when she didn't want to be 'that wife.' That I already had her Christmas present tucked away on my bookshelf. To make sure that I didn't lose her too.

But one truth finally marched to the front of the storm and planted its words on my lips. "We are going to find out who killed Ethan."

She put her hands over her mouth as tears welled up in her eyes. She nodded. "Take my car. There's a bag in the backseat. Take that too."

I looked into Emily's eyes, the Charm crackling to life at the new lead, the new trigger, the place to work my magic. Energized like this, I could almost believe that I would keep my word to Ethan. That I would find who was responsible.

"Stay out of trouble, Merci," Emily said.

"You know I can't promise that."

She almost smiled.

CHAPTER SEVEN

Emily had left Ethan's camera bag in the backseat of the car. I recognized it the moment I saw it, that old red woven strap he always had slung across his chest. I pulled out the camera, amazed that it had survived that night without a scratch. I ran my fingers up the neck strap and didn't see any blood. Emily cleaned it. I can't even imagine what that would have been like for her, and then she gave it to me. Why spend so much time on something and then give it away?

Maybe because I knew what to do with it. Without thinking, I prepped the data card and replaced the battery as I'd seen him do a million times before; the green "ready" light glowed. I hung the old camera around Rafe's neck, smoothing the woven band against the wool of his coat, remembering the battles already fought with it.

"Wait. This is..?"

I nodded. "Are you ready?"

There was a swirl of fur around me that ebbed into a steady warmth between us.

Magic or not, I was more Merci Lanard now than I had been in three weeks. Though Rafe could never replace Ethan, he had brought balance back to my life. I was ready to walk once again into the breach.

Covered in the dusk of a recently set sun, we crept down the street and stopped just around the corner from the address. The night was calm, and Atlanta's words about the quiet before a storm floated through my head.

I prepped Rafe for the plan of action. "Now don't say anything. Take as many pictures as you can. I can go through them later. Got it, Professor?"

"Perfectly, Miss Lanard," he said with the flash of a smile.

I steadied my nerves, and we headed for the convenience store. It wasn't until I reached the corner and saw Rutherford's squad car parked outside that it even crossed my mind I might not be able to do this, couldn't be in that place again. I stopped dead in my tracks and Rafe bounced against me.

He walked around, glancing between me and the dilapidated storefront, highlighted by the few streetlights along the dark street. His voice was low and soft. "This is it, isn't it?"

I nodded. I couldn't seem to pull my eyes away from that spot just inside the front door.

"You can stay outside, talk to your officer friend. I'll get inside and take the photos."

I shook my head. "Don't be stupid. I can do this."

"But you don't have to."

I took in a deep breath and focused on the story. "It's not what he would do."

"What would he do?" he asked over my shoulder.

I sniffed. I didn't even know that my eyes had been watering. The words poured out of me. "He'd say, '*Well, are you gonna take a knee, Lanard?*'"

Rafe chuckled softly at my side.

I sniffed again. "He was big on the sport references."

"Actually," he said, "it's an old Wanderer saying. You either take a knee or take a knife. You succumb to the dark or you fight against it."

I sucked in a deep breath and couldn't admit that his smell, his heat enveloping me, helped steel my nerves against what was ahead. "I think you know which one I chose."

"I'm right there with you."

We headed toward the store. I caught a glimpse of Officer Rutherford nervously fiddling with his silver coin, the circle catching the light from the streetlamps. Slipping it back into his pocket, he immediately intercepted us in the middle of the street and quickly guided us to a sheltered corner. He shot Rafe an appraising look. "Didn't think they'd have you partnered up so fast."

"Trial by fire." I squinted into the darkened store. "So what do we have?"

Rutherford lowered his voice even more, searching the night around us. "I don't know how on-the-record we can go with this yet."

I looked him square in the eyes. "I'm good, Julie. I won't get you in trouble. Now tell me what happened."

The description spilled out of him like a confession, and I hadn't even turned on the Charm. There was no sizzle; there was only the two of us. He needed to tell me the truth. "Someone called in the smell, then went to go see what it was. The body is pretty mangled up, like the ones that you were talking about. But the smell is terrible."

As I started writing down the timeline on a fresh page in my notebook, I grew relieved that my reporting wasn't all based on some magical charm. I'd done good work before—Ethan and I had done good work before—and not everything hinged on magic. The storm had never won me any friends, but what I had with Rutherford was trust built around saving this city from itself sometimes.

"Any ID?"

"None that I can't find."

The only reason I knew that Rafe wasn't by my side anymore was that I began to rub my arms for warmth. "Is the M.E. on their way?"

"You took your sweet ass time, so you've got about three seconds with the scene before it rains police."

I saw Rafe already moving through the store. The pit of my stomach roiled as I thought about being in that place again. I couldn't go in there, but there was one thing that I could do. "Could you point me in the direction of the person who called it in?"

Rutherford gestured with his eyes to the stoop next door. "Not the friendliest."

"You would be amazed at how people talk to me and my friend Andrew Jackson." I winked at him before walking away from the store.

There were three of them out on the front steps watching the dancing blue lights of the police car. I sized them up. Nothing I hadn't worked with before.

"Twenty dollars to the person who called the fuzz."

Two of them might as well have raised their hands and shouted 'I know who' like goodie-two shoes in a third grade class. Their gazes jumped to the man at the back of the group while his gaze landed on the step before him.

"I'm not a cop, and for every question you answer articulately, I'll give you twenty bucks and I don't even need your name."

The man looked up at me with his sallow eyes. A sizzle surged up my back. This is where I needed the Charm. I almost didn't want to. I almost kept my eyes on my notebook so I couldn't use magic on another person. How did this make me any different from the thing out there?

But this was important. I needed to know the truth. We needed to catch who was doing this. This was for Ethan, and my Charm had never hurt anyone in the past, except me. No one else had gotten nosebleeds and headaches. And I would gladly pay that price to find the truth.

What happened last night?

The question was written in neon across my brain. The sizzle followed, that was the energy that Piper talked about. The lightning. The thing the fueled the magic covered me. Years of slipping into interrogation mode and it had been magic this whole time.

Then I looked him in the eye. The man on the stoop was wired, twitchy, but he was open, ready. Once our gazes locked, it was like reaching out and slipping a key into a keyhole and turning it until it locked into place. We were good. He would tell me the truth as long as he was on the tether.

I just needed to keep eye contact, keep my hand on the key, and ask the right questions. Right? Like I had on hundreds of people and just never took the time to fully realize my own truth because the one that I was seeking always seemed bigger, and, frankly, easier to answer.

Now for the trigger.

"Do you know the man you found in there?"

His head tweaked to the left with every third word. "Name was Beakman. Used to run through here. Knew him by this necklace he used to always flash around."

"Used to? Where does he run now?"

The man raked his nails along his upper arms. Even though it was nearly forty degrees outside, he wasn't wearing a coat—none of them were. "Southside now. Was surprised to see him again."

"You think he came home to overdose?"

"Nah, Beakman wasn't a user."

"So this for sure was not a drug overdose?"

The man could only shrug, though it looked more like a full body tremor.

"When was the last time you saw him?"

One of the other men chimed in, probably to get in on the money being handed out. "At the Memorial Day thing, he came to see Shirley."

"Who's Shirley?" I looked down to scratch out the name. There was the slightest of snaps when I disconnected with him, like breaking a spider's web that left a feathery residual feeling at my temple. All this time, all these interviews, and it was like this was the first time, noticing things, experiencing it through the lens of magic.

"Girl he used to go around with."

I scratched at my temple and pulled a curl behind my ear. "She still around here?"

The original man shoved at the second shoulder. "No. She flew about two months ago. Haven't seen her since."

I pointed with my pen toward the store front. "Why'd you bother calling the cops?"

"Can't have violence in our neighborhood like that. This is a family place."

I didn't have any more questions they could help me with. I reached for my cash roll in my front pocket. I doled out the money and was about to leave when the third man finally spoke up.

"Was the shadows that did it."

The Charm crawled back up my throat, and I stared down at the man. Our gazes locked. "What did you say?"

"Like what happened a few weeks back. Devils from hell came to collect him."

He wasn't lying. He couldn't. My skin tightened into goosebumps despite my pea coat against the winter cold. Devils had come. And I was coming for them.

The other three nearly pushed him off the stairs. "Don't believe him, miss. He's high as a kite."

I pulled another twenty out of my pocket and handed it to the man. "Thank you."

MacCallan met me halfway between the stoop and the store. He looked worn, sick to his stomach.

"Magic?" I asked.

"And more."

We didn't speak until we got back to my car. He took the camera from around his neck and shoved it at me, then started pacing wildly in front of the car, running his fingers through his hair. "Same everything. Same look. Same position. It was the same spell."

He stopped in the middle of the sidewalk and did a full body shiver.

"Hey, calm down." I reached out for him this time. I allowed myself to catch his arm as he paced in front of me. "Rafe, walk me through it."

He was on me in an instant. One moment, he was three feet away and a blink later, he was pressing me against the side of my car, his heat suffocating, his lips only an inch away.

I fought the panic that jumped into my throat and clawed for air. He would never hurt me, but my heart pounded in my ears. I stayed still against the car, watching him, watching the riptide of emotions that crossed his fair features.

I could feel it, his power, the wolf. The silky feeling of fur against my neck, my side, was rough, sizzling with energy, instead of sweeping across my skin. Was this what he was feeling? This electric bristle raking through him? No wonder he was freaking out.

He'd just been where his brother was killed. Seen the blood stains on the floor. Felt the proof there was something darker involved in his death. He'd finally seen the proof that lived on the insides of my eyelids. I'd been so concerned with my fears and memories that I'd forgotten that he'd lost his only brother there too.

His eyes fluttered closed and he inhaled deeply. His chest pressed against me as he slid his cheek against mine. For an eternity, everything warred within me. This type of intimacy was too soon, too sudden, but there was something in his being, in the way his muscles calmed, in his beating heart that I could feel pulsing around us, erratic at first, then gaining a steady rhythm. This wasn't about bodies and breath; this was about something deeper, more intimate than that. That's what kept me still, kept me from wracking my knee into his manhood and sending him across the sidewalk.

He exhaled very slowly and pulled away from me, his hands pressed against the car, framing my shoulders. His blue eyes finally drew up and met mine. The feeling of bristles was replaced by the silky caress of his power as it retreated to wherever it went.

Dark circles still resided under his blue eyes, but the panic was gone.

I spoke slowly. "What the hell was that?"

He shivered around me once again, like a dog shaking off the last bit of water from a rain shower. He dropped his arms and took a step away.

I diverted my gaze down the street as I sucked in a deep, cold lungful of the night air. It wasn't that a deeply powerful werewolf had invaded my personal space, but that it had also been far too long since I'd been that close to a man who wanted to be that close to me.

He leaned against the car. I could still smell him, but I wasn't sure if it was his proximity or a residual scent left on my coat. Either way, I didn't mind it.

He started slowly and I listened as I had never listened before. "In the apartment, I didn't feel anything but a flutter, but in there ..." He only briefly flicked his eyes up to the store and then they were quickly back to his loafers. "It's bad in there. It's not the smell, it's the sense of the place. Something evil was done there."

"Something evil was done in there."

I pressed my lips together to keep from asking what else would rub a wolf the wrong way, but when I saw the creases around his eyes, the furrow in his brow, I knew that metaphysically, not much could. I sighed. "What does that evil have to do with ..." I didn't have a word for what had happened between us. Nothing seemed as intimate as it felt despite the surprise nature of it.

He looked up at me. "You are a pond of calm in the middle of all this chaos. I needed to focus on one thing, away from everything, away from what I felt and saw in there. I'm sorry if I scared you."

I didn't know how I could be compared to anything calm. I was usually the cause of the chaos, not the eye of the storm.

I shook my head and the truth tumbled out, "I imagined you experienced the world differently, but I didn't realize just how much. I didn't think about taking you to the place he died. I'm sorry."

"I don't know how Ethan dealt with this every day."

This was one body in one crime scene. Ethan and I had seen murder-suicides, gang shootings, every piece of evil under the sun and I had never seen him falter. "We did everything together."

Rafe looked at me like he had something to say. I knew that I could try again to compel it out of him, get the truth behind those troubled blue eyes, but I didn't want to. He didn't need the stress after this evening and, deep down, I wasn't prepared for the answers he might give.

I opened the car door and pulled out the memory card from the camera before I tossed it in the front seat, slipping the small data card into the breast pocket of my coat. "I'm going back to the office to find out more information about our new victim, so I can turn in a story this week. You've got a spell to research"

...

I'd gotten home only twenty minutes before Rafe called to tell me that he was done with classes for the day. When he mentioned we could cover more ground looking for the spell together, I had volunteered my place. What I left out was that I didn't do tidy, I barely had any furniture, and I wasn't sure I even had a mug that didn't reek of whiskey. I was seriously second-guessing my brilliant idea to research at my place.

I opened the door. "I have to warn you, I didn't have time to clean."

Rafe balanced a stack of books so high I could barely see his eyes.

"Did you bring your entire library with you?"

"No. Only what I could find with a reference to spell or theoretical magic."

He followed me into the living room/kitchen area. He set the books on the table and I didn't need any special charm to tell me that he was slightly surprised by the state of the place.

It made me take a brief glance around. It wasn't that bad. It just like maybe a college kid lived here with really bad eating habits and no real eye for décor. I had the basics: a desk, table, couch, and chair. My interior designer mother would hate it. I could hear all of her suggestions already in my head, which was why I had never invited her to visit.

At least he looked impressed by the bookcases. What I lacked in an eye for design I made up for in books. Tons and tons of books. All the classics, all the *New York Times* best sellers. Most unread, of course, but a girl could dream. Wasn't my fault that I'd worked an eighty-hour workweek since the day I graduated college.

Rafe pulled out a few more volumes from his messenger bag. It was so very professorial of him.

"I have a special one for you." He pulled one last book from the inside of his jacket. "It's rare, so you can't keep it, but I thought you might like to see it."

I took the red leather-bound book in my hands. It smelled like rawhide and sandalwood, like Rafe. "What is it?"

"It's an Idiot's Guide to Being a Wanderer."

My heart skipped a beat, and I experienced the missed rhythm in the base of my throat. I could barely get the question out through my locked jaw. "What?"

"It should be a useful guide into the world before you start researching magic. It's got a really good index in it. Pretty much covers the different breeds of Wanderers and their general characteristics and weaknesses." He pressed his lips together before he spoke again. "It might help you understand my world a little more."

I nodded and held the book to my chest. It was still warm from being tucked away in his winter coat. I took a moment to let the warmth sit against me while he unpacked his books and put them into some sort of order I couldn't begin to understand.

"Right, we've got enough to keep us reading for the rest of the night. Should I put a kettle on?"

I snorted. "If you can find one."

I looked down at the red book with the red leather cover. The fancy emblem winked up at me. He'd said "my world," but my life was in this book too. It seemed fitting somehow that it would be as I surveyed my sparse apartment covered in books. It could confirm what I'd been feeling, experiencing, dealing with, and as a journalist, I still really liked to have hard evidence.

I flipped to the first chapter. The scent on the pages was something I hadn't smelled in years—the smell of my favorite library book.

Chapter One: Genesis

When the world was first created, magic was in everyone and everything. The creative energy, The Mother, made beings and creatures that walked on two legs and ran on four. The magics flowed through the Wanderers who were so in touch with their mother earth, there was nothing to stop them from becoming part of nature in the form of a wolf or dancing with the wind. Each possessed a special skill that helped their fellow Wanderer or served the Mother in some way. They spoke the language of the earth and were able to converse with all manner of creation. They lived so peacefully with nature that they needed no home and were free to wander the path the earth set out for them.

When the world was no longer new, creatures called humans began to live among those who wandered among the world. They were small and frail and couldn't weave water or talk to trees, but they were passionate and artistic and resourceful. To make shelter, humans used trees to protect themselves from the elements. To feed and shod their children, they fashioned weapons to hunt animals. To drink, they damned rivers and created havoc on the precious balance of the earth.

As the humans settled into places across the earth, the Wanderers became divided. Seeing how humans were threatening the land the Wanderers were so vitally connected with, some believed humans needed to be stopped, controlled, and still some believed that only total annihilation would save their earth. Others saw humans as creatures of the Mother to live in harmony with, to learn from, to teach.

Blah. Blah. Blah. There had to be a Table of Contents in this thing. I flipped back a few pages. And yep. Table of Contents. I ran my finger down the list of terms. Avion. Cause, The. Demons. Elementals. Fey. Grifters. Guardians. Order, The. Seer. Shifters.

But what about me? None of the terms in the table of contents said anything about truth or psychic powers or anything useful. What I could do didn't really help a fellow Wanderer or serve the Mother in any way that I could think of.

Rafe distracted me from my book with a coffee.

I stared at the steaming mug before me in disbelief. Is there was such a thing as kitchen magic? "I'm not really used to such service."

"Ever think about that?" he asked as he walked back over to his spot at the opposite end.

"What's that supposed to mean?" I asked. Then I took a sip. It was perfect. My mind raced trying to figure out why. At the theater, he'd already had two creamers and two sugars waiting for me there too. That first night at Sam's. I'd had coffee then. Why would he remember that from so long ago?

"Nothing," he said taking off his jacket, rolling up his sleeves. He slid a huge volume off a tall stack and it made a loud thud as it jostled the table.

"Avoiding conflict. Is that a British thing?" I asked as I started turning through the chapters of a red leather Wandering book.

"More of a self-preservation thing." He flipped through a few pages and scanned the text.

"From what Piper says, you shouldn't have a problem defending yourself."

"I don't."

"Good. Ethan always said I didn't have it in me to play safe."

"I appreciate the warning, but you don't have to be nosy."

"You're the one with the great sense of smell."

He looked up from his books, and even at this safe distance, I could see the twinkle in his eye. "Good one, Miss Lanard. Would you happen to have any white paint?

"Why?" I asked as I got up and walked over to the table.

"If we are going to bed down here, I want it to be protected." He pointed to a scribbly looking circle thing on the worn page. "I want to put up a protection sigil above your doors and windows."

I lifted myself on my seat to see the pages from my side of the table. "And you think a hieroglyph is going to do that?"

He only grinned. "These are not hieroglyphs. This is Old Speak magic."

I gaffed. "You are not doing a spell in my house."

"We need to make sure this place is safe, in case whoever's behind this wants to finish the job they started that night."

I gulped and held my arm to my stomach.

"I could carve this into your walls, but landlords tend to frown on that."

"Why do you assume I rent?" I sighed. "Let me see. I think I might have something up in my closet."

I dug around in my closet and had to move the trunk of my dad's journals to find paint supplies I'd bought with the last boyfriend when we'd thought about renovating the place, but only found the supplies. Neither the boyfriend nor the idea had lasted long enough to apparently decide on a paint color.

But I still had my dad's journals. The dad who was apparently magical enough to pass it down to his daughter and leave her with a mind full of questions, a head full of thunderstorms.

I cracked open the leather travel case and there they were; the journals that my father wrote in every day of his life. They were story notebooks I had just barely saved when my mother was throwing away everything that reminded her of him. I'd dragged them from home to college and then up the stairs and here they sat. As I stared at them, it dawned on me that they too could possible hold the answers about who I was.

I savored the smell of leather and whiskey, maybe with a hint of dust and cigars. They smelled like him. Or maybe he had smelled like them. I pulled out the first one and leather was still smooth like I remembered it. I cracked open the cover to see his familiar handwriting.

Maybe there was something in there. Maybe there wasn't. Downstairs, we had enough books to fill another library, but this one was all about me, about my Legacy. About the magic that I apparently carried with me.

I tucked it under my arm and bounced back down the stairs empty handed.

Rafe was standing on a chair drawing something onto the doorframe.

"Hey!" I protested.

"Would you rather be dead?"

I huffed. "I didn't find paint, so carve away, but explain as you carve."

And he did. He pulled a pocket knife out of his pocket and started to etch a circle into my wooden frame. I had to turn away, a new pain of home ownership.

"Old Speak is the language that binds the magic inherent in the universe. It's the language of spells. Words that give name and power to things and can change how the universe reacts to something."

"And what exactly are you carving into my house?"

"Your home contains your energy, it's a place where you feel safe. Unlike where we were last night." His hand paused, then dropped to his side. I knew he was re-seeing, re-smelling, reliving what he'd been through. After a deep breath, he started his work again. "This is a sigil for protection against harm. Nothing with ill-intent to your person as the person who has filled this place with your energy will be able to get through that door or through this window."

It either made perfect sense, or I had been lulled into submission by his accent. How did the co-eds contain themselves around a handsome professor who could lull you into a dream even when speaking of decay? Perhaps they didn't contain themselves.

At least the symbol was small; it was sort of a circle with a Wi-Fi signal around it. He jumped down from his chair and moved to another window.

"So this Old Speak is how they are working their spells?"

"Aye. Like a computer command. Protect, sacrifice, and so on. I mean, it's a wee bit more than that, but we don't have years to teach you the nuance of spellcraft. The basic premise is magic is the catalyst, fueled by the universe's power or potential energy, and driven by the willpower of the practitioner."

"So the 'they' that we have been dancing around would need to know exactly what sigil to carve into something to get the result they wanted, but it doesn't have to be Warlocks if a Shifter like you can know the nuance of spellcraft?"

"Aye."

"And, from the evidence of the body and your assessment of the space, the sacrifice spell sucked the energy out of the place and the person?"

"Aye." Rafe kept carving as I questioned away.

"Then where did the energy go? Or is the conservation of energy not a universal standard when we are talking about magic."

He paused. "Are you a physicist as well?"

"I know enough about a lot of things."

He chuckled and went back to his work. "That's the part of this we need to figure out. It went somewhere, but without the pattern, the will of players, I can't tell you where."

"So we have the how and the what, but we need the who and the why?"

"Exactly. Someone carved that into her arm with the intent to kill her."

As if summoned, the wound on my forearm started to itch. I'd been attacked and carved into. Could Ethan and I have been a target of this thing too?

The fear crept across my skin like spider slowly stalking its meal. Could my attacker have been trying to carve that sigil into me? If I had gone alone that night, could I have been the first in this pattern? Would Ethan and Rafe be investigating my murder? I mean, what if Beakman was just filling in where I was supposed to be?

Rafe jumped down from the second window and pulled the chair back to the table.

"Something bothering you?"

I stumbled into those deep blue eyes and had to gulp to catch my breath before I fell into them. "Can I show you something?"

His eye brow did wicked arch. "Like what?"

My mouth ran dry. "Hypothetically, if maybe the shadows I saw that night were magical, and hypothetically, if maybe Ethan's death was connected to the other bodies, because hypothetically there is something very evil in this city . . ."

God, this was insane. I couldn't believe the words coming out of my own mouth, but without the sour taste of the lie and the questions that swirled around me, it was a line of questioning that I had never sought out, a kite string I'd never followed, but with the openness of his eyes and the warmth of his body beside me, the words pattered out.

"Could those things have been trying to sacrifice me and Ethan?"

I slowly drew up the sleeve of my left arm and peeled off the thin gauze. The wound was crusted now, and within a week, might be only a faint reminder of what had happened.

I held it out between us. "Could they have tried to carve something into me like they carved something into Tay-Tay?"

Rafe was so close that I heard the moisture from his lips as they parted. He exhaled slowly and his breath played along my exposed flesh.

He held my arm as he would a bird, his touch light and open, not exactly holding so much as caging between his fingers so I wouldn't fly away. He ran his fingers down the scar. It was very clearly a straight line with an acute angle at the end, reminding me of a harpoon in this semi-healed state.

I waited unmoving for what he might say.

Rafe finally spoke. "I don't know, Merci. Run me through that night again?"

He gently pulled me into a chair at the table, never letting go of my arm.

"Benny called me and I went, because I'm one of Pavlov's dogs for danger. We were standing there in the store."

The flashback tore across my eyes, and Rafe's fingers lightly gripped my arm, anchoring me as he surrounded me in that warm scent again.

I was still trapped in the dark, but no longer panicked. "It went dark, like pitch black. Ethan told me to run, but I didn't. I turned toward him, reached out for him, and then two guys tackled me."

"Two men?"

I nodded, remembering the feeling of their hands on my body, on my wrists. "Huge hands and they smelled like . . . sausage."

My eyes popped open. "I don't think I've remembered their smell before."

"Keep going."

I closed my eyes and went back there with Rafe's touch as a tether to safety. "He tore my jacket and starting cutting my arm and then there was this noise this . . ." The howl reverberated through my memory. "I think Ethan shifted."

"We are stronger in wolf form."

"One of the men on me went to help out the other two, and then the guy just stopped and the men vanished." I opened up my eyes again. "I didn't even hear them run away, but by then I was concussed, broken ribs, and bleeding out."

His thumb arched up and down the skin on my arm. "I can't say for sure. I mean, this could be a million things."

"But that center stroke, it matches the sacrifice sigil. That angle at the bottom could be the beginning of the diamond."

My heart scampered into a full run and began leaping against my rib cage. My vision tunneled to the red line down my arm and I could see the outline of Tay-Tay's body on my fair skin.

Rafe squeezed my arm and lifted my chin to meet his gaze. "Take a deep breath."

I did and then another. Until my heart was only a light tap dance in my chest.

"Let's maybe get something to eat."

I pointed to the kitchen. "Food's on the fridge."

Slowly, he pulled away from me and went into the kitchen. "Chinese or pizza?" Rafe called out.

I was cold without him, the skin on my arms prickling. I ran my own fingers over the wound, tracing the line where his fingers had just been. "Let's be cliché. Chinese."

"Done."

Before I knew it, Rafe was whistling in the kitchen, probably on hold. I sighed.

I kept my eyes to the line down my arm, letting my mind drift to that night, knowing I was safe here. Had they not finished the job because Ethan had fought to save me? Had they not completed the spell because Ethan was a shifter and it had taken three men to take him down?

Truth or just a story I wanted to believe, they hadn't gotten me and they wouldn't get anyone else.

Rafe walked back out into the living room. "Food should be here in about thirty."

He paused at the end of the table. "Are you sure you're all right?"

I needed a distraction and found it in the red leather book between us. "If you were a Legacy, why did you have an Idiot's Guide to Being Magical?" I held up the little red book.

It was the right question, even with the right vocabulary. It hummed through my skin, the Charm telling me I was on the right path. Even in my head it was already the Charm, Ethan's vernacular still helping me frame this power, this cloud that I'd been living under my whole life.

Rafe's skin paled and something just north of my stomach churned. He hadn't had time to lie yet, so I wasn't sure what it was, but the shade in his eyes made me feel ill. "I'm sorry. I really don't need to know."

His rose lips parted for a long moment before he spoke. "No, it's all right. It actually might help." He went back to the table to stack his books into another order. "As horrifically trite as the story is, there was a girl. And we went out a few times, and then she had her first vision. Turned out she was a Seer, a psychic. Enough wandering blood that she could see the future. I tracked down a copy of the book to help her ease into the world."

"Didn't last long after that?"

His lips quirked up into a half smile. "She didn't like what she saw."

God, I wanted to ask what she saw in his past, but I would wait. Just like divulging that I was a Wanderer was my story, this one was his, and he obviously wasn't ready to tell me the whole truth, so I would wait. That was enough questions for right now. No need to open any more doors. "So what did you order from Chan's?"

It took him a moment to follow the turn of the conversation, his mind on other things. "Oh... Beef and broccoli and orange chicken with steamed rice and an order of noodles."

What was I going to do with him? With this man who had so easily integrated himself into my life and fit so naturally in my Spartan living room? With Rafe it had been less than six weeks and he already knew the layout of my kitchen and my usual order from Chan's. This was getting annoying. "That'll work."

With a little more time before the food arrived, I curled up on the couch with my dad's journal. Despite stubbornly saving them from my mother, I'd never read them before. They were literally his blood, sweat, and tears.

I took in a deep breath before I started flipping through the pages. I wasn't sure what I was looking for, but the familiar smell of the pages and the curl of his handwriting gave me a little hope that the answers I needed might somehow be in these pages. And it was a nice break from Witches, and Warlocks, and Wanderers.

Once back in high school, my dad had walked me through his notebooks, showed me how he organized his thoughts on paper as he was working through a story. The shorthand he had developed. And though I really hadn't needed to use most of it (I was only reporting on football games and academic decathlon winners at that point), I still used the system myself. Questions in the margins on the left, answers in the main section on the right. Answers that needed to be confirmed were circled and facts that were confirmed were put into a square. Random thoughts to investigate later were scratched perpendicular to the rest of the story.

As the pattern went, as he got closer to the truth, the squares gathered at the end, culminating in the perfect opening paragraph containing the five W's of the story. But there were breaks between stories. Ideas. Random questions. Investigative reporters follow the general trends, so it's more like amassing complaints to see if there is a story. Figuring out patterns to see if a tragedy was just a tragedy or if it was a symptom of something bigger. When he got to random tragedy number three, he would start investigating. Three was a pattern.

His past was painfully similar to my present. Painfully familiar to my own process. But the real question remained—Did he have my power? I mean, the guy could crack a story like no one else and never got the recognition he deserved. That had to mean he had the same Charm, but why had he never mentioned it? Why had he remained silent when I was uncovering steroid use in my high school's football program and purposeful lice infestations at the cheerleading retreats? Surely he would have recognized it? Why hadn't he told me anything about it?

I scanned through the pages and saw another familiar sight. A page so filled with questions there was barely any white space left. Questions circling other questions like a story web from hell. Like a thundercloud that swarmed around him.

Just like me.

I wasn't exactly sure when the doorbell had rung or when Rafe had gone to get the food, but suddenly the smell of beef and broccoli filled the room. My stomach growled and I was forced to joined him at the table, leaving my father's legacy on the couch, far enough away that I could avoid psychoanalyzing my entire life.

Again.

Both of us kept reading while we ate, me the Guide and him some crusty looking book in Latin that would have killed my appetite with some of the lithographs. Long after we had both cracked open our fortune cookies, Rafe leaned back in his chair and rubbed his eyes. "What part are you to in the *Guide?*"

I'd read through the first section that covered most of the breeds of Wanderers, your vampires, guardians, shifters, etc. Each section was like a dictionary with their natural abilities, strengths, and then method of death, which I found disturbingly clinical but good to know. Rafe hadn't been lying when he said the book was thorough. "Nearly done with Notable Events. I just finished the Great Shifter War."

Rafe looked away. "Once you know the truth, the world does make a little more sense."

I desperately wanted to know more about what happened during the War. The *Guide* read like a textbook and what Piper had told me was vague at best. I knew he'd been there, but what really happened? But for once I didn't ask. I didn't want to force the story.

I leaned across the table and squinted the text he was reading. "What are you reading? That doesn't look English?"

"It's Russian, actually, but here's our sigil." He pointed to the diamond with a cross sticking out of the top that now automatically came with a flash of Tay-Tay's dead body. I wasn't sure I wanted it to stop. The image rustled up the bees in my brain and kept my skin and the Charm humming.

"I think it might be Demon specific. I haven't found it any Fey lore or Warlock text."

"What do you mean?" I picked up the discarded box of noodles and fished one out. Nothing like research snacks.

He searched the living room for an explanation. "Old Speak is like any language. Certain words have different meanings depending on who says them. Sort of like how I'd call it a torch and you'd call it a flashlight."

"So you know Demon semantics?"

He only shrugged and started to poke around at his remaining orange chicken still cluttering the table with the demon grimoires and spell books. "I know that if a Fey used this symbol for sacrifice, it be a good thing, an offering to the earth. But I can't imagine that a Fey would offer up a human life."

"But a Demon would?"

"In two seconds. Demons are pure hunger. Their power comes from what they feed on and they have abilities to lure their food to them. So, classic example: an incubus Demon feeds on sexual energy, so it has the ability of glamour to look like an object of desire. Following?"

"Unfortunately," I responded.

"But Demons don't have corporeal bodies on this plane of existence. They'd need a host to even survive here."

"You mean possession?"

"Top marks. You know your horror movies. But before they even have a host body, they'd need servants to carve the marks into people so they could feed to gain enough energy to pierce the veil and come across into our world. But I can't find a spell in any of these Warlock texts that matches the pattern we have here."

"Why are you only searching in Warlock texts?"

He looked at me like I had spoken in his mother tongue; part confused and part awe.

I set down the carton of food. "Why does everyone have to abide by what's written in the books? We have evidence they aren't doing things by the book, so why are you limiting your thinking?"

A crease formed between his brows. "Breeds operate by a finite set of rules. Its why we have such a hard time relating to one another. Without rules, there is chaos."

"Why? Maybe this is something brand new that's never been in one of your books before. Maybe this is special." And maybe I was letting my issues bubble to the surface a little too much. I hadn't found anything like what I could do in this book and wasn't sure that I wanted to be limited like these other breeds were limited.

It was a light show behind his eyes and a dance across his brows and jaw. And I felt it— the shift in his energy at the table as he glanced between the books and me. He finally leaned back in his chair and regarded me, this time only in awe. "I guess that is the beautiful thing about this world, Miss Lanard. With enough will, anything is possible."

Rafe rubbed his eyes and ran his fingers through his thick hair. "Good Lord. Look at the time. I've got a long drive ahead of me."

I stretched in my chair. It had been a while since I'd gotten lost in research, like the good old days when I was waist deep in IRS returns and loving every minute.

He stood and reached for his jacket.

"Without you getting the wrong idea, I have a guest bedroom and fancy protection sigils carved into my walls. You're welcome to stay."

Rafe frowned, yet I saw the playful twinkle in his eye. "Are you sure? You seem like a person who likes her space."

And here was where I needed to actually be truthful. I closed the book and maybe stacked a few before I could work out the words.

I would never say that I was afraid, but maybe I didn't need to be so stubborn. "Piper told us to stay together, and even though I have these sigils, I'm not a super-powered werewolf."

He looked down at the stack of books, running his finger along the edge of one, then tossed his jacket on the chair again. "Thank you, Merci. I appreciate it."

"Don't thank me. It's not like I'll be cooking you breakfast."

CHAPTER EIGHT

I woke to the smell of baked goods. I stretched, and as the cobwebs cleared from my mind, I remembered there was another person in my house. Was Rafe baking? In my kitchen? No one made actual food in my kitchen. I wasn't even sure I had anything to bake on. Worst of all, could he be a morning person?

I ran through the shower and dressed for the day, a whole ten-minute process I'd perfected over the years. I did stop to smear some tinted moisturizer to keep the sunburn and wind burn at a minimum and I flicked some mascara on my lashes. Presentable enough for my kitchen at this ungodly hour.

Rafe was not flipping pancakes as I had imagined, and I sighed, slightly disappointed.

A pot of coffee was brewing and there was something in the oven. He looked up from the book he was reading as he leaned against the counter. "It's cinnamon rolls from the corner store. Don't be too impressed."

"You are going to spoil me, Professor MacCallan." I poured a cup of coffee and sat down at the table, still littered in our readings and plottings.

He followed me across the room and sat in his chair from last night. "Well, point of education. Not being hungry keeps me in a fairly good mood."

"You or the wolf?"

"Both."

I pushed through the photos again, the map we had made of the dead bodies. I closed a couple of books and read their titles. *Spellcraft and the Modern Witch.* And something in Russian that looked ominous. But all Russian looked ominous.

It really was the same as writing an article. The subject was different, way different, but the process was the same. Dig in for a few days to really get the dirt, the case would crack, and the truth would always come to me. Sometimes like a sweet whisper and sometime like a punch to the gut, but I would always figure it out. But was that figuring it out me, or the magical power? Did the Charm bring the answer to me, or did I really crack the cases myself? Would I be as good a reporter if I wasn't a Wanderer? Or was it some mix of both?

I felt the frown etch into my face as I glared down at the books before me.

"What's the medallion around your neck?" Rafe pointed.

I took Ethan's charm between my fingers and flipped it around, over and over, the motion soothing me. "Something Ethan gave me."

"Can I see it?"

I pulled it toward him, but didn't take it off. He leaned in to inspect the strange symbols. I had to look away; the heat was radiating off of him with such strength that it burned my eyes. And I guessed he hadn't showered, since his musk was even more potent than usual.

He hmmmed as he pulled away and went back to sipping his coffee.

"Don't suppose you know what it says?" I asked as I went back to flipping through the book. I could still feel the burn of him on my face and no amount of dusty books could take away his smell.

"I recognize the sign for protection, but that's all I know. If you really want me to, I can decipher it."

The timer for the cinnamon rolls went off before I could respond, and Rafe retrieved breakfast with a potholder. Who knew I had a potholder? And one with a chicken on it to boot.

I cleared a place on the table for the amazing smelling rolls. I didn't care that they were a little extra crispy around the edges. When he put the icing on the top, I wanted all of them to myself.

He refreshed our coffees, grabbed two plates and forks, and joined me. "What are you looking at me for?"

I shook my head. "Nothing. I'm ... just ..."

"Merci Lanard lost for words?" He smiled.

I spit out the words even though they were slightly embarrassing. "I don't often share breakfast with someone."

"Well," he said as he divvied out the lot, "I know Ethan's slept in that bed within the past three months."

I accepted my sticky pile of carbohydrates and wonderfulness. "Ethan crashed here a few times, but he never made breakfast."

"Score bonus points for me then."

I snorted. "It isn't a competition. Ethan and I weren't like that." I took a big bite out of a roll.

"So what are you and I like then?"

I shoved the rest of a cinnamon roll in my mouth and pointedly ignored the question, turning instead to the research. Suddenly the notion of dead bodies and the city map was very interesting. I pulled the map to me and studied the locations we'd plotted the night before, the spots where the bodies were discovered, and bit into a fresh cinnamon roll.

Rafe didn't give me a pass. "What was it like between you two? I only got one side of the story."

"And what was that side of the story?" I asked with a full mouth.

"Mostly it was about your work, your insistence on finding the truth, your ability to get in and out of trouble. Sounded as if the two of you were thick as thieves, he'd follow you anywhere."

I swallowed. It was a little early in the morning for honesty, but the truth really would be easier to remember after the caffeine and sugar hit my system. "Ethan was my rock. And since I didn't have a lot of family, he sort of became everything for me. The two of us saving the world."

"Did you love him?"

I snorted. "No."

The lie tasted like how burnt hair smelled, and I gulped down the coffee to wash it away. "Well, not in the romantic sense. He was my family. But I realize now our whole friendship was one-sided, because he had Emily, and a pack, and you. I just had him."

Rafe turned his mug around in his hands. "After Da left my mum, I didn't talk to him. I didn't even know Ethan existed until he showed up at my door. I was already living in Philly, and he was this Midwestern kid without a pack with my father's legacy. He had a letter from my Da about how we were brothers and blood was important and …" His sentence dropped off and I didn't push him.

I knew most of the story, though Ethan had told me he moved out here after college and met Emily camping. I guess hadn't technically been a lie. For all I knew he met her on a pleasant stroll through wolf-infested woods.

"What was his relationship with his mom? Ethan never mentioned her." I wasn't even sure if she had been at the funeral.

Rafe did smile at that one. "Daisy is a massive hippy, in fact. Emily called her for the funeral and she was in India. Is all about following the Mother. I guess when Da died and Ethan felt the call to find his brother, she was all for letting him follow his wolf. He packed up everything after he graduated college and moved to be closer to me. He joined the pack, and then he and Emily happened and, then he found you. We were just really hitting a stride of being brothers, when …"

I put some math together in my head as I sipped my coffee and let my questions distract him from the painful memory. "What came first, the paper or the pack's need for information about the city?"

Rafe sucked on his bottom lip for a moment, his tell that he was holding back some truth but it eventually same out. "The need for information came first. Ethan volunteered to see what he could do at the paper to prove himself worthy of marrying the Primo's sister."

I took in a deep breath. And then I shoved another cinnamon roll in my mouth.

"But he did value your time together. He probably told you things, thoughts, that he never told me. Things more important than magic and shifting."

"Pretty sure it was a proximity thing. It gets really boring on stakeouts."

Rafe almost smiled, and I felt a pang in my chest. When he was alive, I thought I'd known everything about Ethan. But maybe he had just split himself in two, like Rafe had said. Split himself into two people, one half the journalistic photographer and my best friend, and the other half a dutiful pack member who howled under a full moon.

I watched as the furrowed in Rafe's brow got deeper as he looked into his coffee. I knew where that spiral would lead, where that line of mental questioning would go, and I was running low on whiskey. And it seriously was too early to start drinking. We had a mystery to solve.

I ran my finger along the map charting out the dead bodies, the neutral territory where our pasts didn't matter, just the here and now. We'd marked out the dead bodies, trying to predict the next location in the pattern, but without more information about the spell, we didn't know what else to do. The three red Xs created a demented smiling face staring up at me with the river as a crooked mouth.

My thoughts were interrupted by my ringing cellphone. I fished it out of the bottom of my bag. "Lanard."

"Got a catch for you," Hayne started before he even said hello. "Building fire on Sixth."

"Hayne, come on. It's barely seven a.m."

"Go. Now. You need more inches this month to justify what I pay you."

"Fine." I sighed as I ended the call and tossed the phone back into my bag. "I have to go." I started to gulp my coffee and shoved another roll in my mouth.

Rafe stood with me as I slung my bag over my shoulder and dropped my notebook and recorder into its bottomless depths. "Mind if I tag along? I really don't have anything else to do today."

I could only raise an eyebrow with my mouth full.

Rafe smiled. "I could man the camera?"

...

As Rafe and I walked toward the crowd already gathered, I made a mental note that Hayne needed to verify his sources next time. It wasn't a building fire, it was building explosion. The second floor of the brick office building was gone, blown to pieces that littered a one-block radius, and it was still burning. Emergency service had already blocked off the streets, but no firefighters were manning hoses to stop the blaze.

I pushed my way to the barricade and smiled when I saw a familiar face manning crowd control. "Rutherford!" I waved as I quickly ducked under the wooden barricades.

Rutherford jogged over to where I was, a deep furrow in his brow for so early in the morning.

"How the hell do you..." he trailed off as he pushed me back over to the public side of the barricade. He ran his hands along the flat wooden side facing the fire, and stared at in intently, like he was reading something across it that I couldn't see.

He finally turned his glare to me. "Are you the only reporter at that newspaper?"

"Are you the only cop on the streets?" I fired back. "What's going on?"

"What does it look like?"

I studied the scene again and let the questions start to sizzle and spin. "Gas fire? Burning so hot that the fireman can't fight it?"

He glared down at me.

I matched that glare with my own and reveled in that deliciously familiar chill down my spine. After the little trek down emotions lane this morning, I was energized by the storm clouds in my brain that always preceded a story. As new and strange as knowing why this always happened, magic was starting to fit into my life, becoming perhaps a little too familiar.

"Is it a natural gas fire?"

He gulped as my magic took hold. "We already called the gas company to stop the flow to this area. Don't want to blow the whole neighborhood."

"So residents are in danger?"

"Seems contained."

"Anything weird happen before the explosions?"

"A few people reported an earthquake. Windows shook, and it would explain a gas line rupture explosion." The man smacked his dry mouth and gulped again.

I released him from the Charm. As I had a million times before. Just looked away, like releasing a balloon on string.

Rutherford backed up from the barricade. "I shouldn't be talking to you."

"Always a pleasure, Julie."

I scratched down a few notes to myself, making sure to get his phrasing right. I surveyed the crowd for another person to corroborate his story. There was a woman eating her breakfast on her front stoop who looked like she might talk. I turned to Rafe, who was right at my back. "Can you sniff around the back of the building, see if anything's strange?

"Like sniff around for clues or actually sniff around?" he asked, trying to be serious, but the twinkle in his eye was unmistakable.

"I don't see why they need to be mutually exclusive."

He smiled and worked his way in the other direction.

...

I was jotting down the rest of the woman's words when Rafe walked up behind me. I thanked the woman and gave her my card in case she ever needed to report anything like this again.

I turned around to Rafe, grabbed his elbow, and headed to the back of the crowd, away from prying ears. "Did you get anything?"

"Oh yeah. You?"

"An earthquake happened before the explosion."

"In *Philadelphia*?" Rafe asked.

"Resident said there have been a series of them recently, starting about a month back. Building shaking and birds acting strange. Cop said windows rattled with the explosion today, which totally makes sense. But the witness says a big one hit about good ten minutes before."

I watched his lips as he spoke fast, breathless. "The building behind is a warehouse. It's nothing, an old storage place with a big loading dock in the back. But the place is covered in magic."

"What? What happened?"

Rafe shook his head. "I don't know. I wanted to grab you before I went in to really look."

I nodded as I jammed my notepad in my messenger bag and followed after him.

The space was open and reminded me of a rave I went to in college. A dock at the front stood a good six feet higher than the rest of the open area. It was all concrete and metal rafters, decorated with graffiti and shreds of plastic tarp.

"Do you feel anything here?"

"What do you mean?"

He walked closer to me and dropped his voice, as if someone could be listening. "Like any weird sensations. Something that wouldn't be attributed to a drafty warehouse in winter."

I focused. Right now, all I was feeling was the warmth of his figure.

It was hard to turn my brain off, silence the questions long enough to get a sense of the place. I shook my head. No other super powers for me. Bummer. "Not really. It's just cold."

"Right. But what kind of cold?" he pressed.

I raised an eyebrow. "There is more than one kind?"

"There are a million kinds. What kind is it to you?"

I sighed, but closed my eyes. Different kinds of cold? Wasn't sure I read about that in the *Idiot's Guide.*

His voice was in my ear. "Do you trust me?"

My eyes flew open and I whipped my head around to lock eyes with him over my shoulder. "Barely."

Rafe held up his hand and gently put it on my shoulder. "You know how the Primo exchanges energy with the pack?"

I nodded. The pow-wow under the full moon, where Levi communed with his pack. Whatever Piper did to make the place smell like cinnamon.

"I should be able to share my energy with you, enhance you so you can physically sense what I am sensing. It's one of my perks."

"There was a *should* in that sentence."

"Please, Merci. Try?"

It was the please that grabbed me around the middle and squeezed. My breath caught in my throat and I couldn't say no. I closed my eyes and turned to face forward. It was easy to relax with him so close to me, with that intense heat pressing against my back.

When the slip of fur surrounded me, my knees went weak, but I didn't fall. Rafe's other hand rested on my waist to steady me, and I could feel his words curl around my ear lobe.

"I've linked my power into your senses. Can you still feel the cold?"

I could barely focus on anything that wasn't his body at my back and his hand on my waist. I opened my eyes. The lights in the warehouse were brighter, the morning sun cutting sharper lines across the concrete floor. The place smelled worse than before, like rotten eggs and dead fish. "Is this how you experience things?" I whispered.

I wasn't sure I would ever feel cold again with the memory of his heat around me, even stronger now we were connected. But that was not why we were walking through this exercise. I needed to find the cold spot.

And it was there, this cold eating at my right side. That corner of the warehouse was dark. Though by the light in the place, it should appear like all the other corners. Yet darkness was gathered there. I pointed to the spot. "Like sticking your hand into a refrigerator."

But Rafe didn't respond. He pulled away from me and with him went his warmth, the slide of fur against me. I gasped when our powers fully disconnected, my head spinning.

When the world stopped, when I turned back toward him, I was caught in the full force of his Aegean-blue eyes and suddenly I knew exactly how all the people I charmed felt. Trapped, held, and completely unable to look away no matter what was said.

"Why didn't you tell me?" he asked.

"Tell you what?"

His brows crooked into a jagged furrow. "Tell me that you wander."

Of course he knew now. I let him tap into my energy and he must have felt magic there, the other half of me I had been hiding from him. I licked my lips and still tasted cinnamon. Surely that couldn't be from breakfast. Was it his power?

"I didn't know until Piper told me."

There was a question on his lips. Hanging there, and he fought it. I could see it in those wide blue eyes. He wanted to ask it, but he didn't want the answer.

So I shifted to the matter at hand, hoping he would follow, hoping we could avoid this little tiny omission. "Is that cold spot what you felt at Tay-Tay's apartment when you said the place had been sucked dry of energy? Could a spell have been done here large enough to cause earthquakes that eventually ruptured a gas line?"

"This was the rough news you got?" He wasn't being diverted by dead bodies. "That you were one of us?"

I watched my words carefully. "I don't know the truth of it all yet, so I didn't want to distract us from the real story, from finding the killers."

With a deep exhale, he stepped away from me and raked his fingers through his hair. "I'll meet you later."

I grew colder at his distance. "What? Where are you going?"

He took the camera from around his neck and handed it back to me. "I need to go."

"No, you need to stay and help me figure out what happened here."

His expression turned to slate, flat and unreadable. I grew even colder as all of his energy disappeared from the air between us. Had he just put his "shield" up, because I couldn't feel anything from him.

"I can't right now, Merci."

"But Piper said we're supposed to travel in pairs."

Even the edict from his Den Mother didn't help and I watched him walk away, disappearing behind the building. I knew he would be fine. He was powerful enough to be the leader of a pack. Maybe that was why I felt so cold now. He didn't need me.

I needed him, and now I was really alone in this. The camera became a stone in my hand. I'd spent the past two weeks trying to figure out why Ethan would keep all of this from me, and here I was, keeping it from Rafe.

The Mother had given me one face and I made myself another.

Why couldn't I just tell him? I wasn't under Pack Law, no prime directive. Ethan had been. What was wrong with me that I couldn't be honest with the one person who had always been honest with me? Maybe because I didn't want to deal with the truth of it myself.

I huffed. I hated when I went to a place and got more questions out of the deal than answers. I couldn't knock him for feeling betrayed. But I could be just a little pissed that he was putting his own feelings above the story, above the truth. I had dead bodies to deal with and promises to keep.

If only I had a flashlight in this massive bag of mine. But I did have another light source. Ethan had used the flash as a light plenty of times. Not just to test the exposure, but just to light up cars or windows to see in.

I dug into my bag to get the accessories for the large camera. There was something else that Ethan used to do with his flash. Ethan took pictures of everything with different filters. He used to change them out constantly, like shuffling a deck of cards in his long fingers. I never really thought about it, but what if one of them was responsible for capturing me with the red halo? And what if that red halo had been the proof that I was a Wanderer?

Could Ethan have figured out how to capture magic? Is that how he knew? Since apparently even a powerful Primo hadn't caught on until he was all up in my energy and enhancing me—something Ethan had certainly never done.

I ground my teeth and dropped my bag to the concrete as I put the first filter over the lens. I wasn't the expert that Ethan had been, but I snapped a few pictures of the cold corner. I did one circle of the whole room, then changed filters. Ethan's old camera didn't have the best view screen but the pictures looked similar to what I saw with my naked eyes.

I put the camera to my eye again, focused, and snapped a few more photos of the corner then did another spin around the room. I traded out the filter, trying to keep them in order inside the accessories pouch. I did three turns around the room and was getting a little dizzy.

A glass bottle rolled across the cement floor and the noise of it echoed through the wide space. I paused and listened. There wasn't any wind coming in from the busted garage door that Rafe and I had come through. Very little trash in the space, despite being abandoned.

In my former life, I would have said it was probably a cat getting out of the cold air, but this was my PM life, post-magic life, and there were so many more things that went bump in the night. For the first time in my life, I wasn't sure I wanted to risk investigating. I was, after all, taking pictures with a potentially magical camera lens to capture an image of some sort of spell work.

I finished my circle with the second to the last filter. A door slammed shut and the light in the space grew dim as clouds passed overhead.

I paused. "Hello?"

Perhaps it wasn't abandoned after all. Or perhaps the same person, or persons, who had mastered a spell large enough to crack a gas main were coming back to make sure no one was hanging around.

And that was that. I was done. I shoved the camera back into my bag and headed as fast as I could toward the bright light of morning.

I passed by the crowds still watching the building burn, like it was better than cable television. The gas company had a few trucks out there now. I noted the time for my story. I had to put something down on the page. Not all of it could be creative nonfiction.

Now off the office to write a fabricated story about a gas explosion and get these pictures downloaded. Then to find out who owned that warehouse.

And all of it without a lingering thought to Rafe's scent, which still clung to my wool coat.

...

I'd gone back to the office to write up my fictitious story about the gas explosion and study the Bible-thick batch of blueprints that Greta in City Planning had printed out about the warehouse and the building adjacent. She'd handed me the stack under a bathroom stall in City Hall.

"This spy stuff is exciting, Merci," she'd whispered.

"I don't want you getting to use to it. Keep safe and I'll stop by next month."

"May Saint Francis watch over you."

I didn't know if St. Francis would have anything to do with me. But I did have St. Greta of City Planning and St. Fred of Water and Power and St. Sheila of County Records and I was thankful for those intersessions today.

For those intersessions had brought me a name: Cartwright Constructions. The name was like a punch to the gut. It was CEO of Cartwright Constructions, Jeffrey Cartwright, who had been bribing the mayor and was currently under investigation for a dozen other laws broken. It was the story that I should have been working on. Instead I was chasing something darker, deeper because Cartwright owned the building that was now the site of a spell massive enough to crack gas lines and nearly take out a city block. The company owned a lot of buildings all over the city, which struck me as off; the construction district was in a pretty central place, though the addresses were scattered all over.

Filing this new information into my head, I moved on to the next order of business: the camera. Leaning over my desk, I flipped on my computer, and just as I slipped the card into the card reader on my desk, Hayne's voice echoed out across the floor. "Lanard, get in here."

My jaw clenched. I didn't do a single thing wrong this time. I was sure of it. I dragged my feet like a scolded child into his office. "I was about to start working on the gas explosion this morning. What do you want?"

Hayne just snorted. "Sit."

I took the hot seat. "I really am trying to write up that gas explosion story."

Hayne sat in his chair behind his desk. "How are you coming with the dead bodies case?" he asked, leaning over his desk and clasping his hands.

"Pretty well, actually. Found a pattern in the killing but can't link the victims yet."

"They are killings now?"

I'd said too much. There was still no way that I could actually tell Hayne the whole truth, so I avoided it all together. "Why do you ask?"

"Got a call from upper brass to stop you from investigating further. Said you had contaminated a crime scene?"

I scoffed. "Well, we both know what that means."

Hayne nodded. I knew the drill. When he got a call from the commissioner's office, then I was onto something. It usually meant I would hit it harder, keep poking the bear, and everything would roar to light.

"Let's get the gas explosion story out there."

"Aye, Aye, Captain."

Hayne waved me out of his office.

I quietly shut the door and the entire newsroom turned to look at me. It was probably the first time I hadn't slammed the door shut.

I grabbed a terrible cup of coffee from the break room and sat down to write the pretty straightforward gas explosion story that the nice lady on the step of her porch told me.

Once submitted, I wrote down the truth in my notebook, put a big, fat red square around it as fact, and shoved it down into my messenger bag.

Now, it was time to get back to the real investigation. I opened the files from the camera's memory card and started to scroll through them on my massive monitor. Warehouse, warehouse, warehouse, window, warehouse. Then the lighting changed and it was warehouse, warehouse, warehouse, warehouse, window, warehouse. Then the lighting changed again. And it was warehouse, warehouse, warehouse, window, warehouse. And then it was a horror movie on my screen come to life.

Two images were open next to one another on the screen. One was normal picture of the warehouse in the bright light of early morning, and the other was like someone had flipped the exposure to full contrast. In the corner where I'd felt the cold was a black circle surrounded by a ring of white sigils scratched into the cement. The roughhewn edges were like claw marks against the black of the wall.

The newsroom seemed to drop a few degrees as I studied it. I leaned closer to the screen. I couldn't decipher the exact shapes, but I was sure it wasn't your run-of-the-mill, invisible-to-the-naked eye graffiti. It had to be Old Speak. The glyphs radiated out from the central spot as if someone had thrown an ink bomb in the center. So black, it seemed to absorb the light from the flash. I clicked through the next picture and it was the same thing. Old Speak layered in concentric circles with a void in the center. The next one as well, the sigils fanning out across the walls not even connected to the dark corner. On the fourth, I could make out something above a window, something similar to the circle Rafe had carved into my window frames. Then back to the rabbit hole that. Something had to have crawled out of that. Something big.

I sat up and scrolled back through the pictures. I'd taken five pictures with each lens, which meant that the one that revealed the true nature of the dark corner was the fourth filter. I reached down to the accessory bag and flipped through the slim cases. "Deep Ultraviolet," the case read. I pulled out the lens and held it up to the light. To my extremely untrained eye, it was just a camera lens. Like all the others that I'd seen him flip through.

Ethan had found a way to capture magic. He'd probably taken thousands of pictures around the city with this lens, making sure nothing nefarious was happening. Pictures Emily had to have seen, if not while he was investigating, then afterwards when she took the laptop. Pictures that included several of me with a red, magical-looking halo.

This lens was a weapon against what truly skulked around in the darkness.

And Emily had given it to me. Like she knew I was supposed to be fighting the things that went bump in the night.

...

I wasn't going to say that I was drunk, but I was halfway through the bottle I'd picked up on the way home and I couldn't feel my nose. It had taken nearly an hour and five shots for me to stop wondering if Emily knew, or at least stop caring. A few more to convince myself that I wasn't a fighter. I was more like a smoke alarm that just told the real fighters were the fire was. Sure it saved people's lives, but I wasn't the one who had to follow through until the smoke was gone.

As I relaxed into my couch, glass in one hand, bottle in the other, I left my brain to float around to the million other questions that were more important than me in this manhunt.

If it even was a man. The circle had haunted the space behind my eyelids, and each time I blinked it was like a spinning hypnotist's wheel of scratch marks and monsters. But with every drink, the spinning was slowing down and the images were getting less gruesome. Almost to the point that I could look at them again, maybe find them in the books Rafe had left here, but not yet.

Dad used to drink. Mom used it as an excuse to fight with him most of the time, but I'd understood now why he did. Just like Rafe was always radiating, Pipers house always smelled like home, the Charm didn't stop, but the journalist needed to. The magic didn't care about emotional scars or sleep or food. It just cared about the truth. Whiskey dampened the storm for a while, dialed it down a little bit, but it was never really gone.

I'd seen AA meetings scheduled in his journals but most were crossed off as he chased a lead. Lucky for him, I was never involved in dance or sports—there was rarely anything for him to miss. He did miss a school board meeting where I was protesting the decreasing funds for the journalism program. God, even in my youth I was stubborn and persistent.

I wondered what story he was working on then. What was more important than his daughter's big moment? And I could find out. I had his journals. I stumbled upstairs and sat down in my closet. I opened the trunk and ran my fingers across the journals' covers. I found one marked Fall 2004. It was dangerously close to the last: Spring 2005. I looked at it and the Charm roared to life, like someone gunning the motor of a chain saw. What had he been working on when he died?

I found my glass and gulped down the rest. I didn't need the chainsaw right now. One truth at a time.

His notes were a fine art at this point in his career. Questions on the left, answers and facts in the center. And Dad had written the lead-in to the article about his daughter challenging the school board.

Merci Lanard, 15, took on the school board today at an open forum about school funding. The sophomore at EB White High accused the school board of dumbing down the curriculum to accommodate a growing sports program, as evidenced by testing scores and trial budgets that she had in hand. Miss Lanard was promptly removed from the meeting and her mother escorted her home.

I ran my fingers across his swirling script. I'd never understood how he could write so fast and still manage to dot every *I* and cross every *T.* And I had no idea how he knew about the test scores—he hadn't even been there. Mom had taken care of settling down the school board by herself and I was hardly even punished for the stunt.

I flipped a few more pages to see what story had been more important than his daughter's first expose.

Cartwright Construction.

Why was Dad investigation Cartwright Construction?

The Charm washed over me in a cool river. The heat from the alcohol was gone and my laser focus was back. He'd been investigating Cartwright Construction. Twenty years before his daughter had caught their scent. What a way to be scooped.

Whispers of bribes. God, it was like reading my own journal. I searched for the facts Dad had drawn boxes around. Just the facts. The company started about a hundred years ago. Got a city contract immediately. Got another, then another, even though they were underbid by several companies. Started acquiring storage facilities all over the city.

Then, the bribes started. Bribes to city officials, county records, hell, even a few cops to keep the business fronts safe. On paper, nothing sounded strange about them except the fact that twenty years later, I had busted the family for that very thing. Like this Cartwright had just done the same thing that the generation before had done.

But nothing screamed *magical portal spell in one of their warehouses.* Of course, nothing about me screamed *Wanderer* and yet here I was, sitting in my closet just drinking alone to make the magic stop.

...

I'd made it in for seven a.m. pitch. I was showered, rested, even managed a bagel and coffee from the place around the corner, and yet I was still getting hauled into Hayne's office by a yell across the newsroom floor.

Hayne closed the door behind me.

I took the hot seat. This was our dance. I knew the steps.

Hayne sat in his chair behind his desk, leaning over his desk and clasping his hands.

I waited for the tirade about staying out of trouble, or stealing camera memory cards when all I had to do was fill out a form, or any number of things.

That was what I was perfectly prepared for until something cracked under Hayne's façade. It was a glance, a shard of a different color in his tired eyes, but I knew this man. Something was wrong. I didn't know what it was, but it unnerved me, scared me to the point that the Charm crept up my back and wrap around my shoulders like a protective blanket. I scooted to the front of the seat and planted my feet on the floor to brace myself. "What is it, Hayne?"

"It's Dot."

My mouth ran dry, and I clasped the arms of the chair for support at the mention of his daughter. "Dot?"

"She got attacked last night at some party. Cut up. She's at Hahnemann with her mom."

The news pressed against my sternum as if my entire body was fighting the news of Dot in pain. I'd been watching Dot grow up in the pictures over Hayne's shoulder for forever. When she was old enough, she even went on a stakeout with Ethan and me a few times.

I knew this wasn't a pity party. Hayne and I were cut from the same cloth—a cloth that didn't do pity parties. He didn't need a shoulder to cry on, he needed answers. "Are you giving me an assignment?"

"I need my best on this, but I need to know you're back, Merci. That you'll put everything into it."

I hesitated. For the first time in my career, I paused. Could I investigate this? I had three dead bodies, a spell big enough to crack open gas lines, and a werewolf in my life. It was a lot on a very little plate.

But when I looked at Hayne, the man who had saved my ass so many times I'd lost count, watching him crack before my eyes, I couldn't stand it. Frankly, I couldn't think of a single person at this paper but Hayne himself who could actually get the truth behind what had happened to Dot.

"I'll go see her today though I'm not sure what contacts I have at the university …" My sentence trailed off as I thought about the latest in a line of men I'd managed to piss off. "Actually, I recently acquired a contact at Neumann. I'll get you everything I know by sundown, then you can tell me how deep you want me to go."

Hayne nodded. "I'll send a consent form over to the hospital to get you access to her records."

I stood. He was suddenly so small behind his desk, his shoulders hunched, and his gaze on his fists. "You can yell at me if it will make you feel better."

Hayne chuckled, though his voice cracked. "I'll let you off the hook this one time."

"Sundown."

CHAPTER NINE

I knocked on the hospital door and stuck my head in. It had that brilliant, antiseptic smell covered by the overpowering perfume of flowers. I took a handful of hand sanitizer from inside the door and walked to the other side of the curtain.

The scene was too familiar. I'd visited many people in this hospital. Knew exactly where to park and which stairwell to go to avoid charge nurses. But this was different. This was Dot. I knew her name, I knew her birthday without having to ask any questions.

Hayne's ex-wife was sitting at her daughter's bedside. "Can I help you?"

I took a few more steps into the room and saw Dot lying on the bed. It dwarfed her frame and if she wasn't ill, the lightning made her look so. Nineteen years old and I could still see the pictures Hayne kept behind his desk as she grew up into the women before me.

"Merci," Dot said with a soft smile.

Spite was instantly written across her mother's face, in the long crease of her forehead. "Hayne sent you instead of coming himself? Too busy to visit his own daughter in the hospital."

Dot reached out and put her hand on her mother's arm. "It's okay, Mom. I want to talk to Merci."

Her mother got up and walked out of the hospital room, fists at her side.

Dot's swollen features nearly hid her father's gray eyes and her arms were both bandaged up pretty tightly.

I cleared my throat. "I really don't want to be indelicate, but—"

"Can't let the story get cold," Dot nodded. "I am my father's daughter."

I moved closer to the bedside. "He really is worried sick."

"He must be if he sent his ace reporter." She managed a small smile.

"Thank you, Dot."

She chuckled. "Dot is a name for a chubby twelve-year-old."

"I promise not to use any names in my articles if you don't want me to."

Dot nodded. "I already told the police what happened."

"No you didn't. Not the real story."

I clicked on the audio recorder and looked into the girl's tired eyes. The familiar pressure gathered in behind my temple along with a stab of guilt for putting her under the Lanard Charm—especially when the heart monitor faltered as I locked it into place. But I needed the truth and this would be the fastest way to get it, so she could go back to healing. I started in. "Where were you last night?"

"Party in South Philly."

"Any drugs were at the party?"

"The usual. Coke, meth. X."

"Did you have any?"

"No, Merci. I've ever used anything."

I nodded. Now I knew for sure, I could report that back to Hayne and make sure he didn't name himself the Worst Father of the Year. "I believe you. How did you find out about this party?"

"Some guys we were with knew a guy who got them some party drugs. He sort of chatted me up and then he told us about this new underground place."

I looked away. I was trying to take it easy on her. I knew Dot wasn't the party kid. Hayne used to post her straight-A report cards on the filing cabinet behind his desk. "Think he'll talk to me?"

"Maybe. His name's Tricky. We met him at this arcade bar thing next to campus. Wizards. It's where he usually deals."

"What happened?"

"Danced a little, met this guy who was hanging around the bar. Tricky knew him." She frowned. "Started asking lots of questions about the paper."

My skin prickled. "What kind of questions?"

"Who I knew at the paper." Her eyes watered and her chin crumpled. "I might have dropped your and dad's names, trying to front like I was something special."

I reached out to take her hand. "You are something special, Dot."

She chuckled and looked down at our connection. A tear ran down her cherubic cheek, only making the bruise there a darker shade of purple.

"You get this guy's name?"

She frowned. "Byron, Benson—"

"Benny?"

Dot looked up at me. "Yeah, maybe."

I had to let go of her hand for fear that I might break her already swollen fingers. Benny. It always came back to Benny. What the hell had he gotten himself into?

"He started creeping me out with all his questions, so I went to go find my friends and then we went to the party. We weren't there thirty minutes before…" Her voice trailed off as her gaze floated to the window behind me.

She wasn't ready, so I distracted her with another question. "Do you remember where the party was?"

"Not really. Some underground place. It would have been close to where I was found."

I nodded. That was a simple search and some good old-fashioned footwork.

"Did something strange happen?" I leaned forward.

"I couldn't tell the police. I knew they wouldn't believe me."

"I will believe you, Dot."

She finally looked back at me, and I didn't need to capture her in the Charm this time. She needed to tell this truth to someone, to make it true for herself, and I would take it and carry it with her. "It was like I couldn't see. Like my eyes stopped working before they jumped me."

I gulped, and my blood ran cold. "How many?"

"Four. All those self-defense classes Dad made me take kicked in, and I punched a few of them, but they got me. I hit my head pretty hard, and I passed out. I don't remember anything until I woke up in the hospital. The police said that someone found me talking gibberish on a street, assumed it was high on something."

I gulped. It was Ethan and me all over again. I could hear the echoes of Ethan's howls reverberating off the tile floor again and again and again.

My pen cracked under the pressure of my grip and the flying bits distracted me from the pit of fear that I might never be completely free of. I looked into Dot's eyes and knew where she was, could feel exactly what she was feeling. As she relived the trauma again and again.

Her heart monitor started to beep more rapidly and I took her hand and held her gaze. "Take a deep breath."

Dot did as she was told.

"And another."

She took in a deep breath and let it out with a small shudder. The monitor's beeping began to slow.

"I know people keep telling you it's going to be okay, and it's hard to believe that now. But it really is going to be okay."

"Because Merci Lanard is on the story, and she always gets the truth."

I saw hope in her gray eyes.

I smiled and nodded, squeezed her hand. "Is there anything else that you can think of, something that you grabbed while you were there, anything else?"

"You need to see the cut."

She was the editor-in-chief's daughter. She knew what it took to make a full story. Just like I was a journalist's daughter and I would always take what was needed. "Only if you want."

She made her case again. "It's the biggest lead there is. Police couldn't make anything of it."

I nodded and let her carefully unwrap her left arm. My own scar itched as she pulled away the bandage.

It was raw, like a line of hamburger meat down her arm, but it was a shape. A very familiar shape, the long line with the diamond at the bottom and the cross of a T at the top. The Old Speak symbol for sacrifice. A fresh, hand-carved symbol from four unknown assailants that robbed her of her vision and attacked her.

I looked at my forearm, where I knew there was also faint jagged line. Dot needed to see it. I rolled up my sleeve and rested my arm next to hers. My faint pink line was nothing in comparison, mine left unfinished, but the lines were close enough that Dot gasped, and another round of tears streamed down her face. She sniffed.

"I don't know why this was done to us, but I will stop it."

"Take a picture," she said through her tears.

It killed me that in her greatest hour of need, this is still what she thought of first. Others. The faith in that one sentence rocked me to the core. Hayne had said it so much that Ethan and I had almost made it a mantra.

The truth helps more than it hurts.

And it was in moments like this I wished that wasn't true. I didn't want Dot to hurt at all. As quickly as I could, I snapped a picture of with my phone and slipped it back into my pocket.

Dot pulled her arm back to herself and re-wrapped her wound, holding it to her chest. I rolled down my own sleeve and watcher her recover.

She wiped at her face. "What's going to happen to me?"

I told her the truth. "You'll start feeling better, and then the cops will probably ask you the same questions they did before." I reached out to hold her hand again. "You'll be afraid of the dark for a while, so find someone you trust to stay with you. You'll see the shadows as a little bigger, but don't let them get in your way. And call your father. I worry him enough for the both of us."

Dot nodded and leaned back in the hospital bed, slipping her hand from mine. "Thank you, Merci."

I closed my notebook, clicked off the recorder, and stuck both back into my bag. "Get some rest. The next few days aren't going to be easy."

I wasn't sure if I said that for her sake or mine.

I walked out of the hospital and back to my car. I needed a drink. This was all happening so fast. Dot's attack was just like Ethan's and probably exactly what happened to all those others: Tay-Tay, Mitchell, Beakman. Four people dead in the span of three weeks, all with a link to magic. But how had she survived it when the others didn't? Self-defense classes are one thing, but these guys took down a werewolf.

First a person from the paper and now the editor's daughter? Were we close to something? Was this somehow a cross section of Ethan's world and my work?

With a live body to interrogate, I could potentially connect the two. Tracking down this Tricky could lead me to Benny, could lead me to the Shadow Men.

I sat in my car and locked the doors. I wasn't sure what I was going to tell Hayne. Didn't know if his brain needed to process that he'd nearly lost a daughter to the same thing that took one of his staff members, but he could make sure that the others in the office were safe.

But could I do it without lying to him?

I knew I needed Rafe. This was his fight too. This was his brother. His world. He could tell me things about the university. He could confirm information about the mark carved into Dot's arm now that we had a high-def picture of it not on a withered up old corpse. He could probably even tell me why Dot had survived when the others hadn't. He could be the backup that I needed.

Or he could be the next victim. My stomach churned. I couldn't drag another person into this just to see them broken and bleeding on the floor.

Ethan's voice in my head was like a bucket of ice water across my brain. *Everyone is better with a partner.*

I understood why Rafe felt betrayed. I understood if he didn't want to talk to me. But I wasn't going to really give him a choice. The university website had his office hours and when he taught class. The departmental secretary had confirmed it on my drive over.

I got out of my car and walked into the English Departments building at Neumann. He had to appreciate the effort that I had tracked him down. I was coming to him for help this time.

The office hadn't been renovated in forty years and the secretary waved me through to Dr. MacCallan's office with no problem

Rafe was perfectly suited to academic life. Stacks of books covered his desk and floor and he sat in an old brown leather recliner as he read through pages, chewing on the end of a red pen.

I almost didn't want to disturb the perfection of it. But that was who I was, right? It's who the Mother made me. A walking thunderstorm of chaos.

I tapped on the door.

He looked up from his reading and immediately, his eyes clouded over.

"Lanard?"

That hurt. "Back to the formalities?"

He let out a long, exasperated sigh and put down the paper he was grading. "What do you want?"

"I know that you probably don't want to work with me anymore, but I need to show you something." I stepped into his office and closed the door. It was like stepping into a sauna that smelled like sandalwood and sage, his own wolf's den.

I pulled my phone out of my back pocket and opened up the picture of Dot's wound. "There was another attack where the victim was marked with a sigil and it has ties to Benny."

I handed him the phone.

When he recognized the mark, his brows furrowed together. "Attack not murder?"

"She's still alive. Ethan and I knew her."

"Knew her? Another journalist?"

"My editor's daughter."

He exhaled. "All right."

"She gave me a name of a guy. I thought I would see if he was willing to talk, then check out the place where she was attacked. See if there is any magical stuff left over. Take a few pictures." It struck me that Rafe hadn't seen the photos of the spell yet, didn't know the extent of the damage the spell had done. God, it had been a long two days.

"Do you not know this could be a trap?"

I laughed. "What?"

He rose from his chair and handed me back my phone. "Maybe she didn't survive. Maybe she was left alive. Whoever is doing this might know you can't stop yourself and might be trying to finish what they started."

I gulped. "If they were after me specifically, they would have already found me. I haven't exactly been hiding."

"Maybe they can't. Maybe they don't want you dead. Maybe they are setting you up to be part of the spell. Maybe there are a million things we don't know about you because you've been keeping the truth from me."

I exhaled and gave in. "If you want to be mad at me, fine. I can deal with that. I wanted to give you the chance for the closure I know you need too. We finish the story. You go your way. I go mine."

His eye brow arched as he gave me this dead stare. "Piper ordered us to work together."

"I'm not pack, I don't have to follow her orders. I can do this on my own."

"No," he said quickly. "You shouldn't have to. Where are we going?"

"Just around the corner, actually."

...

Wizards was every college bar I'd ever been to. It reeked of beer, stale clove cigarettes, and cheap cologne. My boots stuck to the floor as I crossed the bar, Rafe following close behind, and we perched in a corner table. It was still too early for any real debauchery, but there were a few co-eds already getting their Saturday night buzz on.

"Who are we looking for?" Rafe whispered.

"I'll know him when I see him."

I scanned the bar scene, sorting through the growing crowd. Life and work had given me a sort of radar, a talent for sorting out the just and the unjust, but chiefly the unjust—they were the ones with the shifty eyes who didn't want to be seen. Only one character pinged as one who might not belong: a lanky young man trying to chat up a girl who was busy beating the high score at Ms. PacMan. She kept waving him off, and he kept leaning in her way, his gaze darting to every dark corner of the bar.

Ping. Guilty party at two o'clock.

I leaned over to Rafe. "So, if this guy is in cahoots with dark magic, would you be able to sniff him out?" I pointed to the boy in jeans that fell off his too skinny hips.

"You want me to sniff out an informant?"

I shrugged and nodded. Technically I wasn't looking for an informant, I was looking for bait that lured in innocent girls. But semantics. "Could you?"

"Depends on the level of infestation, some don't and some smell like black mold and gym socks."

I gestured with my chin. "White rapper at two o'clock with the trucker hat. Why don't you try to get us a few beers to blend in?"

"This early in the evening?"

"Fine. Make mine a whiskey."

I situated my bag to appear casual, trying out the blending into plain sight that Rafe had talked about, but I didn't take my eyes off Rafe. My leg bounced furiously with anticipation.

He slowly walked around to the bar and put in an order. He casually walked around a few of the other games, then made a quick pass by the young man.

There was no need for a secret code or hand signals. The expression on Rafe's face when he passed by him was all I needed to know. He was the one we were looking for. He had to be the Tricky boy who could lead us to Benny.

Rafe picked up the amber drinks from the bar and headed back to my table.

"You have impeccable luck, Miss Lanard."

"It's not luck, Professor." I checked my watch. "College bar. Everyone in here has books or bags. He's got nothing."

Rafe shook his head and took a sip of his drink. He winced.

"What? Couldn't impress a girl by getting the top shelf stuff?" I took the tumbler and threw back the amber liquid in one large gulp.

Rafe's eyebrow rose. "Do we need to have an intervention?"

"Only if you want me to punch you again." I smiled sweetly.

Rafe set his untouched glass on the table before us. "How do you want to play this?"

"Same way I play everything. Direct and to the point."

I stood, pulled out my recorder, and walked toward the young man.

"Are you Tricky?" I asked.

The young man swung around with a half-drunken swagger that came naturally to some. But when he saw me, his casual cockiness turned into wide-eyed fear. "Holy shit. It's you."

"How do you–"

He was running to the back entrance before I could finish the question. Rafe was nothing but a blur speeding past me as he chased after the kid. He grabbed the extra-large shirt before he could reach the door and threw him into the men's bathroom.

I looked around at the other patrons. They were too busy with their philosophy study group or their video games to notice the fray. I slung the strap of my messenger across my chest and readied for my millionth bathroom interrogation. Just another day in the office.

I walked through the still swinging door to see Rafe cornering the young man.

"You may not realize that running really makes you seem really guilty." I locked the bolt on the bathroom door and leaned against it, sliding my running recorder into my pocket.

"Nah, man. I ain't done nothin'."

Rafe winced. "Except murder the Queen's English."

I caught myself in a chuckle. "Why did you run, Tricky? We didn't even flash brass or anything."

"You. They told me to stay away from you."

I beamed with pride. "My reputation precedes me. Who told you to stay away?"

"Nah, man. I ain't tellin'."

The kid tried to make a run for the door. Rafe caught him easily by the throat and slammed him hard against the wall, rattling the condom machine that sounded fairly empty.

"You are not telling," Rafe corrected. "And yes, you will."

I walked toward the kid and smiled calmly. "Did you meet a girl named Dot recently?"

"I meet alotta people." His voice kept its casual swagger, though wide eyes betrayed his fear.

Rafe slammed him against the wall again—at this point, his ball cap was the only thing preventing a concussion.

I reached up and grabbed his chin, forcing his eyes to mine. He tried to pull his head away, but I caught his gaze. The Charm trapped him easily and I locked into him hard. It echoed like a metal jail cell door in my head—a sound I hoped this kid learned very soon for putting Dot in the hospital. "Did you meet a girl named Dot and convince her to go to a club?"

"Yeah."

"Do you know Benny?"

The kid smacked his lips and relaxed against the wall. "Yeah, man. I know Benny. He's the one who told me to chat her up."

My insides seized for a moment and I was nearly sick. Benny was the bad guy here? I wouldn't believe it. He just wasn't smart enough.

"Why would they want the daughter of the paper's editor-in-chief?"

"I dunno."

"Do you know where Benny is?"

"Nah."

"Could you text him to find out where he is?"

There was a pause and I shoved power down the line of our connecting, startling him into submission, like a mental slap up the side of his head.

He jammed is hand down into his pocket and pulled out a burner phone.

"He's the only number."

I cut our connection quickly and turned my attention to the flip-phone. With a few key strokes, I found the contacts. The number was neon across my retinas.

I knew that number. I'd dialed it a thousand times after I had copied it from Tay-Tay's phone. This was Benny's new number. And though he wouldn't answer my text, maybe he would answer one from Tricky.

As I was texting, he struggled against Rafe but to no avail. Apparently, all the heavy lifting of textbooks and magical volumes made the professor much stronger than he looked.

"What are you doing?"

"Drawing out Benny like he drew me."

I hit send just as keys jingled at the door. The kid broke away from Rafe and made his break. I hooked my ankle around his and, thanks to those too large pants and his too skinny hips, he crashed face-first onto the floor, his face smacking the tile and making me wince. Tricky didn't move. That was more than unfortunate.

I quickly undid the bolt of the door and the bartender pushed open the door. I pulled Julie's business card out of my coat pocket. "Call Officer Rutherford. Kid's dealing drugs out of your bar."

I grabbed Rafe and pulled him quickly outside before that bartender did something like remember my face. When we reached the car, I wasn't ready to get in yet. My body was sizzling and defaulted to pacing in the parking lot. The thoughts ran around so fast, I could barely keep up with them.

"How do you know he'll come?" Rafe growled.

"You know Demon semantics. I know dealer semantics."

I could feel it. The truth. It scampered around like spiders along my skin. I was close to getting answers. I just needed to focus.

And Rafe MacCallan's glaring eyes were not helping that process.

"You did something to that lad. Mind control? Is that your ability?"

I could only shake my head. "I can't do this right now, Rafe. We've got a direct lead to the man who might have lured Ethan to his death."

"I think I have a right to know what I have been working with for the past month."

"Why?"

"Because it changes everything," he roared.

"I don't see how," I snapped back. "I worked beside Ethan for two years and I never had the luxury of knowing."

He huffed in frustration and ran his fingers through his hair. "Because you don't know anything, Merci. Can't you see anything that isn't right in front of your nose?"

"Fine, Rafe. What do you want me to tell you? Piper doesn't even know what I am. All I do know is there is this storm in my head and when I focus it on a person, I can get them to tell me the truth. I also have to tell the truth myself."

"You can't lie?"

"Funny how it works that way," I said turning toward my car. "I need to go,"

"Where? Another abandoned warehouse? A corner store? Are you trying to get yourself killed?"

"No, I'm trying to get information about your brother's death. Are you going to take a knee on this or take the knife?"

I watched my words slice into him, it was cruel. I knew it was, but this was Benny. This was the leaf on the wind I needed to catch so badly I could taste it. And I couldn't stop.

...

The *I Don't Know Yet* was a particular favorite of mine – and I didn't even have to lie about the bar's name.

Though specifically, we weren't headed to the bar, but to the illegal poker rooms above it. I pulled out my roll of twenties and the bouncer, Hector, let me in the door and made me promise that Elbow Patches wasn't going to touch a card. I crossed my heart and hoped to die.

I walked back to Room 6.

"Why this place, Merci?" Rafe asked as we made our way down the long, red velvet hallway. It was quiet, but the bulletproofing the owner had done tended to muffle the goings-on in the rooms.

"This was the first story I bought from Benny."

"He knows you're coming?"

"If he's smart, he does."

Rafe grabbed my arm and jerked me around to face him. "How could you be so stupid?" Rafe snapped.

"I'm done with it," I spit back. "I'm done with the books and the magic, and I'm doing this my way. I've been trying to hunt down Benny for a month now, and he's here. I'm going to talk to him. Warlocks be damned."

I tore my arm from his grasp and went to go see what was behind door number six.

Benny had seen better days. He was gaunt, like he'd been running scared for weeks. And maybe he had. His dark eyes sank into his skull as they darted from me to Rafe to me again. But he wasn't surprised to see me, wasn't thrown off that I was the one walking through the door and not Tricky.

"Sort of shocked you showed up this time," I greeted.

"Knew you'd find me eventually. Hoped you wouldn't be stupid enough to try."

Pleasantries exchanged, I waved Rafe in and he pressed himself into the shadowy, velvet walls of the ten-by-ten room. The rooms were meant for two things: playing poker and drink service. Nothing more cluttered the space than the two tables and the necessary chairs.

Carefully, I sat across the table from Benny, flipped on the recorder in my pocket, and laid my hands out on the green felt of the poker table. The harsh light of the single bulb dangling from the cord wasn't flattering. It made his black hair greasier and his features more angular.

I smiled. "Benny. It's good to see you."

He leaned back in his chair. "Aw no. Not that Lanard smile. I'd rather have that guy beat on me." His eyes darted to Rafe.

The familiar chill settled around my shoulders and crawled up my neck. My heart wasn't racing, my focus was on one thing. It was like dancing with a partner you'd been practicing with for years, smooth, without thinking about the steps. If this was a magic show, I was the headliner and Benny had always been my willing assistant. "How are the streets treating you?"

He adjusted in the chair. "Fair shake."

I nodded pleasantly. The nice thing about looking for someone is you have enough time to really whittle down the answers you needed. I didn't need my notebook or anything to help me count the questions. "What happened to the last crew you were running for? The Lone Dawgs?"

"I started asking around, like you asked."

"What happened?"

He sniffed. "I found the new outfit you sent me after."

He'd found them? The whispers Ethan and I had heard. My instincts had been right – there *was* a story. "And their payroll is better than mine?"

"It had a different set of perks."

I remembered Atlanta saying that Benny had been rolling in money lately. But that didn't explain why he looked like he hadn't eaten in two weeks. "All I need is one name and whoever it is will get their day in court."

Benny snorted. "He'll never see a courtroom, Lanard. No matter how many exposés you write."

I needed that name. A chill ran down my spine as I leaned forward. Slowly, carefully, I found that open spot in Benny's dark eyes. I slipped in and locked the Charm into place. Just like that. Like I had thousand times before with Benny, before magic was in my vocabulary, when all this was just a compulsion to find the truth.

"Who is he?"

The answer popped out of him like a ping-ping ball. "Cartwright."

It all clicked into place. The clear picture flooded through me and created a sizzle in the connection between us. "Cartwright. Jeffrey Cartwright as in Cartwright Construction is the new ring leader?"

"Yes."

"So this has ties to City Hall?"

"Yes."

"Is he responsible for the decrease in gang activity lately?"

"Yes."

"What about the missing girls on the Trade Streets?"

"Yes."

All three? Benny was confirming that all the shadows lately had been connected, all the little side stories in my journal were connected. City Hall I could deal with, had dealt with, but the fact that Cartwright's reach was already permeating the other lower layers of the city – that was terrifying.

And it was all under my nose.

Rage began to boil through my veins. I wanted to punch him, but that really wasn't the best way to get the information that I needed. I had to keep it together. I needed answers. I needed the truth, which meant that I was perfectly fine using my magic to get it.

The contact I had with Benny sizzled like a live wire in the rain; I held on to it tighter.

"Why did you call me to meet you that night?"

Benny struggled against our bond but couldn't break it. Or didn't want to. "Cartwright knew about you, needed to get you alone. Paid me to get you there."

"So you did rat us out?" I confirmed.

"I didn't know anyone would die, Merci. You have to believe me."

I did believe him. Benny didn't know that Cartwright was going for the jugular, at least not at the beginning.

"Why did he want to get us alone?"

"He didn't like how you jacked up the bids for the city planning."

This had to be more than just business, right? What about the mark, what about the other bodies, what about the Shadow Men? I had to calm the questions down for a moment. I didn't need to reveal everything I had learned about in the past three weeks – I just needed to get him talking.

"So you call me knowing that I'd come, and Cartwright sends men to rough up Ethan and me for exposing him, but it goes south and they run?"

"He told me later that he only wanted you dead. Ethan wasn't supposed to be there."

"Me? I was the target?"

I thought I was going to be sick. The guilt washed over me in thick, green waves. I had gotten Ethan killed. My work. My insistence. My obsession. Rafe had been right this whole time.

Benny continued. "He wanted to use you as an example of someone who crossed him, but after that night, it changed hardcore."

There were several people who were not in the Lanard Fan Club, but enough to kill? Like Rutherford I said, I was more like a yappy dog than a wolf, more of an annoyance than a threat. Why would I be a target? What could I have possibly done differently from every other story I had written? Was were so special about those construction bribes?

"What changed?"

"Everything. After that night, it wasn't just business anymore. He kept talking about how the soul of the city was his." Benny sniffed and leaned forward on the table. "He wanted you, like *wanted* you."

The magic zipping around in my brain started to sputter and short-circuit. I closed my eyes for a moment, recalibrating. I'd questioned people when I was juiced like this before, but I had never been so desperate.

Benny. Ethan. It was like trying to harness a tornado in my brain to help pull the answers. I needed control. Focus.

I opened my eyes back up; Benny was right there, ready to be put on the hook again. "So, you've seen him? In person?"

Benny nodded. "It's like looking into a void. He's not human anymore."

Not human? Like a Warlock?

I took in a deep breath. It was time for a big push. If my magic could hold out for a few more questions. "How does Tay-Tay fit into all this?"

The little color he did have in his face fled and water filled his eyes. "How you know about that?"

"I went looking for you after that night in the store. Make sure you were okay. Instead, I found her. I made sure she got a proper burial. Paid for it myself."

He gulped, his scrawny neck only highlighting the slow descent of his Adam's apple.

"What happened to her, Benny?"

The words crawled out of his mouth like a bag of nails, rusted and painful. "New guy drives a hard bargain."

"Magic does come at a price, doesn't it?" Rafe finally spoke.

The moisture on Benny's forehead started to bead and run down his face. I wasn't sure if I could handle these two stories actually intersecting, but the look in Benny's eyes was unmistakable.

"So, you know?" Benny asked.

My stomach reeled, but I kept myself stone still, hands still splayed out wide on the poker table. Ethan and magic. They were connected. Of course, it was all connected.

"I know enough to know it's dangerous." I looked straight into his black eyes. The foreplay was over, the storm in my head needed to be sated. "Question is, is Cartwright a warlock?"

Benny frowned and nothing came out. Maybe Benny didn't know the details, the breeds and the semantics.

I tried again, being as specific as possible. "Did he kill Tay-Tay by sucking the life out of her with a spell that was carved into her arm?"

A tear streaked down his grimy cheek, leaving a clean trail in its wake. His voice cracked with pain. "Yeah. They got my princess. I tried to convince him that with your partner's death, you wouldn't come snooping around, but .... He wanted you so bad ... When I said I didn't want to help him anymore, they took her, right in front of me."

I looked back down at the table, breaking the connection; afraid I might actually pull out some of his pain and not just the truth. Tay-Tay had died because Benny didn't want me dead. Was he trying to protect me too?

"Two guys held her down and carved something into her arm and then she was gone."

I traced my own white mark down my forearm and shivered, overcome with the tragedy of it all.

Rafe saved me for a moment, stepping up behind my chair and resting his hand on my shoulder. "What do you know of the other victims, John Mitchell and Beakman?"

Benny only shook his head. "That wasn't on me. I'd managed to keep my head down for a few days before he caught up with me. Before Tay-Tay."

Rafe kept on with the interrogation as I recovered. "How did he find you?"

"It's like he sees everything. Weird shit like talking mirrors and chicken scratch into walls. Its why I didn't reach out. He couldn't find you and I didn't want to lead him to you, even after he killed my Princess. I lied to him, said you left town after Ethan died. I deleted your contact info, burned your business card. But you are just so damn persistent."

Settled, I finally looked back up at him again, ready for a final push of truth, a final admonition to finish this, to get the information that I needed. "Why did you go after Dot?"

Benny shook his head. "I didn't want to, Merci. I'd been trying to get him more people, used my ins with dealers to find him more followers. Used my contacts with the gangs to get him muscle, but he still wanted you. I bought you as much time as I could, thinking you would figure it out."

His faith in me hurt, like a small, smooth blade slicing into my midsection a centimeter at a time until it was up to the hilt. It was difficult to breathe.

"But in the end, he wanted to draw you out. I didn't want to offer up the girl but... he's got punishments worse than death."

He pushed up his sleeves and laid them out between us. There were marks up and down his arms. Dark needle punctures ran up the inside of one arm and disappeared into his hoodie. There were also carvings, some still weeping blood, some looked like they had been there for weeks.

"Fuck me."

I looked up at Rafe. "Language, Professor."

He pointed to the old speak carved into Benny's arms. "It's an immortality spell, a servant linked to a master."

Immortality. Being linked to the creature who had sucked the life out of your lover would be worse than death. And potentially make you hand over an innocent girl. I stared at the swirling mark carved into the Benny's skin. Servant. "As in servant to . . ."

"The Devil." Benny's lower lip began to quiver. "I'm tired, Merci, tired of running, tired of hurting people, tired of trying to die. I just want to do one last good thing for my princess. I don't care what he does to me now."

And it was truth. It was more than just the connection between us, it was the trust that we had built, the faith in me that had gotten Tay-Tay killed, the way his shoulders were so burdened he couldn't even shrug.

"Why me, Benny? What's so special about me?"

"I don't know, Merci. He said that without you, it all burns to the ground."

"Don't worry." I leaned forward. "It's all ash now I know the truth."

I looked away from Benny, letting him take a moment to recover. I felt like socks that had been in the dryer too long, dry and full of static, like I'd spark if anyone touched me.

Rafe spoke again. "We need to know where he is."

I didn't have the energy to even lift my gaze to Rafe. "Why? So you and the pack can go play heroes?"

Rafe didn't answer. Perhaps he knew something that I didn't.

"Please don't, Merci," Benny begged. "Please don't make it easier for him to get you, to finish what he started."

One last push. It was all I had in me. I sniffed and focused. I brought the power to a point again. Once last question. For Ethan. I locked with Benny's exhausted gaze.

"Where can I find him?"

Benny fought his tether again, fought against the answer bubbling up his throat, but he couldn't look away.

I pushed. Focused more than I even had before. It was like dumping a bucket of ice water over my head. I stopped breathing and compelled the truth from him, like funneling all the static in my head down and through the live connection between us, straight into his brain.

He turned red in the face and his lips pressed together. He was holding his breath along with the answer.

"Where can I find him, Benny?"

The truth erupted from him like a cat hacking up a hairball. "Schuylkill and Bainbridge."

Benny panted and his face turned back to his normal shade of slimy with the release of information.

I leaned back in the chair and exhaled. My head immediately began to throb as the Charm was broken, and I lost control of the tornado in my brain, its force spinning out of control. A wave of nausea hit me. Magic did come at a price. This wasn't charming anyone, this was pulling the truth like teeth.

My nose started to run and I held my wrist to my face; blood dripped into my hand. I jumped up and grabbed my bag. I walked to the other side of the room as I dug for my Kleenex pack.

I squeezed my eyes shut, my head spinning a moment in the storm of answers. They had ordered a hit on me because I was messing up their family business. Rafe had been right. It wasn't about Ethan being the Riko of the pack. It was about me. I was the intersection of the two stories. They'd meant to kill me, but Ethan saved me.

I held the Kleenex to my nose and tilted my head back. As much as I hated to admit it, it sounded like Ethan's death was just the tip of the iceberg. More missing people. Taking over gangs. Bigger plans for the city. For me.

I cracked open the bottle of water I kept in my bag and gulped down three pain pills, hoping they would dull the throbbing. I had a feeling this was nowhere near the end of my day. Benny's answers had just led to more questions, deeper questions.

We could give it a moment, but a cloud of unknowns was still swirling in my head, like the pressure of a coming storm. I was beginning to believe it would never be sated.

Rafe walked over and leaned against the wall next to me, crossing his arms across his chest and never taking his eyes off Benny's slumped form. "You okay?"

I ignored the obvious answer as I pinched the bridge of my nose to stop the bleeding. "We've got our answer now. It was both my story and your magic."

He ground his teeth.

"Are the nose bleeds a part of it?" he asked.

I dropped my head back down and studied the bright red Kleenex. Another drop fell on my hand and I put the Kleenex back as I side-eyed Rafe. "I don't know, but this one isn't the first."

I sniffed one more time and tossed the Kleenex into the trash bin, avoiding Rafe's stare as I turned back to Benny. He didn't look so hot. No one ever suffered after I asked questions, but he was shaking and sweating. There were a million things wrong with this scenario, but the blood on his hands was the only one that I could focus on.

"Benny?"

His head jerked back and his legs went straight before he started convulsing. Rafe and I rushed to his side and we managed to get him on the floor.

"Benny!" I put my hand on his arm and found it wet.

The sigil for sacrifice was gouged into his arm with what only could have been his own fingernails.

I unzipped his hoodie to check his airway and watched as the ligaments in his neck strained, his face turning purple. Dark lines crept up his face, running up through his veins and spidering up the side of his face.

I pulled my hands away from him when the blackness seeped into his eyes.

"His death is on you, Merci Lanard." It wasn't Benny's voice. It was dark and heavy; the hair on my arms stood on end, the air in the room went refrigerator cold.

With one final arch of his thin frame, Benny let out a piercing shriek and fell limp on the floor. His skin turned ashen and his body withered before our eyes, like all the other bodies. Like someone had rammed a straw in his chest and sucked out all the water.

"Oh god!" I scrambled away from the dried corpse as it contorted into its final position like Shrinkie Dinks in the oven. "What the hell was that?"

Rafe clenched every muscle in his body and his jaw locked hard enough I could hear the pop.

I jumped to my feet, suppressing the urge to vomit. "What is it?"

"Demon possession," he growled. Actually growled as if the answer was ripped from his gut.

"What?"

"I've seen it before. Felt it before. In the Shifter War." Rafe explained.

I focused on Rafe, fighting to keep the questions in my head from spinning me into a nauseous oblivion.

I took a step toward him and my head felt like a twenty-pound bowling bowl wobbling around on my shoulders. I had to stop to hold it steady for a moment.

Rafe finally spoke. "We need to get this to Piper."

"Why? This was about me. Not the pack. You don't have a responsibility here anymore."

He rose from the floor and I was assaulted by his glare. "There is a Demon involved, Merci. You have no idea what that means for the innocent people in this city."

I looked down at Benny. He hadn't been one of the innocent people in this city, but he was one of mine. A vital soul that kept my city running and breathing and he'd been taken.

A strange ruckus echoed down the hall, like a shuffling of chairs and a murmuring of voices. Then gun fire. Nothing quite muffled the distinct sound of gun fire.

Rafe paused and cocked his head. Like Ethan used to. I was enveloped in the brush of fur as he pulled his animal senses in tune with his human ones and listened.

"Someone is searching the building." He sniffed the air. "I smell fear. And mold."

That's when the lights went out. I had just enough time to grab for my messenger bag and sling it over my shoulder. I jammed my hand down into it and curled my fingers around my familiar Taser.

They weren't taking me. Not after tonight, Not after Benny had just sacrificed himself to tell me everything.

"Merci!" Rafe said. "Go."

I heard the door swing open. There wasn't light in the hallway, either. A rush of bodies entered the room. I might be blinded, but they weren't going to get the drop on me again. I flicked off the safety on the plastic weapon and started to make my way along the wall, following the chair rail around the edge of the room.

"Orders are not to hurt her," one said. He was at my left and close.

"And the other one?"

"He just wants her."

A wave of heat filled the room and I knew Rafe had gathered his power to him. Maybe even shifted. It made my hair stand on end, and even though I couldn't use my eyes, I could feel more. The texture of the wall, the rough groove of the trigger on the Taser.

Had he just enhanced me? Everything was sharper, tighter. The slightest movement, like a feather, tickled my extended left hand. I swung my right arm around and triggered the Taser. Its light managed to fill the space and my eyes adjusted fast. Any part of the anatomy would do the trick, but I nailed the guy in a deep angle of his neck. He stopped in his tracks and fell.

It was too easy. The light from the Taser gone, another tackled me from the side and the contents of my bag scattered across the floor. At least it was carpet this time and not the hard tile of a store.

His weight did most of the work as I wriggled and tried to keep his hands from catching mine.

A growl echoed in the dark space and the man on top of me hesitated for two-tenths of a second. The two-tenths I needed to grab a pen from my pocket and start ramming it into every part of his soft tissue I could. Wasn't going to break the skin, but it was better than just a fist.

He grabbed my neck and tried to make my windpipe meet the floor. Gasping, I scrambled, prying at the hands around my neck. The room grew hot as I fought for breath.

I scratched at his hands and then his own face, but his arm length was greater than mine. He straddled me and held me down.

I tried to call out for Rafe as my hands searched for anything else on the floor to use as a weapon. But from the sounds from his side of the room, someone was getting pummeled.

Another brush of fur preceded a surge of strength. I pried at the man's meaty thumb and he finally broke his grip on my neck. He fell onto his fist next to me and I balled up my hands and swung at where his head should have been, like Babe Ruth swinging for the bleachers.

Knuckles collided with flesh and it was enough to get him to shift his weight so I could wriggle out from under him.

His hands caught my arm once again, but not before my legs cleared his. I rammed my boots into the junction between his thighs and stomped like it was a cockroach.

He cried out in pain. I searched the ground again for my Taser. I kicked the damn thing, plastic tumbling across the carpet toward the door, and found its path unhindered.

"Rafe?" I called out.

I felt another hot blast of power and the thud of a body hitting the wall, though it seemed to have come from the ceiling.

"Run, Merci."

And I did. I followed the noise where the Taser had skittered out of the room and pin-balled my way down the hallway, ignoring the sounds of chaos the shadows had left in their wake. Light slowly returned to the space as I was about to stumble down the stairwell.

I was in my car and down the highway before I even knew what I was doing. My fight or flight had kicked in and I'd actually listened to it for the first time in my life; I'd run away from the danger.

One by one, the questions spinning around me were linked to the answers I'd just gotten. With each mile marker, the answers fell into a line. My brain became a Rolodex of everything I'd learned in the past three weeks, cards flying around in the storm in my head.

Demon, not Warlocks. The spell Rafe and I had discovered in the warehouse was probably a portal that had brought a Demon across to our world. Something had crawled out of it.

Demons can't exist corporeally on this plane. They have to inhabit bodies.

Cartwright had to be that body. Benny had said he wasn't human anymore.

And Cartwright had sent minions because we threatened his growing hold on the city when we exposed corruption on the construction contracts.

I had gotten Ethan killed.

And John Mitchell.

And Tay-Tay.

And Beakman.

And now Benny.

Cartwright had been trying to get to me this whole time. No one was safe. The paper wasn't safe. The bar certainly wasn't safe. I couldn't trust anyone who wasn't buck-naked to prove they weren't demon fodder, so I went to the one place I knew was safe because Rafe had made it safe for me. Scratched runes into my walls to keep out the bad guys even though they knew my name, my face, my editor.

I walked in through the back door of my house and locked every bolt I had and went straight to the liquor cabinet. Rafe had told me to run and hide, and I had run – now I was going to crawl into the bottom of a bottle for a while.

I was four fingers into the amber liquor as it burned through the practical information Benny had revealed. The Who's, What's, When's, and Where's.

Now it was time for the Whys. Why was the demon after me? Why was it unable to target me? Why did it need me so badly that it killed its own servant?

And even the whiskey I threw down into my gullet couldn't quench the one fact that stayed motionless in the fury of the storm.

I was the dangerous one. Everyone around me got killed. Rafe could be bleeding right now in the upper room of an underground poker club and it was my fault because I had gone there following my gut.

It was all my fault.

CHAPTER TEN

The ring of my cell phone jerked me awake and I fell off the bottom stair where I had been keeping guard with my bat and a bottle of whiskey.

The phone had slipped from my fingers and slid across the floor. I shuffled over to pick it up, my fingers faintly aching from dialing Rafe's number into oblivion.

Hayne didn't even say hello. "I've got a catch for you. Grisly murder in South Philly. Four bodies. Sounds like an open-and-shut gang violence."

"Nothing is open and shut, Hayne," I croaked.

I slowly stretched, my shoulders, my legs. Everything hurt and my neck was stiff and probably bruised. The morning light made me feel a little safer, but I kept my bat handy.

I heard Hayne's TMJ actually get worse over the phone. "You're the only one who can handle this one."

"Not today. Give it to Bill or Brian. Is that his name? That new intern."

Hayne sighed. "Are you really passing on this one? It's eight inches of prime real estate. The pictures are going to be gory as hell."

I shook my head. "I've had my month's fill of gory."

He heard him scratch his chin, which meant he hadn't shaved, which meant he hadn't slept. "Is this because of Dot?"

I confessed. "I found the informant, Hayne. Got more questions than answers, so I need a few days. You should too."

I started my shuffle toward the kitchen to get my first round of fuel to figure out what the hell I was going to do next and stopped. I wasn't drunk. Hungover maybe, but drinking had never made me hallucinate before. Yet there was definitely a naked man on my back porch, the body strewn across my glass patio door.

Oh God. Rafe.

"Merci, I—"

"Go . . . see . . . your . . . daughter," I ordered.

I disconnected the call and stuck the phone in my back pocket. I grabbed a blanket from the back of my couch and rushed to the glass door.

Bruises covered his pale side and I looked away before I couldn't unsee parts of him.

Was he alive?

I unlocked the back door, but he didn't move. Slowly, I slid the door open and he still didn't budge. I dropped the blanket over his more censorable areas and knelt at his side. Blood was everywhere. His face, his hands. One eye was swollen shut and his hand was purple and crooked. It was Ethan all over again.

My heart raced and my vision grew dark for a moment as my brain flooded with images from that night, the smells from that night.

"Merci." Rafe's rough voice sounded through the darkness. This wasn't Ethan. This wasn't what happened before. Rafe was alive, and he needed my help. I could save him.

The winter air perked my senses, focused my thoughts. I felt for his pulse, my triage training kicking in. Finally. I had to wait until my own calmed enough to catch his beat. Steady. And he was breathing, but strained. Broken ribs?

"Rafe?"

He moaned and rolled onto his back, through the open doorway and onto my feet. I hated to do it, but I searched his body for marks, for Old Speak, for anything that might indicate that he wasn't who he appeared to be. Nothing but large red welts down his arms and blood all over his hands. And the protection sigil above the back door hadn't stopped him from crossing the threshold, so no demon. Just Rafe.

"Can you move?"

He tensed, but his body didn't actually move. Guess that was an answer.

Every fiber in my being echoed one truth.

"We need to get you to Piper."

I tried to be gentle, but he was as big as me. I rolled him to his knees, and then pulled him up to a standing position. I threw his arm over my shoulder and sort of swayed him toward my garage.

Piper could fix him, help him, help me in ways I didn't even have questions for yet. More importantly, as I challenge the speed limit through my neighborhood and to the highway, I needed him not dead.

...

Piper was already waiting on her front porch when we drove up. Even in this early hour, even unannounced.

Levi and Xenom swarmed my car and carried Rafe's still unresponsive form from my back seat. I followed his body and Piper caught me and wrapped me in a warm hug. "Thank you for bringing him home, Merci."

She ushered me toward the door. But I paused at the threshold, her arm still around my shoulder. I didn't want to go inside. I didn't want to feel that sense of home knowing I could destroy it. That what was coming after me could come after them, all those innocents in danger because of me. Hell, I'd delivered one of them broken because he had been protecting me.

"What is it?" Piper asked.

I looked to the house. I knew what was on the other side. It wasn't just a pack, it was a family. A family I didn't deserve.

"I should go," I said, clutching my car keys in my hand. "I've got a million leads to—"

"No," she said firmly. "Rafe went to you. You are in this."

Her words were monosyllabic, yet still cryptic, reminding me how much I still had to learn about this world. About him. But I was relieved she wasn't going to make me leave his side; I needed him to be okay, to be arguing with me, researching with me.

Piper pulled me toward the house, and with one last glance over at my car, I stepped through the doorway.

The welcoming sent of cinnamon made me feel mildly better, but the edge was still there. "What exactly is the plan?" I asked.

"I don't know," Piper said, keeping her arm around my shoulder as she guided me through the house behind the parade of other men. "We need to assess the damage."

That didn't exactly make me feel comfortable with the situation. But at least Piper was honest. And the truth helped more than it hurt.

We flooded into a guest bedroom with a nautical theme. Rafe's body was put on a twin-sized bed and the bed was pulled from the away wall into the center of the room with a quick tug by Xenom.

Others started to come in, encircling the room with their warm energy. All without words, like nosey neighbors who wanted to watch the fireman at work. Levi and the bear stood at the head of the bed like sentinels.

Emily appeared next to me at the edge of the room. My skin grew hot and I flushed as all the words and truths started beating around in my head, everything that had come to light in the last twenty-four hours about me, about Ethan, and I wasn't sure I would be able to say them out loud to her. Was so sure that she would see the state of Rafe and know it was my fault too.

Levi actually saved me, finally making some sense with his gruff words. "Maybe she shouldn't be here. We don't know what happened to him."

Emily defended me. "She's not leaving."

"And she shouldn't." Piper's gaze sliced up at Levi, then at Emily.

"She's taken the knife," Emily said as she looked down at me. "She's one of us."

For a moment, I was lost. It all went quiet and the questions stopped. For a moment, I believed she could forgive me, we could go back to being the people who exchanged cheesy Christmas presents, but she didn't know the role I'd played, why Ethan had really died. Why Rafe was broken and bleeding. None of them did.

Piper sat on the edge of the bed. "Then let's see what is going on. I need a circle."

The others did as they were told, the leaders of the pack sitting on the floor around the bed. It took me a moment to realize that being part of this meant I was going to actually be a part of this. Join the circle.

Emily scooted over on the floor and I took a seat next to her. It felt surreal, sitting next to Emily, trusting her to guide me through this. But as I looked at Rafe, I knew I would follow all sorts of crazy to make sure he was safe again.

"Are you really?" Emily whispered to me. "One of us?"

I nodded.

Emily shook her head. "Hold on to your stomach then. I used to get a little queasy."

I took in a deep breath, expecting the same thing that happened to my knees when Rafe's power brushed against me. But nothing could have prepared me for being hit with a wall of Shifter power. My stomach turned over on itself and I grabbed my knees. It was like hitting the top of a roller coaster upside down but then going backwards.

Then the smell of my Grand-Mere's Dutch baby pancakes and my father's pipe filled my nose.. No one needed to tell me focus on that feeling of home. And I did. I focused on feeling safe, warm, and all of it guided me back to the kitchen where the cinnamon wasn't coming from Piper, but the breakfast Rafe had fixed me now felt like a lifetime ago. Before I wandered. Before I was the target of a demon.

I didn't even realize I had closed my eyes until Rafe cried out and they flew open. Dark lines streamed up his arms, just like with Benny. I watched as they threaded up his stretched neck and worked up his clenched jaw. I moved to go to him, but Emily's arm shot out across my front to hold me to the circle, like a mother protecting her child as she slammed on the breaks.

He cried out in pain, as his body arched, his hands in white balls at his side. Piper leaned forward and put her hand over his chest.

"Oh. Hello there."

Then there was this heat, like fire that sizzled against my face, though my back remained cool. The heat, the power, was only within this circle.

"Get out of here, you little leech," Piper whispered.

The darkness shot out of his mouth like a snake and hovered for a moment in midair, then exploded into a fine mist of ash. The heat from the circle intensified and I watched as this shadow vanished into thin air.

When it was gone, the desert dry heat faded from the circle and Piper sat up straighter. She took in a deep breath as she rubbed her hands along her jean-clad thighs. "There now."

Rafe was limp again, but there was a peace in his body though his eyes remained closed.

"Emily, will you get the first aid kit?"

Emily jumped up and left, breaking the magic of the circle. I rose to my feet and just stood at the foot of his bed.

"Everyone can go about their business. I need to speak with Merci alone."

I could hear Levi grumble as they left the room. The room grew cooler without the large bodies filling the small guest bedroom.

Piper closed the door. "What happened last night?"

There were a million answers I wanted to give her, but I waited. She was processing too. So I only gave her the truth of what she asked for. I kept my answers to facts and not the wild speculations that had been dancing around in my brain. "We got attacked by the same men who killed Ethan. I got away. I found Rafe on my doorstep this morning."

Piper was silent for a moment. "He went to you?"

I focused on the rise and fall of his pale chest in the morning light. Despite what he knew, he came to me.

Piper studied his pale frame, drew her fingers up his arm, across the marks. "Do you know what these are?"

My mouth went dry, but I pulled out the truth from myself. "We were meeting with an informant. He had the same marks. I think it was a kind of torture by a Demon."

Piper's jaw clenched and her eyes fluttered shut. She inhaled through her nose and exhaled through her mouth. "What I could feel was horrible and then it just blacked out."

"You can feel him?"

"I can feel everyone in my family. Feel them, but can only protect them to a certain extent."

There was a knock at the door. Emily slipped in with a large white box. Piper took it and Emily disappeared again.

Piper walked over to me and handed me the box. "When you are done, I can help answer some of those questions dancing around in your brain."

"Done with what?"

She looked down at Rafe's bloody body. "He went to you, Merci."

"Is he going to be okay?" I need him to be okay. Even after everything Piper had done, I needed a verbal confirmation that he wasn't going to disappear on me like Benny.

"I don't know." And with that, she left and closed the door behind her.

It wasn't the answer I wanted. Since Piper couldn't confirm or deny, it left me with one choice: do everything I could to help him make it through this, though I wasn't sure I should be the person administering first aid. Surely, there had to be a doctor or nurse among them. I was also the last person Rafe probably wanted to wake up to right now. The person who had gotten his brother killed, who had nearly gotten him killed to.

But as I sat down on the edge of his bed, set out the supplies, I realized I didn't need help. I'd patched up Ethan a million times. And he had iced more than one of my sprained wrists or busted knees. I remembered what he had always told me. Wear two pairs of gloves. I'd thought he was just being really careful about blood-borne pathogens after the training sessions we'd had at work, but as I pulled on the second set of latex gloves, I realized he'd wanted to prevent me getting it, the thing, the big furry.

I started on Rafe's wounds. I carefully wiped at his face with an alcohol pad. Most of it was blood, blood that had pilled in the scruff of his beard. I gently wiped away at his nose and the open gashes on his eyebrow and cheek. With a deft hand, I pinched those together and put a butterfly bandage on each, then extras just to make sure. I worked my way down his face then moved to his hands.

That sinking anchor feeling sat heavy in my stomach again. Outside of punching him, this was the first time I'd touched him. First time I'd touched anyone in a very long time. It was a strange thought, something foreign I'd never thought about before. I didn't touch people. I punched people and grabbed a few to force eye contact, but virtually nothing was done with affection. I'd cleaned up Ethan a few times, but it wasn't like this.

As gently as I could, I lifted his hand into mine. Up close, they were nice hands. No calluses, just a writer's bump on his right ring finger. They weren't soft like other academics', so he had to have a hobby rougher than turning the pages of those mystical texts. As I started to wipe off the blood, I realized I knew more about what he was than who he was, and that was on me. That was my fault.

I took special care to clean off his palms, to get the blood out from under his nails so he'd have one less reminder. I could at least do that for him.

The angry welts down both arms were hot and feverish. I wiped them down with alcohol, and then put some Benadryl cream on them. I ran my fingers across them – needle marks, large gauge. Drug needles.

When I was done, he appeared to be peacefully sleeping. Like he'd fallen asleep after a wild night. I pulled the blanket up to his chin.

I tossed all the trash and my gloves into the small waste basket underneath the desk.

I sat down on the floor next to the bed and rested my head on my knees. What had happened after I ran? How had he survived? What was all that blood?

None of that mattered. I just wanted him to wake up so I could explain everything to him. I could find a way to make him understand why I'd never told him, why I held back. Tell him the whole truth. That I was sorry for everything.

...

Piper was cooking when I found her. She looked natural behind the kitchen counter, like food was her life. And with this many people under one roof, I'd imagine it might be a significant part of it.

"Our boy okay?" she asked as she stirred a sizzling skillet of ground meat. On closer inspection, she was stirring the meat a little too forcefully. Maybe she wasn't as calm as I thought.

"He's resting."

Piper nodded. "I felt it. Last night. Couldn't pinpoint what it was. I didn't want to believe it was a Demon again."

I licked my lips. "We saw it. Rafe said he had encountered a Demon before in the Shifter War."

Piper nodded and turned, wiping her hands on a towel over her shoulder.

"Demons can't exist on this side of the Veil. Their hunger needs a vessel in this realm, and their vessel is their only limitation."

"We also found what I thought might be a portal spell, but Rafe hasn't had a chance to decipher the glyphs yet." God. Rafe hadn't even seen the pictures of the portal spell yet. It had been a very hard few days.

"If it's already here, then it must think that the city has turned already. That it can sustain itself on this side of the Veil."

"What do you mean *turned*?"

"That the city is dark enough for it to survive here, potentially feed enough to not need a host body." Piper shivered. "You get more powerful when your questions get personal."

I hadn't even noticed that I was using my power. I was exhausted and smelled bad and attacking others with my magic from across the room.

I let the smell of cooking meat and pasta fuel my own physical hunger for a moment as my thoughts marinated in spellcraft and blood.

"So what we saw today, was that a part of the demon?"

"Some essence of the Demon, yes. Maybe blood from the original host, or," she sighed. "I just don't know."

"How do Demons possess someone? How does it get inside?"

"There are a few ways I know of. Spells, or blood, or sometimes as simple as a host saying yes, but once they are in, Demons lock onto the missing parts of people, hold on to their emotional scars." Piper stopped stirring the tomato sauce. "Otherwise they can't possess and they can't feed."

Another piece of the story clicked into place. With wholesome, healthy Dot, maybe the Demon spell couldn't touch her. Sigil or not, maybe her innocence protected her somehow and she couldn't be taken, couldn't be a sacrifice to a demon. I sat back in the chair. If Demons got into broken things, I would have been a prime target.

"Why would someone just say yes?" I asked.

"Power, mostly. Once locked in, a demon could make a Wanderer extremely powerful. And a human nearly invincible. Depends on the wound."

My thoughts trailed to Benny. To what I knew of his life, how Cartwright's money and the demon's power would make a lower level snitch more of a force to be reckoned with, but he still didn't deserve to die like that.

After draining the meat and tossing it into the sauce, Piper took a seat at the small table and gestured that I join her. As I sat, the smell of Dutch Babies wafted around me. "What is that? I smell my Grand-Mere's baking when you're around."

Piper nodded. "I am home. I am a safe and welcoming place for those who need it." She leaned back in her seat. "How did you find your way back here?"

I had to think. "I just drove. Rafe was hurt and I needed him to get better and I knew that you could do it. I just threw him in my car and drove."

Piper smiled that wonderfully welcoming smile that was like standing in a pool of sunshine. "You and Rafe both need to remember this is your home. You are safe here and welcomed."

"Is this a Wanderer thing?"

The mirth slowly faded away and this grave gray covered her face. "Do you know who my sister is?" she countered my question softly.

This was going to be a big conversation. I'd used the same skittering horse voice on several people as I guided them through traumatic lines of questioning.

I shook my head. "Turns out it's really hard to Google stuff about Wanderers."

Piper smiled and I got a whiff of cinnamon again. She was trying to keep me calm. Why?

"My little sister, Kenzia. One of the big Seers of our generation. Think psychic who can see the future."

"Okay." I understood that. Psychic was a pretty straightforward thing.

"When I mentioned I met you, and you wandered, she offered to look into *The Book of Names* that records all wanderers when they are born and their breed potential."

A stone formed in my stomach and sat heavy on my insides. "So you found out what I am?" The words squeaked out.

Piper nodded. "Lilin. Only one-sixteenth, which would explain why you only have the one ability and why other Wanderers don't pick up on your power."

I didn't remember that breed from the book. I mean, I'd been focused on Warlocks and Demons and Shifters, but not Lilin.

"What's a Lilin?"

Piper adjusted in her chair, move the towel to the other shoulder, classic sleight of hand to draw one's attention away from the truth. "You know how Demons need a physical host to be on this plane?"

I nodded.

"Well, sometimes when a Demon host and a human are intimate, a Lilin is born."

The truth echoed through me like a gong and it rattled my teeth. "I'm a Demon?"

"Demon-spawn doesn't sound much better, but someone in your bloodline at some point had relations with a Demon host and now you have a residual ability."

I thought I was going to be sick. I thought the world couldn't get any worse, but here I was, being hunted down by another Demon? And this gift I had been using this whole time, willingly and gleefully, was a demonic power?

Piper moved away from the table, as I thought she should, now we both knew the truth, and I leaned my head on the gingham tablecloth. I was a Demon. I was no different from the thing I had been fighting, the thing sucking the life out of people. The thing that had killed my best friend and tortured Rafe.

The familiar scent of whiskey traveled across the table and I brought my head up. Piper had poured us both a drink in a short juice glass.

"I know what you're feeling, but I need you to remember something." She leaned down and matched my eyes with her, those golden green eyes that were warm summers and lilac breezes. "It is not the power or the blood that runs through your veins, Merci Lanard. It is how you use it."

I'd never felt such a strong truth before in my life, like she was able to push my power into me to make me feel it.

She leaned back in her chair and lifted the whiskey to her lips, throwing back the shot like a pro. She set the glass on the table and it was the first time I understood this was not Piper's first apocalypse.

"I know Demons. I died by one's hand. You might have some demons of your own, but you are not a Demon."

"Isn't that how they get in though, the weak spots?"

"Yes, but your weakness is that you care too much, you fight too hard to get the truth for others. I'd like to see the Demon who would try to take on Merci Lanard and threaten her city."

I sat back in the chair to match her position. The storm in my head was silent. As if this was the truth it had been waiting to hear for twenty-eight years, something that would explain who I was, and why.

"I know this is a lot, but I'm going to need you to do what you do best," Piper said.

"Get people killed?"

"Find the truth. Rafe and you were tracking down the informant who drew you out the night of Ethan's death. What happened?"

I looked at the amber liquid. The familiar scent called to me, but I didn't want to calm my edge, I wanted to remember everything so I could give her all the information she would need to protect her family. I walked her through it.

"Benny said a man named Cartwright hired him to get Ethan and me out in the open. Cartwright originally wanted revenge on me for exposing his bribes to the Mayor, but after the attack, Benny said it got personal, that Cartwright just wanted me."

She frowned. "Where does the Demon come in?"

"Cartwright is the Demon, or actually, the demon's host. but I don't know why a Demon would want me."

Piper digested the information. "If Cartwright knew you were a Lilin, it would make sense."

"Why?"

"The Demon blood within you would make you the perfect host."

I gulped. "He wants me for a meat suit?"

Despite the calm look on her face, she didn't sugar coat it. "I'm guessing meat suit."

Piper rose again and went back to the stovetop to inspect dinner. I sudden realized that cooking was her coping mechanism. No one needed that much spaghetti at noon.

"What else do you know?" she asked as she salted a pan of boiling water.

I took in a deep breath and focused on what I did know was the truth at this point. I lined the facts up in my head like sugar packets on the table. "There are four dead bodies all marked as a sacrifice. There is a spell of some sort. There is a Demon wearing a man named Cartwright."

"What about Cartwright?" Levi interrupted as he came to stand in the doorway of the kitchen. He was the last person I wanted to talk to about this.

Piper spoke. "Merci is updating me on what she has found so far."

Levi glared down at me and crossed his arm over his chest, waiting for the report. I'd still never get the image of his wolf out of my mind.

"Rafe and I found what I think is a portal spell at one of Cartwright's buildings in Old City."

"Why he would need a building there? They've got his huge outfit on the edge of Grey's Ferry."

"Think he's the Demon type?"

"Would explain why he's always able to outbid us."

I stifled a laugh. Levi wasn't the laughing kind, intentional ornot.

"What?"

Piper rescued me. "It was funny, Levi. You made a joke."

Levi put his hands on his hips, then scratched behind his ear.

Piper got up and went back to her cooking, dumped two boxes of pasta into a now boiling pot. "So we have a name?"

"And potentially a location. Benny said they were at Schuylkill and Bainbridge."

"What are we waiting for?" Levi asked Piper. "We have a location. We strike tonight."

Piper turned on him with her steaming wooden spoon between them. "You will do no such thing. We need to know which kind of Demon, how to kill it, and what it really wants before can do anything."

Levi stepped into the kitchen, but something hot passed between them, passed over me as I sat there, trying to be perfectly still in the swirling, silent argument above my head.

"I don't want to hear it, Levi," Piper finally said. "She's one of us, I don't care how, she and Rafe are going to get answers before you go charging in there."

Levi exhaled through his nose, the snort of an angry predator. I half expected him to paw at the ground.

"Listen. If you need to go blow off some steam, I have about ten loads of ironing that need to be done."

Levi took in another deep breath and let it out, the aggression leaving his shoulders. "Forgive me," he said to her.

"We'll talk about it later. Now, you can go or help me with lunch."

Levi seemed to slink out of the kitchen.

Piper took the towel off her shoulder and wiped her hands. "My word, that boy. I don't know how he's made it this long with that fire under his tail."

I snickered. But it faded fast. "He isn't wrong. Cartwright is after me, killing people I know. You could be in great danger."

"Nonsense," she said with a wave of her spoon.

"How can you be so sure?"

She turned to me and smiled. "Because you are going to fix it."

I looked up into her eyes and the Charm, my demonic harpoon, leapt through me trying to connect, but I held it back, pulled the rope back into my soul so that it was just me, Merci Lanard and her years of training asking the questions, getting her answers.

"Once Rafe and I figure out what this guys is, why does Levi think he has to take care of it? Wouldn't you do a better job?"

Piper gulped as she slipped into the chair next to me. Her voice was soft, not like the skittering horse voice from before, but more like the hushed tones that I'd get in Sam's diner.

"My power isn't like yours or Levi's. I'm human. Flesh and blood. Vulnerable to more attacks and spells that you are."

"But I just watched you extract Demon essence from Rafe."

She smiled and drew her nail down a seam in the table. "I am only a vessel for their power. It's not my own. I am not a fighter, Merci. I'm a glass vase."

It made sense. Sort of.

"Don't you think I'd rather live in a big city with a theatre and decent WiFi? Don't you think I'd rather be putting myself in danger instead of my family?" She shook her head, her graying strawberry blonde hair falling over her shoulder. "Seventeen years still hasn't been enough time to heal the schism that The Great War caused. Packs are getting better, the leadership stronger, but I am still their Den Mother. And they still need me alive."

She looked up at me, a light of hope in her eyes. "I can make my people stronger, increase their power, but I can't take part in this fight. You can. You have the will and the gift to figure this out. To keep fighting. And do you know what you really need to solve the mystery?"

"An easy button?"

She only quirked her eyebrow above those wise green eyes that looked a little more fragile in this moment than they had that morning.

I didn't want to. Alone I was safe. Alone was the best place for me to be, but there was still so much I didn't know. "I need Rafe."

She smiled this sort of maternal I-told-you-so smile and went back to stir the pasta.

...

Footsteps drew my attention away from the *Idiots Guide* as I ate my spaghetti. I stared as Emily walked toward me and sat in the chair next to mine.

"They whisper when I'm around," Emily said as she stabbed her spaghetti. "It's like they don't know how to talk to me anymore. I'm that poor widow instead of the pack Shala."

I forced down a forkful of noodles through the shock of her sitting with me. Like old times. Perhaps this was the opportunity to open up with a bit of truth about myself, to ease us into the conversation I so desperately wanted to have, needed to have. RE-BUILDING RAPPORT 101. "Loss breaks off a part of you. The grieving process is you figuring out if you're going to fight to be who you were or be comfortable with who you are now this piece missing."

Emily stared at me like I'd started speaking in tongues.

"I lost my dad when I was young. It changes you. And people stare because they're trying to figure out what you're going to fill that hole with." I set my bowl on the table between us. It was beyond strange talking about this with Emily, but this is what friends did, right? "If we're being honest, I filled the hole with Ethan. He gave me a family I didn't have. Philly gave me something I could fight for so I didn't have to think about how lonely I really was." Am. I wasn't sure about the verb tense on that one. We'd have to see how the day went.

Emily looked down at her bowl. "I'm just angry. I just want to punch someone."

"And I will hold them down for you when we find them. It's okay to be angry. Lord knows I was."

"How long does it last?"

"Until you find something else to lose."

Emily chewed slowly. I usually loved shocking people with the truth, but this was more of a confession that sliced off a hang nail in my soul. Like a stone that just needed to be out in the world so it could be polished and made smooth.

"Guess you've found someone new to fill it."

Did she mean Rafe? I snorted. "It's not what you think."

"Whatever." Emily smiled into her dinner. "He went to your house."

I watched Emily for a moment—the freckles sprinkled across her nose, the hair that stuck out of her ponytail because it really wasn't long enough to go into a ponytail. She wasn't perfect. She was just a woman. A woman who, despite all the love and family going on upstairs, chose to be down here in the damp basement with me.

I opened my mouth to ask a question then shut it again. I needed to work on that. Now that I really knew where the power came from, I needed to be more careful with it. I started again. "Can I ask you a question?"

Emily nodded as she took another bite of spaghetti.

"Did you know Ethan had figured out a way to take pictures of magic?"

Emily took a moment, licking the pasta sauce from her lips before she answered. "About a month before he died. He said someone made it for him. Someone he met on the job."

"Who? Where are they in this fight?"

"I don't know. Guess he even kept secrets from me." A flash of anger flicked across her brown eyes as she stabbed at her food.

"And you gave the lens to me?"

"And I gave it to you." Emily's brown eyes studied my face. "Ethan told me that you wandered. Showed me a picture he'd taken. I almost didn't believe him."

My jaw nearly dropped. "Why not?"

"Because it speaks too much to fate. Our lives are already so predetermined by our breeds. I had a hard time believing a girl who could make people confess their darkest secrets could would grow up to be a news reporter."

"Don't forget that she has to tell the truth herself."

She gaped for a moment. "You can't lie?"

"I can, but it is really not pleasant."

There was one question buzzing around and I kept my eyes to the red leather book in my hands. "Then why not tell me? If he knew I wasn't human and I obviously didn't know, why didn't he give me this book?"

Emily scanned the title. "I think it had something to do with my brother."

"Figures."

"Shifters don't do well with other breeds, hell, sometime we don't even get along amongst ourselves. It's hard enough to deal with the innate magic the Mother has given us. It's one of the reasons Levi keeps Ethan and Rafe on the outside of the pack. They asked questions no one really wanted to answer." She gulped. "*Kept*, why he *kept* Ethan on the outside of the pack. He asked too many questions."

The verb game was one that I knew well, the adjustment from *is* to *was*, so I distracted her for a moment. It was the least I could do.

"Yeah, asking too many questions doesn't exactly garner you friends."

Humor glimmered in Emily's eyes for a moment, but the glimmer faded fast. When the ashen tone covered her face, I knew what she was going to ask. "So we know who killed Ethan?"

"Yes."

"And we know who they are working for."

"Yes."

"So why are you here?" she asked frankly. "Why aren't you beating down a path to his door? Calling in all those favors you have amassed. Why isn't his name on the front page yet?"

I had to smile at that; our two great minds *did* think alike. I repeated Piper's answer, one that had settled within me as new truths I had to live with now. "I want to do all of those things. But that's what got Ethan killed in the first place – rushing in, head down and pen out. I need more information. I've been chasing the symptoms—bribes, decreased gang activity, missing people. I don't need the scoop on this one. I need the solution."

The hair on Emily's skin stood on end and I could see it across the side table between us. "You really have taken up the knife."

I nodded. "I have to. For Ethan."

Emily's eyes flooded with tears immediately and she looked up at the ceiling to keep them from falling down her cheeks.

I took one more moment of bravery. "I know you're grieving and I'm a walking, talking reminder of what happened to Ethan, but I miss you. I miss the stupid texts and ganging up on him. And when this whole demon thing is put to bed, I want us to see if we can be friends again."

Emily ran a knuckle under her eyes to catch the tears. "I'd like that too." Emily smiled. "After you catch this bastard."

"After I catch this bastard."

Emily chuckled, a weight lifted from both our shoulders. "I've got a box of books in the trunk of my car. You and MacWolf can snuggle over them."

I glowered at Emily. "What is it with you and Piper?"

She only smiled. "Must be a sixth sense."

CHAPTER ELEVEN

I was not just sitting in his room, watching him sleep. I'd come up to his room with a book and a bowl of spaghetti because I wasn't sure this group believed in leftovers, though the bowl had gone cold hours ago. He needed his strength. I sat in the chair by his bed and willed him to get better. I needed him walking and talking. Even if talking meant yelling at me. And while I could see with my own eyes his chest rising and falling, I could at least be sure that he was still with me, assuage my fears I'd lose him for good.

I'd been reading through what I could of the books Emily had brought in. Reading his *Idiots Guide* lead me to the current tome that I was wading through. The book was thirty pounds of breed indexes including information on Lilin, a.k.a demon spawn, and it was like reading a horoscope; everything about them seemed to pertain to my life somehow. The compulsions. The drive. The self-destruction when the hunger wasn't met, like drinking too much to make the storm stop. Rafe had said that Demons were hunger, but I wasn't sure what exactly I was craving.

Without knowing the Original Sire, the demon granddaddy, I still didn't know much about my ability, my hunger, just that it was there. Depending on the purity of the blood line and the generations from the original host, there wasn't a gauge that really said how much power a Lilin might have, or even what form it would take. It depended on the person.

It was oddly reassuring to see that magic was a fairly stable concept across breeds and spells. The power was innate, like a battery, which fueled the abilities specific to each breed, and the practitioner's will drove it all. Piper's confession came into crisper view. She'd said she was a human with power, which meant she lacked a vital part of the equation, the ability of a breed. She was more like a battery to fuel the others connected to her.

From what I could gather, Rafe had all three. Power from his Legacy, Ability from his breed, and a will that was strong and open. A will to protect others which had landed him in the bed before me.

As if summoned by the smell of book dust, Rafe moaned, and I sat up straight in my chair. He strained, struggled against something invisible. His wide blue eyes popped open and darted around the room, his gaze slamming into me like a lead weight.

A dark shadow crossed his brow. "What the hell happened?"

I slowly closed the book on my lap and stuck to the facts. He couldn't be mad at the facts. "I found you on my back porch. Brought you to Piper. She..." Now wasn't the time to sugarcoat anything either. "She extracted Demon essence from you."

Rafe slowly sat up, the blanket falling from his bare chest where the bruises were in the healing shade of purple. He looked down at his hands, his scabbed knuckles, studying them. He ran his fingers up the inside of his forearms as if trying to read the marks like Braille. "Who cleaned me up?"

"I fixed up Ethan a few times, so I knew what to do, what precautions to take." I leaned forward. "Do you remember what happened?"

"Why don't you just glamour me and find out?"

No need to ask if he was still pissed. Check. "For the record, you might actually be the only person in Philly who hasn't been under the Lanard Charm."

I got up from the chair, setting the large book at my feet, and went to get him the bottle of water and pain pills that had been waiting for him. "And it's not a glamour. That's what fairies do apparently."

I handed him the pills and the water. "I thought I was just a hotshot reporter, turns out I was more of a one-trick pony."

He glared up at me and I was surprised he could even get the pills down with the way his jaw was clenched. He gulped down half the bottle of water and handed it back.

"Will you please tell me what happened last night?" I set the bottle on the nightstand next to the cold bowl of spaghetti and lowered myself back into the chair, gazing at him intently.

He finally looked away from me and at the blanket before him. I watched the tension roll across his freckled shoulders as he remembered. "I remembered the Lux Stelen spell and the lights disappearing."

"That's what happened the night in the store. The lights just vanished."

His gaze only flicked up to me, then back to the bed. "I fought them and then there were these big steel traps and a cage, and I don't know what happened." He clenched his fists, then put his face in his shaking hands. "I just don't know."

I took in the state of him. Underneath his steely exterior, he was terrified. Confused. If he was taken, maybe they tortured him like they tortured Benny. I hadn't seen any carved marks on him, and I'd gotten a fairly comprehensive look at his body, but whatever they had done to Benny was enough to make him want to die. If a wolf saw a steel trap and a cage, what did poor Benny see?

"What is it?" he asked sharply.

I shook my head and looked away.

"God dammit, Merci," he yelled. "Stop lying to me."

I slammed my hands on the arms of the chair. "Fine. You want the truth? I think they tortured you with the same thing they used on Benny. Those are textbook needle marks, and a lot of needle marks means a lot of drugs, or in your case, demon essence. It could have made you hallucinate, which explains why you remember steel cages."

He stared at me. "And being lost in the shift."

A kind of fear I had never seen before crossed Rafe's face and it tore through my chest, made me think that maybe the truth did hurt more than it helped. His face twisted as he turned away from me.

"And I was scared out of my mind because I didn't know enough about magic to be sure it couldn't take you like it took Benny. So I motored it here as fast as I could."

He lifted his arm to run his fingers through his mane of hair but winced and held his mottled side. "How could you even hesitate to tell me what you are?"

The truth was pulled up through my mouth like steel wool on a string. "It scares the hell out of me. First, a new magical world to process, then an ability, and now knowing I'm connected to something so big the city's soul might hang in the balance. It's enough to blow anyone's mind. Forgive me for needing time to process. Not all of us were born knowing this stuff. "

His oceanic gaze drew up to mine and I felt a twinge that had nothing to do with the Charm. "Merci Lanard never runs scared."

"I'm not running now. I've always known the darkness was there, but I've faced it alone."

"You had Ethan."

I exhaled the truth. "And look what happened to him. To Dot. To Benny."

Rafe slowly swung his legs over the edge of the bed and I think it was then he realized he was naked underneath the navy blue comforter. He pulled it across his lap and leaned forward on his knees.

"Look what happened to you when you tried to protect me."

I could feel the heat radiating off his bare chest, like standing in front of an oven. I didn't want to admit that feeling his energy, his power around me again, gave me hope that maybe we could eventually get back to that journalist and professor tag team.

The storm in my head was quiet, I was warm, as his heat flowed around us. But he was injured and I needed him better. I needed Rafe at full strength.

I pushed myself up from the chair and grabbed his bowl of spaghetti. "I'll go warm this up for you."

"So you *do* cook?"

It was only a moment of levity, but it brightened my suddenly darker world. "Brush your teeth. Put on some pants. Meet me downstairs."

Rafe leaned against the doorframe. He'd managed a tee shirt and a pair of lounge pants.

"It's still in the microwave."

He shuffled into the space and pulled out a fork from a drawer, then the steaming bowl of noodles from the microwave.

I stayed out of his way and sat on the far counter by the window as he spun a huge fork-full of noodle and devoured half the bowl in one bite.

"You know your way around this place pretty well."

I waited while he chewed. "I spend a lot of weekends here."

"Why?"

Rafe only stuffed his mouth with another huge bite. His eyes fluttered closed as he relished the homecooked meal. His energy emanated from him and slipped around me like a warm, welcomed blanket.

"What were you researching?" he asked after he swallowed.

"Don't you want to wait to talk shop until after the spaghetti?"

He took another huge bite, polishing off the bowl. He set it in the sink and licked his lips. "I'm a day behind, and there is a deadline, literally speaking."

I sighed. I didn't want to get started on it. I didn't want to get my brain back on the murdering Demon who was after my head. But Rafe was willing to talk to me, which felt like a good first step.

"Piper wants us to look into different kinds of Demons to crack which is possessing Cartwright."

"Look at you, all fighting with the big lads."

"I'm just a—"

He was standing before me in the blink of an eye. He was so close, he nearly wedged himself between my knees. "No. You are in this, you are the one who can take them down. You can't deny that anymore, Merci."

I frowned. "What are you talking about?"

He reached out and grabbed my arm and pulled it into the moonlight streaming through the kitchen window. His hot fingers crawled up my arm as his thumb caressed the inside of my forearm where the white streak gleamed.

I studied the deep line. I'd never really looked at it, never wanted to look at it, never really even wanted to acknowledge its existence. But it had healed to be part of me now. This had started it all and I was going to end it.

Rafe looked down at the wound. "I have made it a point to know about evil, in all its forms. If they were after you because you pissed someone off, then they must have discovered something in your blood. Something different from the rest of us, Merci. It makes you a—"

"Lilin." The truth sprang out of my mouth like a jack-in-the-box.

Rafe dropped my arm and stepped away, his eyes wide in disbelief.

The truth was out now, no need in keeping the rest of the story from him. "Piper told me while you were resting. One-sixteenth Lilin."

He leaned against the counter and turned his gaze to the sink and the moonlit window. He distracted himself by getting a small glass of water and gulping that down.

I could feel my face, my body cool down now that he'd pulled away, and it made something flutter in my stomach, anxiously awaiting what he would ask, what he would say, or how fast he would run.

Even though he kept his gaze from mine, I could feel his tension, but was it anger or fear? I was growing more aware of what state his inner wolf was in. Maybe I was getting a little too used to being around his energy. Accustomed to the way he radiated all the time.

"Ethan pegged me."

"No ordinary human could be as fearless as you."

He finally looked up and there was a hint of a smile in the very corner of his eyes, but something else was keeping him from actually revealing his mirth.

"All I got was the Charm and the penchant for self-destruction. I don't have power like you guys do, or at least not enough anyone can detect. But apparently, it makes me a great target for a demon."

I was waiting for him to get angry, for him to tell me a Lilin shouldn't be here, that Demons should be burned at the stake like they'd burned so many others.

But he wasn't running. He was looking at me with this expression I couldn't read. "How does it actually work, your Charm? You mentioned a storm."

I had the words now to tell him what had been happening since I was a teen. Though I described to Ethan what I thought it was, some obsessive compulsive behaviors, the books and Piper had given me language and a context to understand what was actually going on in my brain. More importantly, I wanted to tell him. I wanted him to know everything.

"Something will happen, like a question or adrenaline, and the magic swarms in my head, like a thunderstorm. Then I have to look someone in the eye, focus the storm, and lock into them. Then I ask them a question and I pull the truth from them. I've been using it my whole life and never even knew it was magic."

"And that is everything?"

"That's all I know as of this moment."

His hands tightened around the edge of the counter. He seemed to be formulating something, working his own words around into the right order. I only hoped it wasn't another argument.

"When the Great Shifter War happened, I was on Jovan's side."

"What?" I questioned reactively, immediately putting my hands over my mouth; I didn't want the Charm to get in the way of his truth.

"When the call to arms went out, my pack and I were on his side, not Piper's. Jovan didn't just call all the Shifters, he'd been recruiting for months. He came to me and I said yes. I've been possessed by a Demon before. Voluntarily. Knew exactly what was happening the whole time."

I slipped off the edge of the counter and shrank the space between us. I knew about the Great Shifter War, but I hadn't expected this. Rafe was so kind all the time, so gentle, so funny and considerate. I couldn't believe that he was evil. But I did remember something that Piper had told me, that a person with something broken, something scarred, could easily be controlled.

I wondered what Rafe's something was. He had never mentioned his life much before Philadelphia, never gone into details about Scotland. But then again, I hadn't offered many details either. But I knew the truth of it in my gut. And I was possibly the only person who could prove that to him.

I would know a lie if I heard one and I was willing to risk him seeing me as a monster to help him understand what I had always known.

"Are you under his control now?"

"No," Rafe said quickly.

"Have you been at any point since the day that Piper saved you?"

"No."

"Do you want to be under his control?"

"No."

"Then why are you worried about it? According to the *Guide*, half of the Shifters on the planet were under Jovan's control."

Rafe turned away. "Because I was supposed to be strong. I was Primo and I should have been stronger than that. It was my responsibility to keep my pack safe, but I was weak and they all suffered."

"The book said no blood was shed that day."

"No one was hurt, but because of me, my whole pack fell to him like dominos. They will carry that stain with them for the rest of their lives."

"So afterwards you stayed here as penance?"

"I figured if I was that weak once, then maybe I should be here, close to the Den Mother, to keep me out of trouble. My pack chose a new Primo and went back home. I haven't spoken to them since."

"So why does Levi hate you? You did the right thing for your pack."

"Piper is the only one who knows the whole story. Levi thinks I stayed because I wanted to control this pack. He's always been jealous of Piper's attention toward me."

I watched him stare out the window at the moon for a good while. I had to know. Had to know if the Demon still had a way to control him again, not just for me this time, but for the whole pack, once and for all. "What gave him a way in?"

"Pride," he said, still looking out the window, his arms crossed over his chest. "I was young, twenty-two and barely had enough power to be Primo." He turned back to me and leaned against the counter. "He offered me enough to be the strongest Primo in Britain, to take over the other packs even."

"But you're good now. You just said so to a human lie detector."

His jaw dropped for a moment and then he closed it. He watched me and I didn't even dream of trying to figure out what he was thinking. He would tell me if he wanted and I would be patient for that. Patient for the first time in my life.

He was good now, had been fighting the good fight for seventeen years. But now I was here. This Demon in sheep's clothing. His darkest secret was that he fell victim to a Demon, and one was standing right in front of him. He wasn't safe with me. No one was.

"I need to sleep." I winced at the bitterness that flooded my senses from my own deception.

He frowned. "No, you're running. What did I say?"

I had to look away from him because the answer was on the very tip of my tongue.

He grabbed my arm and took my chin, forcing our eyes to one another's. His words were low yet piercing between us. "This might be the one time in your life where someone will understand the truth about what you are and will never judge you."

My pounding heart kicked the confession out of my mouth. "I saw the Demon speak through Benny, be inside his head and control him. And I knew exactly what that felt like because I'd been there moments earlier, compelling him. It puts me in league with a Demon, Rafe. A Demon who is feeding and corrupting and killing its way across the city."

"But, Merci, it's not the ability, it's how you use it."

I pulled my face out of his grasp. "You all keep saying that. But it's not, is it? This isn't an ability. This is me, this is who I am. My job, my drinking, the hunger for truth. This is who I have always been."

He didn't seem to have anything to say to that.

I straightened my shirt, pulling the knit sleeves down over my hands, hiding the scar and the memory of his fingers. "You have fought your one temptation and built a life for yourself. But me? I will use the demonic ability every time, no matter how much it hurts me, no matter how much chaos it causes, because it's who I am."

I pulled away from him and took a few steps toward the door. "Get some rest, Rafe. You'll need it for tomorrow."

I was almost out the door, was almost free of the weight in his gaze.

"Don't you want to know why I got angry with you?"

My feet stopped moving. I willed them to go, to flee, but they seemed to want to hear his answer. I turned around but remained in the doorframe. "I lied to you."

"Well, yes. I mean, I had told you everything about our world and then I find out about this huge secret. So yes, I was pissed. But it wasn't like I had told you everything either. I don't run from anger, Merci. I deal with it. It's part of the package."

I looked up at him and our eyes locked.

"I ran because I was scared. Classic animal instinct."

"Of me?"

"Of the fact there was nothing keeping me from getting what I wanted."

I gasped, catching the last bit of oxygen as it left the room. Rafe crossed the kitchen as he spoke, a slow stalking as he joined me in the doorframe. "When you were Ethan's human partner, I could do what I wanted, be open with you, and didn't matter what I felt because I couldn't do anything about it. You were human, and I can't be with a human."

He ran his fingers up my arm and his hand rested at the base of my neck. "But when you weren't, when you were one of us, you suddenly became a freedom that I haven't let myself imagine in a very long time."

My cheeks burned and a different sort of sizzling covered my skin, another sort of magic I hadn't experienced in years.

"I'm surprised you haven't asked the one question I was sure you would."

The moment our eyes locked, the question was pulled from my tongue. "Why did your wolf find me and not Piper?"

Everything about him softened. "There's my brilliant journalist. Ask me with the Charm."

I couldn't fight it. It was like ringing a doorbell in a house full of dogs. It was summoned, and even with his heat around me, I still knew when the magic settled in. I didn't flinch when the chill ran down my spine, when the Charm gathered up inside my head. I had to tread water for a moment in his blue eyes before I found the spot and dived in. Our connection wasn't static but more of a smooth rope tethering us together.

I licked my lips. "Why did your wolf find me?"

His eyes watered, and I knew he felt the Charm this time, had opened himself up to the truth as well. He was going to face it, head on, and not look away.

He smiled as he answered. "Because you have become my home, Merci. Where I feel safe and welcomed."

Rafe leaned forward and I kissed him. His lips were soft but firm, and it was obvious he knew what he wanted too. My knees went weak when he lowered his shields, bathing me in his scent, the feeling of his warm fur again my neck, the taste of him in my mouth.

He wrapped his arm around my waist to hold me and turned us to press against the doorframe, bracing me with his solid body, keeping me close and upright. He brought the other hand up to my face, to curl around my jaw, to kiss me deeper.

I wrapped my arms around his middle, ran my hand around those wonderfully wide shoulders. I wanted to lose myself in that warmth, where the questions stopped and there was only blissful silence.

He hissed and pulled away, leaving me wanting in midair. We were both panting, skin hot. Rafe looked at me in the moonlight with those sparkling blue eyes, his cheeks flushed.

"What's wrong?" I pulled my hands away from him.

"Even Primos need time to heal."

He nestled his face against mine. Our chests pressed against one another as he kept me pinned to the frame of the door. His body felt delicious, the long line of his muscles, his strength. And knowing exactly what was underneath the tee shirt didn't take away from the heat of the moment.

It was freeing. A wave of emotion hit me hard. Safe. I felt safe for the first time in a long time. I was relaxed for the first time in a long time. Like I had someone to share everything with. I felt lighter.

"That was really nice." His breath caressed my neck, and my skin tingled behind my right ear.

"I was afraid I'd be rusty."

He smiled. I could feel it on my cheek, in the shift of his chest muscles as he slid his hand down into mine, our fingers entwining. I'd studied his hands, but I couldn't imagine how perfectly they would fit into my own.

It was that exact moment I knew I was sunk. I knew there was no avoiding this truth now. He had his own wounds and he knew everything, my truth, my heritage, my issues, and yet he was still standing here, weathering the storm.

"I think we should get you to bed, Professor MacCallan. We have a long day of book reading ahead of us."

I'd never seen an eyebrow arch quite as high as his did as he asked, "Will you be staying with me?"

I shook my head. "You're injured, and I need my sidekick back to one hundred percent."

I pulled him toward the stairs with our joined hands.

"Sidekick?"

"Fine. Partner."

He stopped walking across the living room and turned me toward him. "Is it really partner, Merci? Not to sound needy, but for all I know, you just have a soft spot for wolves."

He did have a point. I exhaled and looked as deeply as I could into those eyes, nearly pulled myself into them so he could feel the truth behind my words with me. "You, Rafe MacCallan, are the first person I have ever wanted to tell the whole truth to."

Rafe nodded and tucked a strand of hair behind my ears.

"Were you expecting a sonnet? Shall I quote you some pentameter?"

He leaned in to kiss me again, curling his hand into my hair. I memorized everything. The way he smelled of musk and tomato sauce. The way his beard tickled my chin. How he was so thorough when he kissed that every part of my mouth felt sated before he pulled away.

"Leave the Shakespeare to me."

...

They'd left the Ping-Pong table to us and frankly the entire entertainment room, like pictures of dead bodies and magical textbooks weren't the most normal sight first thing in the morning. The children were back in school, most of the others were at work, but I knew that Emily was still pacing the upstairs bedroom and Piper was cleaning up from the seven-course breakfast that she had fixed everyone.

Rafe and I spread out everything I had on the bodies, the buildings, the books.

"You were busy in the one day I was gone." He pointed to the map of the city, highlighted with the Cartwright holdings according to the information that St. Greta had given me. I'd circled the one that Benny had specifically named and the one where we'd found the spell.

"I have a singular focus when I'm on the hunt."

He came around the table and stood next to me. "So I've realized that the warehouse you took pictures of is perfectly aligned on a leyline that cuts across Philadelphia."

"A leyline?" I asked.

"Err ... like an electric current though the landscape, only magical. And you can plug into them to strengthen your spells. Several of the buildings are along this line. Probably why they look so randomly dispersed."

I shuffled the Ultraviolet exposures of the warehouse to the top of the pile and pointed to the scratched sigils in a circle. "And the symbols on the walls?"

He trailed the outside circle, the white ring of exposed sigils scratched into the energy of the space. "Most definitely a portal spell."

"So Demon *is* already here in Cartwright."

"But we can't track it, stop it, or kill it unless we know which kind of Demon. There are as many kinds of Demons as there are hungers."

It was the first time I thought about killing something, that all this research was leading to an execution. My stories had gotten people thrown into jail, run bankrupt, but never dead by my hand. I looked up to Rafe. Had he killed before? He spoke about it with such resolve. "And you think we can kill it?"

He looked back up at me. "Well, yes. How else do you suppose we stop it?"

I licked my lips. "I ... It's just not what I usually think when I think of justice."

Rafe pointed to the pictures on the table. "There isn't a prison for things that do this, Merci. There isn't a rehabilitation program for them. There is only one way to stop something that is all hunger."

I'd been thinking of this as something with a deadline. I'd file the story and that would be it, but this was bigger. More final than just seeing my name on a byline. This was the solution that I told Emily I'd fight to find. This was the knife that I had taken up.

"Stop," Rafe said simply.

I looked up at him. "What?"

Concern was written across his wrinkled brow. "Where ever your head is right now, just stop. This is not about you and your Legacy. This is about Ethan."

"But—"

"No, Merci. I won't have it."

"Right." I turned back to the work and focused on the dead bodies, a welcomed distraction. I had plenty of time to figure it out. And I would, with Rafe right beside me. One story at a time. "Could sucking people dry be an MO? Maybe it's just thirsty?" I asked.

He smiled softly. "It doesn't work that way. And for all we know, the super-dried bodies are a result of the sacrifice mark, not the Demon's hunger."

I sighed. We had nearly all the puzzle pieces. We had the who, what, and where, but it was the whys that scared me. Why did the Demon want Philadelphia? What was it thinking it could do here? What did we possibly have here that other big cities didn't have? New York had drugs and gangs, what hunger could it be following to my doorstep?

"What are you thinking about?"

"Why Philadelphia? What's a special about The City of Brotherly Love?"

"Well, I have read that Demons are creatures of habit. When they find a steady source of food, they tend to come back over and over and over."

It was like I'd stuck my finger in an electrical socket and the Charm was static and sizzle around me, making connections, making my brain work that much faster than before. "Philadelphia is one of the oldest cities in the country. What if the Demon likes it here because it's always been inhabited?"

He frowned. "I think I just said that."

"But what if it had always gone to the same family like each time it tried to come back. Like it would stay with a family?"

"What do you mean?"

"What I mean is, if this Demon likes the Cartwrights now, maybe he has use them as hosts before?"

"Familial hosts would make sense."

The Charm flared before the question even hit my lips. It wasn't even a question yet, but more of a need to know. If this generation of Cartwrights was into bribery and in bed with a Demon and the last generation of Cartwrights was into bribery and possibly also in bed with a Demon and the generation before that and the generation before that.

I got up, closed my laptop, and unplugged it from the wall. The Internet was horrible out in the country. I needed the newspaper database and Piper was right, this dial-up just wasn't delivering.

Rafe rose as fast as he could, broken ribs and all. "Wait."

I pushed the laptop in my bag. "The Demon might have tried to come through before. I can search for another rash of bodies through the archives."

"Hold on."

I was already in the doorway as I glanced back to Rafe. He was still in pajamas.

"I have to go, Rafe. I'm burning daylight."

"Is this how it works? Is your power always so tangential?"

I stopped. Less than a month and he understood me. It had taken Ethan nearly a year to realize what happened when a question took hold, how deeply it was rooted. "You don't want to see me when I'm not allowed to chase a story. It's not pretty."

"I'll go with you." He started gathering up the books and the maps.

"You're still under lockdown."

"You need a partner." He chuckled after he realized what he said. "You need someone with you. Piper's orders go for you too now."

I had to smile. "Aren't we cute with our little partner thing?"

Rafe wasn't smiling when he looked back up at me. "Give me ten minutes with Piper, and I will meet you outside."

"Ten minutes."

...

After I unlocked the door to my place, we fell into a strange pattern. He put his books on the dining room table and went into the kitchen to make a pot of coffee. I dropped my bag into a chair and went to take a shower.

When I came out, I was ready. Relaxed. Focused. Ready to ask the question again.

"Has the Demon tried to come through before?"

I shivered as the Charm covered my skin and sank in to help me do my work. It really was like a hit of Ritalin some days, like life through a magnifying glass, focused and clear. I knew exactly where I needed to start looking first. My friend, county records.

Rafe and I sat across from each other as we searched. I clicked and he flipped and we would sort of bounce an idea off the other and then go back to work. It was a familiar process.

After an hour, I pushed back from my computer screen and rubbed my eyes.

"Something wrong?"

I ran my fingers through my hair. "Do you know how many serial murders there have been in Philly? Like, a million. I've got stranglers, and stabbers, and smotherers, oh my."

I rested my head on my hands and closed my eyes. "The Cartwright family goes back to the founding of the city with fingers in everything: construction, railroad, politics. There are probably hundreds with the same blood but different surnames across the metroplex and we don't have enough time to make a family tree."

Rafe sipped his coffee. "So no pattern to help determine the kind of Demon?"

I looked at my gruesome notes. "There are no other news articles in the archives that link Cartwrights to dead bodies."

The moment I said it, I knew. Like a gong had been struck and my entire body vibrate with the truth. The answers wouldn't be in the archives if the story never got published. But I knew who had been investigating the Cartwrights thirteen years ago. And I knew where he kept his notes.

I needed my father's last journal.

I was in the bedroom before I knew it, staring down at the old trunk, breathing in that whiskey and pipe smell from the leather. I knelt down and opened it up. My hand paused over the last book. Spring 2005. The last story Dad had worked on. The last story he'd been hunting before he died.

Rafe had followed me upstairs. His reassuring heat pressed at my back. Urging me forward. "What are you doing?"

I rocked back and sat on my heels. "My dad was a journalist. Did you know that?"

"You don't talk about yourself much."

"Welcome to my biggest flaw."

I cocked my head. The questions were beginning to swirl again, the hum of the hive filled my ears. "He died when I was in high school. Right about the time my Charm kicked in."

Rafe furrowed and knelt beside me. "Your father never said anything about it?"

I shook my head. "We never talked about it."

"Would you like to tell me what happened?" He curled his hand into mine.

It was so strange. Just putting my hand in his calmed the butterflies that would have prevented me from thinking about Dad, prevented me from thinking about myself at all and made me focus someone else's problems. But with him there, I could finally face this one truth.

"He was working at all hours. He and mom got in this huge fight that night. I snuck out the window and went to a friend's house. Back when I still had friends. When I got home, the police were already there. He'd gotten hit by a train at a station. They said alcohol was involved."

"Could he have been drunk?"

"No. Alcohol is part of the thing, the job, the Charm. He drank because it's the only thing that stops the questions, but I never saw him drunk."

The Charm flared before the question even hit my lips. I needed to find out. It burned through me. "He'd been investigating the Cartwrights for bribes twenty years before I nailed them for it."

"Talk about a legacy," Rafe said.

I looked at the trunk again. I could do this.

Why had he been at the train station that night?

Rafe rose to hover in the doorway of my closet with a cup of coffee. "You need any help?"

"To fuel my delusion that I'm going to find the key to the history of the city in my closet? No, Mr. Tumnus. Go research spells."

He set the coffee down on the dresser just outside the door and then left. A man who respected my process. And a man I was quickly realizing might finally be enough to handle the hailstorm named Merci Lanard.

I reached in to slide out the last notebook, Spring 2005. I needed the last story, what hadn't been published. The last few days before he was found at the train station.

Starting at page one, I skimmed through his notes and my eyes landed on the name that confirmed my fears.

"Cartwright," I muttered.

Bingo. Dad had been investigating a series of fatalities associated with Cartwright Construction. But the end of the story never came, he'd never written an intro paragraph for it.

He'd been investigating the same story I had been. Following missing people and missing money, but twenty years ago it all seemed to revolve around train tracks instead of city hall. I sat in the middle of my closet and read through his notes slowly, trying to use everything I knew about him, his death, and our power, to fill in the blanks.

One side of his notes was dedicated to figures and truck designations and the other contained lists of dead bodies, like he was chasing two stories at once. The dead bodies were warehouse attendants, sex workers in the area, and a construction owner's son—all found in different holdings across the city. As I flipped through the pages, iron seemed to be the common factor in his story, the link that connected all his missing pieces. Triple orders of iron coming into the city and it was all being stored at a warehouse. At a warehouse that, thirteen years later, would be covered in Old Speak and serve as the location to pull a Demon across dimensions and into the heart of the city.

I zipped downstairs with my coffee and my journal, nearly spilling one on the other.

"Is iron special in the magical world?" I asked Rafe, breathless.

Rafe laughed at my entrance. "It has several magical properties. It's elemental, so it's easy to enchant, and it's wicked strong for fairy magic. Why?"

"While investigating missing people, Dad discovered the Cartwrights had been using iron to construct train tracks and bribing inspectors to ignore it."

Rafe exhaled. "Train tracks are usually made out of steel."

"What would happen if they were made out of iron?"

I knew it, when the idea hit him. I didn't know why. That wasn't part of my power. So it had to be part of the strange us-ness that had settled in between.

"The city would be crisscrossed by iron tracks, by a mode of magic." Rafe's nibble fingers were typing away at my laptop. He pulled up a map of the city. "What's at Jefferson Station?" he asked.

Ice covered my skin as I looked up at him. I gulped. "That's where they found him. It was Market East then."

He ran his fingers through his hair, his thick mane sticking up in shock.

"If they were replacing iron for the steel tracks, Jefferson Station would have been the epicenter. It would have been a perfect place to conduct magic."

It was all fitting together too perfectly. Except for one question. "Did Dad know it was magic?"

"Is there nothing about it in his notes?"

To me they were my dad's notes, the books he always had on him, the books he used to flip through over the dinner table, scribble in during every phone call. I knew I wasn't looking at this as a reporter, I was looking at it as a daughter.

It took everything I had to hand the Moleskine to Rafe. If it contained any hint of magic, he could read it better than I could. Find magic where I only saw memories.

He crossed the room and sat next to me before taking the notebook and scanning through the notes. I could tell he was just about to say something as he flipped through the pages when storm clouds covered his face. His eyes lighted on something that had him across the room by the time I caught the journal, which he'd tossed back to me.

"What?" I asked.

He didn't answer, only flipped furiously through the biggest and most dangerous looking book on my kitchen table.

I looked down at my Dad's journal and flipped the worn pages back open, remembering the scent I had always associated with reporters and the newsroom, to find what Rafe had possibly seen.

Dad had made a drawing, with four names and numbers and then sketched lines between the names. A web of dead bodies creating something that resembled the design on the back of a black widow spider, an angled infinity rune across the train tracks of Philly. Four corners and a big X in the center.

Everything slowed down as I looked at the drawing and substituted the names of our dead bodies. John Mitchell, Tay-Tay, Beakman, and Benny. The four boroughs in four different corners of Philly.

The Demon was doing this all over again. And, if Dad's drawing was to be believed, he only needed one more sacrifice.

But beyond that, did my father know it was a Demon, or was he just trying to see the pattern of it? Had he known about this whole world and never once told me about any of it?

The Charm sizzled down my spine as my anger flared.

I searched to see if my dad had known it was a Demon, looked for sigils or weird names or anything in those square boxes that clearly stated "Magic was real", but there were no additional names, just the drawing of the bodies and the initials JR next to a phone number so old it didn't have an area code.

"It's called a Gia'r DLoom."

My skin tightened and tingled when I heard Rafe's voice pronounce the Old Speak.

"I should have looked earlier. This Demon likes his magic ancient, like the Lux Stelen, the light stealing spell."

He slammed his hand down on the volume, loosing dust and who knew what else all over my kitchen table.

"Fairies use it to protect their homes from evil magic. You plant stones charged with your energy around your home so the ground has a piece of you in it, and then charge a center stone under your house to activate and fuel the spell. Like an electric fence to keep the bad guys out.

"This Demon is twisting the ritual. He's setting up death spots, using the sacrifice sigil to create spots devoid of any energy at all strategically located around the city."

"What would that do?"

Rafe exhaled and ran both hands through his hair. "Well, once he activates the center of the spell, it would create a lock on the city. Instead of keeping bad energies away, it would draw good energies to him."

"You mean like suck the life out of everyone?"

Rafe nodded slowly. "Every human here would be his. He could feed at will."

And he wanted to do that in my body? Kill all those people wearing my face.

I'd stopped breathing and had to suck in a gasp of air. The oxygen hit my brain and the Charm seemed to explode into a million pieces before drifting down around me like dandelion seeds.

"Your dad was probably trying to stop the Cartwrights from completing the last step of whatever their plan was the night he died. And since nothing ever happened, he must have succeeded."

Too many emotions were running rampant. Too many feelings, unnamed and untamed. I hated that he hadn't told me any of this—that he'd left me alone. I was scared that they were still out there. But a sense of pride was also welling up in me that my dad, the jerk reporter, was in fact a hero and not just in the eyes of his little girl.

Rafe joined me on the couch and took my hand.

That's when the real pain hit. "If I really am a Legacy, then he was doubly as powerful as me. How the hell am I going to find this thing that has infected the city when it took him down?"

Rafe stood and pulled me to my feet. "You're going to start by not saying things like that."

He grabbed my chin and forced our eyes to lock. The Charm sizzled to life and connected us.

"You are strong—and not because of what you are, but because of who you are."

And I knew he believed it to be true, believed it so readily despite what he had heard and seen. It scared me to death.

"But I don't know who I am."

That was the last straw. The pressure of it all pushed on my chest, and it was hard to breathe. I needed more open space. I pushed myself away from him and leapt from the couch to pace. Halfway through a lap, I leaned over the back of the couch and tried to draw in a full lungful of air, but I could only manage shallow ones. My vision tunneled to the coffee table and the stacks of magical texts strewn everywhere. I was drowning in a sudden floodgate of answers, in the truths that swam around and didn't let the air in.

My father had died saving the city from a Demon who threatened to possess it.

A Demon who now wanted me to finish his plan.

Going back to the couch, I dropped my head between my knees and assumed the position. Contrary to what airlines say, this is neither a calming nor comfortable way to panic.

"Is this you freaking out?" Rafe asked.

"Yes, this is me freaking out. I think I'm allowed. I was nearly killed. My entire life has been a lie, which is hilarious if you really think about it. The one person I trusted with almost everything turned out to be the one person hiding the most from me. And I got him killed. Now his brother and I are hunting down a Demon who wants to kill me and then there's the whole Dad thing—"

In little more than the blink of an eye, Rafe was beside me. He swept me up into his arms and his lips were on mine faster than I could blink. As his wolf surrounded me, my stomach flipped over on itself as he leaned me against the back of the couch. I ran my fingers through his hair and let him take my lips, let him suckle them softly as he ran his hand along my jaw and tightened his arm around my waist. My heart stopped racing and the questions faded to gray as I inhaled his scent.

When my pulse beat normally and I was able to breathe again, Rafe pulled away. His lips were pink and his eyes were the bluest I had seen them since his shift.

"How do you do that?" I exhaled.

"Kiss someone?"

"Make everything stop."

"I was about to ask you the same question."

I sighed and leaned my head against his forehead, closing my eyes.

"Did you really mean that? About not knowing who you are?"

I nodded. "Since Ethan, it seems to be the underlying question of my existence. I really don't know. I never really wanted the answer. Total unexamined life."

Rafe's chuckle echoed in his body, and in his power around us. "You have a razor wit and a love of words that so infuses your being you misquote great literature without thinking. You always put others first, to a fault, and you need evidence to believe anything. You're the daughter of a Lilin and one hell of a reporter. You are Merci Lanard, the girl who always finds the truth."

It was hard to hear, like petting a cat backwards. Hard to believe. One month and he knew me better then I knew myself.

I wanted to pull away from Rafe. This was messy and rough and raw, but I couldn't find a reason to distract myself from it. I wanted more. More of this peace he brought to me, more of this certainty that anchored me to reality. I tilted my head and kissed him. Took those perfect lips with mine and pulled him against me.

I pulled at the edge of his shirt, wanting to feel his soft skin against me. His muscles rippled under my fingertips as he pulled me to him tightly. His excitement grew between us and his embrace grew wild and rough. He twisted his hands into my hair and when my exploration of his body hit a bruise on his side, a growl thrummed between us.

But he didn't stop this time. We both were on the same page, needing the same thing from each other, a moment of respite, a moment of something honest between us. No fate. No destiny. No legacies.

He slid his hand down my thigh and his firm hand cupped my ass. He squeezed then lifted, shifting us backwards on the couch. His body fully against mine, it was a warmth and pressure that called to life parts of me that had long been slave to the Charm, to the work, to the everlasting parade of evil in my life.

But not this, not the taste of him in my mouth, the weight of him against me, the feeling of him ready. There was only good in that.

I reached for the tails of his shirt and pulled upwards, wanting more of his warmth around me, against me. He leaned up and pulled the shirt over his head and I was able to take in his broad shoulders, the expanse of pectorals and the still lingering purple on his ribs.

He dropped his shirt to the ground beside the couch and pulled me up to a sitting position. He skillfully pulled my thermal up and over my head and down my arms in quick movement that left me completely exposed while he studied me with those eyes, pupils blown with contentment.

"You might actually be paler than me."

"I'm a bit of a night owl."

He smiled down at me as he knelt between my legs. Slowly, he reached out and took Ethan's medallion. "I think this is ready to go."

I took his hand and we pulled off the silver chain. As I watched the medallion hit the ground next to my shirt, a brush of his animal surrounded me and covered my bare skin in fur for a moment while my skin goose bumped.

He pulled me closer to him and sat up on his knees and buried his nose behind my ear and drew in a deep breath that brought his chest to mine, skin to skin. Everything tingled, everything sizzled and it had nothing to do with the Charm.

"You smell like roasted marshmallows." His words cascaded down my neck and my nipples hardened on the inside of my thankfully padded bra.

His hand tangled in my hair, and he brought his mouth to mine and kissed me hard, needing. My hand slid up and dug into his shoulders and around his waist, wanting that hot skin against mine. He leaned us back on the couch again, and I could feel his hand work my bra strap down my shoulder and make its way around my back. His lips trailed down my neck, and his teeth grazed my throat.

Pleasure flooded through my body and my vision swam in colors, then lights, reds and blacks, and white streaks.

And then pain. Not from Rafe, god, everything he was doing was heaven and soft and warm.

Another streak of red across my eyelids and then a cold, icicle sharpness stabbed through my chest.

CHAPTER TWELVE

I had the strangest dreams about running and climbing. I rolled over to find the cool side of the pillow and was met with rough rocks. My eyes flew open, and I sat up to find the twinkle of city lights. The roof. I was on a roof in in my jeans and Ethan's medallion danced cold against my bare chest.

I wrapped my arms around my legs and shivered in the frozen night. I scanned the rooftop and found Rafe crouched in a corner. I could see his bright eyes from across the space and his pale skin glowed in the faint moonlight.

"Rafe?"

"Merci?"

"What the hell happened?"

Slowly, he rose. He was only wearing his pants, but his feet were bare on the rocky surface. He paced around the side of the roof, his eyes never leaving me. As he came closer, I could see fresh blood on his cheek and forehead and more bruises up his arms and across his midsection.

"Are you okay?" I asked.

"No. Are you?"

I looked down at my hands. My nails were crusted in blood and my arms were scratched. My mind was blank; I had no memory of how it happened. "I don't know."

He walked carefully toward me, less like a wolf and more like a bird who would fly away at the slightest provocation. He knelt down beside me and carefully reached out, stroking my hands, my cheek.

I waited until I was ready to match his gaze. "What happened, Rafe?"

"You were controlled."

I was going to throw up. I grabbed at my stomach and curled away from him. The silver of Ethan's medallion burned against my bare skin.

"Let's get you home."

My skin was sore where he touched me. Getting back to the fire escape hurt my soft feet and the cold made every step a stabbing pain. He wrapped his arm around me as we walked the block back to my house, covering my more essential parts with my arms.

The door of my place was off its hinges and Rafe had to fight to get it back into place to lock it. I stood shakily on my own and surveyed the living room. It looked like a night after a bender. The picture on the wall was crooked, the couch was on its back, and books were all over the floor.

"Did we fight?"

"We? No," he clarified. "But someone really didn't want me to get in the way."

My stomach churned again, and I ran for the bathroom. I made it just as my stomach contents reversed their resting place. The biscuits and gravy Piper had made from scratch that morning were pretty much the same color the second time around.

I rested my head on the cool porcelain and tried to breathe. Controlled? Like possessed? How the hell had that happened? Possessed by what? The same Demon that sucked all those people dry? Something else? How much about this world didn't I know? And how much of it wanted to kill me?

My head started to spin and my stomach flipped over again, but with nothing to purge. I rested my head on my arm and a cold sweat made my skin sticky.

Rafe haunted the doorway of the bathroom. "I have some clean clothes, but you'll feel more like yourself after a shower."

I moved slowly, treating my stomach like a very full glass of red wine over a white carpet. Still in my jeans, I stepped into the tub and turned on the water. The full pressure of cold stream jolted me awake, made everything sharper. Through the stream of water, I looked at Rafe, who stood watching me carefully.

"Shower. Check."

He shook his head and put the clean clothes on the counter. "Let's get you cleaned up and into bed."

I hurt from my hair follicles to the balls of my feet. Everything. My heart, my head, my body. I was a balloon that had been blown up and then let go to fly recklessly in circles, stretched and shriveled. I closed my eyes and leaned back against the tiles. Even the Charm seemed beaten back for the moment, like I didn't have enough energy to even raise an eyebrow let alone a question.

I heard Rafe move and I was sure it would be to run far away from me. And I'm not sure that I would have blamed him. Instead, I heard the clink of a belt against the tiled floor and the shower warmed up as he slid in next to me and started to unbutton my jeans. My skin goose bumped in surprise, despite the steaming shower.

"Why aren't you running? My living room tells me I kicked your ass."

"I'm used to getting my ass kicked."

I let him pull the jeans off and then leaned against him. I rested my head on his shoulder and he wrapped his arms around me. I didn't know what to say to him. I'd never been here before, never been so lost, so exhausted and yet the only thing I feared was him leaving.

"I'm sorry."

"There's no need to apologize yet."

"Yet?"

"We'll have to see if I scar. You can apologize to me then."

I sighed. "Aren't you afraid it will come back?"

Rafe shook his head. "One thing at a time, love."

A week ago, I would have protested. I was a grown woman. I didn't need to be bathed. I didn't need to be treated like glass. I'd been through hell before and no one had been there to pick up the pieces then. But this was different, this was bigger, darker. Even if I had the energy to work the Charm, I didn't know what questions to ask, where to start.

His thumbs hooked into the waistband of my underwear and he slid them as far down as he could. I shook them from my legs as he took off his boxers.

Everything was so slow, so gentle, like he knew I was wearing my nerve endings on the surface.

He reached for the loofah and soaped it up with my honeysuckle shower gel. Even as he washed me he was slow, careful to draw the soapy ball across my skin, down my arms, in the curve of my hip. He had to scrub a little at my elbows to get some tar or dirt off, but he followed the rough actions with his fingertips, running them over the raw skin to soothe it.

I couldn't do anything as he massaged his strong hands around my body, around my arms, my shoulders, as if he knew exactly where I hurt. He used the bubbles to lubricate his strong hands as they worked at the tension in my lower back and backside.

He paid special attention to my hands, making sure to carefully wash away the dirt, the blood, until they were pink and pristine between us. He brought my palm to his face and softly kissed the roof rash.

My breath caught in my throat at the intimacy. Here we were in the shower together and that's what caught my attention as shockingly intimate. I trusted him. I was entrusting him with every part of me and it was the most intimate thing I'd ever done.

He stepped forward and brought our bodies flush in the water. He ran his hand up my throat and face, then gently pulled my head into the stream to wet my hair. As he worked up the suds in my hair, I felt the muscles in the length of his body, the overall restraint in his being as his fingers massaged my scalp. He was a perfect specimen of man and he was in the shower with me, really with me.

As I leaned back again in to the flow of water, he ran his fingers through my hair to get the soap out. I let the water carry away the pain, the guilt, the pride. Let it run over me, over us, and circle down the drain with the rest of the dirt.

Rafe ran his hand down my neck, my chest, and came around my waist to turn me around, toward the spray. He reached around me and pulled my toothbrush from the holder and laid on a stripe of the fresh mint.

He handed me the toothbrush. "I do have my limits."

I nodded and I started to brush my teeth. It was only then that I became painfully aware of our nakedness and I tried to shift away from him.

"No, you don't." He grabbed my hips and pulled me against him again.

His body fit around mine like two pieces of a puzzle, the curve of my back and shoulders pressing against his chest, his arms looping around my waist, his hip bone pressing into the fleshy part at my own hip.

"This is weird."

"That you are taking a shower after having been blood controlled or that you're brushing your teeth," he said, his lips brushing my ear.

I chewed on the brush for a moment. He was something else. I leaned my face into the spray to rinse out my mouth. "Weird that I've never brushed my teeth in front of anyone before."

"So a lot of firsts for today."

I turned to put my toothbrush back in its holder in the shower. The mundanity of the act made me feel better. More like Merci. I'd needed the shower and the minty fresh breath. How had he known?

I turned back around to face him. I reached up to run my thumb over his busted lower lip. "I am really trying to keep the questions at bay here. But I can only keep them down for so long before I go crazy."

Rafe reached around me to turn off the shower. "Get dressed. I'll fix you something hot to eat. I'll tell you everything you want to know. Then you sleep."

When I'd finally managed clothes and enough courage, I joined him at the kitchen table, still strewn with our research, but now bearing two bowls of soup.

He sat close to me, closer than he had ever before. His thigh pressing against mine and his heat surrounded me, massaged away the ache in my body, in my chest. I wrapped my hands around the soup as he wrapped an arm around my waist.

I blew across the top of the soup to give me two more second to formulate words. "I remember us, you know ... and then waking up on the roof. Nothing in between. What happened?"

Rafe's voice was calm, but his energy itched around him. He was as scared as I was, but he wasn't running this time. "We were getting to the interesting part and you had this seizure and your eyes started bleeding. So that was a hint something was off. You launched me across the room and headed for the door. When I tried to stop you, we struggled. You ran, I grabbed the medallion and followed. When I finally caught up to you, that's when it got viscous."

I looked down at his forearm and reached out to run my fingers over scratches on his forearm obviously made by my nails. His skin goose bumped under my touch. Less than twenty-four hours after declaring his affection, I was drawing blood. I had warned him that being with me was going to be hard, but I didn't think it was going to be this dangerous.

"I did this."

"You did not. I'm not going to blame you for it, so you shouldn't either."

His instant forgiveness didn't settle well, but I wasn't sure why. "What was it trying to do?"

Rafe licked his lips and I could see that he fought with the truth, fought with the temptation to ease me into the truth. "I am assuming he was trying to bring you to him."

A shiver racked down my spine, like someone hitting a pipe with a metal bat. It reverberated through my skin.

He pulled me close and rested his head on my shoulder. "I thought I was going to lose you."

"Guess we're even now." Just a day earlier I'd been thinking the same thing about him. How is it that someone can work their way in so fast? Like a demon, Rafe had worked his way into me, filling the spaces in my soul. Maybe everyone was better with a partner.

I leaned back against him, pulling his arm tighter around my waist.

"How did you stop it?"

Rafe reached out for the medallion that swung from my neck and flipped it over in his fingers. He held it up the light. The symbols on it had never looked darker before. "It's a protection charm against magic. A seriously strong one, iron covered in stainless steel. The Demon couldn't make the spell work while you were protected. But when I took it off when we were, you know . . . it left you vulnerable."

"What kind of spell was it?"

He ran his finger over the scar on my upper forearm. "Blood control. It's literally the oldest trick in the book. It allows the controller to take over another's body like a puppet. But it's not possession, he wasn't inside you—"

"Just using me as a meat marionette. Nice distinction." I closed my eyes and watched the lightning storm crackle across my brain.

"You've been wearing this, which protects you from location spells, control spells, anything they could have been doing to find you." He spun the medallion around in his fingers and then dropped it, letting it swing against my stomach. "The moment after I managed to get it back around your neck, the spell was broken. I've never seen the likes of this before."

"So Ethan's medallion protects from magic?" The truth snapped me like a rubber band, sharp and quick. "This was why he could lie to me."

Rafe nodded, rubbing his scruff along my shirt. "I don't think he wanted to lie to you, but it probably made it easier to keep the whole truth from you."

I curled my fingers around the medallion and held it tight. Two years and how many lies later and he was still protecting me.

"I have no idea where he got something like that," Rafe said softly.

"Probably the same place he got the camera lens that photographs magic. Ethan had a guy on the side, someone else who was putting these things together for him. Emily didn't even know who it was."

Pain, loss, the essence of grieving rippled across his energy. He nestled in closer. The longer we were together, the calmer he grew. He hadn't been lying; I was a safe spot for him, a dock in the harbor on a stormy afternoon. His arm curled around my waist. He was nearly sitting on the same chair as me now. But he was still there, despite the horrorshow of tonight.

I took in a deep breath and shuddered able to finally see the truth of what was going on. "So it really is out to get me?"

"Wanted a more hands-on approach this time."

"Too bad he didn't pick up on my penchant for wolves."

Rafe chuckled and rested his head on my shoulder. "We really need to identify which Demon this is," he said calmly, like talking about Demon blood was an everyday occurrence.

"And how the pack can defeat something that has permeated the city without hurting anyone else."

"And how to kill it."

"And I'm going to have to figure out what to do with you in general."

Rafe took my hand and nuzzled his nose against my palm, then held it to his face, his budding beard tickling my wrist.

A chill ran through my core and I tried to pull my hand back to my lap, tried to pull my body away from his.

A streak of anger flashed across his eyes and he held my hand tightly. "No, Merci. You're not running from me. I've had enough of that for one night."

I didn't know what to say to him. Being around me had almost gotten him killed and I couldn't live if I lost him too.

I closed my eyes and tried to find the actual truth, the actual words that I needed to say. It was like looking for gold coins in a haystack. And when I did find the words, it felt more like a glacier I was trying to haul out of the ocean than gold. "I'm scared."

"You said you weren't afraid of me. That I made everything stop," he protested quickly.

"No, I'm scared of what I will turn this into. No one can tolerate truth all the time. It's Chinese water torture. You will break at some point. And I'm afraid of what will happen without you."

He looked down at our hands in my lap. "I'm already broken, Merci."

"Rafe, I—"

"No, Merci. I mean I have been broken and the scars make me stronger. I know my penchant for temptation, which is why you will always have to tell me the truth. The good and the bad."

I let out a shuddering sigh that reminded me of the burn in my body and the tremble in my hands. "Wow, the truth is scary as hell."

"Amen."

My head spun in the honesty of his affection and the ache of the evening. "I'm exhausted."

"Then sleep. It's nearly three a.m."

"I want nothing more. But there is a story to chase, Rafe. *Hell is empty and all the Demons are here.*"

He smiled, then chuckled, then leaned back in the chair, still holding my hand. "Like a dog with a bone."

"At least I don't avoid the truth like a plague?"

He looked up at me. Those brilliantly blue eyes so full of every answer I think I'd ever been searching for. "Are we done with the wordplay?"

"I hope we aren't done with the word play for a very long time."

...

My feet were cold. That is what technically woke me up. My feet were ice cold and sticking out from under my blanket. Which meant I had kicked my socks off in bed, which means I was hot, because I'd fallen asleep last night curled tightly in Rafe's embrace.

The memory surrounded me like his smell on my pillow. I'd slept dreamless dreams, which has probably for the best, and I was more like Merci than I had been in a month. I stretched and tested myself. My legs, my arms, my toes. Everything seemed to be in working order.

I sat up and adjusted Ethan's medallion to hang forward. I got my tank top into the right place as well and reached for a hair tie to pull my curls out of my face.

There was an energy in the air, something that flicked at the Charm like a fly to a horse's hide, something on the edge of today I could already feel. I'd gotten the feeling before. Before a big break in a story. Before my mother had called to tell me she was getting remarried. So today could go either way.

After freshening up, I joined Rafe at the kitchen table. He was awake and dressed and already halfway through a pot of coffee.

"Oh, God. You're a morning person," I grumbled as I poured myself a mug.

"It's not morning anymore," he said as he caught my hips and turned me toward him. "How are you feeling?"

I didn't need to lie to him. "I feel good, rested, stronger. Thank you."

He smiled and I thought I saw a faint blush on his cheek. He was never going to survive me if that was going to make him blush. He took my empty hand and nuzzled his nose into my palm.

"Why do you do that?"

"It's a universal sign of affection in my breed. Does it bother you?"

I could still feel his breath against the inside of my palm and the scruff of his cheek on my fingers. "No. It's just different."

"You really should rest. Doctor's orders."

I snorted. "You have a doctorate in Literature. And I am . . ." I had to glance at the clock on the wall. It was nearly four in the afternoon. "Seriously behind."

"No worries. Haven't really missed much. I've just been reading. I rang Piper and let her know what we found out about the spell."

My skin tightened. "What about the blood control?"

He shook his head. "We handled that. You don't dare take this medallion off until that Demon is dead. Agreed?"

"Agreed." I surveyed the books on the table. "What language is this one in?"

"An archaic version of Welsh. It takes a wee bit to translate, but they have the best fairy lore, so I thought it was worth the read after what we found last night."

"How far have you gotten?"

"Not much farther."

He pulled me to the table, and it literally took me two seconds to get from snuggly mode into dead body mode. That was how my brain worked. I could go from tender to torture in under thirty seconds.

"If I am translating everything properly, the Gia'r DLoom needs five, not four. Everything refers to five. So we just need two pieces of information."

"Where and who?"

"Close. Where and, considering the twisted nature of the spell, who is going to be the last sacrifice?"

"What?"

He flipped the magical book toward me and pointed to a passage handwritten in a language that was beyond dead. "I knew the center stone needed blood to seal it, but it appears that the person who gives the blood fuels the spell, like they are the battery that keeps the protection spell up."

"Okay." I reoriented my brain to what that meant for the Demon. "So he is looking for the blood of the person who will be feeding *from* the spell to complete the spell? Wait. Is that me? Is it my blood?"

Rafe nodded slowly. "This really is a type of elegance in magic that hasn't been used in centuries."

I glared at him. "Can you not wax poetic about the demon who wants me as a meat suit?"

He looked down at the table appropriately scolded.

I studied the runes, at the map, at the books. Something was off. It itched at me and I let the static of the Charm fill my brain, as every one of my neurons sizzled with the magic.

But it was my journalist training to lay everything out like dominos, to make sure that every inch of the investigation was covered.

"Let's walk through it. The demon probably got the blood the first night, when I was supposed to be the first sacrifice."

"Ethan fought them off, but they would still have your blood on them."

"So Demon gets a whiff of the blood, goes, *I want that meat suit* and tries to do a spell to find me. But he can't because I've been wearing Ethan's medallion since that night."

"Could you please stop calling yourself a meat suit?" he asked.

"Fine. Is *corporeal host* better?"

"Yes, thank you. Continue."

I turned back to the maps. "So he goes back to Benny, and when Benny refuses to help him, he takes Tay-Tay."

"You're missing one."

Four bodies. "Right. John Mitchell attacked me the night before he died."

"Do you think he was possessed?" Rafe asked.

"No. Mitchell was an ass, but that night he was just doing his job. He ripped the bandage from my arm. If any of my blood had gotten on him, could the demon have tracked that?"

"Yes."

"So the Demon works the spell to find me, finds Mitchell instead. Drags him to the first sacrifice point and the spell is begun."

"Then Tay-Tay, Beakman who was obviously some sort of statement, since he was killed in the convenience store, and then Benny."

"And it's been game on since then. Demon tortures Benny and uses Dot to find me. We're drawn out. It find us, his minions take you, you come back to me, it tries to take me, I come back to you and ..."

Running my finger over the map, the information clicked, the big picture, the last domino lined up perfectly. I flipped through my notebook for the addresses of the death spots. The truth trickled down my arm as I pointed to a popular area of town for dance clubs and the place for young co-eds to get attacked in the dark. "This is where Dot was supposed to die."

Rafe licked his lips and travelled the city with his fingers. "But this is where Benny actually died. The fourth death spot."

He grabbed a black marker from his pocket and we transcribed the locations of the four dead bodies on the Cartwright holdings map. Using the edge of a folder and referring back to the sigils in the book, he connected them like the hourglass drawing I'd seen in my Dad's journal.

When he was done, I slid the map back in front of me. "Oh that's good."

"What?" Rafe asked.

"As far as Benny knew, the epicenter was supposed to be at Schuylkill and Bainbridge, based on where Dot was supposed to die. But we forced a change of plans and Benny's death shifted the epicenter of the spell five blocks north."

I wanted to do a happy dance. "It's not highlighted. Cartwright doesn't own that one. He might be scrambling, rushed, getting desperate."

Rafe finished my thought. "He might make a mistake."

My journalist muscle flexed. "I could case the new place, see what I can get from the cops around the area. I've done more with less."

Rafe didn't have to say how unhappy he was with that suggestion, it was written in bold furrows across his brow.

"What? We know where he is now. We can find him."

"Just listen to yourself. You really want to run toward a demon who wants to kill you. Have you no self-preservation?"

I stopped. "But if I stay put, he'll just use Jeffery Cartwright's blood and finish the spell anyway. And he could feed off anyone within the Gia'r DLoom perimeter, have any number of hosts."

Rafe brushed a curl behind my ear. He opened his mouth, but before he could speak, he clutched his chest and his body was ripped from me, like some invisible lasso had yanked him backward and out of my arms.

"Rafe?" I gasped.

He took in a deep breath and his shoulders relaxed. "Piper is sounding an alarm."

"She can do that? Just pull a string or something and you know?"

Rafe nodded. "Every Shifter."

"Wow," I breathed. Now that really was a Den Mother.

My cell phone rang. Levi's name appeared across my phone. I stared at it for a moment and then answered the call.

"It's Levi. The troops are gathering."

"Why? What happened?"

"Get here ASAP. I'll text the address."

"Aye, Aye, Captain."

Levi hung up without any more ceremony. I dropped the phone to the table.

Rafe was staring at me.

"Must be huge if Levi is calling me."

...

I buzzed at the door and waited. I kept my eyes peeled to the darkening street and buzzed again and again until finally someone answered. Even Rafe's heat at my back couldn't stop the new caution of shadows, the exposed feeling of the night.

"Yeah," the speaker box barked out.

"It's Lanard."

The speaker went dead and the door buzzed open.

The elevator was cold and rickety and I took a moment just to take in Rafe. His eye was still bruised, but on the purple side of healing. His lip was split and he had the ancient Welsh book tucked under his arm.

I'd been unable to hide the new fingermark bruises on my throat and no amount of concealer could cover the circles under my eyes. I had my usual arsenal cluttering my messenger bag, including Ethan's camera.

But we were here together. Partners.

When the elevator stopped, Rafe threw his weight against the metal door and I caught a whiff of that musky sandalwood. I inhaled deeply and took the strength I needed to walk into the loft space. Following Rafe, I organized my thoughts with each step, separated facts from speculation, guilt from truths.

The familiar faces of the pack were gathered around a table, the same faces I'd seen around the Ping-Pong table. Other packmates huddled in the corners and watched as I joined Levi and the other pack leaders. The table was scattered with the familiar printouts I had given Piper two days ago. It seemed so long ago. So much had happened. I'd pissed off a Demon, gotten a declaration of love, been blood controlled. It was shaping into a very strange week.

Xenom, the other Riko, spoke. It was the most I'd ever heard him say. "Piper got a distress call from a few pack members. We think they've been taken. We've got a few people out still searching, but even Piper can't locate them."

I looked to Levi, who turned away from me. I was never going to win over Levi, no matter how many times I saved his ass. But I didn't need friends, I needed people I could trust. Speaking of people I could trust.

"Where's Emily?" I asked.

No one answered my question. I scanned the faces again. "Where's Cleo?"

Levi's only response was a clenched jaw hard enough to break teeth.

Emily? They had taken Emily. Cartwright was going after them to draw me out, probably irate that I had been rescued by a Shifter again. More innocents on the line because he wanted my blood. By taking the first person who truly accepted me, who I could call friend.

The storm started to brew, but it was different this time. Darker, deeper. It came from a place that wasn't my head, but more from my chest and I felt the thunder of it in my bones.

"How did it happen?" I asked. I wasn't going to push anyone for answers, but I used the static to keep my ears sharp and my brain focused.

"After school. Emily and Cleo went to pick up the kids for their lessons. They didn't make it to the park."

"He took kids?" I clarified.

"The three youngest of the Thompson pack."

I could feel the lightning crack up my spine, the sizzle of it. Something to chase and this bastard didn't know what was going to hit him. Cartwright was getting desperate. He didn't need the kids for the spell. He only needed me. This was just to guarantee that I would make it there. I looked at Rafe and confirmed that he was thinking the same thing as I was.

The moment of silence between us was the breaking point for Levi and the façade cracked. He thrust his finger over the table between us. "If you and MacCallan are holding back any information, I will personally rip your throat out."

And he was telling the truth. Didn't need the Charm to tell me that.

Levi shoved the maps at me. "Your informant said they were holed up at Schuylkill and Bainbridge. It's a solid Cartwright holding. We go in, get our people out."

"We have new information. We can't go rushing in," Rafe said.

"They can't take our people and think they can get away with it," Levi roared, pushing out a hot wave of energy that was far from puppy and more like vicious guard dog.

I waited until everyone's fur settled before I stirred the pot. "Rafe found the spell Cartwright might be working. It spans the city and could point to where our people might be. But we still don't know what kind of Demon we're dealing with, we don't know exactly how to kill it."

"And I'm just supposed to believe some book in a language no one can read?" Levi said.

Finally, something that Levi and I had in common: a need for proof.

Rafe looked up at me and my entire body hummed as the Charm wrapped around me. It was time for the truth. My truths.

"They tried to do it before," I said. "Thirteen years ago, my father found evidence that the Cartwrights were setting up iron train tracks on leylines to magnify a spell. This generation is doing the same thing, four dead bodies, same quadrants of the city, same spell."

Levi seemed to gnaw on the information as he ground his teeth.

Rafe's voice was the most professorial I'd ever heard it, keeping the tone neutral. "It's the Gia'r DLoom, an ancient fairy protection spell. This time. however, based on the Old Speak we have found and the state of the bodies, we think they are twisting the spell to turn the city into a permanent feeding ground for the Demon."

"Feeding on what?" Xenom asked.

"Without knowing the demon, we don't know for sure," Rafe admitted

Levi's fists turned white. "I knew it," he growled. "You two don't know what you're talking about."

My hand hit the table between us – a grounding point for the storm in my head. "My father was fighting Demons long before the Shifters came to Philly."

A general gasp circled the table.

"He figured this out all on his own and died protecting this city."

In the shocked silence that followed, Rafe placed the book on the table, opening it gingerly, as if the pages would turn to dust.

He pointed to one of the sacrifice sigils in the book. "To complete the spell, a blood ceremony takes place at the center of the stones.

The Bear shook his head. "But Demons using fairy spells? How is that possible?"

I was beginning to see what Emily said about the magic being hard for Shifters to handle. I finally had an answer to all this. It rumbled through me like thunder on the horizon. About why it didn't matter who the Original Sire was in my bloodline. About why it didn't matter that we didn't exactly know what kind of demon we were just about to hit. Using Piper's words made the skin on my shoulders tingle as I finally understood them. "It's not the power, it's how you use it."

"All we need to know is where they took my wife and my sister," Levi growled. "I don't see how the spell is connected."

Rafe eyed me from across the corner of the table. He wanted me to tell them the truth. Tell them about the blood control, about my heritage. And the truth of the matter was that if they knew what they were going up against, they might actually make it. If they understood how determined this Demon was, why Emily and pack were really taken, they might actually take a moment to make a plan and not run in there half-cocked. Like I had with Ethan. If they knew the truth of it all, they might make it out of there alive.

But it also meant they would totally bench me. Or worse, duct tape me to a chair for being another one of the Demon's conduits.

Or they wouldn't.

The truth helps more than it hurts.

I nodded at Rafe and took a step away from the table. I'd seen angry mobs before, seen tides turn with one piece of the truth. I knew that my place in this fight was teetering on the edge. The Charm raked across my skin like steel wool at the thought of not going toward the danger.

"He is after Merci." Rafe kept speaking and I kept listening. "The night Ethan was killed. It was supposed to be a hit, but when he got her blood, everything changed. They've been trying to lure her out into the open."

"Why?" Levi asked. "What is so special about a reporter?"

Rafe laughed. "Haven't you met her? Everything we've gotten so far has been because of who she is, not what she is."

My heart fluttered. It was ludicrous and childish, but there was a palpitation in my chest that couldn't be explained away by too much coffee. It was probably the most romantic thing anyone had ever said to me.

Levi stared at me and I stared back at him. I knew I wasn't supposed to stare a predator in the eyes, but I wasn't afraid. Because Rafe was right. Before all this crap, I was Merci Lanard, investigative reporter and defender of the weak. That was who I was, my pen was just a little sharper now.

"I'm Lilin."

There was a slight decrease of oxygen in the room as the other nine people gasped at the information. Rafe looked at me like I was some sort of angel.

"The Demon found out and has been honing in on me and mine since." I pointed to the first. "Jon Mitchell attacked me the day before he was killed. Tay-Tay was killed because Benny wouldn't give me up. Beakman was killed in the same place I was supposed to die, and I was interrogating Benny right before he was sucked dry."

"The spell was circling you. Why not just attack you again?" Levi asked.

"If Rafe is correct, he wants me as the last sacrifice to the Gia'r DLoom and his permanent host." My entire skin was a mix of goose-bumps and hot flashes as I looked into the eyes of everyone at the table. "He needs me alive and willing. Emily, the pack, they were taken because he knows I'm working with you and this is his last-ditch effort to draw me out and complete the spell."

The pack hadn't strapped me to a stake yet, but Levi's nails were threatening to pierce skin his fists were so tight. But the only way to go on from here on was through and hopefully, they would follow.

I usually made a complete disaster of public speaking, but this was too important. My palms grew sweaty as I looked them all in the eye and pieced together my final argument to solidify my place in this fight, and maybe with this pack. "Piper might be your home, but this city- this is my home, where I am safe and welcomed. I've dedicated my life to keeping bad things from happening to good people."

Levi crossed his arms, still glaring at me. "This isn't one of your little stories, Merci."

The Charm flared to life and the hair at the back of my neck rose. "Not a story, my ass. It's the big story, the monomyth. Everyone fights for what is important to them. I will not let the soul of my city be devoured by some demon. I lost Ethan to it, and I will not lose Emily."

Everyone's eyes were on Levi. He tightened his clasp on his upper arms and looked away from me. They always looked away. And I now I knew why: some people really can't handle the truth.

I softened my tone, calmed my own storm; neither my ego or my Charm needed to convolute my intentions. "You called me, Levi, and I want to believe it wasn't just a mandate from Piper. I know I am an outsider, but you have to trust me on this. We both want this city and the people in it safe. Together we make sure it ends tonight. I cannot lie about this."

Levi was silent and I watched the struggle in his eyes. I couldn't blame him. Emily had told me it was hard for shifters to trust outsiders, and I was a part-demon outsider who had four dead bodies surrounding her like an albatross. I had been the cause of Ethan's death. And I was asking for trust with little more proof than a book in a language no one read.

"Please don't let pride get in the way of doing what is right for your pack," Rafe said.

I curled my hand into his, more sure of him with every breath I took.

"This is your call, Levi," Xenom said.

The silence was deafening and I could hear the lightning in my head, waiting for a grounding point, a plan.

"Where is the new epicenter of the spell?"

A sliver of relief streaked through me, as if Levi's words provided that release and I felt it all the way through my feet. I pulled out a map from my bag with the new location on it. "The last body, Benny, shifted the epicenter of the spell. So here is where it needs to finish. I think you'll find our people here."

Levi looked down at the maps and his demeanor changed. It wasn't the angry wall we'd been talking to and nor the wolf I had seen that night. Instead, a General stood before me, studying the maps of the city. It struck me like a tuning fork: he'd been through a real war before.

"We've already searched their homes and residential areas, so it makes sense that the warehouse district could hide an operation big enough to make ten shifters disappear."

I waited. Patience was never my virtue, and this was like waiting for Hayne to okay a story, but so much hinged on the plan and if he was going to let me be a part of it. Not that I could stay out of trouble and that duct taping to a chair might actually be a decent proposition.

"With decent construction crew, you can get a lot done in a very little amount of time," Levi scratched at his chin and I could hear the stubble pressing through at the late hour.

"I can take a few pictures, see if they have sigils already in place." I offered.

Levi's eyebrows drew closer together, but I didn't think he wanted to know exactly the how. I knew he was having a hard enough time accepting the spell part of this evening.

"I think we let Lanard go in and do her thing," Levi said.

"What?" Rafe barked. "He's after her."

"We need to know what protection it's got in place. So we dangle what he wants in front of him while we surround the building and get a plan of attack into place." Levi looked out at his pack. "This isn't going to be pretty. This might get bloody very fast, but they have taken our people. Get everyone else. You have an hour."

The faces dissipated from the table and Levi's hard gaze landed on me.

"After this is all done, we need to talk."

"You got it." I promised, though there was the echo of something like banana toothpaste on my tongue.

Levi left us to the research spread out before us.

I curled around Rafe's arm and rested my head on his shoulder.

"I'm not sure this is the best move, Merci."

"What?" I asked, keeping my voice between us. "You're one of the strongest here. Why do you want to take the knee?"

"I need you safe, Merci."

"I need me safe, too. Without you there, you're risking us not getting this thing."

"You don't understand."

I grabbed his chin, forcing his eyes to mine. He didn't fight me, but I fought the Charm from locking in. I wanted this to stay between the two of us, without the magic to muck it all up, and this time, the magic seemed to agree.

"Explain to me why in the thick of it together isn't the best plan in the world."

I watched goose bumps rise on his pale neck. He swallowed, then nuzzled hard into the palm of my hand.

I lowered my voice. "Here's the truth, Rafe. I need you there." I took in a deep breath and let the truth settle around me and form as words between only us. "It's not just a powerful protector thing. I need someone there who reminds me to think of everyone, including myself. Because the Charm gives me tunnel vision that leads me to trouble, like I'm a magnet for the stuff."

He closed his eyes and leaned into me.

"And I can't throw myself away because there are people who still need me, people I haven't met yet, stories that need to be told."

"Finally, you're catching on."

My eyes started to water. "And I have to save Emily. I made a promise to Ethan that I wouldn't them hurt anyone else. I've failed him. I can't fail her."

I bit down on my lower lip. It was the closest thing I'd ever gotten to my own truth and it hummed along my skin, finally out in the open, finally free.

I wrote down everything Rutherford said about the building at the epicenter of the spell in my notebook. "Is it registered to a security company?"

"Do I want to know why you need that information?"

"I am not planning on any criminal mischief, Officer."

"Then, no. It doesn't seem to be on a security system. Doesn't mean it doesn't have something."

"In that neighborhood, probably D&B security." I thought for a moment to see what else might be useful while I had Rutherford on the phone. "I think that's it."

Rutherford sighed. "Please stay out of trouble, Merci."

"You and my boss need matching tattoos. Goodbye, Julie." I hung up the phone then scratched out the notes into full ideas.

"What's D&B security?" Rafe asked as he walked back from the final regroup of the shifters who had trickled in over the past hour. Maybe this wasn't going to be Rafe's last pow-wow with the pack.

I glanced at my notes again to make sure they were in order. "Dog and Bat. Old school. Not going to discount cutting the power though. The entire block is nothing. It's an old warehouse with a scrap metal yard. They were trying to rejuvenate it but lost funding and it foreclosed to the bank. A company bought it about a year ago but hasn't really done anything with it."

Rafe leaned against the table that had become my makeshift desk. "You found out all that with a few phone calls?"

"I'm a professional, Rafe." I shoved my notebook back into my messenger bag and repulled my hair back into a pony tail. "So what's the plan?"

Rafe wasn't happy with everything, but this was a battle, it wasn't supposed to be puppies and rainbows. "We are to find out what kind of protection they have set up, break it. The pack will come in when I give the all clear."

I glanced down at my watch. We had to save the pack mates and hopefully put this thing down for good, somehow. Even though we had no clue what he was, or really how to kill him. Here goes Merci Lanard running into danger again, but this time, I had back up. It was a strange thought. That this wasn't me against the world. This was me and a bunch of really powerful shapeshifters against one demon and untold numbers of minions.

But there was something else, something that itched at him. I focused on him, trying to figure it out, testing how much I'd come to know him and his energy. It was right there, in the pull of his teeth on his lip. "You're keeping something from me."

He crossed his arms over his chest. "Levi assigned me to protect you."

"Good call."

"And kill you if you actually get possessed."

My breath caught in my throat. Failure had not actually occurred to me. The Ego of Merci Lanard shining through. But Levi wasn't wrong.

I said the words fast, like ripping of a Band-aid. "We can't walk in there without a plan B, Rafe. You know me. You will know if I am not me."

"No, Merci. We will stop it before it gets to that."

"Then if you can't, I'll just have to ..."

I was going to say 'do it myself.' If I had any semblance of not being me, I would just jump off a building, right? Or maybe get myself hit by a train ... Rafe had said he'd known what was going on when he was possessed by Jovan, still regained his consciousness. So if I was actually possessed, I would know, right?

The truth was like a bee sting in my brain, infecting everything I had known about my father and making it throb for a moment before it settled into a new formation in my brain. Hot tears welled up in my eyes.

"What if he'd had to ask himself the same question?" I asked Rafe. "To protect this city, to protect me, what if my Dad killed himself so the demon couldn't possess him or couldn't complete the spell?"

Rafe grabbed my hands and held them hard.

I took in a deep breath laced with the heat of him, laced with the hot scent of leather and books. I let it out and dried my eyes. "I guess I really am my father's daughter."

Because I knew that I would do the same thing. For this city. To protect Rafe. I would do anything.

I pulled my hands from his to wipe my eyes.

"*Once more into the breach*?" he asked.

I nodded. I was ready. "Just remember, I have one advantage you don't."

He scoffed. "And what's that exactly?"

I pointed to my person. "The bad guys can't really lay a hand on the their boss's custom meat suit, so no real harm can come to me. You however, don't have that protection."

"I'm used to getting my ass kicked, remember?"

CHAPTER THIRTEEN

I balanced myself between the brick ledge and a small shelf on the side of the Dumpster. I lifted the lid and leaned it back against the wall. I clicked on my flashlight and took a good whiff of the contents.

"What are you doing?" Rafe whispered as he covered his nose.

"Checking for freshness. The trash gets picked up in this neighborhood only once a week." Smelling what I needed, I dropped the lid of the dumpster and dropped back down to the pavement.

"What exactly did that tell you?"

"Trash is fresh. You can still smell pizza. After two days, the smells started to mush together and it just becomes that trash smell."

Rafe grimaced.

"It means someone had pizza in this building in the last two days. So not abandoned. Squatters might take out the trash, but squatters will be easy to deal with."

I pulled out some hand sanitizer and rubbed my hands down with alcohol.

"Do you always go through the trash?"

"What people throw out is more telling than what they save. No one gives a second thought about it. Caught one guy on embezzlement by finding where he cut and pasted a logo."

"By going through the trash?"

"My job is strange. I won't lie, but I saved retirement funds with a Dumpster dive."

He followed me around to the front of the building. A small window had a pane of glass missing. I listened at it for a moment, trying to detect any hum of life. "Wait, why am I doing this? You're the one with the super hearing."

"Not super," Rafe whispered. "Just better."

I stepped back and plastered myself against the wall while Rafe leaned forward and listened. I had never seen such a dark look cross his face. "Whimpering and boot steps. But they're faint."

"Are they ours?" I whispered.

"I didn't know."

My jaw locked. I was right. I mean, it happened fairly often, but how many times was it because one of your sources happened to be your dead father's journal detailing how he'd battled Demons?

"You can't burst into a dark building with god knows what inside?"

I rolled my eyes. "I'm not going to burst in there. I've got super-secret weapons, remember?"

I pulled out the camera from my bag and clicked on the Deep UV lens from Ethan's stash. I carefully tiptoed out from the side of the building, then walked a little away from the front. I snapped a few pictures of the street and looked at the images on the screen. Nothing glowed.

I snapped a few more of the building itself. Nothing there. I snapped a few through the broken window and sure enough. "Bingo."

There was a symbol above the door on the inside. I focused in on it and snapped a few more for Rafe to interpret.

Rafe reached out for the camera. He studied the glowing images on the screen. "Protection spell."

I pulled out Ethan's medallion. "I can pass through that Protection spell, break it from the inside to let the pack in. If I run into anyone, I've played the wrong person at the wrong time a million ways."

Rafe frowned. "Is that really how you get some of your stories? That's practically dishonest."

"And I'm still kicking."

"I'm not just going to let you walk in the front door. We've confirmed that there are sigils on the door. I'm texting Levi."

"We need to break the protection spells or Levi can't get in at all." I leaned over and kissed Rafe quickly. "Please. Rafe. Now let me do what I was born to do."

And then I ran along the side of the building. I peeked around the corner as my phone buzzed eleven.

This was like every other story I had done, every other evil I had hunted down. And though I was armed with little more than my sharp wit and a Taser, I knew I had to do this; I was supposed to be doing this. I wasn't nervous. My hands weren't trembling. I was Merci Lanard.

Still, I was glad Rafe was right outside with ears sharp enough to hear me scream.

I couldn't feel the protection spell as I turned the handle of the old door, not particularly surprised that it was unlocked. The hinges protested as I shoved the large door open enough to fit through. The space was dark, save for some streetlights bouncing around the open rafters. Unfinished office space. Eight-foot drywall turned part of the open flooring into a maze, not reaching up to the ceiling. Light glowed behind one of the walls.

And it smelled. Not like trash, but more like rot. Rafe mentioned that evil smelled like gym socks. And this place smelled faintly of a junior high locker room. I tried to figure out how I was going to get up above the door when a shadow passed across the glow of light from the corner.

My heart skipped a beat. And then I put on my Totally Lost girl voice.

"Hello?" I called out.

A man, or a figure that looked like a man, came around a drywall corner. I couldn't see him clearly in the space, just the shine of the light off his bald head.

"Oh, hi!" I greeted before I pasted on a smile. It was always good to start with a smile.

"What are you doing here?"

"I am totally lost and I saw your lights on." I pointed to the far corner with the soft glow. I kept my smile through the taste of rotten SPAM on mealy bread.

"Who are you?"

I needed him to get about three feet closer so my Charm could catch him. "Seriously, just totally lost. These downtown streets are all one way." I pulled a piece of paper out of my pocket and walked toward him. "These directions are crap."

He snorted and walked toward me, reaching out for the paper. Above the black dry-fit shirt, he had a black rose tattooed on his neck. The Flower Boys? The Demon had been recruiting muscle from other gangs for his wet work. Just like Benny said.

That's all it took for me to get him close enough to catch his eyes. The sizzle rose between my shoulders and I shoved the Charm at him with all my might. It slammed into him and I clamped down hard on his beady little brain. "What are you doing here?"

"Waiting."

"Waiting for whom?"

"For our Master."

Crap. I gulped and blinked in disbelief. That was too easy. Was evil really this stupid?

The man looked away from me and shook his head. "What the hell? Wait. It's you."

I turned to run for the door. Evil might have been stupid, but it was fast. The man caught me around the waist and slammed me to the ground. My head banged against the concrete and I saw white lights again.

His hot hands grabbed my face and turned it into the light from the street. "You're the girl."

That night flashed behind my eyes again, how the meaty hands grabbed me and held me down. It wasn't going to happen again. His fingers closed around my throat.

With one hand pulling at his fingers, the other reached into my coat pocket and fingered the Taser. This was going to hurt.

I flicked on the charger, then pulled it from my coat. I pulled the trigger as I rammed it into the side of his neck.

His cries of pain echoed out only moments before my own as the current passed through the both of us. The electricity seared through my body as I lost control of the small weapon and it clattered to the floor.

He fell away from me on to the floor and it took me a moment to recover from the short burst. I rolled to my stomach and pushed up from the floor, getting my knees under me. I wasn't sure my feet were quite ready to hold me, but it wasn't like I had a choice. I needed to get out to the street.

"He wants you," the man growled from the floor, four feet from me, panting and holding his chest.

"I've already got a special someone." I scrambled to my feet just as he jumped to his.

I ran for the door, but the man was faster again.

He shoved me to the floor as he beat me to the door, slamming it and shutting off most of the light from the street.

My knees cracked against the cement and I skidded a few feet. My palms turned to fire as the roof rash was reignited.

Quickly, I pushed myself up to my feet, wiping my palms against my coat. He was blocking my only exit from this place and Rafe's only entrance.

I needed time to come up with another plan. Levi had said eleven fifteen he'd be ready. I stalled him like I stalled most people. "Did you really think I'm dumb enough to come alone?"

"Dumb enough to bring a Taser to a demon fight."

I gave him a small chuckle. "Got me there."

I backed up and scanned the place. Drywall, some left over supplies. Nothing as handy as a two by four with nails sticking out of it. Nothing that really looked like it could hurt this wall of a man.

"I remember you. From that night."

This was one of the Shadow Men. They hadn't really been this talkative before. "Big things come in small packages."

"Your mutt went down pretty easy. Nothing I couldn't handle." A silver blade appeared in his hand, a viscous jagged thing with teeth that I could see from where I stood, as if it collected the little light in the big space. "I like doing things the old-fashion way."

I clutched my fist so tightly I felt like I had a fireball in my hands. This was the man who killed Ethan. This was the son of a bitch who ripped through his throat.

Now is not the time to be stupid, Merci.

My own voice echoed in my head. They will pay. I was surer of it now than I had ever been, but that could have been the concussion talking. The knife was just a show, just a threat. Mentioning Ethan was just thug intimidation, probably why the Demon had recruited him in the first place.

I needed to play this smart. He might have that knife, but I had my words. I needed to keep him talking until Levi and the rest of the pack showed up. It was as simple as that.

"So the tattoo? Your big boss man stole you from The Flower Boys. Do Demons have better dental?"

"Master has promised we will be gods after this."

"What's a little murder when he's going to give you your own turf, right?"

"And more."

I nearly felt sorry for this servant. No doubt he'd been marked like Benny and no doubt he would probably die like Benny. But maybe I could stop that too.

We circled each other and I looked for a way to break the protection spell at the door to let Rafe in. I saw movement in the window where we'd been listening. Rafe was here, I still had back up.

Which I needed because two more men the size of refrigerators walked out into the dark space. Shoulders as wide as a doorframe sauntered up to join their brethren. Seriously, where was the Demon finding his minions, the Eagles defensive line?

Flower Boy grunted. "It's her."

I licked my lips. Nope. No getting out of this one. No running or fighting or Tasering myself to freedom. I held my hands out and up so they could see that I wasn't going for my weapon, just my wits.

They circled around me and I turned slowly assessing them, trying not to feel like a steak in the middle of a dog fight. I wasn't sure that I needed the Charm, I just needed them to hear me. Because I had a really stupid idea. But for a good reason this time. Not because of some tunnel vision for a story. I wasn't chasing a byline. But because of Emily, and Cleo, and the Thompsons and for all the families of all those missing people.

"Listen, you want in with the big man, right? And he's probably not too happy about losing me the last time, right?"

The first man clenched the knife in his fist, but started to spin it like an informant spins a coffee cup. He was listening.

"So why can't we be civil about all this? He wants me. I'm here. He doesn't need all those hostages."

They seemed to be listening.

"So why don't you just let everyone go and I'll come with you willingly? No need to bruise the merchandise."

I kept scanning the place just above their heads as I turned. The windows. The windows didn't have protection sigils on them, only the door. There were seven other possible entrances to this floor alone and that didn't include the sewers. Rafe was small. His wolf form could probably fit between the bars on the outside. Back-up could get in even though I hadn't broken the protection spell. Why hadn't I thought of that earlier?

Or right - penchant for self-destruction.

"Get her."

All three pounced on me and I was grabbed three different directions by hands. I was shuffled across the space and then pulled down a narrow stairwell, my feet barely tapping against every third step.

I was being pulled down into a roughhewn basement because the center stone had to be buried at the center of the spell.

Suddenly, I was airborne until I hit iron bars. This time, I landed on something soft and warm that also let out a cry.

A person. I landed on a person as I heard the clang of a door closing. I'd been in lockdown enough times to know a jail cell when I heard it.

I rolled off and squinted through the dim light. I gasped. "Rutherford?"

"Lanard," he growled through a bruised mouth and bloody teeth.

The floor of our cell was an unfinished cement and the light filtered through from poorly placed work lamps, flooding the open space with harsh yellow lamps. It was not the posh evil lair I was expecting for an operation poised to take over the city. But then again, I had made them reorient their plans at the last minute.

"Man, you move fast." I whispered as I gained my bearings. Iron cell. Several other shadowy cells with several people. "Any backup on the way?"

Rutherford only glared at me and pulled at his vest under his uniform shirt. "No. Just me. Following that gut instinct of yours."

"It's going to be okay. I have back up this time."

I carefully stood, testing my ankles and shoulders to see what I could still use. Everything still seemed to be in working order and they hadn't taken my messenger bag. At least this cell didn't have the communal toilet I was used to.

"Merci?"

The familiar voice was like a cool drink of spring water on a hot day. Emily rose from a crowd of bodies in the next cell over. I darted over to her. She curled her hands over mine on the smooth bars between our cells and managed a smile through her bruised jaw.

"Why are you here? You know he wants you, right? This is all a trap?"

I nodded. "I made a promise."

"To Ethan?'

"No. To you. I said I'd hold the guy that killed Ethan while you punched him."

Emily squeezed my hands. "Cleo and the kids are okay, but..."

"Levi is right behind us," I whispered. "Rafe is waiting for him."

There was a general ruckus that drew both our attentions.

Four huge guys were dragging Rafe across the rough basement floor. They dropped him at the feet of a man whose back was to me, but even in the dim light I could make out his blond hair and well-cut suit.

I flew to the front of the cell and shook the metal bars as hard as I could. Rafe was supposed to wait. This wasn't part of the plan. He was supposed to be safe upstairs while I did the stupid things.

"Hello, Merci."

I knew the voice. I knew it because it reverberated in my head, not just in the space between me and the man who turned slowly.

He started toward me, his black eyes shallow and his gold Rolex gleaming. This was Jeffrey Cartwright. He was every stereotypical construction-front mobster ever portrayed on film.

His slender frame moved with grace but I could see his clavicle, his hollowed cheeks. Blood was crusted in his crow's feet as he smiled at me with more teeth than he should have.

Correction: this wasn't Cartwright. This was the Demon in his meat suit and it was sucking the life out of this body too. This was what was after me. For a moment, I was glad for the blood in my mouth, masking the taste of bile.

"I'm so glad you came."

"Didn't want to miss the big show."

He cocked his head. "How does all that sarcasm work with the truth you carry with you?"

I shrugged. "Never really had a problem."

Cartwright was at the bars now and I could smell it inside him. He smelled like a load of laundry left in the washer, like a moist, dank hole of darkness. My stomach churned with the rejuvenated images of what had crawled out of the black hole in the warehouse.

"If you can't bring the reporter to you, you can always find a way to get the reporter to come to you willingly. You people are like taxis, just needed to give a little whistle. Figured kidnapping some pack members would get your attention since you seem to have a soft spot for Shifters."

He hiked a thumb over his shoulder at Rafe, who was still struggling against the four men. "He's just the icing on the cake."

"What are you going to do?" I prodded.

"Let you watch while I completely possess lover boy there. Shouldn't take too long."

I fought reaching through the bars and tearing at his face. It wasn't my style. I'd looked guys like this in the eye before. I'd get my answers. "Why?"

He slammed himself against the bars and I stumbled back. Rutherford caught me.

"Because I need you broken, empty. I'm burning through these bodies. Even this body can't hold me for too much longer. But yours," he grinned as he looked me up and down. "Your blood is strong enough to hold this much power."

I pushed away from Rutherford and squared my shoulders and turned on the Charm. It sizzled around me like electric armor in the rain. Do what I do best? Piss people off with the truth until they make mistakes. "Fine, but you do know there is an entire pack of Shifters on their way, right? Fueled by a Den Mother. So you'd better hurry up with whatever you needed to do."

He waved off the threat. "Doesn't concern me. They won't be able to get through my barrier spell."

"Like I didn't get through your barrier spell? Like Rafe didn't?"

"It only keeps out the goodie two shoes. You're already like us, Merci. And lover boy here's got a stain on his soul so big you can see it from space."

I didn't feel the twist of a lie within my stomach. I knew it was true. I knew Rafe carried his sin with him; it was why we fit so brilliantly together. The Lilin and the lost wolf. It was why we were going to win.

I just didn't quite know how yet.

The Demon walked away and barked some orders. They dragged Rafe across the floor and strapped him to a chair. I didn't want to turn away from him, from those teal eyes as they bore into me.

Rutherford pulled me to the back corner of the cell. "Can you get him over here again?" he whispered to me.

"What?" I snapped as I tried to peer over the Julie's broad shoulders, not wanting to break my connection with Rafe.

"Cartwright. The Demon. I can work a spell that might weaken him, but I need him close."

My neck popped with how fast I snapped my attention to Rutherford. "What?"

Rutherford poked at the pendant bouncing against my shirt. "Who do you think crafted that for Ethan?"

He pulled out the silver coin he was always nervously weaving between his fingers and held it out to me. Even in the dim light, I could make out the Old Speak carved into the medallion, the runes very similar to what I wore around my neck.

I nearly laughed. "You're a Warlock?"

I let the information soak into my brain. Rutherford? My informant from the police department was in on all this? He had to be the person Ethan had been going to for his magical accoutrements. And he'd said I wasn't the only one trying to save the city. Had Rutherford been waging his own war?

My first instinct was to punch him. So I did. His upper arm was firmer than I expected and my knuckles cracked against him.

"You can wail on me later. Can you get him over here?"

Rutherford stepped close to me quicker than I'd ever seen him move before. He loomed over me, his voice low and between us. "I've been after this guy for a year now and damn it if you didn't find him first. Now, I can work a spell that might slow him down if you can get him within two feet of the cage."

I opened my mouth to barrage him with questions: questions about him, magic, lies. My father.

Rutherford grabbed me and covered my mouth. "Listen, Lanard. I will let you question me until next Tuesday, but after. We have the same mission now. We have always had the same mission."

When I didn't fight him or move to ask another question, he slowly let me go.

"How do I get him over here?" I asked.

"I don't know. Use that sparkling personality of yours. Makes me want to punch you sometimes."

I glared at him. Rutherford. But seriously? Straight-laced, steadfast Rutherford was a Warlock? Crap, the next thing I was going to learn was that Hayne was some sort of headline predicting psychic.

I snorted. Why not? My life was upside down anyway. "Two feet?"

Rutherford nodded as he picked up a rough looking piece of metal from the ground and held it to his wrist.

Instead of watching Rutherford cut himself, I hurried to the front of the cell, my mind running on overdrive. Demon Cartwright was preparing a table, well, actually, it was a thick board of wood on two wood horses. He had book open and was marking the makeshift altar with symbols in white chalk. My good old friends the Old Speak runes probably. Complete with black candles. Joy.

But now was not the time for sarcasm or speculation.

So I had to go on the facts, what I did know? Who? A group of minions stood around, like they were waiting for a show to begin, and not the best-looking people. Thirty at a rough count. Those higher up on the totem pole of evil were very apparent. They were fed and decently dressed, but his thugs only numbered ten.

Where? Emily and Cleo and the children were trapped in the adjacent cells. The cages were well constructed, so this Cartwright family really was handy with a welding torch considering he's had less than a week to change his location. We were in the tunneled-out basement of the office building.

When? I looked down at my cell phone with no signal. It was fifteen minutes after eleven. Levi should be ready to invade. Any time now.

What? What could I do to get him to come closer?

The plan became a lot clearer when one of the thugs walked forward and plunged a needle-full of something dark into Rafe's arm. I cried out. "No!"

Rafe stiffened and shook as if the darkness were burning through him. His eyes locked with mine. He put his hands up as if to say 'stop' and nodded.

But nodded at what? He couldn't possibly be telling me that he wanted this. Wanted the same thing to happen to him now that happened before. To be so full of this Demon blood he went feral again.

A feral wolf wouldn't be strapped to a chair for long, though. If he thought his wolf was stronger than a few thugs, he might even the odds until the others got here. And if I knew anything, it was that I could bring him back. He didn't have the weaknesses that had made him easy prey for Jovan. He would come back to me. Like he had the first time.

The truth of it echoed through the power itching along my skin and turned it to silk for a moment as the plan solidified in my head. Play to our strengths: me being a pain in the ass and Rafe's experience with magic's dark side.

I put on my softest face. It wasn't one I used often. I called through the bars, "Just no more, okay?"

The Demon slowly strutted closer to the cage. "Why not?"

"If you're going to kill him, just kill him. But not that."

One of the men prepared another syringe from the tray. I'd seen freebasing before, but I'd never seen blood used as the liquid. The man sprinkled in a white powder before he held it over a white candle to purify the mixture. He pulled the plunger up on the syringe and it filled with the dark liquid.

I stared at Rafe as the man injected him, this time in the neck. Even from across the room, I could see fingers of darkness streak across his pale skin.

"He'll let me in. They all do, and then maybe . . ." The Demon paused to think. "Maybe make him kill himself."

So not only was this Demon cocky, he really didn't think things through. The last time they had done this, Rafe had escaped in wolf form and the blood on his snout hadn't been his. How could Cartwright forget that? Or did he just not care how many minions he lost, if it meant he gained a permanent host?

I was momentarily offended at the notion of someone so stupid was trying to steal my body and the truth flew from my lips. "You're not the brightest bulb in the chandelier, are you?"

The Demon cocked his head and smiled again, if you could call it a smile. His gums were yellowed and bloodless above his brown, rotting teeth. The demon's hunger was sucking even the nutrients out of this body.

When his eyes turned toward Rafe, mine followed. At the silent command, the man pushed in another full syringe of the drug. Rafe's face flushed red, but even as he struggled, he looked up at the ceiling. From the corner of my eye, I saw as the other Shifters did to. It was that synchronicity the pack had. Reinforcements were coming.

Thank you, Levi, and your pointed head.

I hoped Rutherford's spell was almost ready, because I didn't want to have to keep pushing the Demon, who in turn was pushing the blood into Rafe.

"Well, first off," I started. "If you are going to put up protection sigils, you have to put them on all the entrances into the space, windows included."

The Demon looked up and with a flick of his hand, the loitering minions in the back sprang to life like marionettes, charged through the door, and started scrambling up the stairs.

"And secondly, you're pumping that into a Primo, not just some Shifter. And his wolf is more powerful than your proxies."

"Doesn't matter. My men can handle it." The Demon looked over to Rafe and laughed, before taking a step closer to me "Besides, he doesn't believe he can beat me."

"It doesn't matter, because I do."

The Demon moved even closer and his eyes met mine. He was within an arm's reach. I actually had annoyed him into striking distance. Perhaps that is a new superpower I hadn't discovered yet: being both annoying and armed to the teeth with portable electronic weaponry.

"Not sure what the security situation was last time you were on this plane of existence, but you really need to have someone do pat downs at the door."

I jammed my arm through the bars with the Taser crackling.

The Demon was too fast and grabbed my hand holding the charged weapon. The Taser's blue light gleamed against his face. It illuminated the real Demon behind the thin skin, the gruesome thing that wore the face. A dark skeleton of something not human, not of this realm.

My heart stopped for a moment at the sight. My skin prickled as he took the plastic box from my hand and threw it across the floor, his fingers wrapping around my wrist.

"And you're supposed to be the bright one in this situation?"

"Yep."

His grip tightened on my arm. "You know your father talked too, tried to distract me with his words. In the end, I found his weakness and climbed in."

"What was his weakness?"

"His precious family. When I threatened to possess your mother, he volunteered, carved the mark himself."

"My mother?" I snapped.

"Her Lilin blood would have made an excellent host – and those curves ..." he whistled through thin lips.

"My mother's blood." I couldn't believe it. My June Cleaver of a mother without a pearl out of place was the true Lilin.

"Ripe with demonic power that one."

The truth sunk in my gut and made me a stone for a moment. "My father was human."

"Clever little man with that train trick. Took me nearly a decade to get all my bits back together and find another willing Cartwright. This one was *ready* for me. At his lowest, thanks to you destroying his plans with the Mayor. He was all too happy to make you my first sacrifice."

The timing. The timing was all making sense to me now. It really was all about me. "The construction bribes."

"Slipped into sonny boy here right after he was found out, and now we are dancing, Miss Lanard."

My mother was the Lilin, my father was the human, and I was Merci Lanard. Ace reporter who never even had a clue.

A tear pooled in the corner of my eye and I sniffed. "I loved my father, but he didn't have what I have."

The Demon laughed. "What's that?"

"Backup."

Light coursed around us, and for a moment, I was showered in lava as the spell burned through me and enveloped the Demon. Though the pendant protected me from the spell, it didn't protect me from the melting flesh of his hand locked around my wrist. I yanked my arm away, pulling a layer of his skin with me. The strip of flesh ate at my skin like acid and I rubbed it against the bars to get it off.

Skin dripped off the figure before me. Half his face gone, light danced along the Demon's black cheekbone and the socket of the once steel-eyed man was replaced by a void that my eyes ached to behold.

The Demon pulled away and clawed at his face, creating a clearer divide between Demon and man. I was too focused on the teeth that went all the way back to where the man's ear was still hanging on like a bad Halloween mask. The figure shook and I could feel as the Demon pulled energy to him, to heal himself or to ready himself for a little pay back, I didn't know.

Three people at the edge of the room shriveled into piles of bone. The Demon laughed as he stood straight and looked over at me. "Good one, Witch."

Rutherford pulled me away from the bars. I held my burned arm as I watched the Demon recover. It was hard to watch, like looking into a black hole not quite formed yet, but it was solid nonetheless. That was how much he had already taken from humans, taken from innocents in my city—enough to be half corporeal on this plane.

A growl echoed across the room.

Everyone's gaze jumped over to Rafe, or where Rafe used to be. The chair was on its side and a wolf stood over the body of the thug who had been injecting the serum into his system. Blood covered his snout and I couldn't see Rafe in its eyes.

Another growl caught my attention, another wolf. In the cages at my right, the children had shifted, caught up in the ripple of Rafe's power.

Emily stood there, her fists at her side. "Levi is here."

"Ready to punch something?"

"Hell yes."

That's when the building rumbled and the ceiling caved in. Rutherford grabbed me, throwing himself over me as the rubble fell.

Something heavy landed on us, but Rutherford bore the weight of it. It was deafening and I cursed Levi for not using the stairs like a normal person. But then again, I hadn't broken the protection sigil upstairs so guess he'd had to compromise with explosives. Bless his furry little construction foreman head.

As the dust settled, I watched the flood of animals pour through the hole in the ceiling. The explosion loosened one wall of my cell enough to make it fall. Gingerly, Rutherford pushed the wall of bars up so I could slink out from under him.

It was chaos. Beautiful, rescuing chaos.

As the dust still settled, I could smell cinnamon in the air. A reminder that Piper was protecting her people the only way she could, by fueling them with her power, through her connection to them, making them stronger, faster. And it was incredible to watch.

The animals went for the thugs, the puppets, for everyone. Like a chaotic wave of fur and maybe a few feathers, they flooded the basement and crashed against the men standing unprepared. Screams ricocheted through the dust.

As I tried to find Cartwright in the chaos, I stood there for a moment reveling in the cacophony of howls and screams and hissing pipes. Just taking it in, letting the melee of it all soak into me and sizzle across my skin. The bear rose up on its hind legs and took out two minions as if they were made of paper. Three wolves moved on a Shadow Man like a synchronized swim team as two pulled at his arms and one went for the throat. The smell of blood and rot filled the air as bodies dropped to the floor. There was a perfection in it, a life that I appreciated on a cellular level.

I finally saw Cartwright, for an instant across the battle floor. Honestly, it was pretty easy to find blinding white hair in the dim room. He was staring at me, across the river of wolves and prey, seething.

Emily appeared at my side. "Come on. Let's go."

I had to shake my head to focus on her words. "I can't leave until Cartwright's dead. You go. Take the kids."

"You need to not be here with him," she said logically, as she should have argued to any sane person.

But I was not that sane person. "This needs to end."

Something crossed her eyes, something between awe and frustration. It was a look I was getting used to. Emily nodded. "What do we do?"

"Go. Kick some ass. I'll be—"

A baseball bat hit me in the back and I stumbled forward on the rubble. Emily eyed my attacker and there was almost a smile on her lips. "I'll be right back."

She swooped around me and I followed her with my gaze, turning to watch. There was a unity in her motion as she ran at him in human form and jumped at him, shifting in midair to her wolf form. It was beautiful.

"Get the girl," Cartwright screamed over the howls and hisses, desperation pinching his voice into something gnawing and thin.

With his own dwindling army of warriors synced to his will, the human minions turned toward me. The animals scrambled to pull at clothing and legs, dragging them away from the new hoard to be dealt with one-by-one.

Wolves appeared between me, the fray, and Cartwright. A furry line of Roman soldiers. A black one stood directly before me. Levi. He howled and the howls of the others echoed through the night, making my hairs stand on end.

That wasn't going to attract attention at all.

Rutherford came up to me, shielding me with his body. "You got any idea how to take this guy down."

"Not a clue. But Rafe…" I looked at my line of protectors and didn't see his silver shape.

"I need to find Rafe. He's…" I didn't really know the phrase for it. "Lost."

I searched the basement. In all the commotion, it was hard to pinpoint him. I closed my eyes. He was Rafe. His energy was as much a part of me now as my truth was. I could find him. Just like I had days before in the warehouse, I breathed in and reached out.

There was an itch at my elbow and I turned to the left.

A silver wolf paced along the far wall, climbing over the rubble, nose to the ground.

I climbed over half a wall of drywall and had to pull my coat off of iron bars, but I finally got to him.

"Rafe."

The wolf stopped and slowly turned to me. A slow snarl curled across his muzzle.

I gasped. He didn't recognize me. Not yet. But I could do this. I would bring him back to me.

The chaos of the fight around us faded away, the whole world becoming him and me, the quiet hum of us together. Nothing else mattered except him coming back. I needed my partner to finish this.

I ripped off the pendant. He needed to feel me, my power. He would know me then, I was sure of it. He had come to me before. He would again. I let the Charm fill me, pulled all my power to me as best as I knew.

He slowly looked up and sniffed the air. I knew he knew me.

I knelt down and met that cool blue stare at his level. He turned to face me and his head sank lower than his broad shoulders. I reached out my hand to him, my skin pale in the light.

He filled my vision and echoing across my mind was a line from Byron. "*Love will find a way through paths where wolves fear to prey*," I whispered the words.

The wolf's ear flicked and his head rose. He took a hesitant step forward.

"So that's what it's going to be? My strange predilection for misquoting literature. Well, here's some Foster. *I love you with too clear a vision to fear your cloudiness.*"

He nuzzled my palm and slipped under my hand until he was nearly nose-to-nose with me and my hand was resting behind his massive ear. His fur was so soft and I could feel the life of him beneath it.

I licked my lips and could feel my wild pulse in them. "*Real love and truth are stronger in the end than any evil in the world.*"

It was the Dickens that did it. His figure shimmered, a mirage before me and I blinked and turned away.

His hot face ran beneath my fingertips as he leaned into my hand. His whisper trailed down my inner wrist. "Merci."

His hand shook as he reached out to me. Our hands met in the middle and I wove my fingers into his. I pulled him to me.

His nose pressed into my neck. "I thought I was lost."

"Nope. I'm right here."

He pulled away from me and his blue eyes were back. He was back. "I'm really naked."

"Why does that happen sometimes but not others?"

"I have a book about it."

"Of course you do."

I pulled off my coat and he slipped it on. There were certain advantages to your boyfriend being the same size. Whoa. I'd just thought the boyfriend word.

I helped him to his feet, and as one, we turned to the rest of the battle. Except there was no battle. The room was still and everyone was looking at us.

Rutherford was among them. I searched the pack to find the familiar faces, and not a single dull-eyed puppet or thug was left standing. These Shifters were thorough and brave. Maybe I shouldn't be so hard on their leader.

I carefully moved over the rubble, around bodies I couldn't tell were alive or dead, and over to Levi.

They had the Demon cornered and trapped in a circle of white crackling energy. I stopped next to Rutherford and stared at what was left of it after the fight.

"You're pretty handy with a protection spell," Rafe said to the cop as he leaned against me.

"You don't think that police tape really keeps the public away from a crime scene." Rutherford looked down at us.

"How do we kill it?" Levi growled. "I don't think we can save Cartwright, but I want it dead."

"Get in line," I snapped.

"Spell's not going to last forever," Rutherford said. His knees weakened and Emily caught him around the waist. Someone pulled up a broken stool for him to sit on.

I wiped my hands down my shirt, the burn still sizzling around my wrist. That was going to scar. "Well, let's ask him."

I walked to the edge of the protection spell. The Demon glared at me. In the fight, he'd lost more of chunks of his face and the other eye. Just watching him made my eyes water and I wondered if my Charm could even work on a Demon. Seemed to work on all other manner of beastie, but this thing didn't even really have eyes to look into.

I let the chill of power wash over me. Let the lightning storm cover me. This was demon against demon, now.

I found what I thought was the grounding spot in what was left of his eyes and pushed toward it. "What are you?"

The Demon just laughed at me, the human vocal cords still intact enough to make the eerie noise echo off the now quiet room. But it didn't look away.

I stretched my neck and tried again, pushing harder this time. "How do we kill you?"

The Demon fought his words and was able to swallow them back down.

Rafe's shields opened up around him and I was met with the hesitant feeling of his wolf against me. He was trying to enhance me, like he had done before.

I ask again. "What is your name, Demon?"

"Cartwright."

I pushed even harder. "What is your real name?"

The word clawed out of his mouth. "Kalimore."

I smiled. It was going to take more than just two of us to get out the real information, but a name was a good start. I had done more with less.

"It isn't going to work, my love," the Demon's voice rasped out. "You are nothing. You are a hint of what you could have been with me. You will never—"

Emily's hand clamped down in my shoulder and it felt like someone thrust a furry book against my chest, but Emily's power flowed easily with mine, mixing with Rafe's. The chill between my shoulders grew to my entire back.

I was just about to ask another question when Emily backhanded Levi's shoulder. With a glare, he put his hand on Emily's shoulder.

Then as one, the entire pack opened their power to me. The heavy book on my chest turned into an anvil and the anvil turned into a cement truck and the cement truck nearly threatened to suffocate me with the weight of their animal essences. Then there was a pop, and my entire body went cold, my power pulsing through every ounce of me like never before.

Locking my eyes on the burning voids of the Demon's, I asked again. "How do we kill you?"

The Demon fought fruitlessly. He couldn't turn away. He couldn't move. He was frozen in the stare of forty Shifters and one very pissed-off Lilin.

"How do we kill you?" My eyes began to water and a trickle of blood ran down to my lip as I pushed the truth into him, twisted the harpoon of my gaze straight into the void.

"Fire," he finally cried out.

The entire group took a collective breath and pulled away from me. All the air rushed out of the room as their power retreated back into them. My knees went weak and Rafe was there to catch me, or more accurately, we weakly leaned against each other.

The Demon threw himself against the protection spell and it threw him back against the concrete wall.

"You can't stop me. My thirst will live on."

It didn't take long for the Shifters to pile up a makeshift pyre around the Demon's circle. Anything that would burn. Wood. Clothing, a small pile of newspapers.

He pressed his hand against the spell and it sizzled and burned away the rest of the human flesh on his palms, exposing the smooth obsidian of his claws. "You are nothing more than a parlor trick, Lanard."

I did my best to ignore him. To not let the truth of his words get to me.

I turned toward Rafe and shoved both hands into the pockets of my coat, much to his surprise. I winked at him and pulled out an old book of matches from McTaggert's. It was the first time I'd thought about alcohol in days.

I ripped off two matches and folded the cover back. With a deep breath to make sure I didn't blow out the flame, I ripped the matches against the striking strip and watched them catch fire. I lit the rest of the matchbook on fire and tossed it on the pyre.

The flame was instant and I jumped back and into Rafe. The flames caught quickly around the protection circle.

The Demon stood still and glared at me. "This is not the end."

"It's the end for you, Kalimore. You will never hurt my city again."

A spark from the crackling fire jumped up onto his leg and it was like he had been doused with lighter fluid. His entire body ignited in one flaming pyre and he screamed in pain.

I covered my ears and pulled away from the heat. I watched as the Demon fell to his knees before collapsing into a rotten, ashy corpse.

It was over so fast. I stood over the ashes, absorbing the destruction I had caused. I had taken a life, a demonic-going-to-kill-lots-of-innocent-people life, but a life nonetheless. The truth of that sank into my core as the pack started their withdrawal, climbing over rubble, making their way out of the basement.

"You did good, kid," Xenom, the bear of a man, said. He curled his fingers into what was left of the mouth and braced his other against the shoulder and wrenched the skull off. For good measure, I supposed. He tossed it in a black sack and followed the rest of the people out of the half-collapsed building.

"Thanks," Levi managed before turning away.

I wanted to yell the loudest I-told-you-so at him, but softened when I saw the delicate way he cradled his wife's limping frame toward the exit.

The others moved away, hobbling and carrying the children from the cages as they went up the still intact staircase. Rafe wrapped his arm around me and pulled me away from the sight. Slowly, we made our way across the basement and followed the rest up the stairs.

"Don't think about it, Merci. Not tonight," he said.

"So you read minds now?"

"I know the look. It's going to be okay."

And it was the truth. I saw it in those amazing eyes of his. The ones that never lied to me and never looked away. "I know."

Rutherford loomed over us. "Cops should be here soon. Think we've got half the most dangerous felons in the city in that basement, so you and your friends need to scoot."

Rafe nodded and we headed for the front door. Before stepping outside, I stopped and turned toward Rutherford.

"One question," I started.

"We don't have time, Lanard."

"Did you know my father?"

Rutherford studied the night sky, probably calculating the impending swarm of police, but I wasn't going to budge on this. I needed to know this above all other questions in this moment. I needed to know if Rutherford was the missing person that could have saved my father.

"No. I came in after he died, but I knew about him. Why else would I have put up with you all these years?"

Maybe it was a concussion setting in, or exhaustion, or trauma, but I didn't fight as that truth settled into my view of the world.

Rutherford nodded and his tone was completely different when he spoke again, something softer, sympathetic almost. "I'll answer everything later. But the last thing I need is them seeing you at a crime scene before there is a crime."

I could deal with that. Could deal with it much better when Rafe slipped his hand into mine and pulled me toward the warehouse door. "You and I are going to have that talk."

"You can buy me coffee. Now go."

And for the first time in our relationship, I actually did what Rutherford said; I walked away from a crime scene.

The cool night air seemed to cleanse my nose of the scent of brimstone as Rafe and I walked back to the car. I tried not to think of the bodies left in that basement. I tried not to think that, because of me, pack mates had been kidnapped, battled a small army of lost humans, and were going home right now to lick their wounds.

Instead, I dug through my bag to find my keys. I readjusted the messenger across my chest. The weight of the camera inside settled against me, and I felt better, was comfortable.

We were at my car when my cell phone rang. "Seriously." I pulled out the glowing thing. "Hello?"

"Lanard, I've got a story for you."

I groaned. "Hayne, stop listening to the police scanners and go be with your daughter."

"Some explosion. I need you to cover it."

"No, Hayne. I need a few days."

"But Merci—"

"It's about my dad."

"Oh."

But there was more in that 'oh' than the monosyllabic sound. Part sadness, part surprise. Maybe I was reading into the one word too much or maybe it was exhaustion and nostalgia mixing together tonight, but I owed Hayne for all these years of protecting me, of putting up with me, and letting me chase the leads that lead to the closing of my father's final story.

"I'll cover the story, but then I'm taking a week off and that Brian kid can be your lap dog." I hung up and turned to Rafe who was smiling as he leaned against the car next to me.

"Working late, honey?" he asked.

"Seems so, darling."

He reached out for me and wrapped his arms around my middle. I rested against him, against his warm, strong frame. He brushed his nose against mine. "I'm going to take shower and go to bed."

"The pack doesn't do some sort of celebration when they win back the city? Howl at the moon or something?"

Rafe smiled. "Not quite."

I watched him. I'd used the 'l' word and the 'b' word in the same day and I was still standing. It still held the potential to be a decent night. "My bed or your bed?"

"My shower. My bed."

I almost pouted. I liked the idea of finding him in bed when I got home. Whenever that would be. Like the idea of how warm and safe that bed would be because I was going to sleep for a week after tonight.

He slid his hand up to my face and brushed his thumb over my lips. "We are going to take this slow."

I could do that. Maybe.

"So, I have question for you, Merci Lanard. Would you go out on a date with me?"

The End

EXCERPTS FROM TRUTH ABOUT BLOOD: AVAILABLE XXX

I had my list of questions prepared. Every single question I had come up with in the past month. The who's and what's and why's and how's.

I had done all my research, with the help of state records and Rafe. It was good to have a boyfriend who was handy in the library.

I'd even managed a new pair of shoes and a messenger bag to handle all of my usual interrogation paraphernalia: wad of cash, breath mints, and the lens from Ethan's camera, just in case I suspected anything other than what met the eye.

I was going to nail the truth of all this and I wasn't going to take no for an answer. I'd been waiting long enough.

The drive down there was longer than I remembered, or maybe it was because I was dragging the storm clouds of the Charm with me. Not exactly at full tilt, it was enough to make me think twice about taking the plastic bottle of whiskey I had hidden away for a rainy day. The storm clouds were gathering, but I'd been nearly a month without a drink or a nosebleed.

This wasn't going to be the thing that broke me.

I pulled into the visitor's lane at the entrance of the gated community. I shuffled my driver's license out of my purse and rolled down my window as a guard twice my size and half my speed leaned as far as his little torso would let him out of the window, not risking actually getting up from his seat.

"What can I do you for?" he asked with a thick, Southern drawl.

I'd nearly forgotten that eight hours were enough to get you below the Mason Dixon line, which was far too south for me. I preferred my winters cold and bitter, but this was where the story lead me, so this is where I followed.

"I'm here to see Margot Weber. She said she would put me on the list."

He nodded and pulled his head back into the booth like a turtle, slow and with a few double chins.

I tapped on my steering wheel and waited for him to check the list. Still not a patient person.

He eventually stuck his head out again. "Can I see your license?"

I produced it faster than he probably thought a human could move. He flinched away from the small card.

Eventually, his sausage fingers removed the card from my own and I watched as his eyes glued to the slick scars around my wrist.

I pulled my hand back into the car and pulled my sleeve down over them. The Demon had left its mark in more ways than one. Needless to say, this summer was going to be pretty unbearable if I had to keep wearing long sleeves all the time. Piper said she might be able to help a little, but I told her I didn't need it. If they were going to heal, they would heal, and if they didn't, they would just add to the story of who I am.

"We don't get too many visitors from the great commonwealth of Pennsylvania," he said.

"Interesting," I plastered on a fake smile and waited as he looked at the license, then looked at me, then back at the license, then back at the list, and then at me again.

"Well, everything seems to be in order," he said as he returned my license. "Do you need any directions from here?"

"I'm good," I said as I plucked my license from his fingers and tossed it back into my purse. "Thank you."

The gate had barely reached its halfway point when I drove around it to get on my way. I knew it was just his job, but this couldn't wait any longer.

I needed answers and I needed them now and there was only one more person I could get them from.

As I was driving the twenty miles an hour speed limit through the gated community, a word rested on the tip of my tongue for the manicured lawn and the perfectly placed trees that were still coming into their own and the sheer fact that each person I drove past waved at me. Who does that?

I turned down Magnolia Way and counted the perfectly crafted cottages, each in a coastal pastel. The fourth on the left was my destination, if memory served me.

I turned into the driveway and parked in front of the third garage door. Then I did a three-point turn and backed into the same space. You never know when you needed to make a fast exit and this wasn't the mean streets of Philly where darkness and a stun gun was all I needed. This was the burbs and it had its own rules.

I triple checked my EDC in my messenger. I ran through the questions in my head and finally mustered the courage to get out of the car.

I caught a reflection of myself in the window and pulled my hair back into a curly pony tail to keep it out of my eyes, if this encounter resorted to that.

I took a deep breath, relaxed my energy, and held Ethan's silver medallion to my chest.

The truth helps more than it hurts.

With one last glace to the road as a potential way to walk away from danger, I threw my messenger bag over my shoulder and walked quickly to the porch. The wooden wraparound probably telegraphed my arrival more than the three quick knocks I made to the door.

When no one answered after three seconds, I thought I could turn around, but a shadow passed across the frosted glass. I jumped away, heart in my throat.

The knob turned, and slowly, the door opened revealing a woman in her mid-fifties doing everything right because she didn't look a day over forty. Her pastel pants and white chiffon blouse were a little formal for the occasion, but she had to do something to make the six-carat rock on her ring finger look like it belonged here on earth and not supporting its own solar system. The flare of it alone nearly blinded me as she brushed her still strawberry blonde hair away from her face.

My mouth ran a little dry as I locked with her pale cobalt eyes.

The questions surfaced as I stood there on the porch, began to buzz around like a hive on a live wire, began to swarm and the familiar feeling of it seemed to give me the strength to finally speak.

"Hello, Mother."

CPSIA information can be obtained
at www.ICGtesting.com
Printed in the USA
FSHW011953050121
77444FS